ACCLAIM FOR KELLY IRVIN

"The awesome power of faith and family over personal desire dominates this beautifully woven masterpiece."

—PUBLISHERS WEEKLY, STARRED REVIEW

"A moving and compelling tale about the power of grace and forgiveness that reminds us how we become strongest in our most broken moments."

—LIBRARY JOURNAL FOR UPON A SPRING BREEZE

"Irvin has given her audience a continuation of *The Beekeeper's Son* with complicated young characters who must define themselves."

—RT BOOK REVIEWS, 4-STAR REVIEW
OF THE BISHOP'S SON

"*The Beekeeper's Son* is so well crafted. Each character is richly layered. I found myself deeply invested in the lives of both the King and Lantz families. I struggled as they struggled, laughed as they laughed—and even cried as they cried . . . This is one of the best novels I have read in the last six months. It's a refreshing read and worth every penny. *The Beekeeper's Son* is a keeper for your bookshelf!"

—DESTINATION AMISH

"Kelly Irvin's *The Beekeeper's Son* is a beautiful story of faith, hope, and second chances. Her characters are so real that they feel like old friends. Once you open the book, you won't put it down until you've reached the last page."

—AMY CLIPSTON, BESTSELLING
AUTHOR OF A GIFT OF GRACE

"*The Beekeeper's Son* is a perfect depiction of how God makes all things beautiful in His way. Rich with vivid descriptions and characters you can immediately relate to, Kelly Irvin's book is a must-read for Amish fans."

—RUTH REID, BESTSELLING AUTHOR
OF A MIRACLE OF HOPE

OTHER BOOKS BY KELLY IRVIN

ROMANTIC SUSPENSE

Her Every Move

Closer Than She Knows

Over The Line

Tell Her No Lies

Trust Me

AMISH

AMISH BLESSING NOVELS

Love's Dwelling

AMISH OF BIG SKY COUNTRY NOVELS

Mountain of Grace

A Long Bridge Home

Peace in the Valley

EVERYAMISH SEASON NOVELS

Upon A Spring Breeze

Beneath the Summer Sun

Through the Autumn Air

With Winter's First Frost

THE AMISH OF BEE COUNTY NOVELS

The Beekeeper's Son

The Bishop's Son

The Saddle Maker's Son

STORIES

A Holiday of Hope included in An Amish Christmas Wedding

Cakes and Kisses included in An Amish Christmas Bakery

Mended Hearts included in An Amish Reunion

A Christmas Visitor included in An Amish Christmas Gift

Sweeter than Honey included in An Amish Market

One Sweet Kiss included in An Amish Summer

Snow Angels included in An Amish Christmas Love

A Midwife's Dream included in An Amish Heirloom

The
BEEKEEPER'S
son

KELLY IRVIN

ZONDERVAN®

ZONDERVAN

The Beekeeper's Son
Copyright © 2014 by Kelly Irvin

This title is also available as a Zondervan e-book. Visit www.zondervan.com.

This title is also available as a Zondervan audiobook. Visit www.zondervan.com.

Requests for information should be addressed to:
Zondervan, *Grand Rapids, Michigan 49546*

ISBN 978-0-3103-5183-2 (repack)
ISBN 978-0-310-63735-6 (custom)

Library of Congress Cataloging-in-Publication Data

Irvin, Kelly.
  The beekeeper's son / Kelly Irvin.
    pages ; cm -- (The Amish of Bee County)
  ISBN 978-0-310-33945-8 (softcover)
1. Young women--Fiction. 2. Beekeepers--Fiction. I. Title.
PS3609.R82B44 2015
813'.6--dc23
                              2014028959

All Scripture quotations, unless otherwise indicated, are taken from The
Holy Bible, New International Version®, NIV®. Copyright © 1973, 1978, 1984,
2011 by Biblica, Inc.® Used by permission of Zondervan. All rights reserved
worldwide. www.Zondervan.com. The "NIV" and "New International
Version" are trademarks registered in the United States Patent and
Trademark Office by Biblica, Inc.®

Printed in the United States of America

22 23 24 25 26 27 / LSC / 20 19 18 17 16 15 14 13 12 11 10 9 8 7 6 5 4 3 2 1

For Tim, Nicholas, Erin, Shawn, and now, little Brooklyn Jane. Love always to my Lone Star family.

── *DEUTSCH* VOCABULARY* ──

aenti: aunt

bopli: baby

bruder: brother

daed: father

danki: thank you

dawdi haus: grandparents' retirement house

dochder: daughter

Englischer: English or non-Amish

fraa: wife

gmay: church district meeting

Gott: God

groossdaadi: grandpa

groossmammi: grandma

guder mariye: good morning

gut: good

hund: dog

jah: yes

---

*The German dialect spoken by the Amish is not a written language and varies depending on the location and origin of the settlement. These spellings are approximations. Most Amish children learn English after they start school.

kaffi: coffee

kapp: prayer covering or cap

kinner: children

lieb: love

mann: husband

mudder: mother

nee: no

onkel: uncle

Ordnung: an Amish district's set of written and unwritten rules

rumspringa: period of running around

schtinkich: stinks, smelly

schweschder: sister

suh: son

FEATURED BEE COUNTY AMISH FAMILIES

Abigail Lantz (widow)
Deborah
Leila
Rebekah
Caleb
Hazel

Stephen Stetler (bachelor)

Mordecai King (widower)
Abram (and wife, Theresa)
Phineas
Esther
Samuel
Jacob
Susan King (Mordecai's sister)

John (Abigail's brother) and Eve Mast
Obadiah

Rufus
Joshua
Frannie
Hannah
Rachel

Leroy (bishop) and Naomi Glick
Adam
Jesse
Joseph
Simon
Sally
Mary
Elizabeth

Solomon Glick (Leroy's father)

Andrew and Sadie Glick
Ruth Anne
Will
Patty
Henry
Catherine
Nehemiah

ONE

Getting lost might be a sign.

Deborah Lantz wiped at her face with the back of her sleeve to hide her grim smile. Getting lost might be a sign *Mudder* shouldn't marry a man she couldn't really claim to know—not in recent years, anyway. Abigail Lantz would call such a thought pure silliness and she would be right. Why would God send them nine hundred miles away from their home in Tennessee only to give them a nudge in the wrong direction so they ended up lost deep in south Texas?

Not likely. God had a plan for the Lantz family. Deborah need only be patient. At least that was what she'd been told hundreds of times.

As if it were an easy task.

Deborah wiggled, trying to get more comfortable between Hazel's booster seat and Rebekah, who had her nose pressed to the van window, not wanting to miss a single thing, even after watching the same monotonous, flat countryside for hours. Deborah longed to feel the excitement of her younger sisters. At nineteen, she was old enough to know what she'd be missing back home. All the singings with her friends, the buggy rides with Aaron afterward, the frolics. She would miss the chance to become Aaron's *fraa* and mudder of his children.

All the things she'd ever wanted.

Wrinkling her nose at the scent of sweat and warm feet, she leaned toward the window to watch the barren countryside now that their driver, Bert Richards, had slowed down as much as he dared on a highway where the speed limit signs read seventy-five miles per hour.

"There! There it is." Despite being only ten years old, her brother, Caleb, served as an able map reader. He pointed with one finger and clutched the map with his other hand. "Tynan, County Road 796. Turn there. Turn there."

"Got it." Bert whipped the steering wheel to the left. The force of the turn sent them all listing in the same direction. Hazel crowed with laughter and clapped her chubby hands. Bert hazarded a glance back, his forehead wrinkled above bushy eyebrows only partially hidden by thick, black-rimmed glasses. "Sorry about that. I didn't want to miss the turn a second time. Is George still behind us?"

Deborah scooped up her notebook from where it had lodged against the van door and turned to peer through the back window. The van that carried their bags of clothes and the boxes of household goods still followed at a steady pace. "*Jah*. Yes, he's still behind us." Her tone sounded tart in her ears. She worked to soften it. "George is a good driver."

Too good. Maybe a second or third wrong turn and they could wheel around and go home.

Deborah hugged her notebook to her chest, thinking of the two letters she'd begun. One to Josie, her best friend, and one to

Aaron, who'd been well on his way to being her special friend. If only she could write to them and say it was all a big mistake and they were coming home. Then she could erase the look on Aaron's face as he watched her get in the van and wave until she couldn't see him anymore.

One more turn. One more turn and she would meet her future.

"Gaitan Road," Bert sang out as he made a sharp right turn at a corner that featured a yellow sign that read SUPPORT BEEVILLE BEES. BUY LOCAL HONEY. "We did it. We're here."

"Indeed we are." Mudder clapped her hands, her face lighted with a smile. The weariness of the trip dropped away, and Deborah saw an Abigail Lantz she hadn't seen in a long time—not since *Daed's* death more than two years ago. "We made it. Praise *Gott.*"

Praise Gott. Deborah hoped Mudder wouldn't read her face. If coming to Bee County made her mother happy, then Deborah would make the best of it.

Make the best of it. That was what Daed would've said.

Whatever *it* was.

Even if *it* involved leaving behind the only home they'd ever known and all their friends and most of their family because Mudder wanted to marry an old beau who'd stepped aside long ago when she married Daed.

The van rocked to a stop in front of a long, dirty white building with rusted siding and a tin roof. The sign out front read COMBINATION STORE. A broken-down black buggy sat in front of it as if someone had parked it there and left it to waste away until it collapsed and disappeared into the earth.

"Come on, come on, don't just sit there. Let's get out." Mudder slid open the door. "Stephen will be waiting."

"He's waited this long . . ." Deborah bit back the rest of the sentence. Mudder did what she thought was best. Deborah had no business questioning. "Are you sure he's meeting us?"

"I told him we were dividing the trip into two days so we would arrive middle of the afternoon today."

Deborah slipped from the van, glad to stand on solid ground. Dirt puffed up around her bare feet, then settled on her toes, turning them brown. If it was this dry in early June, what would it be like in August? A desert? Grasshoppers shot in all directions. Two landed on her apron. She brushed them away, more interested in the deafening sound in the air like a buzz saw cutting lumber. She'd never heard such a ruckus. The smell of manure mixed with cut hay hung in air heavy with humidity. She glanced back at Leila, who climbed down with more grace. She had the same bewildered look on her face as Rebekah. "What is that noise?"

"Cicadas, I reckon." Rebekah shrugged. "Leastways, that's what I'm thinking. Caleb was reading about them in his books."

Bugs. No doubt, her little brother would love this place.

The letters Stephen had written to her mother had talked about Bee County as if it were a garden oasis. Deborah had imagined groves of citrus trees so laden with oranges and grapefruits that the branches hung to the ground. He described wild grapes, olives, and figs, filling Deborah's mind with images of something downright biblical—an Eden sprouting up in Texas. Eden with palm trees. After all, Stephen said the Gulf of Mexico wasn't far. He even said they could wade in the salty water if they had such a hankering.

Deborah definitely had a hankering, but it didn't involve the ocean. She sidled closer to Leila. "This is the promised land?" She kept her voice down. "Citrus and orchards?"

Leila stuck Hazel on her hip and hoisted her canvas bag onto her shoulder. "Mudder sure thinks it is." Despite the sweat on her face and the scraggly blond hair that had escaped her prayer *kapp*, Deborah's younger sister didn't look the least bit concerned about meeting the people who would be her new community. "She's as happy as a bee on honeysuckle."

Rebekah tittered and Hazel joined in, even though at three, she couldn't know what was so funny.

"Are those twisted things trees?" Leila wrinkled her nose as if she smelled something bad too. "They sure are stunted looking."

"Live oak, I think." Caleb loved to share all the tidbits of information he squirreled away in his head from his beloved books. "The cacti are called prickly pear. The fat parts are nopales."

He stumbled over the pronunciation of the last word. It came out *no-pails*. Whatever they were called, they didn't look like they would be featured in the garden of Eden. They were more like the wilderness Deborah imagined when the bishop preached about the Israelites wandering around for forty years.

More thoughts she would keep to herself.

"Stephen mentioned the drought." She tried to fill her voice with bright hope for the sake of her brother and sisters. After Stephen showed up in Tennessee for a wedding, Mudder had started to smile more. Deborah liked her mother's smile. "Some of the fields are green. Look over there—see that garden. It's nice. They irrigate. And there's a greenhouse. I'm sure that's what Stephen was talking about. That's probably his farm there across the road."

The farm would one day be their home if Stephen had his way. And he would. Otherwise, why had Mudder agreed to move here?

The door of the Combination Store opened and Stephen strode out, one hand to his forehead, shielding his eyes from the sun. *Onkel* John marched right behind him, along with their cousin Frannie. Stephen had the lightest white-blond beard Deborah had ever seen. It matched blond hair that curled under his straw hat, and he had eyes the pale blue of a summer sky. "You made it. I've been waiting for you. We didn't know what time you would get here, or the whole district would've turned out to greet you."

He stumbled over some invisible rock. His face turned a deeper radish red under his sunburn. He hadn't changed at all in the four months since they'd seen him back in Tennessee. "It's good . . . very *gut* to see you again."

Mudder's face turned a matching shade of red. "I thought you might be in the midst of chores."

"I'm here." Stephen stopped short a few feet from where Mudder stood, arms dangling at her sides. His massive, sunburned hand came out. Then, as if he thought better of the idea, he wrapped his fingers around his suspenders and snapped them. "I've been waiting to see you . . . and the *kinner*."

Mudder wiped her hands on her apron, then smoothed her prayer kapp. Deborah opened her mouth to try to break the strange pause. Leila elbowed her. She closed her mouth.

"Well, don't just stand there. Say hello to Stephen and your Onkel John." Mudder slipped past Stephen and accepted a hug from her brother as if to show her brood how to do it. "I'm so grateful to be here. What a long drive. My legs couldn't take much more of that. Come, kinner." Mudder grabbed Deborah's arm and tugged her forward. "Onkel John is offering us a place to stay in his home. I reckon the least you can do is say hello."

Squeezing past Stephen without meeting his gaze, Deborah nodded to her onkel, who towered over her, the sun a halo around the flat brim of his straw hat. He settled for a quick wave, while Frannie studied her sneakers as if caught in a sudden fit of shyness.

"Let's get your things out of the vans. That's our place right there yonder." John pointed to an L-shaped house down the road from the store. "No point in moving the vans. I'm sure the drivers are ready for supper and a place to lay their heads. They'll have to drive back to Beeville for that."

"I'll take care of it, John. Y'all visit." Stephen strode toward the back of the first van, Caleb, Leila, and Rebekah straggling behind him. "I imagine the kinner are hungrier than bears and tired enough to hibernate for the winter."

He chuckled. Deborah searched for the humor and couldn't find it. Mudder had packed plenty of food for the trip. They'd turned the meals into picnics at the rest stops along the way. If she admitted the truth, those picnics had been fun.

"I'm Frannie, remember me?" Frannie had her mudder's wiry frame, upturned nose, and freckles. She had grown taller since the last time Deborah had seen her, but she was still a bundle of sharp corners. "Come on, I'll help you. Careful where you step. The horses have been decorating the road today. Don't worry, y'all will get used to this heat."

Thankful for a friendly face on someone close to her own age, Deborah veered in Frannie's direction, careful to avoid the horse droppings she'd been so kind as to point out. Deborah wanted to put off the moment when she would have to enter one of the houses with rusty siding, desiccated by the wind and sun, and submit to the reality that this would be her home from now on.

Appearances meant nothing. She knew that. Still, hard-scrabble dirt and the buggy junkyard next to the store and the sorry-looking houses bothered her. Because they didn't look like home. She liked her district with the neat yards, freshly painted wood-frame houses, plain but clean. She liked the pinks, purples, and yellows of the flower garden Mudder planted every spring. Would God find fault in these folks for not picking up the place a little, making it more pleasing to the eye? He created beauty, didn't He?

God didn't make mistakes and God made this place.

If God didn't make mistakes, why did Daed have to die? What kind of plan was that?

Too weary to try to sort out her disconcerting thoughts and impressions, all tangled up like fishing wire and piercing hooks, Deborah led Frannie around to the back of the second van. A strange, shelled brownish-black creature with a pointy face, pink nose, and long, scaly tail trundled toward her on four short legs. It stopped within inches of her bare toes and sniffed.

She stumbled back, arms in the air, screeched, lost her balance, and plopped on her behind in a heap on the hard, rocky ground.

The ugly animal changed directions and scurried into the scraggly, brown grass, apparently as afraid of her as she was of it. "What was that?"

A man with a shock of dark hair hanging in his eyes under the brim of his straw hat tugged a trash bag of clothes from the van and plopped it on the ground. "I've never had anyone scream at the sight of my ugly face before." Despite his nonchalant tone, a scarlet blush burned across his face, deepening the ugly hue of the thick, ropy scars that marred it. He had the same twang as Frannie, but it was at odds with his hoarse voice and the harsh sarcasm that underlined his words. "Guess there's a first time for everything."

TWO

Embarrassed heat coursing through her, Deborah scrambled to her feet. She brushed dry leaves from her dress with shaking hands. It had taken her less than two minutes to show her cousin and this stranger how clumsy she was. She tried to look away, but the man's marred face seemed to hold her gaze hostage.

Deep, angry scars sprawled across his cheeks, nose, and chin. Gashes had healed in brownish-red ridges that made his stretched skin pucker in painful-looking zigzag lines. One misshapen ear hung at an odd angle, and the bridge of his crooked nose sported a permanent knot. "It wasn't you. It was that strange animal . . ."

His gaze jerked from hers toward the overgrown weeds that lined the dirt road. "You're telling me you screeched like a girl over an armadillo?"

"I am a girl, but that has nothing to do with it. It just . . . I've never seen an armadillo before. I've heard of them, but you don't see many in Tennessee." She shook her head, willing herself not to stare at the vicious scars. He had blue-green eyes that reminded her of the lake back home when the afternoon sun shone on its shimmering water. They studied her with an unnerving, unwavering neutral stare. She forced her gaze to float over his shoulder. "Are they common around here?"

"You see them now and again." He had a sandpaper-rough voice that suggested little use, or maybe his throat had been damaged by whatever had done this to his face. "That's why they're the mascot of the Lone Star State."

"On the trip here, my brother read to us all about the Lone Star State. Sam Houston, the Alamo, Santa Anna." It had passed the time, and whether she wanted to admit it or not, Deborah had found the history lesson interesting. And knowing more about her new home made the move seem less intimidating. "He didn't mention the armadillos, though."

"We eat armadillo all the time. It's a delicacy. Eve's serving it for supper in your honor. She'll be awful offended if you don't ask for seconds."

"Give her a break, Phin. Daed asked you to help with the bags, not badger the new folks." Frannie pushed past Deborah, her hands on her skinny hips. "She'll figure out what's what."

"I know people don't eat armadillo." At least not where she came from. Deborah didn't need her cousin to defend her. "I came here to help my family get settled. I'm going home as soon as I can."

Even though the thought of being separated from her mudder, *bruder*, and *schweschders* was almost too much to contemplate. Nothing was more important than family. Not even her own happiness.

"It's just as well then, if you think you're too fancy to eat armadillo. Around here we eat what God provides and count ourselves blessed." Phin tossed two bags over his broad shoulders and strode toward her in an easy long-legged stride, as if his burden weighed nothing.

The rolled-up sleeves of his faded blue shirt revealed more scars on his hands and lower arms. "Besides, we have enough mouths to feed, and you're too scrawny to be much of a workhorse."

"I am *not* scrawny." Deborah planted her feet. It appeared he would sideswipe her with the bags as he passed by in a straight line for Onkel John's house. Certain she'd end up on her behind again, she took one quick step to the left. "I do as much work as the next person."

"Don't mind him." Frannie hitched up the skirt of her gray dress, climbed into the back of the van, and dragged another bag toward Deborah. "He's always like that."

"Who is he?"

"The beekeeper's son." Frannie grinned. "Name's Phineas King. Most folks call him Phin. He was dropping off some jars of honey at the store, and Daed asked him to stick around and help with the unloading. He was none too happy about it, but no one says no to my daed."

"His daed raises bees for a living?" Deborah knew folks who did this, but it seemed impossible anything would thrive in this barren countryside. "You can do that around here?"

"With three hundred apiaries—that's what you call the hives—you sure can. They've got them spread out all over their farm and ours too." Frannie's tone was matter-of-fact, not like she was rubbing in Deborah's lack of knowledge on the subject of bees. "They sell the honey in the store. Folks come in from Beeville and all around the area to buy it. Mordecai—that's Phin's daed—sells bees to folks who want to start their own hives. They even make candles from the beeswax and sell them. Lip balm too. Spearmint." She smacked her lips as if she could use some balm right at that moment.

Deborah nodded and hoisted the bag on her shoulder, but Phineas caught her interest more than bees or lip balm. How much of that contrary nature came from having those scars? Plain folks didn't set much store by physical beauty or looks in general. She didn't even own a mirror. But she could see how Phineas might feel an outcast. Not that anyone would make a ruckus about his looks. Still, he might feel a bit self-conscious about it. She would.

No reason to take it out on her.

"By the way." Frannie grunted as she hopped from the van and grabbed a battered leather suitcase. "He was joshing you about the armadillo. We don't eat them. Some folks say they carry disease, and it's not like they've got a lot of meat under those shells."

Thank You, Gott! At least she didn't have to eat armadillo. That was something. "What happened to his face?"

"The van he was riding in got hit by a semitruck when he was small. It sent him right through the windshield. Threw him up on the bumper of the truck and then out on the asphalt road. He landed on his face. Messed him up good." Frannie dragged the suitcase through the weeds, the wheels bumping over the uneven ground making it twist and turn. "It killed his mudder and almost killed him. Some of the others were banged up, but not hurt bad like him. He hasn't been right since."

"What do you mean, he isn't right?"

"He was eight when it happened, and he never did talk much after that. He keeps to himself." Frannie wiped sweat from her face with the back of her dress sleeve as she tugged the suitcase up the steps to Onkel John's front door. The bags Phineas had been carrying were stacked next to it. He had disappeared from sight. "He talked more to you just now than he has to me in the last year."

Her sly expression and half-suppressed giggle made Deborah stop with her hand on the green screen door with its black netting that made it impossible to see inside her new, if temporary, home. "He was just making fun of me."

"Phin doesn't make fun. He's a big sourpuss. Open the door. Mudder made pulled-pork sandwiches with barbecue sauce, lemonade, and pecan pie to welcome y'all. We don't get meat too often and my belly is growling."

"He thought I was horrified by his looks when it was just the armadillo that took me by surprise." Deborah slung open the door and waited for Frannie to drag the suitcase in, then dragged her garbage bag of clothes in behind her. "I didn't mean to make him feel bad."

"He's had a good twelve or thirteen years to get used to the idea. If he'd be a little nicer to folks, they might forget about it too."

"Did you tell him that?"

"*Nee.* We don't talk."

If a girl let him court her, then he would know his scars didn't matter. "Does he have a special friend?"

"Not that I know of. You interested?" Frannie shoved open the first door at the beginning of a short hallway. "This is where you'll sleep. With me and Hannah and the baby."

Deborah hoped to be Aaron's special friend when she returned to Tennessee. Not that she would tell anyone that. "I don't even know him."

She stared at the tiny room. It held two double beds crammed wall to wall with only a slender walkway between them. Nothing else graced the space but a wooden crate bearing a kerosene lamp and a flashlight and hooks on the walls already full of dresses on hangers. One meager window stood open on the far side, but it didn't matter. No breeze lifted the wrinkled white curtain. The air, smelling of dirty diapers, hung just as still and hot as it did outside. "Thank you for sharing your room with my sisters and me."

"No reason to thank us. We aren't fancy. If we had more room, we'd spread out, but this will have to do." Frannie slapped the suitcase on top of the first bed. "You and Rebekah can share this one with me. We'll put Leila and Hazel with the other girls."

Deborah nodded.

"You can tell me all about Tennessee when we go to bed at night, and I can teach you all about Texas and everything you need to know to live here." Frannie had obviously given this a lot of thought. "I want to know all about what it's like out there. I haven't been away from home since that one trip to Tennessee I barely remember."

Deborah wished she could say the same.

THREE

Phineas brought the buggy to a halt next to the corral and hopped out. Despite himself, he'd spent the entire ride home picking at the memory of the new girl and how she'd reacted to him. The way her blue eyes widened in shock and horror when she first saw him. The way her hands flapped as if she was nervous. No excuse existed for the way he'd treated her. He couldn't say what had come over him. Something about her . . .

Nee, he couldn't blame her for his bad manners. When John had asked him to help out, Phineas knew exactly what was coming. He liked to help people out. It was their reaction to him that got old.

He could handle the horror look better than the sick look or the pity look. A whole range of looks existed. Phineas had seen them all. In fact, he kept a running catalog in his head. The pity look definitely took the cake as the worst one.

At least the new girl hadn't given him the pity look.

Phineas tied the reins to the post and headed across the gravel road that separated the corral from the house. Let these folks have a good supper and a nice welcome. With any luck they'd stay. That's what everyone wanted. New blood. New folks to grow this little district before it disappeared like dust blowing in a hot wind the way other Plain communities in Texas had disappeared from the map long ago. With little more than a dozen families holding out, their community fought to survive with the closest Plain district being in Oklahoma.

Leastways, that was what his daed said.

"What are you doing here?"

As if thinking of his father could make him appear, Phineas looked up to see Daed headed toward him. He slowed, then stopped. Phineas might be able to avoid the new folks, but not Mordecai King. The man could not be denied. "Chores and supper, I reckon. I'll take care of Brownie and the buggy after I get some water."

"I thought you were headed to John's for supper after you dropped off the honey. To greet the new folks."

Phineas met his father's gaze head-on and kept walking. It was the best policy when it came to Mordecai. The man in front of him could've been his reflection in a mirror—without the scars and twenty-some years older. They were the same height, same broad shoulders, and work-hardened bodies. Same skin tanned by the sun. The same untamable black hair sticking out from under straw hats. The differences were in his father's long black beard decorated with a few strands of silver and his unmarred skin with wrinkles just beginning to touch the corners of his eyes and lines around his mouth. Under different circumstances, Phineas could've looked like that once he married. If he married. "Done met them at the store. I even helped with the bags."

"And then you scuttled home like a bashful little boy?" Daed did an about-face and kept pace with Phineas. Nothing mean emanated from his words. Daed always said what he thought and did what he said. "We need to make these folks feel welcome."

"You think a few kind words will make them stay?" Phineas chewed the inside of his lip. No need to get snippy. None of this was Daed's fault. "Didn't make the Yoders stay or the Schrocks."

"Being neighborly goes a long way toward making folks feel like this place could be home despite the way it looks, the way it is." Daed matched Phineas's stride. His tone didn't change, but the gaze he leveled at Phineas said he was counting to ten before he lost patience. "We can't afford to have any more families leave."

"Maybe we should let this district die. Maybe that's Gott's will."

"What's gotten into you?" Daed flung his arm out in a wide arc. "This is home. Our home. We will survive. Leroy won't let it die. Gott called his daed here. Our family as well."

Nothing had gotten into Phineas. He loved the land on which he stood. He loved the apiaries. He never wanted to leave. He couldn't tell his father what really ate at him. "That was a long time ago. Maybe Leroy isn't listening to what Gott is saying now. Maybe He's saying, 'Good job, faithful servant. You can move on now. Go some place where the ground is meant to be tilled and crops reaped.'"

"More likely He's wondering why you're whining when He's given us so much. He's thinking work harder and talk less. He's thinking He never said this walk on earth would be easy."

True enough. Daed had that way about him of getting to the kernel of truth that counted. "I'll check on the hives and feed the chickens. I should probably check on Millie too. She's to have that foal any day."

"I did all that already." Daed twisted a piece of straw between his teeth, then tossed it to the ground in an abrupt motion. "You didn't die in that accident. Time to get on with things."

No, Mudder did. Neither would say those words. They never talked about her. "Maybe it would've been better if I had."

"It was Gott's will that you survive." Daed's jaw worked, but his even tone didn't change. "And I praise Him for that."

That was Mordecai. A man who could find the good in any situation. He never showed anger. Even when Phineas woke up in the hospital, tied to tubes, his face and head swathed in bandages, his father had expressed no anger at the semitruck driver. He expressed no anger that not one of them had worn seat belts. No anger at the sudden, violent death of his fraa.

Praise Gott, he'd muttered over and over again. Mordecai would not have been praising Gott had he known about the last few seconds of his fraa's life. Phineas shoved aside the thought that accompanied him every waking minute like an unwanted visitor who refused to leave. "A better plan would've been to save Mudder and take me."

"You think you know Gott's plan?" Daed's voice dropped to a whisper as if he feared the wrath of God would rain down on his stubborn, belligerent son. "His will, not yours."

The same answer, always the same answer. "I'll bring some squash and cucumbers over later. Eve will want to fry up a batch for her company."

"It's about what's inside you, not on the outside. A woman worth her salt will know that."

Daed didn't see the look on the girls' faces. As if they were petrified Phineas would ask one of them out for a walk home after the singing. They were good girls with true hearts, but they couldn't see past his ugly face. Nor had Daed seen the look on the new girl's face as she tried to blame her horror on a silly armadillo. No matter what anyone said about appearances when it came to man-woman things, they mattered. What woman would want hands like his touching her?

"We're fine just the way we are."

"You have a birthday coming up." Daed reminded Phineas of a barnyard dog worrying a big stick. "You'll be twenty-one."

"I'm aware."

"It's time to start thinking about having your own family." He threw a glance in Phineas's direction. "Abigail Lantz has three daughters close to the age."

"You want me to marry so the district doesn't die out?"

"Nee. I want you to marry and be what Gott intends you to be. A *mann* and a daed." His father cleared his throat. "I want you to be content."

Content. Everything Phineas wanted was encompassed in his father's words, but he'd learned long ago not to hope—or even to think—about such things. To do so was to invite disappointment. "I *am* content."

At the house, Daed did another about-face.

"Where are you going?"

"To John's. Don't bother yourself about the buggy. I'll take it. We're invited to supper. I reckon it wouldn't serve to be disrespectful of their hospitality."

"I'm sorry."

"No need."

"I'll be fine." He wanted to do something to make up his failings to Daed. "Like you said, Gott has a plan."

"The Bible makes it clear. Gott intended for a man to marry." Daed threw the words over his shoulder as he strode away. "No man wants to be alone forever."

Phineas didn't bother to point out Daed should take his own

advice. They were both alone. The fact stood out like poison ivy in a field of clover.

Phineas didn't mind being alone. They had the bees and the horses and the goats and a couple of cows for fresh milk and a litter of new kittens. The chickens he could've done without if it weren't for the money fresh eggs brought in at the store. They had the rest of the family. Abram had married and soon there would be a grandchild, although not a word had been said of the impending birth. Esther was courting, even if she didn't want them to know. Samuel and Jacob were hard workers, and their love of a good practical joke kept them all on their toes and laughing around the supper table. *Aenti* Susan made good okra gumbo and better pie. All kinds of pie.

Pie alone made life worth living on a good day.

All this foolishness over fraas was overrated.

The Lantz girls weren't livestock brought to Bee County to grow the herd and ensure the district's future. Deborah Lantz's face, pink with exertion and embarrassment, danced in his mind. Her pretty blue eyes had filled with horror upon seeing his ugly face.

That look said it all.

FOUR

Aware of Stephen's gaze watching her every move—along with her daughters' disapproving glances—Abigail leaned past him and picked up his dirty plate. She inhaled his scent of man sweat and soap. He'd sopped up the pulled pork and barbecue sauce with the last of his oversized bun, polishing the plate to a shine. The fried potatoes, pickles, and red beets had disappeared in short order. He liked to eat. Abigail appreciated that in a man. She'd left her home and spent two days in a van filled with unwilling children for this moment.

Stephen smiled up at her as if he knew her thoughts. *Mercy me.* Despite the years that had passed since they had courted as youth, he still had the same nice smile with even teeth and full lips. *Ach, you're full of flights of fancy, Abigail.* Hands shaking, she grabbed John's plate, stacked it on top of Stephen's and the one in front of Mordecai King.

Susan King, seated next to her brother, stood and picked up her plate. "I'll help."

"Nee, my girls will help. You visit." Abigail cocked her head toward Deborah. "Help your cousins with the dishes. Come on now, there's work to be done."

Without a word, Deborah dropped her half-eaten sandwich on her plate and scooted from the bench where she sat next to Leila and Rebekah at the second table along with two of John's three girls and Mordecai's daughter, Esther, on one side and the boys on the other. They were crammed in like peas in a pod at both tables. The entire house seemed to burst at the seams between the three families.

"Nee, nee, y'all just drove halfway across the country to get here." Eve made shooing motions with red, dishwater-chapped hands. "My girls have got this. Frannie, get a move on. Abigail, you take yourself a piece of pecan pie and go on out to the yard. Take a load off. You got plenty of time for chores tomorrow."

Her brother had done well for himself. Eve tried so hard to make Abigail feel welcome. The same seemed true of Susan, who would be Caleb's teacher come fall. The thought gave Abigail comfort. There would be women here to whom she could talk. They would fill the vacuum created when she left behind the tight-knit group of friends she'd been quilting, canning, and sewing with her entire life. "I can't let you do all the work—"

"We'll let the girls do the work. Susan and I will oversee." Eve shooed again. "Cut a piece of pie for Stephen here and get him some more sweet tea. I'm thinking he won't turn it down."

"You'd be right about that." Stephen patted his lips and beard with his napkin and tossed it on the table. "You do make a fine pecan pie. Brings back memories of my *groossmammi's* pie, rest her sweet soul."

"I want pie." Hazel reached for her glass of water with both chubby hands, misjudged the distance, and knocked it over.

Water ran in rivulets across the tablecloth and dripped on Stephen's pants. Caleb snorted with laughter. Abigail shot him a look. He slapped his hand over his mouth.

Stephen stood, knocking the bench back in his haste, and righted the glass. He shook his head, his expression stern. "Well, child, I reckon you should clean that up."

Abigail normally put the smaller children at their own table, but John's front room didn't have the space. Hazel's face crumpled. She scrambled to her feet, knocking over Hannah's glass in the process. More water spilled. "Mudder!"

"Accidents happen, little one." Abigail grabbed the tablecloth and folded it up, blotting the water as she went. The less on the floor, the less to clean up. "Get a washrag from the kitchen. I'll clean this up."

"Let her do it." Stephen tugged the tablecloth from Abigail's hands, his hands gentle but his tone firm. "Accident or not, little girls who make messes should clean them up, don't you think?"

Abigail stopped, caught between the desire to make sure her daughter didn't cause extra work for her sister-in-law and not wanting to get off on the wrong foot with Stephen. He nodded at her, his eyes kind, but it felt as if this was some sort of test. At three, Hazel did simple chores, but she tended to make more of a mess when she tried to clean.

"No harm done." Mordecai set the second glass upright. He scooped Hazel from her bench and set her on her feet. "Go on, little one. Bring your mudder a towel."

The little girl, eyes wide, her face stained with tears, sniffled and scurried to the kitchen.

Abigail opened her mouth to thank him.

"You were getting pie."

Stephen pointed his long finger in the direction of the kitchen. His tone held an unmistakable note of authority Abigail hadn't heard before. Timothy had never ordered her to do anything. He'd been more likely to bring her around to his way of thinking with a kiss on her neck or a hug from behind. She could never refuse him under those circumstances. "Why don't you go sit in the yard? I'll bring it out."

"That is a good idea." He paused at the screen door and looked back, smiling. "It's been a long time. We have some catching up to do."

He slipped through the door, letting it shut with hardly a sound.

Abigail took the washrag from a still-tearful Hazel and wiped at the water on the bench and floor. Mordecai picked up a piece of bread he'd spent more time shredding than eating during most of the meal. Abigail, her skin hot with embarrassment, forced her gaze back to the mess her daughter had made.

"It'll dry. No harm done." Mordecai picked up the stack of plates so she could dry under it. His eyes were blue green and brilliant against his tanned skin. "The girls will clean up."

Timothy's eyes had been the color of freshly turned earth and always held a questioning note, as if he couldn't quite believe she'd chosen him. Abigail gave herself a mental shake. She had to stop comparing. "I hate to make extra work for anyone, that's all."

"You brought a lot of helping hands with you. We're all happy you're here. All of us are."

Something about the way he said the words eased the knot of apprehension between her shoulders. He smiled. He had a kind smile. She found herself smiling back.

John cleared his throat. "Weren't you getting pie and tea for Stephen?"

"Tea, right. Tea."

She fled to the kitchen. There she encountered accusing stares from her four daughters, squeezed into the narrow kitchen with Eve's three. Ignoring them the best she could, Abigail cut a thick wedge of pie and refilled Stephen's glass. She inhaled and let out a breath. It had been only two years since Timothy's death. She knew how to acquiesce to a man's will. She'd done it for years, but somehow she felt out of practice. She'd best relearn the skill, no matter what the girls thought.

"He doesn't have kinner." Deborah looked as if she'd bitten her tongue.

"What?" Abigail had heard the statement, but she needed time to find a response. Stephen had never married, true, but that could be her fault. He'd asked her to marry him once before and she'd chosen their father instead. He'd moved away not long after Abigail married. Then he returned to Tennessee for a wedding a year after Timothy's death. The same quiet man of faith he'd always been. A man who'd never fallen out of love with her. She had been sure of that when she left home or she would never have come. Could she learn to love him the way she hadn't loved him the first time? She cared for him. Wasn't that enough?

It had to be. She had to have this new start in this new place. A place far from the pond where Timothy had asked her to marry him and far from the house where their children had been conceived and born. Far from the cemetery where he'd been laid to rest twenty-four months, one week, and six days ago.

"What does he know about what a little girl should do or shouldn't do?"

"You best hush." Abigail picked up the saucer, avoiding her oldest daughter's dark look. "He was right. Hazel needs to learn."

"Will he tell the rest of us what to do too?"

"Do the dishes."

Deborah plunged her hands into the water so hard it slopped over the edges of the tub. Leila grabbed a plate and started wiping it down with a furious motion while Rebekah scrubbed the prep table with enough force to remove the varnish. Abigail wanted to reprimand them, but she couldn't come up with a specific reason. They were doing as they were told. She bit back angry words. It would take some adjustment, this living in a new place, for all of them. Adjustments would have to be made if—when— she married Stephen. Deborah would learn. She would learn to respect Stephen, even if she couldn't love him the way she loved her father.

They all would.

Not wanting to dwell on what that meant for herself, Abigail marched out to the front yard where she handed the pie to Stephen, all the while giving him her best smile. "Here you go." She set the tea on a battered crate situated between the two lawn chairs. "I hope you have room for a big slice."

"Always." He settled into the faded plastic chair and waved his free hand toward the other one. "Sit with me."

She sat. Despite the hour, the sun sinking in the west still bathed her in heat. Sweat pricked her forehead and trickled down the back of her neck. Flies buzzed her face. She swatted them away, only to see them dive-bomb the pie. The chair creaked under her, loud in the evening air laden with the sound of cicadas buzzing endlessly in the distance. What would they talk about? She'd imagined so many conversations for so long, it never occurred to her that at this moment her mind would be blank.

"Where's your pie?"

Her stomach churned. She felt like a girl about to go to her first singing. Stomach full of butterflies, mouth dry, hands sweaty. As a widow with five children, she could barely remember her first singing. She felt more like a filly for sale at a horse auction. "Eve's pulled-pork sandwiches were so good, I couldn't eat another bite. The fried potatoes really hit the spot too."

"You've gotten thinner." A bit of pie crust teetered on his lower lip and fell into his beard. He brushed it away, his head still cocked as he stared at her. "You know what they say: A skinny woman must be a bad cook."

"A skinny woman is a woman working the fields with her *dochders* because she has no mann and only one young *suh*." She tried to temper the tartness in her voice. He wanted to make conversation. He didn't really mean it. "I ate plenty this spring, but between the fields and the garden, I burned it all off."

Stephen chuckled. "You got a little vinegar in you. I like that. I'm only giving you a hard time. It's good to laugh a little, don't you think? Especially when things are awkward."

She heaved a sigh of relief. He liked her vinegar. How he would feel about her daughters, who all possessed that same vinegar in varying degrees, remained to be seen. As hard as she tried, Abigail had never been able to cultivate placid dispositions in her daughters. She'd prayed and admonished and punished, just as her mudder had done with her. Deborah, Leila, Rebekah, and Hazel—they all reminded her of herself. And Timothy. "I'm sorry about the water."

"I expect I'll have to take them in hand when the time comes."

"When the time comes?" Abigail's heart banged against her rib cage. Blood pulsed in her ears. In his letters, Stephen had asked her to come out west, but he never actually proposed marriage. The rest of his meaning sank in. "Take them in hand?"

"If we're to make this work, they'll have to respect me as the head of the household."

"Getting a bit ahead of yourself, aren't you?" Again she worked to keep her tone soft. "We hardly know each other after all these years."

"We both know why you're here." His hand rested on hers for the merest second, then lifted, leaving behind a faint, lingering heat. "I need a fraa. You need a mann. We need each other. We have a second chance to make that happen."

His declaration lacked romance, but Abigail wasn't a young girl in the throes of her first love. Stephen spoke the truth. So why did her throat hurt with the effort to hold back tears? "A woman with five kinner can't dispute that."

"You know I've always cared for you."

"I know you did a long time ago."

"I never married."

"Because of me?"

He leaned back in his chair, his gaze fixed on some distant point she couldn't see. "For many reasons. I reckon I felt . . . uncertain . . . about trying again. Time passed. More time than I intended, but I never found the right woman. Until now."

"I hate to think of you being unhappy on my account."

"I wasn't unhappy. I learned to be content. I learned to wait upon the Lord." His gaze came back to her face. He smiled. "And Gott has rewarded my patience."

His happiness at this thought shone in his face. That he thought of her as a reward from God was almost too much for Abigail to contemplate. He'd thought of her as some ideal for all these years. Now he would know the real her. The one who burned the bread on occasion and often snapped at the kinner before she'd drank her *kaffi* in the morning.

"Sounds like you did real well with the sale of the farm." He eyed a huge chunk of the pie. Apparently deciding against it, he cut it into smaller pieces. "Did you bring the money with you?"

The sale of the farm had been the hardest thing she'd ever done—next to putting Timothy's body in the ground. "Nee. John advised me to go to the bank there in Ethridge and have them set up an account for me at one of the branches they have here in Texas. The lady at the bank said they have one in a place called Victoria not too terribly far from here."

"Too far to go by buggy." A bee settled on the remnants of Stephen's pie. He shooed it away with a gentle swish of his big hand. "You'll have to hire a driver to get your money out. It's another expense."

Did he think she would carry that kind of money in her canvas bag across three states? She'd kept out money for their expenses, to pay the drivers and to help John with feeding her brood. Beyond that, she hadn't thought of needing more. "Get it out?"

"When the time comes, I mean. I was thinking we could irrigate another five, ten acres of my property. Plant more fruit trees."

"What happened to the olive trees you wrote about in your letters?"

"It takes six or seven years before they start bearing. I should have olives next year." He set his plate on the crate. "We're doing good selling onions and such to the grocery store chain. But I'll need to do more to feed five kinner. Or more."

The last two words sent heat coursing through Abigail once again. She hadn't allowed herself to think beyond a wedding. To being the fraa of a man again. To the days and the nights that would follow. Memories flooded her. Timothy holding her hand as they walked into their home for the first time as husband and wife. Timothy removing her kapp and taking the pins from her hair with the gentlest of touch. Timothy, tears in his eyes, holding Deborah in his arms minutes after her birth, and sixteen years later holding Hazel with the same look of awe and joy on his face. Timothy's big, callused hands on her shoulders, his kind eyes dancing with laughter and love as he bent to kiss her, sure any minute one of the kinner would walk in the kitchen and discover them acting like teenagers.

"Abigail?" Stephen leaned toward her, his forehead furrowed. "Are you all right? You look done in. Maybe we should put off this conversation for another evening."

"Jah. Jah, that would be good." She choked out the words, horrified at the thought that tears might follow. She popped from the chair. "It was good to see you again."

"I've waited a long time for this." Stephen caught her arm as she turned toward the door. "I don't want to wait much longer."

"I know." She nodded and tried to summon the optimism she'd felt as she packed up all their belongings and closed the door behind her on the house that had been filled with memories of a life that had ended with Timothy's sudden heart attack. "I'm just tired."

His hand dropped. "You can't stay in your brother's house forever. It's too small."

"I know."

"I have a decent-sized house." He smiled at her, his expression begging her to see the future he imagined. "Big enough for five kinner and then some."

"I know." She forced a return smile. "You said that in your letters."

"One of these nights I'll take you for a buggy ride." He ducked his head, staring at his dusty boots, sniffed, then looked her in the eye. "You'll see. The house needs a woman's touch. Some elbow grease to shine the floor, pies baking in the kitchen. The vegetable garden needs weeding. You'll find it suits you."

He was trying so hard. She swallowed the lump in her throat. "I'm sure I will."

He picked up his plate and handed it to her. "Don't forget the glass."

"I won't."

Stephen walked away, grasshoppers scattering in his wake, leaving her standing in the front yard, his dirty dishes in her hands. Caught in the moment, she watched him drive away in his buggy.

A woman her age couldn't expect romance.

Shouldn't expect it.

Should she?

She was being ridiculous. She slid the glass on top of the plate, intent on heading inside. Gott had blessed her with the chance for a new start with a good man. The Stephen she remembered was a steady, decent man. The kind who would take on a ready-made family and step up as the head of the house. That was what she needed. Not romance. Her season for romance was over. She should be content.

She closed her eyes, burning with unshed tears, and sought comfort in the place she always found it. Gott's grace covered Texas every bit as much as Tennessee. She had only to seek His will and be content with His answers. *Gott?*

A mosquito buzzed her ears. She flapped her free hand, trying to ignore it. Bees, flies, mosquitoes. Like Texas's version of the plagues.

Gott, Thy will be done. If this is Thy will for me, let me find contentment in it. Let it be enough.

The screen door slammed. Abigail jumped and nearly dropped the plate. John stomped down the steps, Mordecai behind him. "What are you doing, standing there with your eyes shut? You look silly." He glanced around. "Stephen left already?"

"He did." Hoping John would be satisfied with an answer to his second question and not his first, she started to squeeze past the men. "I'll take these dirty dishes in."

Mordecai tipped his straw hat toward her with one finger and nodded. "Esther and Susan are still jawing with Eve, but I best be getting home to my chores. Joshua says he'll give them a ride home."

"It was nice to meet you." Abigail swallowed, sure she couldn't say another word without doing something silly like sobbing. Mordecai's gaze looked so familiar. So . . . wanting. She recognized the look. Nee, not the look. The feeling that went with that look. Drowning in loneliness in the midst of a crowd. A knowing. He knew. Because he had felt what she felt. But not for two years. For twelve, according to Eve. If it took a man like Mordecai that long to overcome his fraa's death, why did everyone expect her to snap out of it so quickly?

Mordecai nodded again. He hauled himself into his buggy and set off, his hat pulled low over his face against the setting sun.

John looked from Mordecai's retreating buggy to Abigail, his face scrunched against the brilliant light. "You didn't scare him off, did you?"

"What? Who?"

"What you mean, who?" John scratched at his ribs with one long finger, his gaze perturbed. "Stephen, of course."

"Nee. Nee. I'm tired, that's all. Long drive."

"You liked Stephen before, didn't you?"

John had known about her dilemma in her courting days. Courting might be private, but her brother had been friends with Stephen back in the day. He couldn't help but know. Still, he hadn't meddled when she chose another. "Jah, but I chose Timothy for a reason."

"And now Timothy's gone. I'm sorry for that. But Stephen's a good man. Being a bachelor and all, he comes over here pretty regular for supper. He's a good friend."

"I know. You've mentioned that before." More than once.

"It took him a long time to get over being hurt the first time." John's face reddened under a deep tan. Her bruder had never been one to talk much about feelings. "But he's willing to forget it. I'd like to see you settled. Taken care of. Stephen's willing to take on a fraa with five kinner with only one boy among them. That's not worth nothing."

"I know. It means a lot to me." She'd hurt Stephen once. The last thing she wanted was to do it again. She managed a smile for her brother's benefit. John studied her right back. She forced the smile wider. "I'm so happy to be here."

"It's a tight fit, but we'll manage." He slid his hat back on his head and rocked on the heels of his boots. "I'm off to feed the livestock. Your room is at the end of the hallway. It was intended for storage, but we squeezed a bed in there."

He trotted away, light on his feet for such a tall, burly man. "It's not for very long, anyway."

His words floated on the air behind him, surrounded by the words not said. His house was full. Abigail needed to accept Stephen's offer.

After all, that was why she'd come.

Wasn't it?

FIVE

The plagues of south Texas abounded. Deborah added fire ants to her list as she dropped her empty basket into the dry, yellowed grass that crackled under her feet. Trying to avoid the fire-ant mounds that dotted an open field that went on forever, she hopped on one bare foot so she could remove a burr from the tender skin along the arch of her other foot. She tried not to feel so aggrieved at this tiny prick of pain that seemed like punishment somehow for her sour disposition this fine June morning.

Lifting her hand to shield her eyes from the sun, she surveyed the winding, leaf-covered vines that curled around a saggy fence that seemed to lead nowhere. The vines, heavy with purple and green grapes, had taken over, stretching from the fence to a dead ash tree, winding upward and resting on gray boughs as if they owned the place.

"They don't look like any grapes I've ever seen." She worked to keep the disdain from her voice. Everything about this place seemed to disappoint her, and that wasn't Frannie's fault. "I mean, they're kind of small and peaked looking."

"That's because they're mustang grapes." Frannie snatched

one from the vine and held it out. "They don't grow in clusters like Spanish grapes. Daed tried planting that kind, but they died out—too hot, I reckon, or not enough rain. These grow wild, which is a blessing for us. Try one."

Thinking of the grapes they used for jelly back home, Deborah popped it in her mouth. "Ewwww." Her tongue curled and her lips puckered. She spit the skin at her cousin's feet. "Frannie! Sour!"

Frannie whooped and did a two-step to avoid the offending grape. "What's the number one thing we put in jelly and jam?"

"Sugar."

"So what does it matter if they're sour? We just add more sugar. The *Englischers* who come to the store even ask for it special."

"Well, the other grapes we can eat plain." Deborah sounded like a spoiled child and she knew it. "I reckon all that sugar isn't good for us. It rots our teeth and makes us fat."

"I ain't got an ounce of fat on me, and I eat butter-and-jelly sandwiches all the time."

Fresh, hot bread slathered with butter and jam did sound good. They'd left the house right after breakfast and the sun looked to be well overhead now. Deborah was hungry and thirsty and surely had a whole new batch of chigger bites. "Is it time to go back yet?"

"Nee, silly, you haven't begun to fill that basket. We need to pick as many grapes as we can. Mudder wants to make the jam tomorrow so we can get it to the store before Friday. That's when most of the Englischers come to buy the produce and honey." The smile slipped from Frannie's face, replaced with a pensive expression Deborah hadn't seen before. "Too bad Leila and Rebekah were busy digging potatoes. We should've brought Hannah and Hazel. They could help carry. The more we pick, the more money we make at the store."

"And then we'd have to carry Hazel, Hannah, and the baskets." Deborah's little sister handled small chores, but her short legs still kept her from being a help on treks like this. Besides, if they didn't have the jam to the store this Friday, there was always next Friday. "What's the matter? You look worried about something."

"Nee. Don't do any good to worry about things. 'Sides, Leroy says worrying shows a lack of faith."

Deborah hadn't spent a lot of time with Frannie, but she knew worry when she saw it. She'd seen it too many times on her mother's face. "Come on, spit it out."

"I heard Mudder and Daed talking." Frannie began to pick grapes with a steady, sure hand that said she'd done this many times. "It sounded like . . . Daed's worried. Daed never worries. He says worrying is a sin too. They were arguing . . . not arguing . . . Mudder never disagrees with Daed. But it sounded like they were tugging back and forth on something."

Deborah copied Frannie's technique and began to fill her own basket. "About what?"

"It sounds like Mudder wants to move back with her schweschder up in Missouri."

Deborah lost her grip on her basket. It tumbled into the weeds. "Ach." She squatted, set it upright, and began to pick up the spilled fruit. "Nee, you must've misunderstood. Your family has lived here forever. Your farm is here. We just came down here because you're here."

"I know." Frannie plucked grapes faster and faster. She didn't look up. "I don't reckon it's my place to say anything—"

"Say what?"

"Before you got here, I heard Mudder telling Daed that he should've told Aenti Abigail not to come. It was foolishness for y'all to come here. He wanted y'all to come because of Stephen. He figured that'd work itself out, either way."

"Why move, though?"

"Look around." Frannie flopped her hand in the air. "The district isn't getting bigger. It's getting smaller. We lost two families this year already. We don't mind working hard, but Mudder says sometimes you have to admit that a thing isn't meant to be. That Gott didn't intend for us to try to farm in a place with rocky soil and no rain. She says we could go back up north and farm where Gott intended food to be grown. She says Daed's just being stubborn because he doesn't want to admit that he was wrong to move here or bring y'all here. That Leroy's daed was wrong to bring his family here from Tennessee way back when."

Deborah worked Frannie's words over in her mind. Onkel John hadn't said anything to her mother. She was sure of that. Mudder never would have moved them here if she thought the district was about to break up. "Why did the families leave?"

"Different reasons." Frannie's voice dropped as if she feared someone would overhear in this great, wide-open space. "The Matthew Glicks left because they didn't agree with the *Ordnung*. They moved into town and started a carpentry business. He even drives a van now and they go to an *Englisch* church. They said Leroy was being too strict. That we needed to find new ways to support ourselves. David Schrock and his kin moved back to Missouri because his mudder and daed were getting old and needed him to run their farm."

"It doesn't sound much different from back home." Deborah wanted to comfort her cousin, but she could see both sides of the argument. "It doesn't matter who it is, Plain or Englisch or whatnot, folks have differences. That's what my mudder always says. Maybe Leroy isn't hearing what Gott is saying now."

"Leroy is the bishop. He was chosen by holy lot. Gott chose him." Frannie shook her head so hard, it was a wonder her freckles didn't fall off. "Still, in a little district like this, we can't afford to lose families. The Schrocks and the Glicks weren't the first to go. From what I hear, they won't be the last. It ain't much." She pointed a finger toward the field with its ornery cacti, black-eyed Susans, and mesquite. "But it's the only home I've ever known. It grows on a person."

Deborah didn't have the heart to tell Frannie she couldn't ever see it growing on her. "Gott will provide." Hadn't Mudder told her that a thousand times since Daed's death? "You know what? We could pray."

"We could."

A sudden hopeful look on her face, Frannie closed her eyes and bowed her head, still clutching her basket. Deborah did the same, waiting. The silence was filled with cicadas. A bee buzzed her ear. Or maybe it was a horsefly. A mourning dove cooed.

Deborah struggled to find words that would help Frannie and still be truthful. God would see through her words to her heart. He would know her true desire was to return home. It could be that God's will for this tiny, dirty place was to let it sink back into wilderness, to let the vines cover the fences and the fierce winds from the south blow down the tin walls until nothing remained of this settlement. *Gott, Thy will be done.*

The familiar words of the Lord's Prayer, repeated at every church service she'd ever attended and nightly evening prayers, ran through her mind. *Thy kingdom come, Thy will be done. Thy will be done. Even if it's this place.* She kept her eyes closed, hoping God read her heart and not the confusion in her head.

"Amen. I feel like singing."

Startled, Deborah opened her eyes. "What?"

Frannie attacked the grapevines with renewed vigor. "After praying, I always feel like singing. That's what I feel like doing now."

"Huh?"

"Singing always makes me feel better."

"What song would you sing?"

"Let me think about it."

Deborah let her think on it. As if singing would get Gott's attention if their prayers hadn't. She had her own thinking to do. They'd driven nine hundred miles across several states to a district that might very well disappear from one day to the next. Did Mudder know? And why would Stephen lure them here if he knew?

Deborah had more questions than answers.

———

The soothing hum of forty thousand or more bees a concert in his ears, Phineas tucked his pants into his knee-high rubber boots, then adjusted the screen over his head. The sun beat down on him, but he didn't mind. Days like this, with the sun shining and the bees as his only company, he felt content, if not happy. He double-checked to make sure his shirt was tucked in all around. Honeybees were a docile lot, and they had no bone of contention with him, but he'd found it was not much fun when one got under his clothing and then couldn't find its way out.

Satisfied that he was sufficiently protected from the unlikely chance the bees would take offense at his intrusion into their home, he picked up the smoker and lifted the apiary lid. The hum reached a crescendo as thousands of bees went about their many duties of depositing nectar in the combs, cleaning the empty cells, and taking care of the queen. Their industrious nature served as an example for humans, in Phineas's way of thinking. Plain folks worked hard, harder than most, but nothing compared to bees, who literally worked themselves to death—as Daed liked to remind his kinner whenever they complained about their chores.

Grinning at the thought, Phineas waited while the smoke puffed from the smoker and drifted over the open hive. The bees settled into the super, retreating toward the level that held the queen bee. Such a life she had. Her every want and need taken care of, followed about by the worker bees who assured that she filled every cell with eggs that would bear new bees and sustain the colony. Plain women worked hard and they had the babies and counted themselves blessed. Phineas pushed the thought away. It would only lead to the path of discontent. Not today.

After a few seconds, he set the smoker aside and picked up the frame grabber. The first frame was covered in thick, white wax. Perfect. Ready for harvest. Ignoring the errant bees that explored the screen over his face and trundled along his sleeves, he grabbed another frame. Equally heavy. This would be a good harvest. Daed would be pleased. They would have a goodly number of jars to sell at the store and in town. They needed supplies to repair the shed and rebuild the chicken coop.

The words of an old Englisch hymn, sung with great gusto, broke the silence, louder than any screeching sirens, followed by peals of decidedly girl laughter. Startled, Phineas lost his grip on the grabber. The frame tumbled from his hands, landed on his foot, then bounced to the ground. Bees, buzzing with indignation, flew in all directions.

Phineas hopped on one foot, teeth gritted. Ignoring the pain in his toes, he tugged on the frame, set it upright, then transferred it to the box. The wax had cracked and honey oozed in rivulets from the gaping crevices.

"Great." He muttered, forcing himself to step away without batting at the bees that now swarmed the frames and him. The worst thing he could do would be to wave his arms around. With measured, careful movement, he picked up the smoker and applied another dose. The bees calmed and retreated into the super.

"Ouch, ouch!"

"Who is it?" He forced himself to keep his voice calm and collected. "Who's out there?"

Deborah peeked from behind a cluster of halfhearted mesquite. Behind her, Frannie popped out. Each held a basket in her arms and had a silly look on her face.

"Sorry, Phin, we didn't know you were out here." Frannie made a bold move away from the trees. "We were just picking wild grapes. Mudder wants—"

"Hush, you've got them all riled up."

"Ouch! Riled up? One of them just stung me." Deborah plopped her basket in the straggly grass, wrung her hand, and then peered at it, her face contorted with pain. "It's already swelling. What should I do?"

"For starters, hush." He spoke softly, much as he didn't feel like it. "If you're calm, they're calm. Stay where you are. I have to close the hive."

To Phineas's surprise, they did as they were told. He applied a bee brush to the frames, gently encouraging the straggling bees back to their home. That accomplished, he replaced the lid on the top and picked up the box of frames. "Let's give them some peace and quiet."

"Peace and quiet—"

"That means no talking."

He stalked toward the two girls. Frannie knelt and picked up the fruit that had fallen from Deborah's basket and handed it to her. The two kept pace with him.

They walked several yards before he decided to take pity on Deborah. He settled the box on a tree stump, removed the netting from his head, and turned to her. "Let me see."

"What?"

"You don't speak the language or your hearing is going?" He held out his hand and wiggled his fingers. "Let me see."

"I'm sorry about the bees. We were singing, and then we both forgot the words to the song at the same time—"

"Stop. Talking." What was wrong with her? Didn't she get that her voice, all high and fast, excited the bees? "Now."

"You can't tell her what to do." Frannie frowned, squinting against the sun. "Me neither."

Men always told women what to do. It was expected. Leave it to Frannie to buck thousands of years of tradition. "Fine, you want to get stung, be my guest." He turned to pick up the box. "I have work to do."

"Wait." Deborah cradled one hand in the other, both clutched against her chest as if they pained her. "Did we hurt them?"

"No, you didn't hurt them, but you could've been stung a lot more. You're lucky honeybees really are mostly interested in nectar and not humans."

"They sting people all the time." Even with a hurt finger, she used her hands to talk. She sure did like to argue, worse than his brothers and sister even. "Caleb got stung at a picnic last year."

"Those were probably yellow jackets." And she didn't know

a thing about bees. She really should go back to Tennessee. "They're the ones who hang around sweet drinks. Honeybees are looking for flowers."

"Well, fine, but it still hurt." She stared up at him, something forlorn in her face that she hoped made him feel small and mean. "Caleb's arm and fingers swelled up and we had to take him to the doctor. He almost cried."

"But not you? You're not going to cry over a bee sting."

"Nee, it's fine. I'm fine."

Exasperated at his own waffling, he gritted his teeth. Her ignorance wasn't her fault and she was in pain. He didn't like seeing anyone in pain. "I've been stung a few times. Let me see."

Her expression hesitant, she extended her hand. Her forefinger was swollen and red. Phineas squinted against the sun as he peeled off the latex gloves he used to extract the frames. "Let me get the stinger out."

"Nee." She jerked her hand away and hid it behind her back like a child afraid of punishment. "I mean—"

"Don't be a baby."

"I'm not a baby."

"Hold out your hand, then." He had work to do. The frames needed to be relieved of their loads and returned to the hive. He silently counted to ten in German and then in English. "It doesn't hurt that much and it hurts more to leave it in. There's a venom sac attached to the stinger. We need to get it out of you."

Her chin lifted and her hand came out. "It doesn't hurt, but go ahead."

Despite his curt words, Phineas hesitated. He'd never touched a girl outside his family. *Don't be an idiot.* Avoiding her gaze, he took her hand in his and bent his head close. Her fingers were thin and fragile looking and her skin soft against his rough calluses. He swallowed, suddenly aware that the first time he touched her, he would hurt her. *The first time.* That made it sound like there would be a second time or a third.

Don't be an idiot.

With as much care as he could muster, he used the nails of his thumb and forefinger to pluck the offending stinger from her finger. Her hand jerked, but she didn't make a sound. When he looked up, she smiled at him.

Her smile enveloped him like an early-morning breeze. He couldn't see anything else. It seemed he might forget simple things, like how to speak or breathe.

Don't be an idiot.

He forced his glance back at her hand. "Better?"

She shook her hand as if that would help ease the pain. "No, but that's okay. It will be."

"If Eve has ice, that's the best remedy. Keep it on there for about twenty minutes." He resorted to reciting facts he knew by heart. No thought required. "If not, make a paste of baking soda and vinegar. It will help with the itchiness and swelling. Calamine Lotion is okay, but it wears off pretty quick."

"We don't have ice," Frannie announced. "But I could run over to the store and get some."

"Nee, it's too far." Deborah blew on her hand as if that would help. "Eve has some calamine I can put on it. It's fine."

Her cheeks were pink from the heat and her eyes light blue like the Gulf of Mexico on a sunny, cloudless summer day. Phineas had never seen a prettier girl. The thought only served to irritate him more. According to Daed, looks meant nothing.

In his case, they meant everything.

"Stay away from the hives and you won't have this problem." He picked up the box. He had work to do. Best to focus on that. Honey to harvest. Jars to fill. He didn't have time to babysit girls. But he couldn't help himself. He looked back. "And don't be wandering around here barefooted. You know better, Frannie. You want to step on a rattler?"

"A rattler." Deborah's voice rose on the second word. "I thought you said they didn't come out during the day."

"Not much." Looking unconcerned, Frannie scratched a red welt of a mosquito bite on her neck. "Everyone knows snakes can't regulate their body temperature, so they stay in the shade when it's hot."

Frannie sounded an awful lot like she was quoting Phineas's daed. They all did it. They couldn't help it. Mordecai was a fountain of facts, some useful, some not.

"Yeah, like under the vines where you've been picking grapes." Phineas barely contained the eye roll that so irritated his daed on many occasions. "You rattle their shade, they'll rattle back."

"I can't wait to go home." Deborah marched past Phineas, the pain in her hand seemingly forgotten.

"Anyone silly enough to howl around an open beehive and clomp around barefooted out here needs to head north to the city." Phineas flung the words after her. Why, he had no idea. "Go on back to Tennessee. We don't need you here."

"I will." Her gaze was glued to the ground in front of her, her pretty face creased with anxiety. "Just as soon as I can."

"Gut."

Her stride lengthened. In a second she'd be running, basket and all. "And I don't howl. Or clomp."

She might as well have said "so there," like a little girl. Phineas almost laughed. Almost. She didn't look like a little girl, and he hadn't been nice to her. He opened his mouth.

"Don't. You've done enough for one day." Frannie brushed past him. "Stick to talking to bees. I reckon you're better at that."

The truth of those words stung worse than any bee.

SIX

Abigail shaded her eyes with her hand, trying to see Stephen's house in a blazing sun hovering near the horizon. Sweat trickled down her temples and buried itself in small tufts of hair that had escaped the confines of her kapp on the buggy ride. The washrag bath she'd taken after supper, knowing this would be the evening Stephen came to fetch her for a ride to his farm, had been for naught. Her dress stuck to her skin and her nose felt sunburned. And this, at eight o'clock at night. The buggy swayed. She grabbed the front board and held on. Stephen did like to keep a pretty pace, not necessarily a safe one, given the deep, rutted grooves in the road.

"That's it. My place yonder." Stephen shook the reins and the horse picked up even more speed. "Not much, but it'll do."

It would indeed. The two-story white and rust house sat back on the road with a huge metal shed that had seen better days behind it. Beyond it were the fruit orchards and the olive trees he had nurtured for several years now. He'd told her all about them in the letters. How he built a windmill and used it to irrigate. The greenhouse he'd built. The work he did for Englischers in their fields to earn the money to do all this so when the time came, he could support a family. The house was a little bigger than John's. Stephen must rattle around in it alone.

"How did you come by such a house?" He'd never told her much about his life since coming to Bee County. "It seems like a lot for a bachelor."

"I bought it from Leroy's cousin Josiah when he decided to take his family back to Tennessee." Stephen turned the buggy onto the gravel road on his patch of land. He glanced at her and back at the road. "I know I've waited longer than most to marry. But I wanted to be prepared. I wanted a family, and it seemed like first things first. Working to have the means to support a family. Buying a place for the family to live."

Always the thoughtful, measured person. A quality to be admired in a man. Yet he'd chosen to move across the country on his own to start a new life. That showed initiative and courage. "Moving here and leaving behind your folks in Tennessee must've been hard."

"Not so hard." He snapped the reins, his gaze on the road ahead. "My daed decided to leave the farm to my older brother. He said it did no good to subdivide it. It couldn't make enough to support a family that way."

Emotion stained the words. Something Stephen obviously didn't like to think about. Abigail understood that. Families could be hard. "But you learned a trade and managed fine from the looks of it."

"And I did. Carpentry. I did a lot of different jobs, mostly working for Englischers." He nodded more to himself than her. "That's why I came down here. This district needed more people and Carroll County was crowded. I had a hankering to have my own place and get a new start."

Staying in Tennessee would've meant seeing her and Timothy at church on Sundays and watching their family grow. A new start would've looked mighty fine. She glanced at the neat rows of trees, heavy with brilliant oranges. "You've made it work. Does your family ever come out to see you?"

"Once or twice, but they're getting up there in years and don't travel much anymore. I don't know if they'll come for the wedding." *Wedding* came out in a stutter. "Not to get ahead of myself."

"We'll cross that bridge when we get there." She tried to see herself walking across that bridge, Stephen at her side, his hand in hers. Her palms felt slick with sweat. *The heat, just the heat.* "We have time."

Stephen cleared his throat. "We'll see, I reckon."

"Your farm is nice. I like it."

"You mean that?"

She wouldn't say it if she didn't mean it. Stephen had a lot to learn about her. The irrigation made his farm an oasis of green in the midst of so much drabness. "I try to always tell the truth. You seem to have a green thumb."

"What I have is Gott's blessing. All this comes from Him." Stephen's face creased in a sudden grin. He hopped from the buggy and scooted around to her side where he held out his hand to help her down. "What it needs is a woman's touch."

His fingers felt warm and moist around hers. "I'm fine, I can make it."

He didn't let go of her hand. In fact, his grip tightened. "It needs a flower garden. Well, maybe a cactus garden would be easier, but you know what I mean. And a good cleaning. The grass needs to be mowed."

Was he listing the chores he expected she would do as his

wife? Or trying to sell her on how the house would look once a woman got ahold of it? He plopped her on her feet so she stood close to him. "It sounds—"

"Shush." He loomed over her, a curious gleam in his eyes. "I've been waiting a long time for this."

He bent down. She opened her mouth to protest. His hand came up and touched her cheek, his skin rough against hers. His eyes closed and he leaned in. Abigail wanted to back away, but the side of the buggy dug into her shoulder. "Stephen." Her voice came out a whisper. "I don't—"

His lips covered hers in a wet, slobbery kiss that reminded her of Caleb's favorite dog back home. Bubba, with his big muzzle all over their faces whenever they'd been away for a while. Abigail closed her eyes and tried to summon the emotion such a kiss should elicit. Her heart chugged faster, but more from embarrassment than emotion. She wanted to give Stephen what he wanted, what he was asking her to give him with this kiss. He wanted her heart. He wanted them to be as one, as husband and wife.

She wanted that too. She'd been sure of that. The kiss seemed to go on and on. Her back hurt and her face felt slick with sweat.

Stephen took a step back, but his hands lingered on her shoulders, his fingers moving in gentle circles until they touched the hollow of her neck.

"There. I've been wanting to do that for a long time—for years, in fact." The grin turned self-satisfied. "What better way to start your visit to your new home, don't you think?"

He turned toward the house with the flourish of one arm. Abigail swiped at her mouth with her sleeve. He hadn't had much practice kissing, that was obvious, and she should be glad of that. He kept his affection special and pure by sharing it only with someone he really cared about. If he had longed to do this when they courted as youth, he'd never shown it. Would she have responded differently if he had? Her mind's eye filled with Timothy's face as he bent his head to kiss her on a moonlit-drenched night on the road that led to her house. Nee, Timothy had made her his with that very first kiss.

And now Timothy was gone and she had to go on. Stephen was a good man, not unpleasing to the eye. So why couldn't she respond in kind? She had more practice, but only because she'd been married to a man she loved for more than twenty years. Maybe it was for that reason. She still loved Timothy. She would always love him. Perhaps she simply couldn't learn to love another. If that were the case, she would be alone for the rest of this earthly life.

Plain men and women were expected to marry again. Families needed to be complete. Kinner needed mudders, but they also needed daeds to be the heads of their homes. If she were to talk to the bishop, he would tell her as much. She knew it in her head, but how did she get her heart to go along?

Stephen grabbed her hand again and tugged her toward the house. "Come on, come on, I want to show you everything."

In his exuberance, he stumbled in a rut in the road and down he went with a thud. For some reason not clear to Abigail, he refused to relinquish his hold of her hand. Down she went with him. Her knees smacked against the hard earth. Gravel scraped her free hand, and her momentum carried her until her nose banged against the sunbaked dirt road hard as brick.

"I'm so sorry. I'm such a clumsy oaf." Stephen scrambled to his feet. He slid his hands around her waist and planted her on her feet before she could protest. "I don't know what's gotten into me. I've never been so clumsy—"

"It's all right." Abigail brushed at the dirt on her apron, leaving a faint red tinge of blood from the scrape on her palm. "No harm done."

"You're bleeding." Stephen grabbed her hand and examined her palm. "I'm such an oaf."

"Nee. Just enthusiastic." She tugged her hand from his once again and hid it behind her apron. "Maybe if you slow down a little, if we slow down a little."

His face darkened. "If we go any slower, I'll be too old to have our own children by the time we marry."

So that was the rush. He wanted children of his own. "I know it's been a long haul for you, but you have to remember, it's only been two years since Timothy passed."

"Two years is a long time. Most Plain folks remarry pretty quick."

As if he had any idea what it took to get to that frame of mind. "I know and I'm trying. But I'm asking you to give me a little more time."

His gaze softened. "If time is what you need, then time you shall have."

"*Danki.*"

"No need to be all fancy about it. Gott will give me the patience I need and you the courage you need."

"Courage? I'm not . . . I wasn't—"

"Let's go in. You can wash your hands and face—you've got dirt on your nose." He swiped at it with his catcher's mitt–sized hands and missed. Much to Abigail's relief. Her nose throbbed as it was. "I want you to see the kitchen. I put in a propane stove next to the woodstove. Two ovens. You can get them both going and have bread and pies baking."

Abigail trailed after him, her gaze on the spreading patch of dark sweat on the back of his faded blue shirt, her aching hands cupped in front of her.

"Come on, don't be shy!" He opened the back screen door and went in, not bothering to hold it open for her. "You can pour us some water from the pitcher on the counter and I'll find the ointment. I've got it in here somewhere."

Finding it might prove to be a challenge. Abigail stopped inside the door, her fingers over her mouth. She wanted to pinch her nose to keep the stench at bay. The kitchen smelled of old coffee grounds, rotting cantaloupe rinds, and rancid grease.

Dirty dishes covered the counter. A skillet filled with dirty cooking oil sat on the stove. An overflowing bag of trash drooped by the prep table. "It's in here somewhere." Stephen rummaged in a cabinet, his back to her. He turned and held up a tube. "Found it!"

His triumph faded after a second. His gaze roamed the room as if following hers. "I told you it needs a woman's touch."

"You did." Her voice sounded weak in her ears.

"The sooner the better, I reckon."

Abigail managed a nod.

The sooner the better, or the cockroaches would carry the place away.

SEVEN

Dear Josie,

I know this is my fourth letter in two weeks, but you said you wanted to know everything that happens to me. It's like living in the wilderness. We picked grapes yesterday and I got stung by a bee. I know we had bees back home, but here they raise them and sell the honey. It was the first time I saw the beekeeper's son again, and he was mad at me because we raised a ruckus with our singing. We were just trying to make the work lighter. Like you and I did when we washed laundry or did the dishes. Phineas King wouldn't know fun if it bit him on the nose.

Deborah lifted her pencil and sighed. That was mean. The accident had wrecked Phineas's nose. Yesterday he had been minding his own business, working hard, and they'd stirred up the bees. She touched the swollen red spot on her finger. It hurt. Still, no need for Phineas to get so snippy with Frannie and her. They didn't do it on purpose. Frannie was right. Phineas was a sourpuss.

So why did she feel so funny about the way he'd looked at her before taking her hand? His touch had been delicate, his expression tentative. He hadn't wanted to hurt her. She shoved away the thought. He had hurt her. With his snippy attitude. Wiggling on the hard wood of the step that led to Onkel John's back door, she bit on the end of her stubby pencil, the taste of paint and wood and lead bitter on the tip of her tongue. Enough thinking about Phineas.

It's the same every day. Get up, help cook breakfast, clean the kitchen, work in the garden or do laundry, make the lunch, sew and mend, clean the house, fix supper, go to bed. I guess it's not so different from back home in that respect, but it always seemed so much more fun when we did it as friends. And we had the singings and frolics and fishing and wading in the pond. Here there're hardly enough of us to have a singing or a frolic, and they haven't any creeks that have water in them. It's dry as bone here. Drier. Dry as sawdust. Dry as ashes. The grass is brown and crispy like straw and the trees are dwarfs.

I wish you could see what I see. I know what's on the outside means nothing and we shouldn't draw attention to ourselves by being fancy. But does that mean we leave junk lying on the ground and let the paint peel off our houses? I wish I could ask the bishop that question. Jonas knows about these things. Gott knew what He was doing when Jonas drew the lot. Maybe you can ask him for me.

That sounds silly, doesn't it, like Gott doesn't always know what He's doing?

Deborah raised her pencil, her cheeks suddenly hot, even though she was alone with her words. She should erase that last part. She stuck the pencil out and studied it. Only a nub remained of the pink end. Not enough eraser to get rid of her words. Besides, she hadn't said what she really meant. She hadn't written down the words that so often did somersaults in her head and made her stomach hurt. How could Gott's plan include taking Daed from this earth so soon? What purpose did it serve? What plan involved moving her family to this dirty, barren, brown place?

She waved away a fly the size of her big toe and squinted against an evening sun dipping toward the horizon. If her old bishop were here, he would say she was full of hubris and needed a good dose of humility. He'd say she had no right to question. That Gott should strike her down with a big bolt of lightning for having a head too big for her kapp, and he'd be right.

What she couldn't figure out was how to make her thoughts behave. They barricaded themselves behind her heart and showed up when she closed her eyes at night and tried to sleep. They pestered her while she picked tomatoes and dug up beets in the garden. They tried to burst from her lips when she saw Mudder serving yet another piece of pecan pie to Stephen, who seemed to have a hollow leg and no use for napkins.

Deborah wiped a drop of sweat from the end of her nose. It might be a tear, but she preferred the idea that it was sweat. She was no crybaby. She took a big swallow of lukewarm, tart lemonade from a Mason jar to ease the lump in her throat. Sniffing hard, she applied pencil to paper, determined to finish this letter so she could walk it out to the mailbox in the morning before the mailman came by.

I'm sitting on the back step at Onkel John's house, smelling the smell of garbage in a rusted trash can. I'm staring out at a broken-down buggy that looks like it hasn't moved in years. Grass is growing up around it and pretty soon it'll be hidden. Maybe I can use it as a hidey-hole place to go and write my letters where no one can see or know what I'm thinking. 'Course, there might be a rattlesnake in there or one of those armadillos I told you about in my first letter.

Mudder has gone on a buggy ride with Stephen. I'm not supposed to know. She thinks I've gone to bed already, but it was so hot I couldn't sleep. I saw them ride away. Mudder says Stephen is a smart farmer who took lemons and made lemonade.

The thing about Stephen is he keeps looking at me funny, like he's trying to figure something out. Like I'm a bug he wants to study or squish under his boot—one or the other, I'm not sure which. He's never been married and if he's been around kinner, it's been a very long time. The first night here, he made Hazel cry because she spilled her water.

Mudder says we have to give it time. That he's trying. I'm trying too. I think I might need to try harder.

When I walk down the road, dirt floats in the air. When the wind blows, grit gets in my mouth and my teeth grind on it.

I keep thinking I'll get used to it. When I wake up in the morning and smell eggs frying and pancakes and kaffi, I can almost imagine I'm back home again. Then I open my eyes and see the sagging roof over my head and hear my cousin Frannie snoring and smell her morning breath and I remember.

Write me. I want to know everything I'm missing. I'm coming home just as soon as Mudder gets settled with Stephen. They'll get married in November and I'll come back. I can get a job cleaning houses or as a teacher, earn my keep on my own. I'll be home soon, you'll see.

Write me back as soon as you can. I'm crazy to know what's going on there. With you-know-who. I should stop now so I can write to him too. I haven't received a letter from him. Yet.

Tickle your little sister for me and eat my share of the ice cream.

Deborah

She hadn't mentioned this plan to her mother. Or her sisters. She tried to imagine getting on a bus and going home without them. She'd never been anywhere in this world without her family. They'd get by without her. They had each other.

She would spend time with Aaron. It'd only been two weeks. Yet his image in her mind's eye had begun to fade and curl up around the edges. Try as she might, she couldn't summon the complete picture. Or how his voice sounded. Or his laugh. How could these things fade so quickly?

She'd written him three times. He hadn't responded.

Maybe her image had faded just as quickly. Maybe he had begun to forget her as well.

Nee. Nee. She would write him another letter.

Right this very minute.

EIGHT

Abigail squeezed the tongs around the wide-mouth Ball jar and lifted it from the cast-iron pot of boiling water. It felt as if her own blood were boiling, such was the billowing heat from the woodstove, combined with the sun-heated breeze that lifted a white curtain hanging in the window in Susan King's kitchen. Almost three weeks here and she still hadn't grown accustomed to the heat.

Eve and John assured her she would. They claimed not to notice it at all. Even though their clothes were always soaked with sweat and their faces red with sunburn. Abigail set the jar on a wooden table that looked as if it had been built from mesquite. By Mordecai? Or Phineas, maybe? The idle thought made her glance toward the kitchen door as if her thoughts could make the King men appear.

Which led to the next thought. Did she want Mordecai to appear? And the next. Why? Just because Stephen's house was a pigpen and the King house was spotless. Sparse, but clean and orderly. No doubt because of Susan and not Mordecai. It wasn't fair to judge Stephen when he had no woman to clean up his messes. No, that would be her job, the second she married him.

Sighing in exasperation with her own inability to think of anything else, she tried to tune into the lively conversation that bounced around the kitchen among her daughters, Eve, Susan, Esther King, Naomi Glick, Frannie, Theresa King, the other cousins, and a few other women whom Abigail had met at the Sunday service. They apparently were discussing if and when another trip to town would be made. Abigail had yet to see the tiny town of Beeville. According to Eve, there wasn't much to see.

"I need to get flour and baking soda." Eve snapped green beans with an efficiency born of years of practice. "And to buy material. The boys are growing so fast I can't keep up. Their pants look like high waders."

"Same with Caleb," Leila added. "Hazel's growing like a weed too."

"Don't you sound like the mudder." Eve chuckled and handed the girl another pan of sliced cucumbers. "I know young men around here who are chomping at the bit to take fraas."

"No rush. She's barely eighteen." Abigail intervened, her hands tightening on the tongs. What was the hurry? Her daughters had time. Just as she had time. She wouldn't hurry them into something any more than she herself needed to hurry. No matter what Stephen thought. "It's important that we settle in and take some time to get to know everyone."

"I thought you were anxious for us to find husbands." Rebekah held up a tomato. "This one is mushy. I think it's too far gone to use."

Susan took the tomato and studied it. "I can salvage half of it. No waste around here."

The tomatoes looked good to Abigail. It amazed her what they were able to grow in this inhospitable climate. "I do want you to find the proper young man, but that takes time. You'll be going to the singings here and the frolics. You have time."

Time might not help. There were so few families in this district and only a limited number of young men. Dread and doubt clasped hands in Abigail's belly. Not only was she in a precarious position of having to marry before being sure of Stephen, but her girls might very well have trouble as well.

Gott's will. Gott's plan.

She turned to check the steaming tomatoes. Time to fill the jars. She adjusted the funnel and ladled tomatoes into the first hot jar, leaving a scant half inch at the top. "Who wants to get rid of the air bubbles?"

The change of topic seemed to lay to rest the sudden pause in conversation. Deborah hopped to her feet, leaving the cucumbers and onions she was thinly slicing for bread-and-butter pickles on the table, and joined Abigail. "I'll do it."

Abigail picked up a washrag, ready to wipe the rims after Deborah pushed out the air bubbles. "Leila, you follow behind with the lids and the bands. We'll get an assembly line going."

"What about the honey jars?"

Mordecai King's deep, graveled voice filled the room. He stood in the doorway, a large box in his arms filled with wooden frames covered with something white and waxy. A bee crawled along his sleeve, then zoomed across the room toward the back door, its buzzing loud in the sudden silence.

"Mordecai!" Susan stood and began moving pots and pans and baskets of produce from the prep table. "I told you I had the canning frolic today."

"So you did." He deposited the box on the table as if it weighed nothing. "But these frames are about to burst. They're almost as good as the ones Phineas brought in the other day. The frolic will have to include honey. Just add a few rows of the honey jars. Esther put the labels on last night."

"It'll be a tight squeeze, but we'll manage." Susan frowned, her upturned nose wrinkling They looked so much alike in the face, but there the similarity ended. Mordecai was tall and muscled whereas his sister was short and round. "I'm sure Abigail and the girls will find it interesting."

"Ach, just because you think bees are the best thing since kaffi doesn't mean everyone else is fascinated with them." Esther set her bowl of cucumber slices on the counter and folded her arms in front of her, the picture of a mother scolding a child. "You're looking to get a taste of Aenti's fresh lemonade, that's what I'm thinking."

"I *am* a bit parched."

"I'll get it." Abigail dropped the washrag on the counter, hustled to grab a clean glass, and poured the lukewarm lemonade. It sloshed over the side and ran down on her fingers. She handed it to him, feeling silly that she'd rushed and, moreover, that he could see that she had. The proof was in the sticky. "There you go."

Mordecai gulped down most of the liquid, then glanced around the kitchen as if taking stock of his audience. "You Lantz girls haven't seen how we harvest the honey, then?"

A chorus of "nees" followed the question.

The girls sounded eager, and Abigail found herself inching closer to the box with its treasure trove of frames from the hives.

Mordecai jerked his head toward the table. "You missed the good part. One of these days Phineas can take all y'all out to an apiary so you can see how we use smoke to calm the bees down and get the frames from the supers."

"I think Deborah saw all she wanted of the bees the other day." Frannie giggled. Deborah glared. "I mean, you know, getting stung—"

"I didn't see anything." Deborah craned her neck and peered over the side of the box. "I got stung before we reached the hive—the apiary or whatever—and then Phineas . . ." Her voice trailed off.

"Phineas was a little peeved you upset the bees." Mordecai finished her sentence. He snapped his suspenders as if for emphasis. "He told me. He's protective of them like that. And it's how we pay the bills."

"It wasn't intentional. Deborah and Frannie were collecting wild grapes for jam. We sell that to support our family." The words sounded lame, even to Abigail as she said them. "And I think Deborah learned her lesson. Didn't you?"

Deborah nodded as she crept closer to the table, her sisters crowding around her. The intensity in her oldest daughter's face as her hand touched the edge of the box, a finger trailing down the side, surprised Abigail. It was the first time Deborah had seemed interested in anything in Bee County. "What are supers?"

"That's where the bees make the honey." Mordecai plucked a long serrated knife from a shelf and dipped it in the pan of water still boiling on the stove. "The supers are above the section where the queen bee lives. That way we can take out the frames without upsetting her."

He proceeded to scrape the white wax into a plastic container. "We'll use this beeswax to make candles and lip balm."

He pointed at the openings now visible on the frame. "See, there's the honey."

"How do you get it out?" Rebekah raised her hand as if at school, then giggled. "Do you have to cook it or something?"

"We put the frames in an extractor and spin them." He grinned as if this thought gave him great joy. "Do you and your schweschders want to help? It's old hat to all these women. They've seen it hundreds of times."

"I do, I do." Hazel crawled out from under the table where she'd been sitting with her own pan of green beans, attempting to snap them the way Abigail had shown her. "I want honey."

Mordecai laughed, a big, booming sound. "Well, that's one thing we've got plenty of."

Deborah, Leila, Rebekah, and Hazel crowded around the table while the others, true to Mordecai's prediction, went back to chatting, finishing up the tomatoes, and starting on the pickles. Abigail longed to watch, but somehow it seemed as if she shouldn't. Why, she couldn't be sure. It was simply honey, after all. *Tomatoes. Think tomatoes.* She couldn't help it. She sneaked a glance now and again.

Mordecai removed all the wax from the frames and then set them in a huge pot he called an extractor. It had a handle that allowed him to spin the frames, flinging the honey against the sides of the pan so it pooled in the bottom.

As he worked, he talked to the girls in a tone that reminded Abigail of a schoolteacher. Had his life been different, had he not been born a Plain man, maybe he would've been a teacher. Instead, Susan had that job in the King family.

"Did you know bees have a stomach especially for honey?" He picked up Hazel from the floor and stood her on the chair so she could see. "That's where they put the nectar when they collect it from the flowers. On one trip, they suck up so much nectar their stomachs weigh as much as they do."

He stuck his hands out as if to mimic a huge belly and the

girls laughed. His gaze whipped toward Abigail. She whirled toward the counter. Lids made popping sounds. *Pop. Pop.* Good. Good, the first batch of tomatoes was setting up fine.

Mordecai's soft chuckle told her he'd caught her watching him. "You know, worker bees only live about thirty-five days in the summer. That's because they work themselves to death going back and forth to get the nectar and then flap their wings to help the extra water evaporate from the nectar once it's in the hive. My point is, I don't want to hear any of you complaining about having to work too hard. I've never seen a Plain child worked to death yet."

Laughter followed this statement. Abigail couldn't help herself and peeked again. Mordecai grinned. Her face flaming, she turned back to her rows of jars.

"How does the nectar get out of the bee's belly?"

Deborah, ever the scholar with the most discerning mind, posed the question. Abigail waited, wanting an answer to that strange question herself.

"The hive bees suck it out with their tongues, mouth to mouth."

"Ewww! Yuck. Gross!"

The chorus from her girls filled the kitchen, followed by laughter from Eve and the other women. Abigail found herself smiling for the first time in days. Mordecai's tone said he relished the telling of this little fact. Probably had repeated it many times. It was so like a man. Still smiling, Abigail picked up the wooden spoon and stirred the spicy vinegar concoction that would cover the cucumbers, onions, and red peppers that would become bread-and-butter pickles. At least they were learning something new. Even Deborah, who'd been morose at best since arriving in Bee County, seemed fascinated.

Susan slid in next to her. "Go on, go watch. I know you want to. I've had enough honey stories to last me a lifetime. I'll take care of this."

Wiping her hands, Abigail turned to watch as Mordecai flipped the frames and did the other side. "There you have it." He opened the extractor and tipped it so the girls could see. "Smell that? What does it smell like?"

Deborah leaned forward, eyes closed, and took a big whiff. "Flowers."

"Yep. The honey will always smell like whatever flowers the bees take the nectar from. Gott's fragrance."

Hazel attempted to stick a finger in the pot. Deborah grabbed her back just in time. Hazel wiggled, arms outstretched. "Want honey."

Mordecai shook a finger at her. "We have to strain it first." He made quick work of that step, demonstrating to the girls what to do, and then poured a small amount in a bowl and set it on the table. "Susan, we're ready for your bread."

The canning frolic temporarily on hold, Susan sliced thick hunks of white bread and covered it liberally with homemade butter supplied by Naomi Glick. The girls took turns letting Mordecai pour a dollop of honey on their slices. Abigail waited until last. His gaze didn't quite meet hers as he ladled a spoonful in the center of her bread, golden, sweet-smelling, and thick. Why be shy now? Or maybe that was her own heart fluttering in her chest. Silliness. Pure silliness.

"Danki." Her voice sounded high and silly in her ears. "For this."

"It's just honey. We have it running out our ears around here." He smiled as if completely at ease, which only made the flutter in her heart turn to a gallop. "Some days we're sick of it."

"Not for the honey." She glanced at the girls, busy stuffing bread in their grinning mouths, their hands and faces sticky. Even Deborah looked like the little girl she'd once been, back in Tennessee.

"For what, then?" His voice had turned gruff. "Sharing widely known, useless facts about bees?"

"For making them feel welcome. Giving them a little treat."

"I moved here when I was a teenager." He stuck his utensils in the tub with their dirty canning utensils and picked up the last of the frames to return it to the box. "I remember what it was like."

"From Tennessee?"

"Jah. My family was one of the first."

"You never thought to return?"

"Once I started raising bees, I found myself content."

Abigail sank her teeth into her bread. The sweet honey oozed onto her tongue, the taste like spring in her mouth. "Mmmmm."

"Nothing like fresh honey, is there?"

She nodded, her mouth full.

"We best be getting back to the house." Eve spoke up from the chair she'd taken in the corner, a pan of green beans in her lap. "I need to see about supper for John and the boys. *Stephen* is coming out."

The emphasis on Stephen's name couldn't have been an accident. "We still need to finish up the pickles and do the green beans." Abigail cocked her head toward the rows of empty jars. "And help clean up. Plus, I reckon this honey has to be jarred."

"The girls can do that." Eve stood and made a shooing motion. "Hazel, Hannah, you come with us. Frannie, you and Deborah and Rebekah and Leila finish up here. Your mudder and I have work to do at the house."

Something about Eve's tone reminded Abigail of John that first night in the backyard. She'd only been talking to Mordecai, nothing more. Stephen might be a friend of theirs, but wasn't Mordecai also? Still, she understood how they felt. She'd hurt Stephen once. She didn't want to do it again.

Mordecai picked up his box. "I need to get these back out to the apiary." He clomped toward the back door. Eve held it open for him, her expression sour. He glanced back. "You girls interested in any more lessons in beekeeping, let me know. Phineas is the real teacher when it comes to the hives. The bees calm right down for him. He hasn't been stung in years."

Abigail touched a drop of honey that had landed on the table. That was what this was about. Mordecai saw an opportunity for Phineas, one the boy would never take for himself. She studied her three girls. Rebekah was still too young, at sixteen. Leila, at eighteen, had been running around for two years and had never given any indication she had a special friend back in Tennessee.

Deborah, on the other hand, showed all the signs of missing someone special. She hadn't said anything since the move, but the moping around and the surliness spoke volumes. Idle talk around the quilting frame back in Tennessee had suggested her daughter had been passing time with Aaron Gringrich for more than a bit, but Deborah had said nothing. How would she feel about a man like Phineas, scarred for life, not only physically, but on the inside?

Her daughters were not shallow. They understood that physical beauty meant nothing. Only the heart counted. Phineas's heart and soul seemed damaged, but there was no damage that couldn't be mended by God Himself. Her bishop back home had told her that after Timothy's death. She tried to live every day as if it were true. Only God's touch could mend her own broken heart, it seemed. She was blessed a man such as Stephen would want her as his fraa.

Blessed.

She sighed as the screen door slammed and Mordecai's broad back disappeared. Only then did she let herself feel that slight, but still ugly, pinch of jealousy. Mordecai hadn't come to sweeten her up with honey. He'd come for her daughters.

Eve had nothing to worry about on Stephen's behalf. Abigail had best get used to seeing herself as spoken for. Everyone else did.

NINE

Deborah put out her hand. She could see the writing on the envelope Onkel John held, the curious look on his face—so like her mother's in the blue eyes and high cheekbones—telling her he wanted to know who Aaron Gringrich was and why he would send a letter to his niece. John's expression said he didn't like her getting a letter from a man. John wasn't her father, but he was the head of the house where she now lived.

She didn't need disciplining. Getting a letter from a friend didn't violate any Ordnung rule as far as she knew. But then, she didn't really know what the rules were in this district. Only the ones back home.

John snatched the letter from her reach. "Does Abigail know of these letters?"

"Jah." Deborah struggled to keep her tone respectful. "She knows I've written to Aaron. We're friends."

John grunted and slapped the letter onto her palm with a sharp crack. "I'll mention it to her as well."

Deborah had nothing to hide. She slid her arms behind her, clasping the letter in both hands. Not to hide it, but because it was private. Between Aaron and her. Finally. His first letter despite the fact that she'd written him four times already. "I better get back to the garden." She edged toward the door. "Danki for the letter."

"Didn't do nothing but fetch it from the mailbox." Onkel John frowned as he thumbed through the stack of mail in his hands. He dropped leaflets and flyers and a tool catalog on the scarred oak end table that served as a desk of sorts. "Don't think I haven't noticed you moping around the house. It doesn't do your mudder any good. She's got a hard row to hoe without her kinner looking like their horse just died."

The words stung worse than a slap. Deborah swallowed a heated retort. "I know."

"You got a roof over your head and food in your belly. You might try appreciating that. Know that Gott has a plan for you and it's prideful of you to question it." His long nose wrinkled as if he smelled something rancid. "Your mudder is trying her best to do right by you and your bruder and schweschders."

"I know and I count my blessings."

"Don't look that way."

"I'm . . . homesick, that's all."

"Best get over it."

If only it were that simple.

Onkel John cocked one long finger at her. "You'd do better to stop mooning over some boy you most likely won't see again and start settling in here. We got some good young men who need fraas. We need new blood, more kinner, to keep this district going and make it stronger."

Deborah managed a nod.

John stared at her a second longer, his mouth pursed in a

frown that made him look like her mudder when Deborah burned the beans. "And don't you be filling my girls' heads up with stuff and nonsense about how great it is in Tennessee. Ain't no better than it is here."

Deborah nodded a second time, afraid if she opened her mouth to speak, she'd blurt out all the words whirling in her head. It *was* better there. Greener. Prettier. Cooler. The colors were brighter and the air fresher and cleaner. Flowers bloomed in purple and pink and orange and yellow. A riot of colors that made her heart squeeze for the sheer joy of it. Here the drabness weighted her down like a heavy, thick, humid fog until she could barely pick up her feet and move. She wanted to settle in a corner and turn into a big lump of clay.

She didn't care what Onkel John thought. She would go home. She would see Aaron again. She would wrap herself in the beauty of a day in Tennessee. Maybe in the fall when the leaves turned orange and red and yellow and the breeze held a hint of winter. They'd have a fire in the fireplace and make fried pies and tell stories.

Soon.

"Ain't you got work to do?" John's frown had deepened. He jerked his head. "Standing there daydreaming won't get the cucumbers and squash picked or the tomatoes and beets canned."

"I came in to get the water jug."

"Tell Eve I'm headed into town to buy lumber."

Deborah wanted to know what the lumber was for, but she didn't ask. Maybe they would build an addition to this house and she'd be able to breathe again. Maybe Frannie was wrong about them moving. Maybe they were expanding this house. It looked like Eve might be expecting again. 'Course, no one had said that

and no one would. No need to speak of those things. Only to
make more room in a house already full to the rafters.

Deborah waited until John stomped through the front room
and disappeared out the door, letting the screen door slam behind
him. She slid into the hickory rocking chair and turned the envelope over in her hands. Aaron's familiar block print was so neat
and tidy, just like him. She wanted to rip open the envelope; yet
she waited, savoring the moment.

Lifting it to her face, she inhaled, imagining she could smell
the mouthwatering aroma of Elizabeth Gringrich's cinnamon
rolls. Knowing Aaron, he'd written this letter sitting at the kitchen
table after everyone turned in the for the night, the pole lamp casting shadows around him, a cinnamon roll on a plate in front of
him next to a tall glass of tea. He'd waited until everyone had been
asleep and then picked up his pencil and paper to write to her.

Slowly, savoring the moment, her heart fluttering in her chest
and her breathing light and fast, she opened the envelope, taking
care not to tear it.

Deborah,

*I hope things are going better for you now that you've had
a few weeks to get used to your new home. It sounds different. I
would like to see the armadillo. I wouldn't mind tasting some
of that wild grape jelly. Especially if you made your rolls and
some peanut butter and marshmallow cream to go with it. I'm
writing now to tell you my news. You know my family moved
to Carroll County from Ohio many years ago, but I don't think
I told you most of Mudder's family still lives there. My Aenti
Ruth's husband died a few months ago and she needs help
on her farm. Daed has asked me to go work her fields for her*

and take care of the livestock, her sons all being married and moved to Missouri with their families now.

I leave on the bus tomorrow. I don't know when I'll be back. Truth be told, I'm excited at this new road. It's a lot of responsibility to take care of Aenti Ruth's farm. One I would not get here, as Daed will not retire to the dawdi haus *for many years. And by then I'll be expected to have made my own way. The farm will go to my youngest brother in the end. I think it will be an adventure, living in a new place up north and meeting new people.*

Deborah wiped at her face. The words wavered in front of her. Her big plan shattered like a pitcher of lemonade and fell to pieces at her feet. What was Aaron trying to tell her? She'd promised him she would be back. He'd said he would wait for her. They would finish what they'd started. Neither had spoken of marriage, but they'd been walking the road that would take them in that direction. They'd been through baptism together. How could he change his mind so quickly? Surely that wasn't what he meant to say. She forced herself to focus on the words, to find his true meaning.

Anyway, I wanted you to know. I'm adding Aenti Ruth's address in Sugarcreek at the bottom in case you get a hankering to write. I will be busy, though, so don't be surprised if I don't write much. Ruth has two hundred acres and pigs and chickens and goats and a dozen horses. I'll be up to my ears.

I imagine plenty of men there in Bee County already have their gazes on you. It hurts my heart to think of it, but I know it wouldn't be fair to make you wait. Being apart is too hard. Especially when others might do just as well. I don't know what

*God's plan is for us, only that He has one for you and one for me.
I don't know if our paths are intended to cross again. It's hard
for a simple man like me to understand. So I'm going to Ohio,
and I figure whatever happens, happens. I know it's hard. It's
not what we wanted, but I figure it'll be a bit of adventure too.
You're having your adventure in Texas, I'll have mine up north.*

Take care.

Aaron

Take care? Whatever happens, happens? A simple man, indeed. Deborah let the letter drop into her lap. To her surprise a wet spot appeared at the top, a blotch of water. She wiped at her face. No sense in crying over spilled milk. That was what Daed would say. She sniffed, stuffed the letter back into the envelope, and smoothed down the flap.

Swallowing the hard knot of disappointment in her throat, she stood and marched to the room she shared with her cousins and sisters. Kneeling, she tugged a red plastic Tupperware box from under the bed and tucked the letter in with the three she'd received from Josie, much dog-eared from reading and rereading. She wouldn't be reading Aaron's letter again. His decision had been carved on her heart with words sharper than the knife her daed used to dress a deer. Aaron hadn't said as much, but he didn't think they had a chance. He made it sound as if he didn't want to stand in the way of her happiness, when it was his that was first and foremost in his mind.

She snapped the lid back on with more force than necessary, then shoved the container back under the bed. With a weariness that almost felt like sickness, she leaned her head against the mattress and closed her eyes.

In the heavy, oppressive heat of the room, the air hung on her like a shroud. She searched for words of supplication but found none. Only a cold, dark void where once had been the little sprig of joy she'd nurtured with hope and the beginnings of love. Something she thought would blossom into love and life with Aaron.

Not likely.

So be it.

She raised her head and got to her feet.

Time to get to work. This place needed some cleaning, so she might as well use some elbow grease to get it up to her standards. They had vegetables to pick and another canning frolic to plan.

She had all the time in the world to whip this place into shape.

TEN

Deborah felt as if she were sixteen all over again, awkward, self-conscious, and stumbling about on two left feet. This wasn't her first singing, so why did her heart pound and her palms sweat?

She took a deep breath and let it out. Frannie giggled for no apparent reason. Deborah exchanged glances with Leila and Rebekah. Her sisters rolled their eyes and shrugged. Their cousin had been giggling as they walked along the sagging fence that divided a field of cornstalks, only knee-high, from a field of milo just beginning to get heads and up the dirt road that led to Leroy's house. Deborah hoped her cousin would stifle those giggles during the singing. It would get embarrassing to be with her otherwise, on this, their first time to a singing in Bee County.

She smoothed the clean apron she donned over her nicest blue dress. It wasn't anything fancy, but it was the least faded. Mudder had insisted Deborah come. Said it was part of joining the community. In an odd little fit of closeness, she had straightened Deborah's kapp and smoothed her fingers across her cheek before murmuring that the dress brought out the blue of her eyes.

Her mother always said Deborah looked the most like Daed.

The blue eyes were his, but Mudder's were blue too, so Deborah could only imagine that Mudder wanted to see what she wanted to see. To her, Caleb was a little miniature of Daed. Even without a single photograph, she would never forget what her father looked like. She thanked God for that blessing, at least.

"What are you looking all moony-eyed over?" Frannie did a hop-skip that made her seem more like three-year-old Hazel than a seventeen-year-old who'd been going to singings for over a year now. "This is supposed to be fun."

It would be more fun if Josie and Aaron and her other friends would be there. *Stop it.* Aaron was in Ohio by now. Farther away than ever. "I'm not moony. I'm just . . . a little nervous, this being at Leroy's house and all."

Having the singing in the bishop's house made it seem more like another prayer service than a time to get to know the other young folks in this tiny district.

"Will there be a lot of people?" Leila looked festive in her lilac dress and freshly ironed kapp. "Will Leroy and his fraa stay around the whole time? Back home we have the singings in the barn and the older folks stay up at the house. Just come down to check on us once in a while."

"Our barns are old and messy and dirty and hot." Frannie waved a hand, her expression airy as if this explanation made perfect sense. The idea of cleaning the barns didn't seem to have crossed her mind. "Besides, Leroy says adult supervision will make sure we stay on a righteous path. There're usually a couple dozen of us, depending on who can make it. Leroy and Naomi most likely will sit out in the backyard and visit with Andrew and Sadie."

Two dozen. Back home there'd sometimes been fifty or seventy-five on a good night.

"How do you . . . I mean . . . doesn't that make it hard . . . to . . . you know . . . ?" Deborah floundered for words. Courting was private, and holding the singings right under the bishop's nose with a handful of young people defeated the purpose. Most all of them would be in their *rumspringas*. "Do the boys and girls pair up? Do you play games?"

"We play volleyball usually."

Those weren't the games Deborah meant, but she didn't want to tell her cousin if Frannie didn't already know of such things. Every district was different, every Ordnung different—one of the things she found most confusing. If a way of doing things was true and proper in God's eyes, wouldn't it be the same for all Plain folks? Another question she never expected to have answered.

She and Aaron had spent some time in the shed out in back of Josie's barn at a singing not long after her seventeenth birthday. It had been hot and sweaty, but Aaron had grinned the whole time and he'd held her hand without trying anything else until the boys outside yelled their five minutes were up and it was time for them to come out. That was when she'd decided he was the one. They'd exchanged their first kiss in that same shed a year later. Now she wished she had those lovely first kisses back. They should've belonged to someone else. Someone willing to wait for her. Not someone who gave up at the first sinkhole in the road.

"You're moony-eyed again." Frannie slapped Deborah on the shoulder with a playful swat. "You know who is pleasing to the eye? Jesse Glick. He isn't courting anyone, leastways so you would notice. Maybe he'll give you a ride home. That's when the pairing-up happens. Or maybe he'll take you for a walk."

"Leroy's son?" Leila's expression perked up. "I saw him at the store yesterday. Dropping off a bunch of eggs. He said hey."

"Besides running the store, they build and repair buggies. They also break horses for the Englisch folks. They do all right."

Deborah wiped at the sweat forming on her upper lip. Her fresh dress drooped. It was a long walk from John's to Leroy's and she still had to make the walk home, unless a boy like Jesse gave her a ride.

Only a few buggies and one wagon were parked in front of the house. Either attendance was light, or the others were on foot too. Deborah longed for Aaron's two-seater. Nee. She banished Aaron from her thoughts and trudged up the two lone steps to Leroy's front door, where she tapped with a shaking hand.

"Nee, silly, go on in. It's unlocked. They're expecting us." Frannie pushed past Deborah and opened the door. "Don't make them keep coming to the door."

Deborah followed her in, Leila and Rebekah close behind. The Glicks had pushed the benches from their supper table into the front room and arranged them in rows along with two rocking chairs, a couple of straight-back chairs, and a footstool. The sparsely furnished room had plenty of space for the dozen and a half or so young folks who occupied it. Leroy stood in the doorway that most likely led to the room where they took their meals and then the kitchen beyond. He nodded. Frannie approached him directly and shook his hand. Following her lead, Deborah, Leila, and Rebekah did the same. He had a firm but quick shake.

"Have a seat." He nodded toward the benches. "Girls on that side."

Feeling like a turnip in a basket of beets, Deborah watched Frannie traipse over to a cluster of girls she'd seen at the prayer service earlier. They glanced her way, gazes open and curious.

"The Lantz girls!" Esther King broke away from the group,

all smiles. "I was hoping you'd come. The more the merrier. We could use some new faces."

Esther looked like Phineas. They had the same blue-green eyes and dark hair, but she was a slight girl, barely as tall as Leila, and round in a pleasing way. She didn't have any of her brother's dark broodiness. But then it would be easier for her—she didn't carry the scars of that day. Had she been in the van? The details of the accident were none of Deborah's business, but life had changed for the entire King family that day, physical scars or no.

She glanced beyond Esther to the boys roughhousing and talking in low voices, glancing at the girls every now and again to see if they were watching. No Phineas.

"It's nice to be here." Deborah forced a smile. Being here reminded her of not being with Josie and her friends back home. It reminded her of Aaron. "It's a nice little group you have."

"Small, but lots of spunk." Esther plopped onto a bench and patted the spot next to her. "Sit next to me."

Deborah did as instructed. She surveyed the group. "Phineas isn't coming?"

"He fancies himself too old, I reckon." Esther's eyebrows rose and she leaned toward Deborah. A smile spread across her face. "Why, did you expect to see him here?"

"Nee, I . . . I just . . ." Deborah plucked at a thread on her apron. Why had she brought up Phineas to his sister? Now Esther would run home and tell him. Phineas got under her skin. Not in a good way. Really. "I just wondered. He's not married and he's the same age."

Esther's smile drained away. "My bruder's not like most men. I wouldn't change a thing about him, but I wish girls could really see him."

"See past his . . . scars?"

"It's okay to say it. He has scars. He also has a good heart. Once you get to know him. Believe me, I know him." Esther's smile returned. "I'll tell him you asked about him."

"Nee, nee, don't do that." Heat scalded Deborah's cheeks. It had been an idle question, nothing more. "He'll think . . ."

"He'll think you're interested." Esther's face darkened. "And you're not because you're like all the other girls. All you can see is his face. Well, he's worth getting to know and it's your loss."

"Nee, I just don't want to be too forward." Deborah grappled for words to explain the strange awkwardness that afflicted her whenever she thought of Esther's brother. "It's not my place. I mean, I'm new and I don't know what's what."

"Isn't that the point of all this?" Esther patted her hand as if she were the much older, wiser woman. "Give Phineas a chance—that's all I'm saying. After all, courting is private. Speaking of which . . ."

She popped to her feet and gave a fleeting, furtive wave to a young man with dark-rimmed glasses and brilliant green eyes who leaned against the far wall, arms crossed, as if waiting. Deborah had seen him at the Combination Store. Jesse Glick's older brother, Adam. Esther had a special friend. Maybe she could explain all the feelings rattling around inside Deborah.

"How do I know—?"

Deborah's words were drowned out by the first notes of a hymn sung by Jesse Glick, who clutched a songbook in his big, tanned hands. Esther sank back into her seat, disappointment apparent in the way she stared as Adam slipped onto the bench next to Jesse. Stragglers eased into their seats and voices immediately rose up to meet Jesse's in the sweet German that came without effort, without thought.

Unaccountably irritated by her conversation with Esther, Deborah closed her eyes and tried to focus on the words of the old, familiar hymn. The words died away and someone else picked another song, equally familiar. She opened her eyes and saw Leroy straighten and ease from the room, probably into the kitchen where he and his fraa would sit and chat within earshot.

The singing went on and on. Deborah grew sweaty and her throat felt parched. Will Glick, Jesse's cousin, left and came back with a bucket of water and a tin cup. He handed it to Deborah first, a tentative smile on his tanned face. She nodded her thanks, gulped a few swallows, and passed it to Leila, whose face shone with sweat. Still, they continued to sing. Deborah could almost pretend Josie sat next to her and Aaron yonder in the first rocking chair.

But no, it was Jesse who sat across from her, Will on one side, his brother, Adam, on the other. Every time she glanced their way, Jesse was looking in her direction. Will seemed to alternate between the floor and the ceiling. She tried keeping her gaze on her hands, but curiosity drove her to take a quick peek again. Jesse grinned at her, his cheeks and jaw reddening.

The last note died away. "Time to eat." Jesse popped up from his seat and waved a hand toward the girls. "Someone want to bring out the snacks?"

Frannie, Leila, and Rebekah, glued to her side, and her knot of friends headed to the kitchen, all the while whispering and giggling. Esther edged toward the door, Adam close behind. They huddled next to the door, heads close together, deep in conversation.

What now?

The music had been a balm to Deborah's heart, but this part, this part seemed too much like being set adrift in a lake in a canoe with no paddles. She'd never been new anywhere before. She'd known her friends her entire life. Her social skills were untested, untried, until now unnecessary. She'd made a mess of things with Esther. No one else had made an effort to include her.

She turned, thinking she'd head to the door, and bumped into Jesse. "Oh, sorry." She stopped. Had he come over to talk to her? It seemed that way. The thought made her palms feel sweaty. "You're Jesse, right?"

"Jah. Jesse. And you're . . . I forget which one you are. I know there's Leila, I met her at the store yesterday . . . and Rebekah and . . ."

"Deborah. My name is Deborah."

"Gut. That's gut." He kept looking over her shoulder. She glanced back. The doorway that led to the kitchen was still empty. She swiveled toward Jesse and he grinned. "How are you liking it here in Bee County? Not as fancy as your district in Tennessee."

"We're not fancy." The words stung, even if they were innocently intended. "Bee County is different, not as . . . green."

Deborah was going to say pretty, but that did indeed sound fancy. Jesse didn't seem to notice her hesitancy. His gaze returned to the spot over her shoulder. Whatever he wanted, he wasn't finding it in the conversation with her. She swiveled again. This time the girls were streaming through the door, Leila at the front, Frannie and Rebekah right behind her.

"That's nice." Jesse squeezed past her and trotted toward the other girls. "Welcome to Bee County."

"Danki." Deborah pressed her hands together in front of her and breathed a long sigh. "For nothing."

He hadn't heard her words because he hadn't been listening. He'd been watching for someone else. He took a plate of cookies from Leila, his words indistinct across the room, but his expression speaking volumes. Leila smiled up at him, her face shy. The dimples in her cheeks deepened. She ducked her head and said something. Jesse answered and stepped back, letting Leila lead the way. Neither seemed aware that Deborah watched.

Deborah edged toward the door and slipped out. She was glad for Leila, but the bittersweet taste in her mouth made the bile rise in her throat. Time to go home.

"Don't mind Jesse." Will stuck his head through the door before she could shut it. "He's like a kid in a candy store tonight."

"What?" She feigned ignorance, not wanting to find herself vulnerable yet again. "That sounds . . . like he's big on himself."

"My cousin isn't big on himself." Will moved so he stood next to her on the narrow porch. "New girls at the singing. It's been awhile since that happened."

"So we're like produce, ripe for the picking."

"That's not exactly how I would've said it." A wide grin split his face, revealing white, even teeth. "But that's one way of putting it."

"I don't care for that way much."

"We don't intend to offend you. It's just that we don't have many girls and we're thinking . . . ahead."

How could she be offended when she'd been doing the same thing? "It's okay."

"Then why do you look so aggravated? You look like you just drank turpentine."

"I'm not mad . . . I'm just . . ." She stared at the gathering dusk. "Tired."

"That's not what you were planning to say."

"I'm homesick."

"You got someone back home?"

"Nee." Not anymore.

"Gut." He cocked his head toward the door. "They're about to start again. Come back in."

"Not tonight."

"But next time?"

He was so eager. He didn't even know her. Just her outsides. Her appearance. First impressions.

Phineas didn't get to rely on those. Most people never got past that first look. Why was she thinking of him now, with his prickly ways? "We'll see."

"We sure will."

Deborah bolted from the porch, the self-assurance in those three words following her. Will Glick didn't know her, but he'd like to change that.

Somehow that knowledge didn't give her the pleasure she once thought it would.

ELEVEN

Deborah stumbled over a tuft of cornstalk. She bit back a groan and strode forward. Burrs stuck to the top of her now-dusty sneakers. The journey home seemed even longer than the walk to Leroy's house. She had no one to blame but herself. She could've stayed at the singing. Instead, she'd slipped away because Jesse was more interested in Leila than her. Deborah didn't even want a special friend. She still cared for Aaron. She wasn't so shallow that she could simply forget what they had one week to the next.

Still, it hurt for some reason. She grabbed at the thought and turned it over in her head as she walked, her gaze on the ground to try to avoid stepping in a red ant hill. It hurt because she felt so alone here. Aaron didn't want her. Maybe no one would. She longed to be a fraa and a mudder. Everything up until she left Tennessee to come here had led her to believe Gott's plan was for her to be with Aaron. Now she had no idea which way to go, where to turn, so she kept walking forward.

Time to get over it, as Onkel John said. Sniffing, she picked up her pace and cut across the field next to Leroy's farm. If she walked along the creek bed, now nearly dry, it would take her in a more direct line to Onkel John's. She slipped past a water tank, sidestepped an old, broken-down wagon, and made her way to the creek bed. The sooner she arrived at the house, the sooner she could go to bed and begin a new day.

Rustling sounds followed by deep, guttural grunts brought Deborah to an abrupt halt. Her breath caught in her throat and her heart, already pumping with the exertion of her walk, clattered into overdrive. In the gathering dusk, several mounds moved. They grunted in a cacophony of conversation that sounded like they were looking for something they couldn't find.

Barely breathing, hands pressed to her chest, her entire body rigid, she peered at the mounds that seemed to be milling about. Pigs. They looked like pigs, but bigger. They had white tusks and big heads with stiff, grizzled whiskers. They were black or dark brown, she couldn't tell. Mostly they were big. She'd never seen such enormous pigs.

A head came up. More grunts and snorts. One of them stared directly at her, the whites of its eyes shiny in the dusk.

Deborah took a step back, then another. Her foot hit something slick. She slipped and staggered, arms flapping.

The writhing in the dirt and the rutting of the tusks against the black earth stopped. Beady eyes studied her. She stilled. The biggest pig raised its head and sniffed, its long snout quivering in the air. Its head bobbed and its massive body started toward her.

Deborah whirled and ran.

———

Phineas picked up his binoculars from the wooden crate next to the hive and slung the strap over his shoulder. Combining work with pleasure had an economy that pleased him. He enjoyed his time with the bees and watching for birds. He smiled to himself as he always did when he thought of the little, silly joke his daed liked to make about Phineas's interest in the birds and the bees. He studied the horizon. The gathering dusk meant it was too late for any more bird-watching.

The thought didn't bother him too much. It had been a long day. Time to roll into bed. Dawn would come early. He strode through the field, humming to himself. When he realized what he was doing, he stopped. Just because the singing was tonight didn't mean he had to partake. No matter how many times Daed and Susan and Esther brought it up. He liked this time outdoors much better. The music of nature suited him, a concert all its own. Birds cooing in the trees, crickets singing, frogs croaking, dogs barking.

He slogged through the weeds, keeping an eye out for rattle-snakes. They liked to come out once the sun started to set and the day cooled. He'd rather not come upon one unawares. They really wanted to be left alone and would only strike if they felt threatened. Still, he chose to wear his work boots when he walked in the fields.

One thought led to another. Deborah and her fear of snakes. Deborah and her bare feet. Deborah and her determination to go home. Last he'd heard, she was still here. Daed had mentioned showing her and her sisters how to extract honey from the frames. Then Susan had brought it up. Then Esther. They acted like they'd never had new folks at a frolic at the house.

Any girl who had as much dislike for this place should go home. Then he would stop thinking about her.

He could admit it. To himself. When he closed his eyes at

night, for some reason, which he couldn't explain, her face appeared. When he worked the hives, his mind drifted to the look on her face after he'd plucked the stinger from her finger. Gratitude, and something else.

Rather, something lacking. She hadn't been thinking about his face or his scars. She'd been thankful for him. No girl had ever looked at him like that.

A shriek cut the serene evening quiet. A woman. Phineas swung right and pushed through withered cornstalks and weeds to the road. Deborah Lantz ran smack into him, slammed into his chest. Out of sheer instinct, he caught her. His arms went around her. She stared up at him, her face contorted with surprise and shock. Her mouth opened but no sound escaped.

"What happened?" He'd been thinking about her and here she stood. The shock of that realization made him stutter. He held her, acutely aware of her warmth and her ragged breathing. Her heart pounded against his chest, making his own race to catch up. He wanted to keep her there, close, within the circle of his arms. After a second or two, something else hit him. She stank. "What's that smell?"

Panting, she tugged free and stumbled back a few steps. A sudden, disorienting sense of loss enveloped him.

"You. It had to be you." Her voice quivered. "Every time I do something silly, you appear. Where did you come from? Did you see them?"

Her words sounded almost like an accusation. Phineas breathed through the desire to snap back at her. She'd been scared, and sometimes people who were scared lashed out. "I was working the hives. I heard you scream."

"I didn't scream." Her cheeks, already scarlet with heat and exertion, burned redder. "I may have . . . yelped a little. They were chasing me."

"Who was chasing you?"

"Not who, what. I don't know exactly." Her chin came up and she stalked away. Phineas stood there for a second, then rushed to match her step. If she walked any faster, she'd be running. "They looked like pigs only . . . bigger . . . and black." She flung her arms out as if measuring their widths and heights. She always seemed to need to talk with her hands. "They were . . . digging around in the dirt, and when they saw me they rushed at me. I ran away from them."

"Stepped in something along the way, did you?"

"What do you mean?"

He sniffed the air. "You're a little . . . smelly."

She groaned, stopped, and picked up the skirt of her dress a few inches. Brown stuff smeared both sneakers. "That's just great. Great."

"It'll wash off."

She started walking again, her face the color of beets now. "I suppose."

"Are you going to your Onkel John's?"

"Jah. What does that have to do with it?"

"You're going the wrong direction."

Her expression saying it was all Phineas's fault, she halted, pivoted, making a cloud of dust around her feet as she stomped. Dust that stuck to the manure. Then, with more grace, she resumed her hurried stride in the right general direction.

"Wild pigs." Phineas whirled and kept pace with her. "Technically, they're called javelinas."

She didn't look at him. "Javelinas?"

"There're a lot of them around here. They rut around, rooting for food. Tear up the fields something fierce. When it's dry like this, it's hard for them to find anything to eat. They're usually down around the creek bed, hoping it'll have water, I guess. By the way, they don't chase people. I imagine they ran the other direction. They only come after people who antagonize them."

"I didn't antagonize them."

"Then you probably had nothing to worry about."

"Right. Now I know." Her pace slowed again. "Are there any other wild animals I should know about?" She waved both arms over her head as if in surrender. Apparently the more worked up she got, the more she had to move her hands. "Anything else that might run me down, bite me, chew on me, spit me out?"

Phineas liked her feisty anger better than the earlier fear. Her tone suggested she was ready to take on any critter who tried to take a bite out of her. Phineas waited a beat or two, letting her catch her breath. "Coyotes."

"Coyotes. Onkel mentioned those." She sighed, a blustery, exaggerated sound. "What else?"

"Mountain lions."

"Mountain lions?" She finally glanced sideways at him, her eyebrows lifted. Her arm swept out in a disdainful gesture. "Are you pulling my leg? This place is flat as a pancake. There are no mountains here."

"They get pushed out of their natural habitats by folks building stuff and go where they can find food. There're not a lot of them, but once in a while, we find a cat or a dog or a goat that's been killed by one."

"How do you know so much about animals and such?"

"I read."

At first because it filled his time, especially when he was in the hospital those long weeks of recovery. His jaw had been wired shut and his nose taped into place, the swelling making it difficult to breathe, let alone talk. And later because it kept the loneliness at bay.

Deborah's expression said she still didn't understand. She wanted him to explain himself. He'd never made conversation with a girl to any extent. He dredged up the words. "They interest me. We also have the two-legged animals you have to watch out for around here."

"What do you mean?"

"The escapees."

"What escapees?"

The real reason she shouldn't be gallivanting around the countryside alone at night. "Once in a while, a prisoner escapes from the McConnell Unit or Garza, the west transfer unit."

"Prisoners?" Her shoulders hunched and her head went down. "There's a prison out here?"

"Just east of Beeville. There are almost as many prisoners as people living in Beeville."

"Why would people want to live around a prison?"

"Jobs." Pure and simple. People were hurting for ways to put food on the table for their children. The folks in Beeville had lobbied for more and bigger prisons. "A way to make a living that doesn't involve sweating on the back of a tractor, I guess."

"Farming is honest work. I suppose guarding prisoners is too." She was silent for a few more yards. "Are they dangerous?"

"They say they put the worst of the worst here, so you shouldn't traipse around at night by yourself. I'm surprised John didn't mention it."

"He's too busy trying to put food on *his* table."

Good point. "Anyway, I think that's it for the dangerous creatures who live in our neck of the woods."

She picked up her pace as if chased by those very dangerous creatures he'd mentioned. "What are the binoculars for?"

He'd forgotten they hung around his neck. "I like to bird-watch."

Her eyebrows rose and fell again. "Just any birds?"

"Unusual birds. They fly through here on their way to Mexico for the winter and come back through in the spring. Even in the summer you can see some interesting birds sometimes." It sounded like a silly thing for a grown man to say aloud. He wanted to kick himself. Birding was something he kept to himself. He'd been doing it since his daed gave him the binoculars and a book on birds the day he left the hospital. Mordecai knew he would need something to take his mind off the grotesqueness that was his face with the new, red, raw scars like braids across his cheeks and nose. "I like the way they look when they fly."

"Me too. I wish I could fly with them."

The knot of embarrassment in his gut dissolved. "Me too."

He'd never told anyone that and she'd said it first. They had one thing in common.

He matched his stride to her shorter one and took a quick peek at her. She marched along, arms swinging, her gaze fixed on something on the horizon. Her breathing still seemed strangely fast and the color hadn't faded from her cheeks. Sweat dampened her forehead, and the tendrils of blond hair that escaped her black kapp curled around her temples. She glanced his way, then back at the road. "You don't have to walk with me."

He slowed. He'd been so intent on making sure she was all right, he forgot to think about whether she wanted his company.

Of course she didn't. Why would she? Fine. The smell wafting from below the hem of her dress didn't make her particularly good company either. Nor did her general air of discontent with him, with Bee County, with the world. "Good night."

She glanced back, her expression much more tentative than it had been only seconds earlier. "But I wouldn't mind if you did . . . walk with me, I mean. If the *schtinkich* isn't too much for you."

"It's not like I'm not around manure every day." She shouldn't be out here by herself. At least that's what he told himself. Phineas sped up. "What were you doing out here anyway?"

"Walking back from the singing." The tiniest tremor in her voice gave her away. This had not been good. She hunched her shoulders, her gaze on the road. "I decided to go home—back to Onkel John's a little early."

"Didn't enjoy it, did you?" He kept his tone neutral. It was none of his business. "That's the funny thing about those singings."

"Nothing funny about it."

"I just mean the idea to start pairing off with the person you might marry someday. Most of us here, we've all known each other forever already. I reckon we should've figured it out by now."

"Not me."

So that was it. She'd felt left out. The new girl. Even with Frannie there and her sisters, most likely. He'd felt the same way and he'd known all these people for his whole life. "Didn't go so well?"

"It was fine. I'm just tired."

"What does it matter?" Deborah didn't plan to stick around here. She'd told him as much the first day she flopped at his feet in horror at the sight of him. And again after the bee sting. She'd seemed pretty set on leaving as quickly as possible. "You're not in the market for friends anyway."

"What do you mean?"

"You don't plan to stay. At least that's what you said."

She seemed to take a sudden interest in the road, sidestepping a twig and two-stepping past a stone. Her cheeks flamed still brighter. "I shouldn't have said that."

"Truth is truth."

"I can't go back anytime soon. My mudder needs me here, at least until after the wedding and probably beyond, given the state of Stephen's house."

"He isn't much of a housekeeper, but surely your schweschders can handle that."

She picked at a burr stuck to the bottom of her apron. "You can't expect things to stay the same just because you're not there anymore. People move on."

She uttered this statement with a faint underpinning of what sounded like despair, or more like melancholy. That was it. Melancholy like he so often experienced when he stared up at the sky and wondered why God had bothered to plant him on the earth, so little did he have to offer those around him who pretended to accept him as he was, but shuddered after he turned away. He found he had no answer for her, none that would make it better.

"I had a special friend."

He figured as much. A girl like her. It surprised him she wasn't already married.

"He left Tennessee and moved to Ohio."

"Sorry."

"Gott's will. At least that's what he says."

"Sometimes people like to call their actions Gott's will because then they can do what they really want to do."

"Aaron's not like that."

"So you thought."

"So I thought."

They walked in silence for a stretch. Phineas didn't try to find another topic of conversation. They had nothing in common, except geography. He had never had a special friend, likely never would. The dusk deepened as clouds blotted the stars and moon. It became harder to see the rutted road in front of them. Deborah stumbled a few times but still said nothing.

At the intersection, she veered right. He followed.

"You don't have to keep walking with me. It's out of your way and it's been a long day. You're surely tired. And I schtinkich."

"I've gotten used to the smell." He didn't want this time to end. Not yet. Tomorrow things would go back to the way they always were, but for tonight, for just this one time, he wanted to walk along the road with a pretty girl. "You can't walk around out here alone at night."

"It's only another mile or so."

"It's dark."

"I'm not afraid of the dark."

"Me neither. Only what's in it."

Deborah chuckled, a soft sound that said she would acquiesce. "It says something about you that you would admit it. Especially to me."

"You, being a woman?"

"Me, being almost a stranger."

"Not so strange. Okay, maybe a little."

They both laughed then, the sound light and more than a little surprised.

The silence grew again, filled only by an owl hooting and barn swallows cooing.

"Can I ask you a question?" Her voice sounded much wearier than it had a few minutes earlier. "You don't have to answer if you don't want to."

"Shoot."

"Why don't you go to the singings?"

The dusky blanket of night worked to his advantage. She couldn't see the firestorm of red that surely crept across his scarred face. He cleared his throat.

"You don't have to answer."

He wasn't a coward. Or maybe he was. He'd gone to one singing when he turned sixteen. Four years ago. "It didn't suit."

"You don't like singing?"

"I don't like making people—girls—uncomfortable."

"Why would you make them uncomfortable?"

"You seem like you're smart enough. You can figure it out."

Her pace slowed. "Because of your scars?"

He fought a sudden knot in his throat. He'd set all this aside long ago. Why would it bother him now? "Because there's no point. The idea that I might show an interest in more than friendship with any one of them scared them silly. It showed on their faces."

The looks. He'd seen them all despite their best attempts to hide them. Pity. *Poor Phineas.* Compassion. *Poor Phineas, it's not his fault.* Fear. Fear he'd want to walk one of them home and they'd have to say yes because they were good girls who didn't want to hurt his feelings. *Poor Phineas, please, Gott, forgive me, but don't let him pick me.* He could play volleyball or kickball or baseball with them, but walk them home and steal a kiss in the moonlight, no, that was a different skillet of fish too hot to handle.

"Like you said, you've known each other forever. If they're your friends, the scars don't matter."

Easy for someone so pretty to say. "I don't want to talk about this."

"Why? I won't say anything." She crossed her arms and halted in the middle of the road. "I miss talking to my friends."

Was she asking him to be her friend? He'd never really had friends. Not that Will and Jesse and the others hadn't tried. Things had changed after the accident, and they eventually left him alone to his books and his binoculars and to the rituals of harvesting honey and caring for the beehives. She was lonely. He understood that; moreover, his heart hurt for her. His heart wasn't used to such a thing. He'd been turned inward for so long, he'd forgotten how to look out. Swallowing hard, he forced himself to gather the words he kept locked inside. "The scars matter."

"Why?"

"Don't play dumb. Those singings are about pairing up. Finding the person you'll court and marry. Who would want to . . . marry . . . this?" He pointed at his face, even knowing the clouds scudding across the sky hid the light of the moon needed to illuminate the ropy scars. "If you said they don't bother you, you'd be lying."

"If you said you weren't feeling sorry for yourself, you'd be lying." Her tone was tart. She sighed, a sound like a small child missing her mother, such a sad sound. "Just like I would be. We both need to stop feeling sorry for ourselves."

"You haven't been here long enough to know what I need to do."

"I know what it's like to be lonely." The tartness returned. "I know what it's like to walk down this road and feel all alone."

"I like being alone." It wasn't a lie. He'd gotten used to it. Embraced it.

"I don't believe you." She stopped at the entrance to the gravel drive that led to her Onkel John's house. "No one wants to be alone."

The clouds over the moon drifted apart and the light illuminated her face. She looked so sad something caught in Phineas's throat. She also looked beautiful. Plain folks didn't talk much about that sort of thing, but she was pleasing to the eye. In a place so desolate, a man couldn't help but know beauty when he saw it. That was why he spent so much time looking for birds. They were beautiful, especially in flight. So many times after the accident, he raised his head to the skies and watched them soar effortlessly and longed to do the same. To fly away from the loss and the hurt and the pain.

And the thought that he'd done this to himself and to his mudder. He swallowed the ache in his throat. "I'll walk you up to the house."

Her head cocked, her gaze glued to his. She didn't move or speak.

"Deborah?"

"I would like to see the birds you watch sometime."

"You would?" Nothing could've surprised Phineas more. "You want to bird-watch?"

"I want to see what you see."

"I do it to be alone."

"You don't need to walk me." Her pique made her voice high. She took two steps away from him. "I know the way."

"Wait." For some reason he couldn't bear to leave her on a sour note. "Fine. I'll show you. We're past the migration season, but there're still a few birds around."

She halted and turned back. "Are they pretty?"

"Some. I'll let you know when."

He turned away, not sure what had just happened.

"Phineas."

He looked back. Deborah waved at him, a quick, see-you-soon sort of wave. "You're wrong."

"About what?"

"It's what's on the inside that counts."

"You been talking to my daed?"

"Nee, but I've heard he's a wise man."

"Good night, Deborah."

She waved again. "See you, Phineas."

"See you, Phineas." She didn't really see him. Not under the inky dark of a cloudy night. For the first time in his life, he'd walked a girl home. Phineas hardly knew Deborah, but they had talked as if they'd known each other forever. His body felt curiously light, as if his feet didn't touch the hard dirt still warm from a sun already set.

Dark. It was dark. She couldn't see his face. That was it. She could forget about his ugly mug when they spoke under the cover of dark.

How he wished it could be the same in the harsh light of day.

The ebullience he'd felt only seconds before dissipated like air from a pierced balloon. He tried to remember the stench of manure instead of the sweet voice and lovely face. The sound of his name spoken by her voice fluttered in his ears like the tiny, silky wings of a hummingbird.

Anger washed over him. He worked so hard not to want what he couldn't have, and here it was again, slapping him in the face at the least expected moment. He needed to stay away from Deborah Lantz. She would go home or she would find someone to be her special friend and he would end up hurting and alone.

Again.

TWELVE

Deborah fanned her face with a section of *The Budget* she'd finished reading for the third time. The news from Tennessee only made her that much more homesick. Right now they were probably fishing at the pond on the Bylars' farm. They would fire up the grill, set a big pan of grease on it, and deep-fry the fish dunked in flour and spices. There'd be red cocktail sauce. Her mouth watered at the thought of the spicy horseradish. And tartar sauce. And potato salad and coleslaw. The Brennamans or the Gringriches would bring homemade ice cream. Josie would bring an apple pie, because everyone knows it goes best with vanilla ice cream.

Aaron wouldn't be there. He'd be long gone to Ohio on his big adventure. Most likely he'd picked out a girl at the first Sunday night singing. By now he was driving her home in his aenti's buggy.

A fly buzzed her face. Deborah swatted it away with the newspaper. Flies and mosquitoes. She'd counted a dozen bites on her legs and ankles. The thought made her bend over to scratch. It only made the itch worse. Still fanning, she leaned back in the lawn chair, watching Leila, Rebekah, and the cousins play a fast and loose volleyball game. She should join them. Fun. They all could use fun. Still, she didn't move, held in her seat by the sheer weight of the humid evening air.

Leila smacked the ball over a net that had holes in a number of places and sagged in the middle. Frannie whopped it back so hard it knocked Rebekah back two steps. She collapsed in a gale of laughter for no apparent reason.

They were having fun. It was Deborah's own fault she was having none. The thought made her squirm. No one liked a whiner. She rose, determined to throw off her sourpuss attitude.

"Want this last piece of watermelon?" Eve trotted toward Deborah, carrying a plate that held a thick wedge of watermelon so juicy liquid dripped off the side. "My eyes are bigger than my stomach."

Deborah couldn't help herself. Her gaze went to Eve's thickening middle. Deborah had found her aunt retching in the sink the previous day. No doubt Eve was expecting again. Her skin looked pale under the flush of heat on her damp cheeks, and her fingers gripping the plate were swollen.

"The first slice was so nice and sweet, I do think I could make room for another." Deborah took the plate and moved aside. "Have a seat. I'll stand over here where I can spit the seeds. I want to play some volleyball in a bit anyway."

"We could have a seed-spitting contest." Eve settled into the chair without protest. "The boys love that."

"The girls are having too much fun with their volleyball game." Susan King chimed in from where she sat in the grass, her legs tucked primly under her. She and her brother, Mordecai, had come visiting in the afternoon. "Too bad Phineas didn't come; he was a good volleyball player when he was in school. They used to have some good games at recess. We could have the boys against the girls."

"Why didn't he come?" Mudder posed the question from her perch next to Onkel John on a wooden two-sitter swing suspended from a frame made of plastic PVC pipe. "There was plenty of food."

"Phineas isn't much for visiting." Mordecai stood with one leg propped against the only tree in the front yard that qualified as a real tree. "He was headed out to the back forty with his binoculars last I saw him. Something about some bird he thought he saw yesterday."

Deborah paused, the wedge of watermelon halfway to her mouth. Phineas hadn't kept his word about taking her on his next bird-watching expedition. Even though this didn't surprise her, it still caused a wave of something like . . . hurt to roll through her. He'd acted so strange during their late-night walk—one moment friendly, the next closed up like a jar of sour pickles with a lid that couldn't be pried off. He'd said he would take her to mollify her. That was all. He didn't need a silly girl like her for a friend. He'd made that clear. He didn't need friends at all.

"Why would he do that?" Mudder patted her face with a handkerchief, her expression perplexed. "Is he hunting? What's in season here?"

"We're so close to the Gulf of Mexico, we see quite a few tropical birds around here." Mordecai worked at his front teeth with a toothpick, his lips bared over a neatly trimmed dark beard shot through with silver. "Mexico isn't too far off. We're right in the path of lots of birds that head south for the winter and come back up to have their babies in the spring."

"Why would anyone go hunting for them with binoculars?"

Mudder asked as she worked the handkerchief along the back of her neck and then under her chin. She sounded only half interested in the answer. The only bird hunting Deborah's daed did was with a rifle when dove, quail, and turkey were in season. "Doesn't sound like those are eatin' birds."

"Nee. But they're right pretty." Mordecai dropped the toothpick and smiled. Phineas would look like that if he smiled. "Sometimes it's nice to gaze on something so bright and pretty in the middle of this dry, dusty place. Reminds us of Gott's hand at work during the creation."

Deborah followed the finger he extended toward the horizon. A dreary, desolate sight presented itself. The ground was so dry she could drop a match and watch an inferno birth itself, blossom, and spread in mere seconds. She inhaled the scent of dirt. So much dirt.

"Look yonder." Mordecai pointed again. The others joined Deborah in swiveling to see what he saw. "Those look like thunder boomers."

Black, menacing clouds hung low on the horizon. A sudden wind kicked up, causing a tumbleweed to flop its way along the fence line. Grit pinged Deborah's face and got in her mouth.

"It's moving pretty fast." Susan wiped at her face with a sleeve, as if she had experienced the same nasty surprise. "We might actually get some rain out of it."

The volleyball game stopped. Rebekah held on to the ball while Leila and Frannie took down the net. A sort of breathless anticipation seemed to hang over the yard. Deborah could feel the hopefulness that ran through each person, connecting them together.

Rain. Sweet rain. She could almost taste it.

The wind grew stronger. The strings on her kapp fluttered. She lifted her face to air laden with humidity. It felt cooler, she was sure of it. A drop of rain splattered on her nose. She closed her eyes.

Please, Gott, let it rain.

Another big, fat drop landed on her lips. She laughed and opened her eyes.

Thank You, Gott.

Rebekah stretched her arms over her head and lifted her hands to the sky. "Rain, rain," she chanted.

Leila and Frannie and the little girls joined in. "Rain, rain."

Caleb tumbled down from the dilapidated wagon he'd been pretending to drive and joined the chant.

Another gust of wind sent the lawn chair end over end. Caleb dashed after it, tackled it, and brought it back. Thunder rumbled. Lightning crackled. No one seemed to notice or care.

The rain came, a sprinkle at first, then harder. The older folks moved toward the house. Torn, Deborah looked back. Frannie, Rebekah, and Leila hopped up and down and shrieked with the sheer joy of it. She couldn't help it. She raced toward them. They grabbed hands and ran in a circle, faces lifted to the heavens.

"Rain, rain, rain, I love rain," Frannie shouted over the wind. "Gott is gut."

"Gott is gut," Hannah chanted.

"God gut," Hazel lisped.

Deborah laughed and scooped up her little sister, now a bundle of wet clothes and hair that smelled of mud and sweat. "You are right, little one."

Rain would mean a fresh growth of green grass and, more importantly, the crops would soak it up. The corn, the sugarcane, the milo, and the vegetable gardens that stretched endlessly behind every house. They would have more produce to sell at the store and in town on Friday mornings.

She only had to look as far as John and Eve's backyard to find something for which to be thankful. She would be thankful and content during the time she spent here. Even if she still intended to return home. Home where she had real friends.

"Let's play tag." She set Hazel on her stubby, little legs and pointed to Frannie. "You're it."

"Hide-and-seek. Hide-and-seek!" Hazel trundled after her. "I want hide-and-seek."

"Next," Deborah assured her.

For once, for one afternoon, they would play childish games until it was time to put childish things aside.

———

Still laughing at the comical way John and Eve had hippity-hopped to the back door, hands over their heads as if they might melt in the rain, Abigail grabbed a dish towel from the kitchen counter and wiped her face. They'd gone on to their room to change while Susan had declared she would take a quick nap if no one minded.

Abigail, on the other hand, felt more wide awake than she had in days. She also felt cooler than she had any day since their arrival in Bee County. Even the toothache that had plagued her recently seemed to subside. It didn't matter where a person lived. Farmers loved rain, but especially in this place. Irrigation and greenhouses were good, but some old-fashioned rain was the best medicine for a dry land.

"Share that?"

She looked up to see Mordecai standing on the rag-piece rug by the back door, water dripping from his straw hat. He grinned despite his soggy beard and rain-spattered shirt and pants.

"Surely."

She held out the towel. His fingers grazed hers as he took it. They were long and thin and callused. Everything about him shouted hard work, from the leathered skin of his face and spidery sun lines around his eyes to the broad muscles of his shoulders and biceps straining against a much washed, faded blue shirt.

The towel hid his expression for a few seconds, but when he handed it back, he smiled. "Much better."

She nodded, not sure where to look.

"It's good to see them act silly and have fun now and again." He nodded toward the screen door. "Their laughter . . . it makes me feel . . ."

"Less sad." She moved to stand where she could see out the window over the sink. The kinner whooped and dashed after each other in a muddy, wet game of tag, celebration in every dash and every skid. "Like Gott has not forgotten us."

Mordecai's startled expression made Abigail wish she'd held her tongue. He wiped his feet on the rug and leaned against the wall, hands folded over his broad chest. "Is that how you feel? Forgotten?"

"I didn't mean to question Gott's will." She stuttered in her race to retract the words. Mordecai would tell Leroy and Leroy would tell Stephen. She wasn't the stout believer her intended thought she was. "I know He has a plan for me and my kinner, for all of us."

"I'm not the bishop. You don't have to pretend with me."

She wasn't pretending. Not exactly. "I try hard to be patient and wait to see how the plan unfolds."

"But you're only human."

Abigail wanted a different conversation with this man she barely knew. Light, easy, simple. "Would you like some sweet tea?"

"Nee. What makes you think I'm sad?"

"Sometimes, when you think no one will notice, you look like I feel when I wake up in the morning and—"

"And remember your husband is dead."

"Jah. Timothy."

"My fraa was a good woman, but she's been gone twelve years."

"As was my husband." She glanced down at her hands gripping the sink. Her knuckles were white. She loosened her grip. "He's been gone more than two."

"The days of his life were complete."

"Jah, and mine are not." He would understand the sentiment behind those words. How strange and sad it seemed that the days of her life had not coincided with those of the man she loved. "Still, it's Gott's will."

"Gott's will."

Thunder rolled in a deep, continuous sound like a train chugging along a track. The rumble filled the air between them. Mordecai cocked his head, his blue-green eyes contemplating something behind Abigail's shoulder. "Time moves on."

"It does." She found herself holding her breath for some reason.

He smiled again and years fell away from his face. "What do you say? Let's play in the rain."

"What?"

"Come on. I figure it's Gott's way of offering us a good bath. I won't even have to take one later."

"But—"

"Nee. No buts."

He opened the screen door and jerked his head. "Last one to the horse trough and back is a monkey's uncle."

No one wanted to be a monkey's uncle—whatever that was—at any age. Feeling lighter than she had in months, Abigail darted past him, pounded down the two wooden steps, and let the wind carry her across the yard. Rain soaked her kapp, her hair, her face, and her dress. She glanced back, Mordecai followed. The wind knocked off his hat and sent it flying. Chortling, he chased it down.

She raced toward the horse trough, dress flapping behind her, hands planted on her kapp to keep it in place. Her feet hit a soft patch and went out from under her. She flapped her arms, skidded, and did a whirly turnaround in the mud, smacking into Mordecai.

His booming laugh told her no harm done. He dodged around her and pounded toward the horse trough. The kinner howled with laughter.

"It's a race. It's a race!" Leila darted across the yard, her muddy dress entangled around her legs. "To the trough!"

All the kinner joined in, laughing and shrieking. Hannah slipped and fell in the mud. She lay on her back, laughing, until Frannie dragged her to her feet. They both went down in a heap.

Mordecai slapped a hand on the trough, now full of muddy water, and trotted back toward the house. Caleb planted himself in the man's path. Mordecai zigged and zagged, lost his footing, went to his knees, then crawled around Caleb, who staggered forward, hand on his chest, gasping for air in his laughter.

"All y'all are crazy!" John's voice boomed from the open

kitchen window. "You're making a big mess of yourselves in that mud hole out there."

"The rain will wash it off." Mordecai paused by the back step, panting. "A little rainwater, a little laughter, both are good for the soul."

"So is quiet contemplation and an early bedtime." John's face disappeared from the window.

"Guess we should call it a day." Mordecai stretched and strolled toward Abigail as if he weren't covered with mud and wet to the bone. His face still shone with laughter. "Wouldn't want to outstay our welcome."

"You haven't." Abigail shut her mouth. This wasn't her house and Mordecai hadn't come to visit her. To her surprise, she didn't want him to leave. "I mean, it was fun."

"Yeah, it was fun." Rebekah wiped at her face, leaving a trail of mud across her check. "You run fast for an old . . ."

"Rebekah!" Abigail hastened to amend her daughter's statement. "You run fast, period."

Mordecai threw his head back and laughed, a deep belly laugh. "I'm no spring chicken, but I can still catch my kinner and turn them over my knee, if need be."

"Do they need be?" Deborah, who leaned against the horse trough with her face lifted to the sky, rain running down her pink cheeks, posed the question. "Phineas must be a handful."

"Never once have I taken that boy to the woodshed." The smile on Mordecai's face died. "Sometimes I wish he would be more . . . Anyway . . . his brothers make up for it. I better get Susan and get home."

He looked down at his muddy boots and pants. "Maybe you better get her."

Abigail squeezed her apron together, wringing it out as she trudged back to the house. "I'm surprised she didn't hear all the ruckus."

"I did." A huge smile on her face, Susan pushed through the screen door and hopped down the steps, everything about her clean and dry. She popped up a black umbrella. "You were having so much fun, I was jealous." She beamed at Abigail. "I haven't heard Mordecai laugh like that in a very long time."

Something in her tone made Abigail's cheeks grow hot. She brushed past Susan. "I enjoyed your visit. Me and the girls will be up on Tuesday for the quilting frolic."

"Gut. We'll see you then."

Abigail found she couldn't look at Mordecai. What had been simple fun a few moments before now took on a whole new context. Through the eyes of others. What would Stephen say? Was frolicking in the rain like a child with a grown man improper?

Mordecai winked as he walked by. Apparently he didn't think so. With a wave, Abigail lifted her chin and stalked into the house, head held high.

Her ribs and cheeks hurt from laughing. She'd like to have that kind of ache more often.

THIRTEEN

Deborah jerked awake and sat up. She fought with the sheet tangled around her legs as she forced open gritty eyes, trying to see what had startled her from a fitful doze. She never slept deeply—not since Daed died.

Rain pounded the tin roof overhead and danced through the open window on the other side of the room, driven in by a wind so fierce it made the curtain stand at attention. Thunder crashed. Lightning crackled low to the ground, lighting up the window so she could see the live oak branches bending to the ground in a long, illuminated stretch. Air smelling of wet earth and leaves inundated the room.

The storm had been over when she went to bed, tired, damp, but as close to being content as she had been since coming here. It had returned under cover of darkness. She shivered at the sudden, wide-awake sensation that something or someone had shaken her from a dream. Had she been dreaming? She couldn't remember.

Nee. Nee. Fragments of the old nightmare—the one where the clods of dirt showered down on the casket that held Daed captive even though he still breathed—wouldn't have disappeared so quickly into the dark night.

Thunder. Just thunder. Another storm on top of the earlier one. God knew they needed the rain in a bad way. The thunder must've awakened her.

Wiggling, she leaned against her lumpy pillow, damp with sweat, and endeavored to get comfortable. Frannie mumbled in her sleep and flung out her arm so hard her hand slapped Deborah in the chest. She shoved her cousin's arm back in her direction. "Hey, watch it."

Frannie rolled over so the schtinkich of her night breath blew in Deborah's face. Sighing, Deborah scooted closer to the edge of the bed. Any farther and she'd fall on the floor. She might be more comfortable there than in a bed shared with three other girls. She closed her eyes and inhaled, trying to grasp fleeting sleep before it disappeared completely as it had so many nights since their arrival in Bee County.

She wrinkled her nose. The fresh rain scent of a few seconds earlier had been replaced by another distinct odor. She inhaled again, sudden fear replacing her earlier irritation.

Smoke. She smelled smoke.

"Frannie, Frannie, wake up!" She grabbed Frannie's arm and shook her. "Wake up. I smell smoke."

Muttering something unintelligible, Frannie rolled to her other side and threw her arm over Rebekah.

Deborah shot from the bed and grabbed her housecoat. "Frannie, Rebekah, Leila! Get up, get up. I smell smoke."

Leila sat up, rubbing her eyes. "Smoke? Didn't you bank the fire in the stove?"

"I did. I think lightning struck the house. Something woke me up and now I smell smoke."

"Hannah, Hazel, wake up!" It took Leila all of two seconds to slip from the bed and bend over the girls sleeping next to her. She scooped Hazel up in one arm and little Hannah in the other. "Where's it coming from?"

"I don't know. You wake the others while I check it out."

Deborah grabbed a flashlight from the wooden crate that served as a nightstand and opened the bedroom door. Smoke billowed in. Thick, dark smoke. Fear gripped her. "Hurry! Get up! Come on, girls. Everyone up."

She glanced back one last time to make sure they obeyed, pulled her housecoat sleeve over her mouth, and scurried down the hallway. The smoke thickened. It stung her eyes and burned her throat. *Lord, have mercy.*

"Mudder! Mudder!" She pounded on the door to the tiny storage closet that served as her mother's meager bedroom. "Fire! Fire!"

The door flew open and Mudder popped out, her long blond braid bouncing behind her. "Where?"

"It looks like it's in the kitchen. The girls are waking the others."

Together they flew down the hallway, through the front room, to the kitchen. Deborah slammed to a halt, Mudder at her side. Flames shot through the door, making it impossible to go any farther. The heat blistered her face.

"We have to get everyone out." Mudder tugged her back. "Caleb!"

"I'll get him. You get John and Eve. Meet out front."

Coughing and choking on the smoke, they ran. Deborah forced away thoughts of what they were about to lose and focused on the fragile, dear lives that were so much more important.

She pounded on doors and rousted her brother and cousins from their crowded bedroom. Together they ran into the pouring rain. Thunder boomed overhead, making Deborah duck for no reason that made any sense. Lightning spiderwebbed across the sky. Were they any safer out here in the elements?

"Let's go to the barn," Caleb screamed over a wind so strong it knocked the boy back a step. "I don't want to get hit by lightning."

"We have to put out the fire." Deborah gasped, her lungs aching for air stolen by the furious gale. "We need to get to the well."

Holding hands with Caleb, she trudged, heads bent against the pelting rain, to where Onkel John had begun pumping water from the well and handing out buckets.

"Will the rain put it out?" Deborah wiped dripping hair from her face, aware of her drenched nightgown and housecoat. She'd never been outside her bedroom dressed this way. "All this water and it won't douse the flames?"

"The inside will keep burning until the roof is gone." Onkel John thrust a bucket at Cousin Obadiah, who slung it down the quickly forming line. "We have to salvage what we can. I sent Rufus to get Leroy, Andrew, and the others. Leroy will get to the store and call the fire department."

"How far away are they?" She slid into the line next to Obadiah and slung the bucket to Frannie on her other side. One bucket of water that would have no impact on the flames now lighting up the front room like daylight.

"It's volunteer. They're all at home, asleep in bed." John's voice grew deeper, more hoarse, whether from the smoke or emotion, Deborah couldn't say. "It'll take them a bit, but they'll be here."

It didn't matter. They had to try. She thrust the now-empty bucket back at John, who kept the water coming. Without speaking, they worked in tandem in a futile assembly line. *Take, swivel, hand off, take, swivel, hand off. Full, empty, full, empty.*

Deborah stopped thinking about anything else, forcing herself to ignore the tickle of the rain on her face and her straggling hair on her cheek. After a while, the muscles in her arms and shoulders burned with fatigue. Her throat ached from the smoke and her lips cracked and bled. Still the blaze refused to be extinguished.

"Let me." Hands tugged the bucket handle from her weary, numb fingers. She glanced back, then up. Phineas towered over her. A gust of wind whipped. His straw hat went sailing across the yard, revealing tousled, too long, black curls. Too late, he slapped a hand to his head. "I've got this." He didn't yell, but his husky voice carried. "You chase my hat."

"Nee, I'm fine. I can do this." He could go to the end of the line with the other men. She didn't need his help. She could carry her weight. "There's room between Obadiah and Caleb. The more hands, the better."

He muscled his way past her and grabbed the next bucket coming down the line, bypassing her without a second look.

She slapped her hands on her hips, prepared to scold him for being so presumptuous. So presumptuous as to take from her a task her arms could no longer bear. "Fine," she sputtered, suddenly aware of her nightcoat and her hair slung down her back in a braid. "I'll look in on the kinner."

"Aenti Susan is bringing food."

She wasn't sure if his words were meant to assure her, to tell her to get something to eat, or to direct her to help. Surely he didn't think he could tell her what to do. She had enough people doing that.

"Go on, you look done in."

The quiet assurance in the words told her he expected her to do what he said, but only because it made sense, not because he wished to lord it over her. Nee, more like he had some sliver of concern in him for her.

Why, she couldn't imagine. He seemed to barely tolerate her presence. He didn't want her around. Certainly didn't want to share anything with her or spend time with her.

"We've got this."

His words were almost drowned out by the sound of sirens still in the distance but coming fast. Deborah whirled. The lights flashed red and white and yellow up and down with the deep ruts and grooves in the dirt road that led from the asphalt highway to the farmhouse.

By now most of the house had been reduced to smoldering flames. She backed away but didn't leave in search of Susan. Her stomach, soured by the overwhelming stench of burning wood, rubber, and fabric drenched in water, demanded she think of something else, anything but food.

More than a dozen Englischers in fireman jackets with thick, yellow reflecting lines on them streamed from two fire trucks that looked plenty worse for wear and several pickup trucks that surely were their personal cars. They didn't unfurl hoses or ask about water. They huddled together, hands on hips, and surveyed the scene. They spoke among themselves and then to Leroy, John, and the other men.

The bucket line slowed, then stopped. Phineas trudged in her direction, his bare feet sinking into the mud, making squelching noises. When he looked up, his expression told her when he registered her presence and he veered to the right, away from her.

"Wait, Phineas, why aren't they doing anything?"

"Too late." He wiped at his soot-covered face. His sleeve came away black. "They'll just stick around and make sure it doesn't spread and treat what they call the hot spots." He paused next to her, his hunched posture speaking volumes about his weariness. "You best go inside."

"Go inside where?" She flung her hands in the air, then pointed at the pile of smoldering remains. "There?"

"The barn." He ducked his head and looked at his feet as if he'd never noticed them before. "You don't want to stay out here in your . . ."

He cleared his throat. Heat scorched Deborah's cheeks and her neck. Her ears burned. "There're no clothes in the barn, if that's what you're thinking."

"The women are gathering clothes right now. Susan and the others, they're bringing food and clothes."

In the drab dawning of a gray day, she saw something in his expression. A genuine concern for her. "That's gut. You're right. Danki."

"Don't thank me. I didn't do nothing."

The sour tone was back.

"Fine."

She turned and slipped and slid her way across the muck, resigned to the thick coat of mud that covered her feet and legs. It matched the soot on her arms and face. Even opening the barn door proved to be almost too much for the shaking muscles in her arms.

Inside, she found Rebekah sleeping, the little ones stretched out around her on old horse blankets spread across piles of hay.

Hazel curled her small body around Rebekah's feet, her eyes closed, her fat fist clutched against her mouth. Rachel and Hannah lined up as if they were in their bed, side by side, arms and legs all tangled up. Deborah wished she could do the same. When she closed her eyes, she saw flames shooting from the kitchen, destroying the braided rug on the floor, devouring the oak table and benches, incinerating the Burpee seed catalog on top of a pile of mail strewn over a battered, old pine table, licking up the walls until it consumed a calendar hung there. The bedding in their small bedroom. Her letters. From Josie and Aaron. All gone. The fire's appetite had been voracious. It had taken everything from a family who had little.

She bent her head and searched for words of prayer. None came. They'd traveled halfway across the country to start a new life here, and that new life hadn't lasted two months. Between the two families, fourteen people were now homeless. No house in this tiny district had room for that many people. It would be better for everyone if Deborah's family of six returned to Tennessee. Wouldn't it?

What now, Gott? Home? Please let it be home.

How dare she ask? Who was she to question God's plan? He had one, no doubt. For the life of her, Deborah couldn't figure out what it was. "Rebekah, Rebekah, wake up." She couldn't stand to be alone with her own thoughts anymore. She knelt and touched her sister's face. "Wake up."

Rebekah stirred. "Did they save anything? One dress . . . my shawl . . . my bonnet? Our Sunday shoes?"

"Nothing." Deborah dropped onto the hay and sat cross-legged, close enough to smooth Hazel's tangled, wheat-colored curls. The little girl sighed and stuck her thumb in her mouth. Something she hadn't done in at least a year. "Not a stitch of clothing."

"What will we do?"

"We'll make the best of it."

"Like Daed always said." Rebekah's face crumpled. A tear slid down her cheek, teetered on her lip, then disappeared. "I miss Daed."

Whatever *it* was. "Me too," Deborah whispered as she hugged her little sister tight. "Me too."

"I miss home."

"I know." Deborah hugged harder. "Me too."

She had to convince Mudder this trip had been a mistake. They would all go home. Together.

FOURTEEN

"There you are!"

Trying to ignore the irritation in Stephen's tone, Abigail smoothed the pile of dresses Susan had given her and climbed down from the buggy in front of John's barn so she could face Stephen. She hadn't been avoiding him. She'd been busy collecting clothes for the kinner. They couldn't traipse around all day in their nightclothes. She forced herself to meet his gaze. Soot darkened his white-blond beard. Smudges on his cheeks looked like black paint.

He held out both hands as if to embrace her. They were black as well. Water soaked his pant legs, the hems were ragged, and his boots were covered with mud. He looked like a horse that had been ridden hard and put up wet. She took a step back. "You look tuckered out."

"I'm fine. I wish I could've done more." He tucked his dirty fingers in his suspenders and shrugged. "We did what we could. Thank Gott no one was hurt. He will provide."

"He will." Her heart knew this, but her head still wondered why it was necessary to take everything in one fell swoop. Hadn't they started over once already? "I do feel for John and his fraa, though."

"It's just stuff. They'll leave it all behind when they leave this earth anyway." He snapped the suspenders as if to punctuate his optimistic statement. "When I first heard, I came running to make sure you were all right, but I couldn't find you and I was needed on the water line."

"Susan took me to find some . . . things for the kinner." Things remained as awkward as ever between them, ever since the kiss in front of his house. The kiss and the fall and the discovery that he lived in a pigsty. "We fled the house in our . . . with nothing more than our . . . nightclothes."

"Jah." His face reddened under the caked dirt and soot. "Gott will provide."

"We'll be fine." Except for the part of her and her five children not having a stitch of clothing to their names or a bed to lay their heads in. That was selfish of her. John and Eve had lost everything too, including their home. "I'm taking these to the barn. The girls need to get dressed."

Heat curled around her neck and warmed her cheeks. Stephen ducked his head, his ears turning red. "Jah, go, go."

Hugging the enormous pile of clothes to her chest, Abigail started toward the barn. She had dresses and fresh prayer kapps for her four girls and Eve's three. They could string blankets across the last stall and make a changing room. She'd brought soap, and she could send Deborah for water. They could scrub up. Everyone would feel better with clean faces and some food in their stomachs.

"Abigail."

Startled, she glanced back. Stephen trailed after her. He

chewed on his lower lip, making his beard bob. She stopped and turned. "What is it?"

His hand gripped her elbow, leaving dirty fingerprints on her sleeve as he steered her away from the barn door and around the corner. She stumbled to keep up. The dress on the top of the pile toppled to the ground. She grabbed at it, missed, and it landed in a puddle of water. "Stephen!"

"It'll wash." He snatched up the dress and wadded it in a ball. "I wanted to say something to you."

"So I gathered."

He turned the balled-up material over in hands the size of bushel baskets. "You have no place to live now."

True. Anyone could see that. Still, she tried to be patient. As patient as she could be after a sleepless night of storm and flame. "That is true."

"I was thinking."

Something in his ruddy face made Abigail wince inwardly. Nee. Not now. Not today. "In the midst of all this upheaval, how could you have time?"

"I can do more than one thing at a time." He sounded wounded. "I think a lot when I'm working. My mind does one thing, my muscles another."

A good skill to have. Abigail worked to soften her tone. "What did you think about?"

"Why wait until November? Why not go to Leroy now? Ask him to announce next Sunday? We could get married two weeks later. Then it would be right and proper for you and the kinner to move into my house. Problem solved."

Abigail's stomach lurched. A marriage proposal born of practicality, not romance. That made sense. She was no young girl in the throes of her first love. She hugged the clothes to her body with one arm and raised trembling fingers to her face to push back straggling hair on her forehead. Seconds ticked in her head, louder and louder. As impractical as it might seem to a practical man like Stephen, she didn't want the rest of her life, her chance at love again, to be a problem the man in front of her had to solve.

Timothy.

She'd thought she would have time. Time to adjust. To get to know Stephen again. To get used to this place. "I'm sorry, I'm—"

"Sorry? You came here for this." Stephen's face reddened even further. His jaw jutted. "Will you find me lacking once again?"

"Nee. I'm tired. That's all."

He stuffed the dirty, wet dress on top of the clean ones with such force, Abigail staggered. "We're both tired. Not a good time to make important decisions."

Relief blanketed her like the gale-force wind of the previous night. "I just want a little more time to get to know you again."

"I understand." His face said he didn't. "In the meantime, you're homeless."

"We're having a district meeting in a few minutes. What to do next will be decided then."

Stephen swiveled and marched away. At the corner of the barn, he looked back. "Beggars can't be choosers, you know."

After a minute, Abigail remembered to close her mouth. By then he had disappeared around the corner.

When had she become a beggar?

FIFTEEN

Despite the clear morning air, the rank odor of smoke lingered in Phineas's nose. He'd been unable to shake it, no matter how much he washed his face and hands after a scant few hours of sleep. Morning brought light, and with it, a clear view of the destruction. He turned his back on the wet rubble that had been John's home and strode to the barn. How did a person see God's hand moving in such devastation? His daed would say God had a plan. Whatever it was, Phineas couldn't fathom it. He let the thought drift away in a fog of fatigue.

He squeezed through a cluster of men standing by the barn doors, discussing the cost of lumber and Sheetrock. They would need plenty of both to rebuild the house. Everyone had gotten the word and made their way to the Masts' barn. They would hear what the bishop had to say about the fire and decisions would be made. They would help the Masts rebuild and provide food and clothes for them and for the Lantz family. That was what they did.

He couldn't help himself. He let his gaze rest on Deborah. She had looked so forlorn during the dark hours before dawn. She was feisty, though, no doubt about it. Swinging that full bucket with all the force she could muster. For a scrawny girl, she was strong. She held Hazel in her arms as if the little girl weighed nothing. Hazel raised her head from her sister's shoulder and smiled at him. He couldn't help it, he smiled back. "How are you, little one?"

"Fire burned up doll."

"I know, but there will be other dolls." He squeezed her plump hand, careful not to touch Deborah. "What's important is that you and all your family are safe and unhurt. Gott is gut."

Deborah looked up at him, her expression bleak. "He's right, Hazel. We'll make you a new doll."

Hazel snuggled against her sister's chest. "Phineas is smart."

Deborah turned back to the front of the barn, but not before Phineas saw the look that flashed on her face. She didn't think he was so smart.

She was angry at him and trying not to show it. He stepped back so he stood next to his father. He hadn't taken her to look for birds. In the hard light of day, he couldn't bring himself to do it. In the dark of night, she could forget what he looked like, but not during the day. She'd see and regret her request. She'd make excuses not to go and he'd feel like a fool and more alone than ever. He was better off not going down that road. Still, he'd started in the direction of John's house twice, but each time he veered off in a long hike to the apiaries.

Maybe he'd thought it would be easier to simply run into her as they had that night on the road. After dusk. But he hadn't and the days had stretched until it seemed awkward to show up at her door. He'd stayed out of sight and kept to himself. That was what he did. Surely, in the light of day, she'd recognized it was for the best. She was going home anyway, sooner or later.

She looked better now. Her dress, faded and a size too big, was clean and neat, but smudges like bruises darkened the skin under pale-blue eyes that held a familiar sadness. She ached for everything she'd lost—not just the clothes and the keepsakes, but her home back east and her daed. He knew how that felt. Even after twelve years he still ached for his mudder's warm, soft hand to touch his cheek to see if he had a fever.

Deborah's head came up, her gaze sideswiping him, then bouncing over to Stephen. Her face darkened and she handed Hazel to Leila. The little girl went without protest while Deborah hugged her arms to her chest as if cold and edged closer to the door.

Something about Stephen's presence in her life made Deborah cold.

Phineas could understand that. If anything ever happened to Mordecai, well, Phineas refused to go there. God's will was God's will and they all were only passing through on this earth, but he couldn't bear to think of Daed slipping away ahead of him.

"Let's get started, then."

The sound of Leroy's voice cut the air. The men faced the front, arms crossed, their faces solemn.

The gentle mutterings of the women on the other side of the barn muted, but the Masts' horses took turns whinnying as if they hadn't gotten the message.

"First, I want to say, though we've had a bit of a rough night, the sun is shining now." Leroy's dark eyes were bright behind his smudged, wire-rimmed glasses. "The Lord is gut. No one was hurt. Those material things consumed by the flames, they mean nothing."

Phineas sneaked a look at John. The big man nodded, his expression serene. What it must feel like to know he not only had his own family of six kinner and a fraa for whom he had to provide, but also his widowed sister and her five. Still, he stood, shoulders broad, hands relaxed at his sides, looking as if he'd had a restful night of sleep. Phineas longed for the man's peace of mind gained from the knowledge that God would provide.

"I've given this some thought and I've prayed." Leroy smoothed his silver-gray beard and smiled. "It's best to open our homes to these two families. We'll provide shelter while we rebuild. We'll start rebuilding as soon as we clear this site of the rubble and debris."

No surprise there. Why call a meeting to state the obvious? Phineas sideswiped his father with a quick look. Daed moved restlessly, his hands on his hips, then dangling at his sides, and finally he crossed his arms over his chest. Something odd tinged his normally benign expression. He looked . . . nervous. Nee, it couldn't be. Not Mordecai King.

"To the question of where John and his family will stay and his sister's family, it is necessary to divide them up. Our homes, while sufficient for our needs, are small and our families abundant. We've been blessed by the gut Lord in that way."

Leroy did have a way with words. When his Sunday came around to deliver the message, he often held them in the throes of his words. But he never got down the road to his point quickly. Ever.

"John and Eve and their girls will go with Andrew. The older boys will stay with Stephen."

Stephen cleared his throat and bobbed his head as if acknowledging grace bestowed.

"We'll also split up Abigail and her kinner. The boy will stay with Stephen. He'll put Caleb to work. He can use more hands with his greenhouse and selling his produce to the grocery stores."

Leroy nodded in Phineas's direction. Startled, Phineas glanced around, then realized his daed nodded back. "Abigail and her girls will stay at the King house. Mordecai has the most room, and Susan can host the frolics to help them make new clothes and the other necessities they now lack. They can help with the honey production."

The most room because Mudder died before she could bear the children she and Mordecai had dreamed would fill his home. The thought blew away in the realization that Leroy was saying that Deborah and her sisters would stay in the house Phineas lived in. He turned to Daed. "Nee—"

Daed shook his head, his expression dark. "Not now."

They would fill up the house with Abigail Lantz and her four daughters. Four girls wandering about the house, taking up space.

They would be in his house, looking at him, watching him, waiting for him to make conversation. His house was the one place he could go where he didn't have to worry about what people thought of the way he looked. His stomach lurched. Hand to his mouth, he squeezed through the crowd and slipped out the door.

Outside, the early-morning sun peeked through clouds that still hung low and thick and heavy as if they might open up and pour out their bounty once again. Rain caught on the brown, wet grass glistened in the light. A steamy fog hung in the air. Soon it would all dissipate in the blazing July sun. Hands on his knees, Phineas breathed the tepid, wet air and tried to calm his roiling stomach.

The air smelled like remnants of a spring long gone. A flash of color caught the corner of his gaze. A pale, achingly thin rainbow hung beyond the trees, slivers of yellow and red tinged with pink and blue in the distance, beyond the sodden, black rubble that stank of burned rubber and wet wood, beyond the road and the halfhearted trees in between. Without thinking, he straightened and moved toward it as if he could touch it and catch this slim sliver of God's creative genius in his hands.

A soft sob wafted in the air. Phineas halted, hand out. The sound came from behind the row of buggies and wagons. Where the horses nibbled at wretched, wet grass. He waited, listening. Nothing. Maybe he'd imagined it.

A second sob, this one softer yet, more muffled as if the person wanted nothing more than to suffocate the feelings that would cause such a sad, sad sound.

Phineas slipped around the wagon. Deborah huddled on the other side, her forehead pressed against the wooden slats. One hand covered her mouth, the other pressed against her chest as if she feared her heart would burst through it and escape.

Something inside Phineas swelled and ached with a familiar sensation of mourning and loss. Deborah was a fellow sojourner on a journey he would not wish on his worst enemy. She'd lost her daed, just as he'd lost his mudder. Too soon. He didn't even know her, but the anguish on her peeling, sunburned face broke his heart.

It was a private moment. She wouldn't want his pity, just as he didn't want hers. He started to back away but found his feet stuck to the ground. His heart fought with his head. Never in his life had he been a coward. "Deborah?"

Her head jerked up. Wiping at her face with both hands, she backed away, taking a long shuddering breath. "I was just . . . It was stuffy in there, so I came outside—"

"There's a rainbow."

"What?"

Phineas pointed. "There's a rainbow. It's only the second time I've ever seen one."

Deborah inched toward him, her gaze following his finger. "It's so thin. It's hardly there at all." Her voice trembled. "It's beautiful."

"It is." Phineas dropped his arm to his side. "They'll be out any minute."

She turned back toward the barn. "I best gather up the girls, then."

Phineas wanted to say something. Anything to wipe that desolate look from her face. He studied the rocky ground under his feet. It was the same solid ground he'd walked on all these years, but he tried to see it as she must. As a strange and foreign land.

"When things settle down, I'll show you where to pick the wild cucumbers."

Her head came up. "Like you took me to see the birds?"

"You really want to bird-watch . . . with me?"

"Who else would I do it with?" She glowered, but nothing she could do would make her face anything but pretty. "If I said I wanted to go, I wanted to go. You must be the one with the second thoughts."

He drew a line in the mud with his boot. "We can do both."

"If you don't want me tagging along, just say so." Her hands fluttered, talking for her as usual. "I don't want to go where I'm not wanted."

"It's not that. I . . . want . . . you to come."

"I can tell by the way you talk."

Frustration welled up in him, mixed with the certainty that he could see how all this would end, and it wouldn't end well. Not for him.

Still, this wasn't about him but Deborah, with her tearstained face and her effort to hide those tears from him. "We'll go. Soon. But there will be work to do first."

Her wary look said she didn't believe him. "You think Susan will still have the quilting frolic?"

"It'll take the men time to clear the rubble. We can't have a house raising until we do. There's plenty of time for other frolics."

"Okay." Her voice softened. She looked so weary. "But you don't have to take me bird-watching. I know you'd rather be alone."

"With so much work to do now, it might be awhile, but I'll try."

"Don't put yourself out for me."

"I won't."

"That's apparent."

"Are you always so . . . plainspoken?"

"Only with people who disappoint me."

He'd disappointed her? How was that possible? She turned her back again and trudged away, head down to the barn. At the door, she looked back. "We'll try not to be a burden."

Before he could think of what to say, she shut the door on him.

He turned. The rainbow had disappeared. The sun broke through the dissipating clouds and light poured out on him.

Truth be told, if he dared admit it to himself, having Deborah Lantz close would be no burden at all.

Only his heart was on the line.

SIXTEEN

The sway of the wagon and the warm early-morning sun combined to make Deborah sleepy. Another restless night squeezed between Leila and Rebekah in a bed meant for two had left her cranky and tired. Her black tights were twisted and her shoes felt tight as if her feet were swollen. That was what she got for going barefoot so much. She felt even less at home in Mordecai's house than she had at her onkel's. Onkel was family. At least Mordecai had a bigger house. Mudder had an actual room to sleep in. Sleep. Deborah closed her eyes, knowing she wouldn't miss a thing. The terrain between their tiny district and Beeville didn't seem to vary. Mesquite, brush, open fields of milo and corn, and dirt, lots of dirt.

Deborah tried not to listen to the strained conversation between Stephen and Mudder on the front seat. Stephen's bass carried and seemed to step all over Mudder's high, breathless voice. She sounded as if she were talking to a stranger, even after two months in Bee County. Stephen wasn't happy about them staying at Mordecai's. Deborah could see why. Mordecai was a kind and decent man. He should have a fraa. God had blessed him with a sister who could take care of the house, the cooking, and the garden when she wasn't teaching, but a man like Mordecai should have a wife.

Why couldn't Mudder be interested in him? It would mean staying in Texas, but at least it wouldn't be with Stephen. Why Stephen instead of Mordecai?

Deborah opened her eyes and peered up at Stephen's back from her vantage point in the bed of the wagon. She tried to see him through her mudder's eyes. Broad shoulders, hair long enough to stick out the back under his straw hat, tall, a hard worker, a farmer who owned his own land. Everything a fraa could want.

Almost. He wasn't daed.

And he never would be. That wasn't his fault.

She switched her gaze to the back of the wagon where she could see Esther and Frannie following along behind them in the Kings' buggy. She should've squeezed onto the seat next to Esther to avoid hearing her mother and Stephen chat, but Mudder had insisted she sit with Susan. Why, Deborah couldn't imagine. To talk about Phineas. Surely not.

"What's a *taquería*?" Rebekah pointed at a dusty pink-and-green building with a flashing neon sign in the front window. Breakfast tacos 3 for $2. "They're everywhere."

"They sell tacos." Susan offered the explanation in her schoolteacher tone. "Taquería comes from *taco*."

Deborah hadn't eaten many tacos in her life, but she would surely like a hamburger now. Stephen had rushed them out of the house and onto the road before breakfast was over.

"Look, Deborah, there's a McDonald's." It was Leila's turn to point. She must've been having the same hunger pains. "French fries and hamburgers."

"If you had money." Stephen swiveled to toss the words at them. "We brought sandwiches. No need to waste money on eating out."

Deborah's mouth watered at the thought. They hadn't eaten in a restaurant since the trip here. Susan King set a good table and they never lacked for fresh vegetables and fresh-made cookies or pie, but they didn't get a lot of meat. Eating in a restaurant would be a treat.

Stephen tugged on the reins and made a sharp right turn. Deborah tumbled against the back of the wagon and smacked her head on the side. "Watch those jars." His tone was curt. Why was he so cranky? He drove the wagon, not her. "Hold the boxes steady—that's your job, not daydreaming."

Rubbing her head, Deborah clamped her mouth shut to keep from saying something she shouldn't. With Susan's and Leila's help, she realigned the jars of wild grape jam, honey, and pickles next to baskets of fresh tomatoes, okra, cucumbers, cantaloupe, radishes, corn on the cob, onions, and squash. Nothing had broken, no thanks to Stephen. The pies they'd spent the entire previous day baking were snug in boxes with towels tucked around them to keep them safe on the journey.

Susan said the Englischers loved those pies. They would earn a nice price and then maybe Stephen could be convinced to buy a round of burgers and fries—they could share orders. She could almost taste the tang of the catsup and the salt as she licked her greasy fingers.

Susan smiled at Deborah as if she were reading her mind. "We'll have a cookout on July Fourth. We always roast hot dogs and make hamburgers on the Fourth. I make French fries. Homemade are better anyway. If we can afford it, we get a few firecrackers for the kinner. They like the sparklers."

Deborah nodded, appreciating Susan's attempt to smooth things over. "Hazel likes the ones you light and they look like worms curling up when they burn."

"We're here." Stephen pulled the wagon to a stop on the street in front of Walmart's enormous parking lot. People trundled out, their carts full of groceries.

"Get the sign up." Stephen hopped from the wagon, his tone brusque. "Folks will be coming by as soon as they see it. They always do."

He was right. No sooner did they anchor the sign Frannie had made with her pretty print on a piece of cardboard box that read FRESH PIES * PRODUCE * JAMS * HONEY to the side of the wagon than folks began to make a beeline for them. A lady who sniffed the pecan pie and gushed over the apple pie, an elderly couple who wanted three jars of honey to give to their children visiting from New York, and a cowboy who grinned at Leila and stuck a toothpick in his mouth before carrying off a pecan pie in each hand. One man carted off the entire box of corn on the cob, even though the ears were small and stunted from lack of rain.

"Not bad," Stephen muttered as he counted out the bills, stuck them in a coffee can, and snapped the lid on with a satisfied air. "All right. We best get to the bank, Abigail. We can walk from here."

"The bank?" Deborah studied her mudder's face. She looked as if she felt . . . guilty. Or unsure of herself. Mudder never used to be unsure of anything. "What's at the bank?"

"Money."

No need to be sarcastic. Deborah chewed the inside of her lip as she forced back the retort. "We're putting this money in the bank? It's not really much yet, and it's not even ours."

"You're right. It's not ours. We're not putting it in." Mudder rearranged the jam jars, wild grape in front of the peach, even though they were perfectly fine the way they were. "Stephen wants to irrigate a few more acres so he can expand the orchards."

Something in her tone explained the pink on her cheeks. "With our house money?"

"Your house money?" Stephen's frown deepened, making his thin lips thinner. "You don't have money. Or a house."

"It's not your money either. My daed built that house." Deborah slapped her hand to her mouth, horrified the words had burst from her. She breathed and let it drop. "I mean—"

"I'll not have disrespect from you. You may be the oldest, but you're not too old to be thrashed." Stephen took a step toward Deborah. "You'll find yourself in the shed."

To her horror, Deborah felt a giggle burble up in her. The idea that this man would attempt to take her to the shed seemed downright silly. Daed had never taken a switch to her. She'd never given him a reason to do so. And now she was a grown woman. She gritted her teeth to keep the giggle and the words from escaping.

"Do you hear me? Answer me when I speak to you."

"Stephen, you're getting ahead of yourself." Mudder's face had turned a deep, ugly hue of red and purple that matched Stephen's. "And not here, not on the street. We'll talk about this at home. Please."

"Why don't you and I go to the Walmart for the material and sewing goods we need?" Susan stepped in front of Deborah. Stephen loomed over them, his face even darker than Mudder's. Susan smiled up at him, the picture of calm. That patient air must have been a King family trait. "We can take the buggy and Frannie can run the stand for us. She has lots of experience."

This couldn't be happening. Stephen Stetler couldn't be her daed's replacement. He was . . . He wasn't the right man. He couldn't be. Deborah ducked around Susan and Stephen so she could crowd Mudder. "I thought we were waiting a bit to see how things go. What's the hurry?"

"No hurry. It's a loan." Mudder shook her head, her expression a cross between beseeching and furious. "We'll be back in an hour or so. You go with Susan. Hazel, behave yourself and stay with Leila and Rebekah. Remember, cars use the street. Not little girls."

"I want to go with you." Hazel grabbed Mudder's apron, her chubby fingers tight around the bunched-up material. "I go to bank."

"Nee, little one." Mudder attempted to loosen Hazel's grip. "You help with the stand."

Hazel's face crumpled and she began to sniff, her blue eyes bright with tears. "Want to go."

"You heard your mudder." Stephen grasped Hazel's arm and tugged her away from Mudder. "You best do as you're told. At least you're young enough to still learn to respect your elders." His glare scalded Deborah. "It's not too late for any of you. Mark my words."

Deborah scooped Hazel into her arms and settled her on one hip. The girl hiccupped a sob and buried her wet face on Deborah's shoulder. "Wanna go home." Her words were muffled, but her meaning unmistakable. "Go home now."

"Me too, *bopli*, me too." Deborah nestled her close and watched Mudder walk away, her head down, a few steps behind her future husband. "We'll be fine."

Fine was a relative term.

SEVENTEEN

Deborah wanted to melt into the ground. She wanted to turn and run and keep running until she reached Tennessee. She'd talked back to a man. A girl didn't do that. But Stephen tried her patience down to her very soul. He did. He wasn't her daed. He never would be.

"Come on, come on, Deborah, we've got shopping to do." Susan scooped her canvas bag from the wagon and tucked the strap over her shoulder. She didn't seem the least bit perturbed by the scene she'd just witnessed in front of Englischers who only wanted to buy pies and cantaloupe. She tugged Hazel from Deborah's hip and winked. A big wink. "Hazel can come too. She can help us carry the food."

"The food?"

"Didn't you know? This Walmart has a McDonald's inside." Susan patted her belly with her free hand. "My stomach is rumbling, and I have my egg money tucked in my coin purse."

"We don't need anything. We brought a water jug and some sandwiches." Deborah didn't want to saddle Susan with any more expenses, and Mudder had given her only enough to cover material, thread, underwear, and socks. It was the last of the cash she'd brought with her from Tennessee. On the other hand, it sure would be nice to eat some of those fries, just because Stephen didn't want them to do it. *Bad, bad attitude. Gott, forgive me.* "We're fine."

"My treat." Susan's smile widened. She looked so much like Mordecai that day they'd played in the rain, they might've been twins. "Later on down the road, you can treat me."

"If Deborah doesn't want her fries, I'll take hers." Frannie looked a little pouty that she was being stuck with the produce stand while Deborah got Walmart. "I'm starved and so is Esther."

Esther nodded, but she seemed more interested in sneaking side peeks at Deborah. She'd been a little cool toward Deborah since their exchange at the singing, but after the fire, she'd offered to help Deborah make new dresses. Now she had to be horrified at how Deborah had talked back to Stephen. It wasn't done, and Deborah would hear all about it from Mudder when they got back to the house.

"I'll bring the little junior burgers for everyone, and we can share a couple of orders of fries. It'll be plenty and not too costly," Susan promised. "You girls just make sure to count the money and make change properly and don't take any checks."

"We know, we know," Esther, Frannie, Rebekah, and Leila chimed in unison. "And no wooden nickels."

They all laughed. The lingering pall of Stephen's rant dissipated.

Ten minutes later Deborah traipsed behind Susan, Hazel between them, past the Walmart McDonald's with its scent of French fries and hamburgers wafting by them. The frigid air made her shiver. It felt like winter inside the store. With Susan's assurances that they would get the hamburgers after they made their purchases, Hazel allowed herself to be settled into the shopping cart with a small root beer. They made their way through the long aisles in the store's sewing section filled with bolts of material in all colors and patterns.

Deborah didn't know where to look first. She touched a bolt of silky pink material and then flannel covered with puppies. Winter nightgowns. She didn't even want to think about what winter must be like here. It took some rummaging, but finally she unearthed a bolt of plain blue cotton. Perfect for shirts for the boys and dresses for the girls. "I don't see any plain black cotton." She tugged a bolt of gingham aside followed by some burgundy material with a paisley print. "Do you?"

Susan lifted a bolt of black fabric from the far side of the display table. "I ask them to keep it in stock. They're real nice about it, even though they don't have much use for heavy black cotton."

Deborah smoothed a nice lilac cotton/synthetic blend. It would make a pretty dress. Not that she had anywhere to wear such a dress.

"You know, Stephen means well." Susan touched the lilac material. "This is nice. We'll get it. Y'all need new dresses. It's on sale. So is the gray material. And look, they have thread on sale too."

"It's not too fancy?"

"It's just right." Susan added the bolt to her pile. "So does Phin."

How did Phineas get into this conversation? "I know."

"At your age, sometimes it's hard to understand why people act the way they do."

"So when you get older, it gets easier?"

"Nee." Susan chuckled and patted Deborah's shoulder. "You just have more patience with it, I guess. I can tell you this, though. I've known Phin his whole life. He has a gut heart."

Esther's exact words. They would say that about someone who belonged to their family. They loved him. Susan shook her head as if she knew what Deborah was thinking. "I'm not just saying that because he's my nephew. Even if he hadn't been in that accident and lost his mudder, he would be a little on the independent side. He loves his family and he's committed to his faith, but he struggles with the need to be solitary. It's his nature. Like my bruder."

"Mordecai seems . . . nice."

"He changed after the accident. My bruder used to be stubborn and impatient with people who couldn't keep up with him. After he lost his fraa in the accident, and almost lost Phin, he slowed down. He began to treat people better. He stops to enjoy the moment, whether it's the sunrise in the morning or sharing honey with some homesick girls. He knows those are Gott-given gifts. Our days are numbered on this earth. We should appreciate the journey as we pass through."

"So Gott let his fraa die to teach him a lesson?" What kind of God did that? The kind who let her father die of a heart attack long before she was ready to let him go? What a selfish thought. Daed had gone on ahead because it was God's will. Why was that so hard for her to accept? "Sorry, I didn't mean that. I just . . ."

"Miss your daed? I understand that. Mordecai misses his fraa and Phin misses his mudder. That's human nature. Our time on this earth is measured in days. Sarah was a gut woman who loved Gott. I believe she went and never looked back. It's just hard for us who are left behind. I reckon it's the same for you with your daed."

"It is. I try not to be selfish." Deborah fingered the lilac material, imagining how it would look in a dress and how Daed would've stuck his hands on his hips, cocked his head, and growled that she was growing up way too fast the first time he saw her in it. "I know what I'm supposed to believe. It's how I feel that I can't change."

"Your heart will catch up." Susan handed the bolt to a lady with a measuring tape around her neck and scissors in her hand and asked for six yards. "And when it does, I hope you're still here. Phineas could use a friend."

A friend. Was Susan matchmaking? Like Esther? Like Mordecai with his hints about Phineas showing them how to harvest honey? Phineas had said he would take her bird-watching. He'd said he'd show her where the wild cucumbers were. Yet he'd been avoiding her since she moved into the house. He barely made eye contact at the table and rushed out the second he finished eating. He spent all his time with the bees. Which was just as well. She had no desire to relive that mortifying moment when she realized he'd seen her crying behind the wagon. Or his awkward attempt to make her feel better.

The beautiful rainbow. That one moment they'd shared something beautiful in the midst of the ugly, sodden aftermath of a fire that took everything. Beauty in the midst of desolation. Nothing before or after could change that. God had sent them a sign that life would go on. That He created new beauty every moment of every day.

Did Phineas think of that moment? Did he think of the night he'd walked her home from the singing? She'd enjoyed that walk, as embarrassing as its beginning had been. The manure on her sneakers. Her headlong rush into his arms. Did he think of that? If he did, he didn't let her see it at the supper table or over kaffi in the morning. It wasn't her fault Phineas was so hardheaded. "He might try being a little nicer."

Susan laughed outright, startling the saleslady who dropped

her scissors. "Sorry, ten yards of the black and ten of that lilac material. Twelve of the gray." She turned to Deborah, her face still creased in a smile. "That will do, don't you think? The lilac is kind of pretty."

It was and so was Susan, with her scrubbed pink cheeks and laugh lines around her eyes. She had to be in her midthirties. She'd never married. For the first time, Deborah stopped to wonder why. "Do you think there's a special someone for everyone?"

"For most folks." Susan took the folded material from the saleslady and laid it in their basket next to Hazel, who sat cross-legged in it, sipping her soda, her cherubic cheeks split in a wide smile. "Don't get that on the material, little one. I don't want to have to wash it before we get the dresses made."

Hazel wrapped both her chubby hands around the cup and nodded. "Gut."

"Very gut."

"But not you," Deborah broke in, anxious to understand. How would she know what God's plan was for her? Maybe she didn't have a special someone. Maybe that was why Aaron went to Ohio. How was she supposed to know? "How come not for you?"

"I had a chance, but I love teaching. I love my scholars and I never felt that longing, that feeling that said this was the one. This was my intended. The one Gott choose for me."

"But you're happy."

Susan smiled. "Content."

"I don't think Stephen will make Mudder content, let alone happy." Deborah blurted the words and immediately wished them back in her mouth. "I know it's not for me to say."

"Your opinion of Stephen is clouded by your broken heart."

"Broken heart?"

"Your heart is still broken for your daed. People walk that path in different strides. Your mudder walks ahead of you. Don't punish her for seeking to be content with her lot in this life. You'd do well to follow her example."

With those crisp words of advice, Susan pushed the basket toward the notions rack. "We need thread. Lots of thread."

"But . . . but it's not that." Deborah marched after her. "Stephen . . . he's so different from Daed and he's not good with kinner. You saw that."

"Of course he's different from your daed. And you spoke back to him in a way I imagine you never talked to your daed." Susan stopped in front of a display of hundreds of different colors of thread. Without hesitation she plucked first a white, then a black, and then a lilac spindle, her forehead wrinkled as if considering her response. "But that doesn't mean your mudder can't love him. Or that he can't learn to be better with you and the other kinner. Have patience."

Patience. One of the many things Deborah had in short supply these days.

"Have patience and be kind." Susan dumped a dozen rolls of thread into the basket, making Hazel squeal with delight. Then she added a package of threaded bobbins followed by a needle for the treadle machine. "With yourself. With Stephen. And with Phin."

Back to Phineas. Deborah opened her mouth, but Susan kept talking. Her expression said she'd uttered her last words on that topic. "Okay, we have material for the boys' pants, their shirts, you and your sisters' dresses. We have the underwear and socks. What else?"

Nothing else. Susan had spoken all that needed to be said. She was right. Deborah owed Stephen an apology for being mouthy.

And her mother for questioning her decision to come to Bee County, how she spent her money, and with whom she spent her time.

How she would ever force her lips to form those words, Deborah couldn't imagine. But she would.

"Nothing? Gut. Time for our hamburgers."

She'd been serious about McDonald's. Deborah's spirits lifted. Not because Stephen wouldn't approve. Nee. Because she was hungry.

She kept telling herself that all the way to the parking lot. Her hamburger was the best one she'd ever eaten.

EIGHTEEN

Rubbing her jaw in hopes of assuaging the dull throb of a toothache she'd been trying to ignore for days now, Abigail stifled a yawn and trudged on bare feet to the kitchen. She'd managed to rise before Susan. That hadn't happened much in the days since they'd moved in with the Kings. Abigail wanted to make herself useful, but Susan almost always rose so early that breakfast was well under way before Abigail could lend a hand. The habit of a schoolteacher who had to prepare meals for her brother's family before spending the day teaching. Not during the summer, but still, Abigail was determined to give Susan a break she undoubtedly deserved.

She would make pancakes, fried eggs, potatoes, zucchini, and squash. A tasty breakfast that would hold the men over until the noonday meal. The only person absent would be Caleb. She missed having her only son at the table. He looked so like Timothy and had his affectionate heart as well.

Abigail picked up her pace. Cooking would take her mind off her situation. She had to do something soon. She couldn't keep living in Mordecai King's house. It wasn't right. Certainly not in Stephen's eyes, and he was quite willing to marry soon, which would get her family all together under one roof again. Was that a good reason to get married? The thought drove her to hurry even more. In the pitch-black of the predawn morning, her big toe connected with a chair leg in the front room.

"Ouch, ouch!" She danced around, foot in the air, then sank into the chair to rub it. Now she had an ache in her toe to match the throbbing of her tooth that wouldn't go away no matter how much she willed it to stop. What was that chair doing there? She wanted to scream, but she didn't. Not living in her own house, she couldn't wander around in the dark without expecting something like this to happen. Her toe felt broken. "Gott, this is no way to start the day!"

"Probably not."

Startled at the sound of another voice so early, Abigail jerked upright, toe forgotten. "Mordecai. I thought I was the only one up."

He stood in the kitchen doorway, a fishing pole in each hand. "I gathered as much." The ends of his lips curled up in the slightest of smiles. "Chastising Gott? I wouldn't want anyone to hear me doing that."

"I wasn't . . . I just . . ." Abigail stood. Her toe ached in protest. She bent and rubbed it some more. "I wanted to get an early start on breakfast. I thought I would make pancakes, eggs, fried potatoes, and some zucchini and squash."

"You don't have to try so hard."

It took Abigail a moment to shut her open mouth. That he'd noticed her effort surprised her. That he would comment on it, even more. She'd washed clothes, sewed, cooked, and cleaned with a fervor even greater than she employed in her own home, but Mordecai had been busy working from dawn to dusk at John's place, helping with the rebuilding of the house. How could he know?

He was wrong, of course. She did need to try hard.

"We're guests here, and I don't want to make more work for Susan and Esther. The least we can do is earn our keep." Five more mouths to feed would quickly become a strain on the Kings. To her great frustration, Mordecai had steadfastly refused to take money to help with household expenses. "I wanted to thank you again for your hospitality."

"No need. We're only doing what's right and expected."

His pained smiled said he meant the words. His generosity went without saying. Or he would prefer that it did. He had a quiet way about him as if he was at peace. He walked in a measured pace that spoke of a certain destination. Today it appeared that destination involved fishing, also to Abigail's surprise. Much work had to be done before a new house could be raised on the site of the destroyed one. "Were you going fishing?"

"It was supposed to be a surprise." He tapped the bottom of the poles on the faded vinyl in a jerky tune. "I hired a van to take us to Choke Canyon Reservoir."

"Reservoir?"

"It's a state park. We can fish and the kids can splash around in the water." Grinning like a child on Christmas morning, he moved into the room and leaned the poles against the wall. A bony, dirty white dog with black patches on its face and back trotted in behind him. Abigail had never seen the animal before. It dropped on the floor next to Mordecai, its mouth open, long pink tongue lolling as it panted. Mordecai squatted next to the dog as if accustomed to having it in the house. "Phin goes birding on the trail."

"Whose *hund*?" The question trumped the half a dozen others that milled around in her head about this plan to take a day off and go fishing and look at birds. "Where did it come from?"

"I don't know. Mine, I guess." Mordecai scratched behind one droopy ear, and the dog's snout seemed to widen in a big, thankful grin. "Folks are always dumping their dogs out here in the country, like they think they can fend for themselves by hunting or something. After being fed store food and table scraps, they have no hunting instincts left."

"So you just decided to adopt this one?"

"He adopted me. He's been following me around since I fed the horses this morning."

"Did you feed him?"

"Yep."

"There you go."

"You don't like dogs?"

"I like them fine, but he is another mouth to feed." Abigail knelt and smoothed a hand over the dog's rough fur matted with burrs and dirt. "He needs a bath. What's his name?"

Mordecai grinned, his face not that far from her own. He leaned in and petted the dog so his hand passed within inches of hers. "Tell you what, I'll let you do the honors."

"You'll let me name your hund?"

"As long as you don't give him a sissy name like Belle or Star or Angel or Jasmine."

"Sissy names." She chuckled. "Is he a he?"

"Jah."

"Let's see." Tickled that Mordecai would trust her with the naming of his dog, she tilted her head and gave the dog a good once-over. He tilted his head and gazed right back at her. "You look like Mutt to me."

"Nee."

"Patch?"

"Nee."

"I thought you said I could name him."

"I did."

She laughed. "How 'bout Butch?"

"There you go. That's a nice, strong name. Butch. Butch it is."

Butch barked, one quick bark, then flopped his head on his paws as if tuckered out.

"What will Susan think of this latest addition?"

"It isn't the first time. She'll just natter on about how he can't be messing up the house, that he needs to stay outside. Until the first hard thunderstorm and then she'll be all worried about how he's doing out in the barn."

That didn't surprise Abigail. People like Mordecai and Susan were helpers by nature. They took in strays. In fact, they'd taken in almost a whole family of strays. This hund was no different. Mordecai could no more turn his back on it than he could a child. "So is Butch going fishing with you today?"

"I expect so. He'll like it at the lake. Lots of critters to chase. Lots of shade for a nap later."

"You plan to do those things yourself, I reckon." The pleasure the idea gave him was so obvious in Mordecai's face. He reminded her of Timothy the first day of hunting season. The thought didn't cause the terrible deep-seated ache it once had. More of a warmth nestled around her heart. "Don't try to say it's for the kinner. You want to play hooky."

"Something like that." He didn't seem to feel the least bit guilty. "It's a treat. People should have a treat now and then."

Like playing in the rain? Mordecai worked hard, but he played hard too. Would the bishop agree with Mordecai's sense of balance between the two? Would John? Or more importantly,

Stephen? "What about John's house?" Abigail couldn't imagine simply taking a day off in the middle of the week to go fishing. It wasn't done. "Susan and I planned to make meals for the men today and do laundry."

"I talked to John. He's hired a van too."

And Stephen? What would Stephen say to this crazy plan? Abigail could only imagine. He'd barely spoken to her at Sunday service. Her refusal to move up the wedding plans had hurt him, something she hadn't intended. She needed to be careful of his feelings. Abigail edged toward the kitchen door. She should stick to her plan, make breakfast, start the laundry, and churn out more clothes for the kinner. Tonight Stephen would come for a visit, as he'd taken to doing on a regular basis. "I'll stay here. I'm far behind in making new dresses for the girls and I haven't even started on pants for the boys."

"They've been given hand-me-downs that will tide them over." Mordecai squatted and did something to the line on one of the poles, his head bent over them. He touched the handle on the spinner and the line spun and whirred, a soft sound that reminded Abigail of summer. His tone had softened. "Everyone deserves a day away. Not just a Sunday of rest, but a day of play."

He didn't say it, but his expression spoke to Abigail. Mordecai thought she needed a day away. Why? She'd tried hard to pull her own weight, not to whine about her situation, to put on a happy face. Something told her Mordecai saw through her facade. "Work first, play later."

"You have worked hard." Mordecai cleared his throat. He worked the spinner some more as if not satisfied with its performance. "You've had loss. You've had more loss. Today, you play."

He had no right to tell her what to do. He wasn't her husband.

Still, she lived—if only temporarily—in his house. "The sooner the new house is built, the sooner we'll be out of yours."

"Everything in its time."

Maybe so, but living in a stranger's house, taking his charity, one shouldn't do that for longer than necessary. "Guests are like fish—they schtinkich after three days."

Mordecai laughed, a deep, rich chuckle that sounded like musical notes. Butch raised his head, his expression perplexed, then let it drop again. "Around here, fish get eaten long before three days. We'll have a fish fry and eat watermelon and spit seeds."

The last time they'd done that, lightning struck John's house and it burned to the ground.

"It doesn't seem right."

"I learned something when my fraa died. I reckon you've noticed it too."

"I suppose I did." She'd learned how to get up each day, get dressed, cook, clean, grow crops, and be a mother and father to her children. She'd had no choice. "I learned to go on."

"I learned to take each day as it comes, to enjoy it, to thank Gott for it, to appreciate the blessings of this earth. We're only passing through, but this is Gott's creation and it is worthy of our praise and thanksgiving."

"I do thank Gott for it."

"Do you?"

His gaze seemed to drill right through her. "I do."

"Then let's go fishing. Today." He'd won the battle, and the smile on his face said he knew it. "Pack the fixings to go with fish. Susan will be up any second. She'll help. The van will be here in about an hour."

A day at the lake with Mordecai King. The thought sent her

mind into a tizzy that made her body feel off balance. "We could invite Stephen and Caleb. Caleb loves to fish."

The laughter in his face died away. He cocked his head side to side, his neck popping. "We could."

Abigail missed her son. Stephen? She didn't want to delve too far into that train of thought. Stephen worked hard and it was good for Caleb to be with him. He would train him up right. He would get practice being a daed, and Caleb would learn to see him as his new daed. A little boy needed a father. She could ignore the over-zealous kiss and the messy house. Those things could be fixed. She had to try harder. Caleb needed a man at the head of their house.

Timothy would always be his daed, but Stephen would raise him. The old ache in her chest returned. Everyone deserved a day off now and then. Her son surely did. "This state park. Does it cost money?"

Mordecai wrinkled his nose as if he smelled something sour. "That's no concern of yours."

"It is. I can't let you pay. You're already paying for the van. You won't let me help with the food—"

"A person should learn to accept a gift with grace." Mordecai straightened and grabbed the poles. "Each time I pick up my earnings from the store, I set money aside for the emergency fund, and for the fun-day fund. That money will pay for this trip. For all of us. Kinner twelve and under are free. Chuck Weaver wants to go fishing too, so he's giving us a discounted rate on the van. Come on, Butch."

He trudged toward the door without looking back, his four-legged buddy close behind.

Abigail followed. The memories of Timothy standing on the shores of the Bylars' pond, casting his line, went with her. "Mordecai."

He swiveled, eyebrows raised as he put his hand on the screen door.

"Do you use lures or fresh bait?"

He grinned, his craggy face lighting up. "Today, stink bait. I got a hankering for catfish. The lake is down, but a guy who came into the store yesterday said the channel and the blue catfish are biting. Phineas and Abram like the black bass. They'll probably use those soft plastic worms. Jacob and Samuel will use a little of both."

"Abram is going fishing too?"

"Yep. Bringing his fraa. The whole family will be there."

The way he said it made Abigail feel included. Right along with the King boys and Abram's fraa. Theresa was expecting soon. Sitting outside in the hot sun while her husband fished might not be her idea of fun, but at least she would be off her feet.

"Pancakes, fried potatoes, and squash in twenty minutes. Don't be late."

"Don't you worry. I'm never late for a meal that involves pancakes."

He shoved his hat down on his forehead and eased the door open with one elbow. Butch trotted thorough and Mordecai followed, letting the screen door slam behind him.

Abigail stared at the empty space where he'd stood. Something more than fishing and breakfast had been said between them, but she had no idea what it was.

To her great surprise, she wanted to find out.

NINETEEN

Deborah wiggled in her seat so she could turn a little sideways. Hazel had dropped off to sleep the minute the van hit the highway's asphalt pavement, and Frannie, who sat on the side, was busy reading the paperback she'd brought—a prairie mail-order-bride story from the looks of it. Phineas sat in the backseat with his brother Samuel who also snoozed, his mouth open, little fluttering snores escaping now and then. So far, Phineas hadn't said a word. Not a word.

He continued to do a good job of avoiding her. He left the house early and often didn't come home for the noon meal. At supper he wolfed his food and slipped from the table the second he finished. Any attempt to start a conversation on her part had been quickly thwarted. Just as well. She didn't really want to go birding with him. Why should she, when he acted like this?

Why was he avoiding her? More importantly, why did she care? She wiggled some more. What drove her to sneak peeks at him now? She turned until her leg touched Hazel's booster seat and leaned into the crook of the seat, her back to the window. By swiveling her head just a tad, she could study him out of the corner of her eye.

In the shadows inside the van, his scars looked more gray brown than red. His blue-green eyes were darker, but still his best attribute, along with wide shoulders and a lean body. His black hair stuck out in tufts under his straw hat. He needed a haircut. He clutched a book in his hand, but thirty minutes into the trip, he hadn't opened it. Did his mind wander back to another van trip every time he got into one now? Deborah could only imagine. Maybe he didn't remember what happened. Maybe God blessed him with loss of consciousness until the pain subsided with the medicine the doctors would've given him.

Of course the pain would come back. Especially when they broke the news that his mother had died.

"It's not polite to stare."

Deborah ducked her head. He'd turned from the window so suddenly she didn't have time to look away. "I wasn't staring."

"Lying is a sin."

"So is being prideful. Why would I stare at you?"

"My ugly mug seems to fascinate people."

"Fascinate?"

"More like horrify."

"Self-pity is a sin too."

His mouth opened, then closed. He went back to staring out the window.

Deborah glanced around. Frannie had fallen asleep, her head resting against the window, one finger still holding her place in her book. Mudder, Susan, and the girls were chattering about who knew what. Mordecai sat up front discussing the drought with the driver, an Englisch man who favored a red-and-blue plaid shirt and overalls even in this heat. She leaned closer to the seat that separated her from Phineas. "Can I ask you something?"

"Nee."

"Are you always so grumpy?"

"I said nee."

"That wasn't the question."

He gave an exaggerated sigh. "What is the question?"

"Were you . . . afraid to ride in a van after what happened to you?"

The blue green of his eyes flared, the color dark, then light and golden like water reflecting in the sunlight. For one beat, two beats, he held her gaze, then looked away, his face throbbing a painful red that made the scars all the more livid.

She shouldn't have brought it up. Even now, it was a painful subject. What had she been thinking? "I'm sorry. I don't have a right to ask questions like that. I just thought, if it were me—"

"If it were you, I'd say Gott had an even crueler streak than I already thought."

His voice was low, hoarse.

"What do you mean?"

"To take a face like yours and do this to it?" He pointed to the scars. "It doesn't matter so much on a man who wasn't much to look at to start with."

He thought God had a cruel streak? She'd wondered about that herself, when He took her father away so soon. "Looks don't matter. They sure don't matter to Gott."

His gaze returned to the window. Deborah eased back into her seat, painfully certain he didn't believe her. No wonder he didn't want to talk to her. She had no words of comfort to offer to a man so in need of them and too prickly to accept them.

"I don't remember much." The words were spoken so softly she could barely hear him. "Before in the van, yes. We were singing songs and acting silly. It smelled like the taco meat Mudder had made for the lunch we were going to eat at the coast. The driver gave us pink Bazooka bubble gum as a treat and we were blowing bubbles. Mine popped on my face and I was peeling it off . . ." The sentence trailed off. His jaw worked. "That's it. Until the hospital. I don't remember the accident. None of it."

"I guess that's gut."

"Yeah, it's a long way to the coast on horseback." The laugh held no humor. "And more dangerous with the way folks drive cars."

"True."

"We're here."

Deborah turned to look out her window. She didn't really know what to expect. How much water could there be in this place, with this drought? Where would it have come from? Not from the sky. Through the sparse trees that lined the highway, she caught glimpses of a vast lake that seemed to wind in the same direction as the road. The sun sparkled on the water, even at a distance.

"It's pretty."

"It's down about twenty feet because of the drought." Phineas's voice seemed closer to her ear. He'd leaned forward. "Still, it's enough for fishing. Makes it easier for the alligators to nip at your heels when you go wading."

"Alligators?" Surely he was joshing her. "You do like to make things up, don't you?"

"You calling me a liar?"

"I think you like to tease the new girl."

"You wait. You'll see the sign that says to watch out for them. The parks department even has a hunting season. You can buy permits to hunt them."

"Yeah, I read in the paper the other day that a kid caught an eight-hundred-pound alligator right here in this lake during hunting season." Frannie's head popped up from the window. Had she been feigning sleep and eavesdropping on their conversation? Deborah felt her cheeks flame. Frannie looked wide awake. "It was the biggest ever."

"What would they do with an alligator?"

"Some folks eat the meat." Phineas's voice held a note of suppressed laughter. He was enjoying her horror. "Tastes like chicken, they say."

The barely perceptible turn-up of the corners of his mouth told Deborah he wanted to laugh at the effect his words had on her. The chill dancing up her spine. The hair standing up on her arms. She didn't want to give him the satisfaction. "That's what I heard about rattlesnake meat."

"One of these days we'll ask Susan to fry some up for us. See how you like it."

"I'm not frying any snakes in my skillets." Apparently Susan had good ears as well. "Don't let him give you a hard time, Deborah. Mostly hunters want the skins. They make boots and belts and such out of them."

"The alligators or rattlesnakes?"

"Both."

Such a lovely place, south Texas. Rattlesnakes. Wild hogs. Alligators. What happened to good old livestock? Even coyotes seemed tame compared to this menagerie. Determined not to let Phineas see her discomfort at the thought, she forced herself to lean back in the seat and fan herself with the notebook she'd brought along, thinking she would write a letter to Josie on the ride. As the days passed, it became harder and harder to think what to say to an old friend. How would she explain someone like Phineas to Josie?

The van came to a stop, brakes squeaking. Mordecai handed a few bills to Mr. Weaver, who in turn handed them through the window to a young woman dressed in a brown uniform. Seconds later Mordecai attached a permit to the inside of the windshield.

Another short ride and they came to a stop again. Phineas squeezed from the backseat first and turned to help Hazel out. He smiled at the little girl and plopped her on her feet with a flourish, but when his gaze met Deborah's, the smile disappeared. Fine, his goodwill didn't extend to her. So be it. Deborah stretched and tried to take everything in. The lake was indeed low. Trees stuck up in the water, their branches barren and white. Even so, motorboats buzzed across the lake, tiny dots in the distance. Birds chattered, sounding very much like women scolding their kinner.

Everyone seemed to know where they were going. The boys took off for the shore, fishing rods over their shoulders. Frannie took Hazel and Hannah by the hand. "Let's play in the water." She glanced back. "You coming? The water will feel great after all this heat. I can't wait to swim."

"In our dresses?"

"Jah. I do it all the time. In the sun, they'll dry fast."

"With the alligators?"

Frannie grinned. "The swimming area is safe. I dunk the little ones there all the time. They love it."

Frannie was one for exaggeration. Deborah glanced back at Phineas. He'd already had his binoculars to his eyes in the direction of the picnic shelters grouped along the shore. Several birds were clustered around a shelter that had a sign FISH CLEANING

Area on it. A couple of elderly Englischers were hard at work cleaning their fish. Phineas veered their direction, but the birds, chattering in what sounded like a fierce argument, took off for the top of the trees.

Phineas stopped and changed directions, headed toward a wooden sign with words etched into it that read NATURE TRAIL with an arrow underneath. He had his book under his arm, a canvas bag on his back, and the strap of his binoculars slung around his neck. He looked perfectly content. She chewed her lip and tugged free of Frannie. "You go on. I think I'll take a walk first, stretch my legs after that drive."

Frannie's gaze went to Phineas and back to Deborah. Her dark eyebrows lifted and her eyes widened. "Are you sure, cousin?"

"It's just a walk."

"Jah, a walk. I'll cover for you."

A silly grin on her face, Frannie giggled and put her hand over her mouth as if to stop the sound.

"I'm not doing anything wrong."

"I know, go on. Take your walk."

Deborah picked up her pace but kept back a few yards, watching as Phineas opened his guidebook and thumbed through the pages, his head down, not even watching where he was going. He lifted his binoculars and looked out at the lake, then back at the book. A few seconds later he glanced up at a tree, then stopped, his gaze lifting toward something in the highest branches. Deborah hung back, stooping to admire a mess of black-eyed Susans along the trail. After a minute or two, he started walking again.

"Stop following me." He slung the words over his shoulder without slowing his pace. "It's annoying."

Deborah slowed but continued to walk toward him. Phineas swiveled and stared at her. "Stop following me."

"Aren't you going fishing?"

"Later."

"What are you doing now?"

"Looking for birds."

"What kind of bird are you looking for?"

His gaze bumped her shoulder and then veered toward the water. "You really want to know?"

"You told me you would take me bird-watching."

He stared at the binoculars in his hands as if he'd never seen them before.

"What kind of bird are you looking for?"

"Bullock's oriole for one. Also a Vermilion Flycatcher."

"Why?"

"Because one is bright orange and the other bright red."

"Pretty fancy."

"I reckon, but they're also easier to see because they stand out against the brown land and the pale-blue sky."

She moved past him and continued on the trail, casting her gaze from side to side, trying to see it as he saw it. "What have you seen so far?"

Giving an exaggerated sigh, he tugged a skinny spiral notebook from the bag slung over his back and produced a nub of a pencil. "So far, some olive swallows nesting in the eaves of a picnic shelter and a Bell's Vireo nesting in the brush. The White Egret, of course, and the wild turkey."

"Not interesting?"

"Pretty average."

"Why is color important?"

"It's not. Some birds are more beautiful to look at. Mostly birders like to find the rare birds, endangered species, ones you don't see too often. That's considered special. But I like the ones that are beautiful too."

"But most of them fly just the same." At that moment a white bird with a long, graceful neck took off from the shore, soared along the bank, and then landed near the dock next to a bird with blue-gray feathers. "What's that other bird, not the white one, but the other one?"

"The white one is a Great Egret. The other one is a Blue Heron. They like the water, and we're close to the coast so we see a lot of tropical water fowl here."

He stopped long enough to scribble in the notebook some more. His writing was tight and narrow with skinny loops. Nothing like Aaron's neat block print.

"Why do you write it down?"

"That's part of birding." He started walking again. "You write down what you see and share it with other birders."

"You do?"

His lips twitched. He almost smiled. "Nee, I mean, that's what the Englischers do. They write about it on the Internet."

She had heard of the Internet but never experienced it. From the beginning of her rumspringa, she'd avoided it for fear of disappointing Daed. He was firm about some things, technology being one of them. He didn't want his kinner to lose their innocence. He'd told her as much on her sixteenth birthday. Took her into the barn and gave her a talking to. *Just remember, there are some things you can never get back and some roads are dead ends. You can't get back your innocence, your purity. Hang on to it. It's a gift you'll give to your husband one day. A gift like no other. One only you can give.*

She hadn't known exactly what he meant by all that, but the love and the angst in his voice and the way he looked at her as if she were the most important person in the world to him, it was enough to make her tread with care. She'd seen some movies, watched TV, even played pool at a little tavern in town, but she'd never dated an Englisch boy or gone to parties where alcohol was served. She'd been good. She'd done her best to please him.

And then Daed had died. And now Aaron didn't want to wait for her. And Jesse was interested in Leila. And Phineas thought Deborah was a pest. She chewed on her lip, holding back tears that seemed to pop up at the slightest provocation these days. She cleared her throat, determined to move on. "You ever been on the Internet?"

"Jah."

"Really?" In this place where they barely had food on the table, he'd been on a computer? "Where?"

"There you go calling me a liar again."

"Did not. I didn't mean that."

"I went to the library in Beeville. The librarian helped me find information about birds in this part of the country."

"After you started your rumspringa?"

He nodded. "But even before."

"What about the Ordnung?"

"At the time I didn't care."

"It was after the accident and your mudder . . ."

He nodded again, his lips curled down in a frown as he let his hand run through the branches of a bush along the trail, the branches popping behind him. "It just seemed like, what harm could it do? I know all about the slippery slope, so don't preach at me."

"I won't." She hadn't personally experienced it, but she'd watched a friend or two hit that slope and end up on their behinds at the bottom. "It's not my place to judge."

"I needed to be away from the house, and I couldn't work in the fields at first so Daed took me to the library."

"To read the books." She stopped to watch a turtle trundle across a fallen log and slip into the muddied water mixed with weeds along the edge of the lake. "And lightning didn't strike you when you got on the Internet?"

"Nee. I didn't see anything that drove me into the arms of the world. But there was information and I did learn some things. I believe in the rules. I follow them every day. But at that time I was . . . so . . ."

"Melancholy?"

His mouth opened, then closed. He shook his head, a sardonic smile spreading across his face.

"What?"

He shrugged. "I thought that about you. You feel melancholy."

Her heart squeezed in a painful contraction. That he'd given any thought to her state of mind surprised her. "What a thing to have in common. It's the same as being discontent with Gott's plan for us."

"I'm not discontent." His sniff held undisguised disdain. "But I'm not always thinking about how ugly this place is or how I want to leave as soon as possible."

"Instead you're always thinking about how ugly your scars are and how no one will ever love you."

He halted with a jerk. His knuckles went white around the notebook in his hand. His gaze seemed fixed on something far beyond the horizon. "You don't know me."

She'd gone too far. Her big mouth needed a muzzle. "I know. I'm sorry."

"Nee, you're not. You're following me around because you think you can fix me."

"Nee, I don't. I feel like . . . I don't know what to call it . . . I feel there's something about you that is like me and I'm like you. I think you can feel it too."

His gaze dropped to the book in his hand. His grip loosened. He raised his head and looked at her. His jaw worked, but his eyes captivated her. They sparked blue green like flames turned up too high on a gas stove. "Well, all I know is we're not going to find a Vermilion Flycatcher standing here yapping."

"Yapping." She breathed again. An invitation of sorts. "You call this yapping?"

"That's what Daed calls it."

"I call it getting to know a person."

Phineas ducked his head, his expression once again unreadable. "I don't understand why you would want to get to know me."

"I told you." And she didn't intend to repeat it. "Besides, you're different from most men."

"I only look different."

"You must think I'm awfully shallow."

"Nee. I don't."

"Then what makes you think I care what you look like?"

"It's human nature."

"You don't set a very high standard for our behavior."

"I've seen the pitying glances."

"It's in your head."

"Nee. It's not. You don't have to pretend you're interested in bird-watching or bees or me. I don't need company."

Deborah stood toe to toe with him. "Jah, you do. You do. Just like I do. Stop pushing people away and you'll see that people want to be friends with you—I want to be friends with you. You're the only one making it hard."

His chest heaved and his breathing sounded loud in the still, heated morning air. He turned his back and walked away.

"Phineas!" She gritted her teeth, counting to five, then breathed. "When I look at your eyes, I don't see those scars at all. Gott gave you beautiful eyes. I look at them and I see right into your heart. I see how you feel about things. You're not hiding anything from me."

His pace slowed, but he didn't turn.

"Fine. Be that way."

Her heart pounded in her chest. She might not be able to draw her next breath, such was the angry welter of emotions that pressed on her. Why did this man make her so agitated? Aaron never did. What did that say about her feelings for him? Or for Phineas?

"Someday you'll stop feeling sorry for yourself and start living the life Gott wants for you." Deborah itched to stomp her feet. Only her last shred of dignity kept her from taking that last childish step. "When you do, you'll let me in."

"Why should I? You're leaving."

Deborah put her hand to her mouth to corral the words banging around in her head. He was right. Maybe her advice to him would be advice well taken for herself. Putting someone else's house in order when hers was a mess. Tennessee seemed so very far away and Phineas King was right here. Right now. And something about him tore at her heart.

Unfortunately, he didn't seem to have the same feelings about her, and Deborah didn't have an answer for his questions.

Until she did, she should stay far, far away from Phineas King.

TWENTY

Inhaling the scent of seasoned salt, fish, and hot oil, Abigail slid the chunks of breaded fish into the skillet and adjusted the flame on the Coleman stove Susan had placed on top of the picnic table. They had done well, considering they'd fished for only a couple of hours. Enough catfish to feed the whole family. The farmer who visited the store had been right. Stink bait did the trick.

Abigail's stomach rumbled. She loved a good piece of fried fish with buttered, boiled potatoes and corn on the cob. The fish and potatoes, her sore mouth could handle. Corn on the cob would be more than her tooth could bear. She needed to go to the dentist, but dentists cost money. She sighed and breathed a prayer for healing.

All in all, it had been a good morning. Mordecai squatted next to a bucket he'd filled with water from a nearby spigot. Butch lay at his side, as if keeping watch, his panting loud in the still after-noon air. A skinny white bird with a long neck ambled toward them, two babies following after. It seemed they wanted their bite of fish too. His ears up, Butch lifted his head and growled low in his throat. The birds trotted away.

Mordecai washed his knife and the board he'd used to skin and fillet the fish in the fish-cleaning area as fast as the boys brought him their catches. He hummed the tune of a familiar German hymn as he scrubbed the knife, then his hands. The off-key, breathy effort made her smile as she scooped another chunk of fish onto a paper plate for Samuel.

Despite the heat, the flies, and the sweat trickling between her shoulder blades in an irritating tickle, Abigail felt content. At peace. Mordecai had been right about this day of rest. The only place she felt closer to Gott than Sunday prayer service was when she worked in the garden. This park, with its lake of lapping water and tree branches rustling in the breeze and birds jabbering from their perches on wooden pilings that stuck up in the water and atop picnic benches, came a close second.

Mordecai looked up at her and smiled. She smiled back. His eyes were more blue than green today against the blue of the sky and lake. The smile spread and became a knowing grin. Her own grew to match. "What's so funny?"

He shrugged and straightened. "You have flour on your nose."

"Do not." She scrubbed at her face with the back of her hand. "Well, maybe a little. You smell like fish guts."

"Best smell around." He tossed the water into the grass and settled the bucket on the cement. "Next to bread baking."

"Nee, the best smell around is cherry pie."

"True. Or pumpkin. I like pumpkin."

He liked pumpkin pie. She made a good one, if she did say so herself. "Maybe come Thanksgiving, I'll bake you one."

"The fish are burning." John approached with a full plate in one hand, the other hand waving the air as if trying to clear imaginary smoke Abigail couldn't see. "What a waste."

"It's not burning." She returned to her task, aware of Susan and the girls crowded at one table, giggling and whispering. What would Susan think of her? She wasn't flirting with Mordecai. She surely didn't remember how to flirt. And she was committed to another. "I like the breading crisp, don't you?"

John stuck a pickle in his mouth and chewed without responding. He looked as if he'd taken a bite of the wrong end of a porcupine. Maybe he'd been goosed by one of those armadillos Deborah went on and on about. He'd been morose and grumpy for days now. Not that she blamed him, losing the house and all. Didn't seem to affect his appetite, however. He'd been standing around shoveling food into his mouth like a starved child for several minutes.

Abigail nodded to an open spot on the bench next to John's boys. "Sit, bruder. It's not good for the digestion to eat standing."

"That's an old wives' tale." The words were muffled by a mouthful of jalapeño-cheese bread Susan had baked the previous day. John swallowed, his Adam's apple bobbing with the effort. He jerked his head. "Come. Talk with me."

Abigail picked up the tongs and turned the fish pieces over with a gingerly touch. "Go ahead. I've got a whole mess of fish still to fry."

"Frannie and Leila can handle it." His tone suggested she not argue. "Or Eve and Theresa."

Eve and Theresa sat at a picnic table in a nearby pavilion, side by side, backs to the table, matching dishwater-red hands on their big bellies, faces damp with sweat. Their conversation had been faint and breathless.

"Leila, take over here." Abigail gave the fish another stir. It didn't look or smell burned to her. Her turn to eat would have to wait, it seemed. What did John want that couldn't wait a few minutes or be said in front of the rest of their family? She handed the tongs to Leila. "Careful not to bump the stove or you'll have hot grease running down your legs."

John stalked away, choosing a concrete sidewalk that led down to the water's edge but ended abruptly with a downturn that went nowhere. Curiosity stirring in her, Abigail scurried to keep up. "What is it? If you want me to help with the baby, I'd be happy to do it. I've delivered a bunch of babies over the past few years. I just thought Naomi would do it. She's helped with others, according to Susan."

"It's not Eve." A dull red crept across John's cheeks. A pulse beat in his temple. He faced Abigail. "We're moving to Missouri."

Her bruder suddenly spoke a language Abigail couldn't understand. "Missouri? What? What are you talking about?"

"Eve's family is from up yonder around Jamesport."

"I know, but you have land here and friends and . . . family." The hunger Abigail had felt earlier turned into a hard, heavy stone in her stomach, leaving her with a desire to retch. John had her and the kinner. His family. They'd only just arrived in Bee County and, at the moment, were homeless. "You told me it would be a good move, to come here. That's what you said."

"I did. I'm sorry." John's hands clenched at his sides, then opened again. "I didn't know what was coming. No one could've. Our family is growing, and I'm hard-pressed to provide for them here. I could barely make ends meet, and now with the house . . ."

"Gott will provide. He already has. We've already started to rebuild. The foundation is still there." Abigail worked to keep the panic from her voice. "The supplies are here. We'll have a building frolic tomorrow. Surely that is Gott's plan."

"Building the house will make the property easier to sell. Eve and I have prayed and we believe moving is Gott's plan."

"Sell? Who'll buy it?" Abigail clamped her hand over her mouth to keep the words from spilling out. Such an ugly place. Even this lake, with its dearth of water and dead trees reaching their shorn gray-and-white branches to the sky, seemed to be dead or dying. She'd kept that opinion to herself for weeks now. She wouldn't criticize God's creation, as much as the drab grays and browns reminded her of a funeral.

She breathed and dropped her hand. "You mean to leave us here with no family?"

"You're to marry Stephen. That's been the plan all along. You'll be settled here with a good man who can provide for you and your kinner." John faced her. Creases around his eyes and mouth made him look older than she knew him to be. "I have a sense of peace over that. Don't you?"

Despite the oven-like heat of midday, a shiver ran through Abigail. Her life stood before her, the road empty all the way to a barren horizon. This was her life from now on. And the life of her kinner. She'd brought them here for a new start. With Stephen. "I thought to have you and Eve close, that's all. Everything is better with family. You can rebuild."

"It's not just the house." John stooped and picked up a rock. He slung it into the lake, making it bounce across the shimmering blue water. "Truth be told, it's been a long time coming."

Something he hadn't shared with her before she uprooted her kinner and trekked halfway across the country to this alien place. "I don't understand."

John chucked another rock into the lake. Like a little boy in trouble, he couldn't seem to look her in the eye. "Eve misses her family. She misses Missouri and snow at Christmas and leaves that change colors and silly things like that. I want to farm in a place where the earth is fertile and meant to grow crops. This is ranching country."

"Are you saying it was a mistake to start a district here?"

"That's not for me to say. Leroy's daed saw something here. Gott called him here." John waved his hands toward the horizon. "I just don't think He called me here."

"Have you told Leroy?"

"Jah."

"What did he say?"

"He's disappointed. We're the third family to leave in the last year."

"Third? Why didn't you tell me this before I moved here?"

"The district has struggled to make it for years. Folks come and go. I thought you and the kinner, especially the girls, would help grow it. The fire was the last straw. Maybe a sign, I don't know. I have decided to trust Gott and move closer to Eve's family." He kicked at the hard ground with a dusty boot. "Besides, you weren't coming here for me. You came for Stephen. Leastways, that's the impression I had. I know it's the one he has."

It was Abigail's turn to stare at the water. Jah, she came to Beeville because of Stephen, but also because she had family here. A fallback. She could admit to herself she'd been counting on John and Eve as her backup plan.

Instead of counting on God. *Gott, forgive me.* "When will you go?"

"Next week. I'd like to get Eve settled before she gets too far along." He ducked his head and cleared his throat. "Eve's brother needs help with his harvest. He can pay me a wage. That'll get us started until I can sell the land here."

Abigail's throat ached with a sense of loss she hadn't felt since Timothy's death. John didn't die. It didn't make sense that she should feel so bereft. So lost. "We can't keep living in Mordecai's house."

"You have two choices." John sounded much surer of himself now that the topic had shifted from him to her. "You can do what you came to do here and marry Stephen. Or you can come to Missouri with us."

Or she could admit coming here had been a fool's errand and return to Tennessee. That would make the kinner happy. What they didn't understand was they had no home left. Some other family lived in the house that had once been theirs.

It was just a house, but somehow she couldn't bear the thought of watching another woman hang clothes on the line outside the house she'd shared with Timothy. Or plant potatoes and peas in the ground Timothy had tilled for her garden.

Or she could uproot the kinner yet again to go to another place to start over once again without a husband.

Or marry Stephen and lie in the bed she'd made for herself.

TWENTY-ONE

"Abigail! There you are!"

The familiar refrain. The familiar voice. Abigail felt as if she'd lived this moment before. More than once. Stephen always seemed to be following after her, pursuing her, a bit of a whine in his voice telling her he didn't like it. As if conjured by her thoughts, Stephen trotted along the path to the spot where Abigail stood with John, gazing out at the lake. He puffed as if he'd run the entire way from the farm. To him, it probably looked like they were having a nice, bruder-schweschder chat beside the lake.

"Stephen came to me yesterday and told me he wants to announce the banns soon. He doesn't want to wait until November." John waved at Stephen, then turned to her. His voice was low, the words meant for her ears only. "He also says you seem hesitant. You should take him up on his offer before it's too late. A man like Stephen won't wait forever. And you shouldn't expect him to. It's best for everyone involved."

He sounded so sure of himself. Abigail wanted that same certainty. She stared at Stephen, traipsing toward them with that loose-hipped, gangly walk he had. Like a kid who'd never gotten used to his height after a growth spurt.

John did an about-face and passed Stephen on the path with a nod. Stephen barely seemed to notice. "When John said everyone was fishing today, I had to join in. I enjoy a gut fish fry, you know. Caleb was anxious to come too. I think he misses his schweschders, even though he's not about to admit it."

"Caleb loves to fish. I'm glad you're getting to do something fun together." Caleb had seemed content with his stay at Stephen's. He helped in the greenhouse, and Stephen seemed to enjoy teaching him how to fend for himself in the kitchen. All good things. Fighting a drowning sensation, she tried to compose herself. "It's nice that it costs nothing for the kinner under twelve to enter the park."

"He's a gut boy." Stephen cocked his head, his expression eager. "I look forward to teaching him how to work the fields and harvest the olives and the citrus fruit."

To treat him as a son. The thought struck her heart as an arrow to its target. "It's gut of you to take him under your wing."

"I care for him." His gruff voice deepened. "As I care for you."

"I'm thankful for that."

He shook his head, the eager look dissipating. "That's not the response I hoped for. How much longer will you make me wait?"

Mordecai's whistled tune filled Abigail's head. Followed by his chortle when the wind blew his hat from his head and the way his voice sounded when he talked about rubber worms, names for dogs, and fishing. She swiveled and faced the lake, hoping Stephen wouldn't see her expression. "I don't know. I'm trying, but I need time."

Time for feelings to grow. Was that too much to ask for?

"I'm trying to be patient, I hope you know that."

He tried so hard. *Gott, soften my heart toward him.* "It's a beautiful day. Come back to the picnic shelter and let me make you a plate of fried fish. It's delicious. Mordecai—"

"You need to be out of Mordecai's house, the sooner the better. I've spoken with John—"

"He told me."

Stephen sighed, a long, exasperated sigh. He didn't say anything for several beats. A bird somewhere beyond Abigail's line of sight chirruped. A fish jumped and disappeared into the water.

"I—"

"You—"

They walked over each other with their words. Abigail halted. Stephen did the same. Another beat of silence. Stephen cleared his throat. "You first."

"Nee. It's only right that you speak your mind. I'm sorry."

Stephen moved a step closer. He had a woodsy scent of leather and sweat. After a second or two, his hand came out and grasped hers. It was damp, but not unpleasantly so. His fingers curled around hers. "When you picked Timothy the first time, I knew then that I would never be the man your heart desired—"

"Stephen—"

"Nee, you said I could go first." His grip tightened. The deep bass of his voice sounded hoarse. "I can't compete with the memories of your husband. I'm clumsy and I don't always have a way with words."

"You do fine."

"Don't lie. You find me lacking. I see it in your eyes."

"I'm sorry. It's been harder than I expected to get used to being here."

"Being with me, you mean." His gaze sideswiped hers and careened back to the lake. "I had hoped you would see me in a new light here. That your affection for me would grow and deepen. It hasn't. It shouldn't be this hard for me to get your attention. I know when I . . . kissed you . . . you didn't feel what I did."

She had hoped it would too. She'd prayed for it. The last thing she wanted to do was hurt this man once again. She'd been so sure she would grow to love him. "I'm truly sorry if I'm hurting you. I'm trying. I'm trying so hard."

He let her hand drop and faced her. "I went too fast. I'm the one who's sorry."

"Nee, it's my fault. I thought I was over Timothy's death, but I'm beginning to see you don't actually get over such a thing." Could he understand that? Abigail prayed he could. She prayed God would give him patience. "You learn to go on and begin a new season in your life. Maybe for some, like me, it's harder than for others."

His arm slid around her and she found herself enveloped in a simple, brief hug. "I'm sorry if I made it harder for you." He let her go and took a step back. "I'm awful at this. I'm pigheaded and used to going about things my way. I hope you'll give me another chance."

Abigail looked into his eyes so blue against his sunburned face. He was as earnest as a teenage boy on his first ride with a girl. She could recall with minute detail everything about her first buggy ride with Timothy. His soapy, clean scent, the way his dark hair curled on his neck, the white of his teeth as dusk fell and stars began to pop out in the night sky. The clatter of the wooden wheels against the gravel and dirt road. His laugh. Mostly his laugh.

The image faded, only to be replaced with Mordecai's laughing face as he raced across the yard, slid in the mud, and fell on his back, his face tilted to the sky, a wide grin stretching from ear to ear. Was it his laughter or Timothy's that rang in her ears?

She shook her head, trying to clear the thoughts from her brain.

"You won't give me another chance?" Anxiety mingled with disbelief in Stephen's voice. "You're leaving with John to Missouri, then?"

"Nee, nee, I haven't decided yet what to do."

"Then I still have a chance." He reached out cautiously and took her hand.

"You still have a chance. We both do. I'll try to do better."

His face lit up and the young man who'd vied for her attention all those years ago reappeared. "I'll do better."

With that, he let go of her hand, grabbed her by the waist, picked her up, and whirled her around. "You'll see, it'll be better." He plopped her on the ground, then leaned down and kissed her lips with the softest brush of a kiss, a kiss a far cry from the one he'd delivered with such overwhelming gusto at his farm. "How's that for starters?"

"Gut . . . I think." She staggered back a step, hand on her chest, breathless from the spin. Not so much from the kiss. He was trying so hard. It was sweet how hard he tried. "It was nice, but go slow, remember?"

"I can be fun too."

"I know."

"I believe in hard work first."

"I know. Me too."

"Then let's go get that plate of fish you offered me, and then I'd like to do some fishing with Caleb. Maybe Hazel will let me show her how to fish. While I'm here I need to have a word with

Mordecai." His voice faltered on the name. "We're to work on the house again tomorrow and he has tools we'll need him to bring."

They rounded the curve in the path and the picnic shelter came into sight. Mordecai sat with his back to the picnic table, his paper plate in his hand, Butch lolling at his feet. He looked up, a piece of fish halfway from his plate to his mouth. A smile formed, then disappeared.

Stephen didn't seem to notice. He forged ahead. "Come on, I'm starved. I hope there's still fish. Have you eaten?"

His words ran on, no pause in between, giving her the opportunity to not answer. Mordecai dropped the fish on his plate, wiped his fingers on his pants, and stood. He tossed the plate into the trash can and stalked away. Butch stood, stretched, and followed, his tongue hanging from his mouth.

Every bone and muscle in Abigail's body wanted to follow. For some outlandish reason, she felt the need to explain, to offer an apology, to say her walk with Stephen meant nothing.

It did mean something. It certainly meant something to Stephen.

She wiped her hand on her apron. As if she could wipe away the scene now burned on Mordecai's memory of her strolling along the lake with another man. She'd come to the lake with Mordecai—with his family—but she would leave with Stephen.

That shouldn't bother Mordecai. She came to Bee County to be with Stephen. Everyone knew that. So why did it bother her?

She couldn't answer that question because it meant fettering out the meaning of the ache in her heart when she realized the look on Mordecai's face had been hurt for that one split second before he shuttered it. Hurt and longing.

Just for a split second. Then it had been gone and so had he. That look. She recognized it. She understood it. She felt it.

Stephen was right. The sooner she left Mordecai King's house, the better.

TWENTY-TWO

Deborah took a quick swipe at the sweat on her forehead with one hand and then returned her fingers to the material she guided under the bobbing needle on the sewing machine. Her hands made damp impressions on the pale lilac. Her bare feet slipped on the treadle and the needle slowed. At this rate, Hazel's new dress would have some seriously crooked seams. Not that Hazel would care, but Mudder might. She was a good seamstress, and she had taught her daughters to be meticulous with their needles and thread.

"My sewing is fine," she muttered. "It's the heat causing the squiggles."

"Are you talking to yourself?" Leila trotted into the front room, a basket of clothes in her arms. "Or do you have an imaginary friend?"

"Very funny." Deborah reached the end of the seam, stopped pumping the treadle, and pulled up on the lever so she could cut the thread. "I think it's hotter today than it was yesterday."

"I don't mind the heat." The smile on her sister's face told Deborah that Leila really didn't mind. The thought only made

Deborah feel even more cross. Which wasn't fair. Leila had a sweet nature, and she and Rebekah had been doing laundry all morning and making fancy handwritten labels for the honey jars between trips to the clothesline. "I'd rather feel the sun on my face than icy snow. The clothes dry faster and they smell good."

"Okay, okay, Miss Ray of Sunshine." Deborah held up the skirt of the dress. Time to pin the bodice and begin on those seams. "How can you be so cheerful? What's your secret?"

"She's in *lieb!*" Rebekah traipsed through the door, her face half-obscured by another pile of laundry. "Didn't she tell you?"

"She did not. It's none of my business." Deborah pulled pins from the material and stuck them in the red tomato-shaped pin cushion. "Where's Hazel?"

"I sent her to the kitchen to get me a glass of water. I'm parched." Rebekah dumped the clothes onto the rocking chair and stretched, one hand on her back, the other raised over her head. She grimaced. "You'd think after the fire, we'd have less clothes to wash, especially with Caleb not being here."

"I told Susan we'd take care of all the laundry and finish putting the labels on the last batch of honey jars while she and Mudder are at Martha's helping deliver her baby. It's all in the timing, a baby coming on laundry day."

"I'm sure Martha planned it that way." Deborah joined her sisters in giggling over her silly comment. She was trying not to think about Rebekah's earlier statement. Leila in love. Already. They'd only been in Bee County two months. "Delivering a baby is a lot of work, you know."

"You want to know about Leila's beau, I can tell." Rebekah shook a finger at Deborah. "You like to know what's going on, same as the rest of us."

"Courting is private."

"I'm not courting." Leila's dimpled face turned pink. She ducked her head and smoothed the pants she was folding with both hands. "Leastways, not yet."

"But he talked to you, didn't he? He's talked to you at the singings and after the prayer services." Rebekah clapped her hands in a quick one-two, one-two as if applauding her own statement. "He'll be showing up here one night to take you for a ride, you watch."

"He who?" Deborah couldn't stand it anymore. "Is it Jesse?"

"I thought you didn't want to know." Rebekah rolled her eyes, her mouth stretched in a wide grin. "Of course it's Jesse."

Deborah focused on pinning the bodice seam. Good for Leila. She was starting her new life here on the right foot. She'd made a clean break. Gut for her.

"Why do you look so sad?" Rebekah's smile disappeared. "Don't worry, schweschder, your time will come. That's what Mudder always says. In Gott's time."

"Besides, everyone can see you like Phin." Leila's tone made the words more of a question than a statement. "You walked with him at the lake that day we went fishing."

"That doesn't mean anything."

"Then why is your face turning as red as a strawberry?"

"Because."

"Because why?"

Deborah slipped the material under the needle, dropped the lever, and began to pump. Maybe the noise would discourage her sisters from pursing this line of questioning.

"Come on, Deborah, I'll tell you about Jesse if you'll spill the beans about Phin."

"There are no beans or peas or radishes to spill." She stopped pumping. "I'm just not sure if he . . ."

"If he what? He likes you. I can tell by the way he stares at you at the supper table when you're not looking."

"He stares at me?"

"Jah, with this strange look like his stomach hurts or something." Rebekah demonstrated by squinting her eyes and scrunching her face as if in pain. "I watched him last night. I couldn't decide if it was staring at you that gave him that look or whether he had indigestion from the wieners and sauerkraut."

The sauerkraut had been particularly sour. "You're making that up."

"Am not."

"Are too."

A crashing sound emanating from the kitchen filled the air. A cry of pain followed.

"Hazel!" Deborah stood so fast she smacked her knee on the sewing machine drawer. "Ouch!"

Another howl of pain from the kitchen made her wince and dart toward the door that divided the two rooms. She jockeyed with Leila to get through it first. There she found Hazel huddled on the floor next to an overturned chair. A glass lay shattered next to her on the cracked, faded linoleum. Blood dripped between fingers pressed to her mouth and ran down the back of her hand. The girl sobbed big, shuddering sobs as she rocked back and forth.

"Hazel, what happened?" Deborah knelt next to her little sister and gently pried her hand from her mouth. She peered at the swelling lower lip, then tugged it forward just enough to see inside. "Ach, schweschder. You have a little scratch."

It wasn't a little scratch, but she didn't want to give Hazel more reason to sob. Her lower front teeth were mashed up against the inside of her lip. They'd penetrated the skin, making a deep, nasty-looking gash. Blood turned the spaces around her teeth red, both top and bottom.

"Leila, get me a clean washrag." While Leila rushed to a basket on the counter, Deborah lifted Hazel into her lap. Not for the first time, she wished for ice. Back home, they always had ice in their gas-powered refrigerator. Did these folks have something against ice? "What were you doing, little schweschder?"

"Needed glass for water."

"So you stood on the chair to reach the cabinet?"

"I fell."

At three, Hazel had plenty of chores and she handled them well enough. But still, short was short.

"I'm sorry. I didn't think of that." Rebekah slapped a hand to her cheek. "Next time come tell me you need help, silly girl."

"Wanted water."

"No standing on chairs to get it." Deborah pressed the towel against Hazel's chin and lower lip, hoping to stanch blood that trickled from her mouth. "There's no shame in asking for help."

A lesson she could learn herself.

"Want Mudder." The words were muffled by the towel, which quickly soaked red.

"Rebekah, go get Mudder at Martha's."

"What happened?" A box of empty jars in his arms, Phineas strode through the doorway. His gaze shot around the room, an emotion like fear making his scars stand out in stark relief against his skin. "I heard a scream."

Deborah hugged her sister close and explained.

"Did you check to see if any bones were broken?" Phineas laid the box on the counter and squatted next to Deborah. He touched Hazel's plump arm with one finger. "Where does it hurt?"

"Mouth."

The word came out *mouf.*

"Anything else? Arms, legs, fingers, toes, your backside?"

"Nee."

"Open up wide, then."

Hazel did as she was told. Phineas peered inside, clucked, and shook his head.

"What?" More tears slid down Hazel's cheeks. Her swollen lips trembled. "Hurt."

"You have a really big mouth." His scarred features softened by a kind smile, Phineas pretended to tickle the girl's neck with two long fingers. "No wonder that's what you fell on."

Hazel's sobs eased and turned into hiccups. "Nee, I don't."

"Do too." He patted her cheek with a hand that looked huge and brown against her small, tearstained face. "You must take after your sister Deborah."

Hazel giggled and hiccupped again, which made her giggle more. Her face scrunched up in a frown. "Owie."

Some of the tension drained from Deborah's neck and shoulders. Phineas had a way with kinner. The brusqueness he used in dealing with adults fell away when he talked to children. "Nee, you're the one with a big mouth."

"Get her into the buggy. I'll hitch up the mule and take us over to Mr. Carson's. He'll give us a ride into the clinic in Beeville so the doc can check her out."

"You think she needs to go to the doctor?" That would mean a doctor's bill. Mudder usually did their doctoring. "I think we should wait for Mudder."

"We need to go." Phineas's tone didn't change, but the look he gave Deborah told her his meaning. "She needs stitches."

"Up you go." Deborah tugged Hazel from her lap and stood, her knees cracking in protest. "Phineas will take us for a ride, and we'll get you all fixed up."

She glanced back at her sisters, standing side by side. Leila looked worried, and Rebekah looked so guilty a person would think she personally pushed her little sister from the chair. "It's okay. You two stay here and let Mudder know what's happened when she comes back."

"Shouldn't one of us go find her and tell her?"

"Get my daed from the field. He'll ride over to Martha's." Phineas spoke with an authority that said he had taken charge of this situation. "It's faster and I don't have to worry about you getting lost or bitten by a snake or stung by a scorpion."

"A scorpion?" The words burst from Deborah before she had a chance to lock them in. "You never said anything about scorpions before."

"I've lost track of the number of critters I've told you about." He grinned, lifted Hazel onto his hip as if she weighed no more than a gnat, and started for the door. "Let's go. This girlie needs to be fixed up."

A sly smile on her face, Leila gave Deborah a push. "Go on, Phin says the girlie needs to be fixed up."

Deborah glared at Leila. "Maybe you should go."

"You're the oldest." Leila pushed harder. "Mudder would want you to go."

"Jah, Deborah, Mudder would want you to go." Phineas mimicked Leila's high voice. "Phineas says."

Leila and Rebekah tittered. They were actually matchmaking

in the middle of this mess. Deborah opened her mouth to protest.

"I want Deborah." Hazel joined in. "Deborah comes."

Fine. A long ride to Beeville might be just what the doctor ordered.

TWENTY-THREE

Swallowing against the nausea that had roiled in his stomach the entire ten miles into town, Phineas scooped Hazel from the backseat, tucked her on his hip, and slammed the door of Mr. Carson's rusted two-tone station wagon that smelled of cigarette smoke and Mr. Carson's feet. The little girl sighed and snuggled against his chest, her face wetting the faded blue cotton. She had been brave on the trip into town, but tears stained her eyes red. Her lip, now a purplish hue, had swollen to twice its normal size.

Horse and buggy might have been faster than Mr. Carson's car putt-putting along the highway, one hand on the steering wheel, one hanging out the window. Phineas's arm tightened around Hazel. He hated to see little ones in pain or sick. Only the need to ease her pain kept him from turning and running home on his own two feet. "It's okay, we're here now. The doc will take good care of you, and you'll be all better before you know it."

Her face furrowed in a frown, Hazel patted Phineas's cheek with chubby, damp fingers. "You got owie too?"

He swallowed against the knot that suddenly appeared in his throat, strangling him. "Jah. I do. I did."

"Doc fix it for you?"

The words twisted and burrowed straight through Phineas's heart. From the mouths of babes. Her sweet face held no disgust or distaste. Her hand didn't jerk back at the feel of his ugly, ridged skin. He cleared his throat. "That's okay. We'll just take care of you today."

Deborah scooted around the back end of the car and held out her arms. "Let me have her."

Ignoring her command, Phineas leaned toward the window on the front passenger side and spoke to Mr. Carson. "I'll ask Belinda to call you on your cell when we're ready to go back."

"I'll be over at the diner having an iced tea."

Mr. Carson touched the tip of his John Deere cap and drove away, leaving the stench of exhaust and gas fumes trailing behind. Phineas whirled and lugged Hazel toward the doctor's office. The slap of Deborah's sneakers on the asphalt told him she struggled to keep up. Despite wanting nothing more than to be done with this foray into a town full of people who would stop and stare, Phineas forced himself to slow down.

She hadn't spoken during the drive in, but he could feel her gaze on the back of his head the entire time. She had some question she wanted to ask but didn't. He could feel it. Of course Mr. Carson kept up a steady stream of conversation centered on the weather, hunting, and fishing, in that order. Hard to get a word in edgewise, even if she wanted to do so.

"Mudder will pay you back when we get home." Her voice sounded breathless. And her tone defensive. "For the driver and for the clinic visit."

"Don't worry about it. There's a district fund for medical emergencies."

Leroy made sure everyone contributed whatever small amount they could spare each month so the community could help each other in times of need. Mordecai always gave more than his share. Phineas appreciated his father's generous nature, even when that meant doing without a new hunting rifle or making the old buggy last another year.

Deborah scurried ahead of him and opened the clinic door. Inside, the smell of cleansers and bleach carried on frigid AC air hit him in the face. Phineas swallowed against the immediate surge of bile in his throat. This wasn't a hospital. He wasn't the patient. He would do it for the little girl in his arms.

Half a dozen people sat in the chairs arranged in rows in the waiting room. A baby wailed on his mother's lap. A boy coughed and whined to his mother about his sore throat. She hushed him, but her gaze lingered on Phineas, then bounced away as her long, horsey face reddened. An elderly man dozed, his head propped against the wall behind him, mouth open wide, his loud snores like a buzz saw. The wait shouldn't be too long. Phineas sucked in air and marched up to the reception area.

"Phineas King, hi, how are you?" Belinda, Doc Peterson's nurse-slash-receptionist-slash-daughter, smiled up at him, her chubby cheeks dimpling, and then at Deborah. "Long time no see, which in my business is a good thing. And this little one. She has a boo-boo, doesn't she? Is this your girl and your wife?"

More pain, this time a razor-sharp arrow piercing his skin over and over again, sliced through him. Hazel's warm weight against his hip felt right. It felt like the most natural thing in the world. "Nee. Nee."

Belinda looked from Phineas to Deborah and back as if expecting someone to elaborate. Deborah's gaze remained on the slick black-and-white checkered tiled floor, her expression pained, her cheeks pink.

Phineas shifted Hazel to his other hip. "This is Hazel Lantz. And her sister Deborah. They just moved here from Tennessee. Hazel hit her mouth. Looks like she needs stitches."

"Well, welcome to Beeville, Hazel. Looks like you took quite a spill." Belinda bustled around the counter where she put one finger to Hazel's chin, forcing her to lift it, and peered at her mouth. "I'll get some ice to help get the swelling down while you fill out some paperwork for me, Deborah. Doc's got four or five folks waiting, but I can work her in. Have a seat, have a seat." She shooed them with both hands toward the chairs.

A TV attached high up on one wall blared a cartoon, so Phineas chose seats that allowed them to sit with their backs to it. Hazel clung to him as if she feared he might abandon her. He removed her hands from his shoulder and smiled down at her. "Time for you to sit next to Deborah."

"I like Phin."

Her flat statement made him want to smile. "I'm glad, but it is more proper for you to sit in your own chair while Deborah fills out the papers. I'll be right here."

Hazel allowed herself to be transferred to a seat next to her sister. Deborah's gaze was pensive as she studied the clipboard in her lap. Did she like Phineas too? *Stop it.*

He forced his gaze to the magazines on the nearby rack. *Field & Stream.* That would do. He picked it up and flopped the pages open to an article about trout fishing.

"You'd rather read a magazine than talk to me?" She pressed the pen against the paper so hard, it was a wonder it didn't rip. "Figures."

Now she wanted to talk. In front of a bunch of Englischers. "I hadn't heard you doing any talking." He kept his voice low. "And remember, we're not alone here."

"I didn't want to interrupt the important discussion you were having with Mr. Carson about how hard it is to find enough time in the day to go fishing." She scribbled some more, then held the pen against her cheek and chewed her lip. "I don't know the answers to some of these questions."

"Just do the best you can. They aren't picky unless there's insurance to be filed. We don't have any and Belinda knows that."

"Fine." She scratched something out. "I don't know why they have to know all this stuff to fix a lip."

"You sure are irritable." He flipped the pages and pretended to be enthralled by a photo of a buck with an eight-point rack. "Are you always this irritable?"

"My little sister is hurt."

"She'll be fine."

"Thanks to you."

He jerked his head up. It sounded an awful lot like she intended to thank him for helping with Hazel but didn't like that she had to do it. He'd only done what needed to be done. No thanks expected or needed. "You did fine as well."

"Did I do something to make you mad?"

"Nee."

"Why do you avoid me?"

"I'm not."

"You are." Her voice rose. She looked around, then clutched the clipboard to her chest. "You make it a point to be out of the house most of the day. Sometimes you don't even come in at noon to eat."

He breathed. The faint smell of blood wafting from Hazel mingled with Betadine and bleach made his stomach rock. He hunched forward, hoping the brim of his hat would hide the sick expression on his face. He tried never to come to places of sickness. Certain smells brought back the agonizing pain and then the murky, underwater blur of the pain medications. The snatches of memories. The sounds of a doctor barking orders over him, hands touching him, cold hands. Needle pricks. Glaring lights overhead that made his head ache and his throat dry.

"Are you all right?" Her voice softened to a whisper. "You look like you're going to pass out."

"I'm fine." He inhaled and let the air out. "When I don't come in, it's because I'm working the hives. Nothing more. I'm going outside."

"Fine. Go. We'll be fine, won't we, Hazel?"

Hazel snatched at his hand. "I want Phin."

"I'll be right outside."

Tears teetered in her big blue eyes. "I want Phin."

He eased back in his chair. "You know how it feels when your stomach hurts because you ate too much ice cream?"

Hazel nodded.

"That's how my stomach feels today. If I go outside, I'll feel better."

"Okay." Hazel didn't look convinced, but she nodded again. "Come back."

He rose a second time. Belinda exited a swinging door that led to the exam rooms. "Doc said to get this little one in there right away. Come on, come on, let's go."

"I'll be right there." His stomach lurched. He had to go. Now. "Deborah, you go with her."

"Phin—"

"I said I'd be right back."

He shoved through the door into the bright, white heat of a south Texas summer. Hoping to leave the smell of pain and death behind. Knowing it would follow him wherever he went.

———

Six stitches. Deborah hugged Hazel. The little girl squirmed loose, busy plucking at the sticker of a flower the doctor had given her for being so brave. He said most kids got suckers, but he didn't want Hazel sucking on candy so soon after getting stitches in her mouth. She'd been a brave little girl through the whole thing. Even Doc Peterson had said so.

"That was a nasty little gash, but you're good to go." He patted Hazel's head, then rolled his stool back to the tiny desk on the wall where he picked up a pen and wrote on a pad. "I want her to take antibiotics to make sure we don't get any infection in there. She needs to eat soft foods. Pudding, mashed potatoes, soft scrambled eggs."

He stood and handed the paper to Deborah with a flourish and slight bow. "Bring her back in a week and we'll have another look-see. Stop by the desk on your way out to make the appointment. Belinda will finish up your paperwork."

And take their money. Money Deborah didn't have. If Phineas didn't come back, Deborah would have to figure something out.

She helped Hazel down, took her hand, and trotted down the hallway to the reception area where Belinda sat behind a computer, pink-rimmed reading glasses perched at the end of her long nose. She hopped up. "All done?"

"All done." Hazel piped up in a singsong warble. "All done."

"All done." Deborah took a quick look around. "Phineas didn't come back?"

"No, but I'm betting he's outside waiting for you." Belinda shook her plump index finger with its long nail painted bubble-gum pink and adorned with a ring featuring a huge green stone that twinkled in the light. "He's not the sort of young man who abandons a lady in distress."

"It's just that . . ."

"He's in charge?"

"Not exactly, but he did say he knew about how . . . the bill is handled."

"Oh, sweetie, is that what you're worried about? Don't you fret." Belinda's chuckle made the rolls of fat under her chin jiggle. "Your folks having a running account here. We'll send you a bill. We know where to find you. You're staying with Mordecai King, right?"

"Right."

"Mordecai will make sure we get paid, don't you worry."

"We don't take anything on credit."

"It isn't credit, honey. It's good faith. Everybody knows that Mordecai King and his kind are good for it." Belinda smiled. "Everyone remembers when Phineas was in that hospital down in Corpus for over two months. The trucker's company's insur-ance paid some of the bills, but not all. You folks took care of what was yours."

Two months. A terrible-long time to be in the hospital. "People still remember after all those years?"

"We remember how heartbroken those folks were and how stoic and brave they were."

Stoic. That was a good word for Phineas.

"Anyway, we know you're good for it. Who drove you in?"

"Mr. Carson."

"I'll give him a call to come get y'all while you go find Phin. Little Hazel here can draw me a picture for our bulletin board while you see how he's doing. He's probably feeling better now."

"This has happened before?"

"Not in a long while. We haven't seen him in years. He doesn't come into town. Not since Mordecai brought him in for checkups so he didn't have to make the long trip to Corpus. He was scared of riding in the van back then. I don't think Mordecai was too fond of it either, truth be told." Belinda handed Hazel a pack of crayons and a piece of white construction paper. Hazel grinned, her fat lip protruding. "I imagine coming here reminds him of things he'd rather not think about."

Yet he hadn't hesitated when Hazel needed help. "Hazel, be good for Belinda. I'll be right back."

Nodding, Hazel barely looked up from the green scribbles she'd drawn on her paper. Deborah slipped out the door, prepared to go in search of Phineas.

She didn't have to go far. He sat on the curb, head down, elbows propped on his knees. Using her hand to shield her eyes from the fierce afternoon sun, Deborah eased onto the hot concrete next to him. "Hazel's all fixed up."

"Gut." He sounded congested, his voice low and hoarse. "Sorry."

"Sorry? About what?"

"Bailing on you."

"You got us here, didn't you?"

He sat up straighter and clutched his arms to his chest as if cold. "I don't come into town much."

Or ever, according to Belinda. "Yet you came because you knew Hazel needed help. I . . . we appreciate it."

His gaze skated across hers and then back at the cars that raced past them, leaving the stench of gas fumes and oil behind them. The pavement shimmered with heat and the air seemed to sizzle over it. His Adam's apple bobbed. "It's like a nightmare I remember in snatches. The smells . . ."

"You have nightmares about the accident?"

His head bobbed, but his gaze stayed on the trash and bits of grass and rock that littered the street at their feet. "I don't remember the accident, but I dream that I do. I see the truck that hit us and I know what's coming and I can't stop it. I feel it smash into us, feel the pain of hitting the dash and then going through the windshield. I hear the screeching of rubber and metal. I see the look on Mr. Jenkins's face and then I turn and I see Mudder. She's all crumpled up."

His voice broke.

The rumble of a truck engine mingled with the conversation of a couple passing by. Apparently they were arguing about whether caffeine increased stress or helped reduce it. Deborah breathed, trying to find words to soothe such a terrible, gaping wound. A wound that had festered for twelve years. What could one say about something so painful?

"I have nightmares too." She plucked at a bloodstain on her apron. It had dried to a rusty brown color. "I dream my daed was still alive when we put him in the ground."

"That's awful to contemplate." He picked up a pebble and flicked it across the road. A truck honked, a strident, blaring sound that made Deborah jump. A car returned the favor. "You know that couldn't happen?"

"It doesn't matter. Just like you know your dream is your mind playing games with your heart and your memories. I know my daed is gone." Saying the words aloud made Deborah feel the pain of that empty spot at the supper table as if it were fresh and new. "He was gone days before we buried his body. Still, I always wake up with this sick feeling in my stomach and tears on my face. I didn't cry at the funeral, yet I cry in my sleep."

"They're in a better place. They're where we all want to be. So we don't cry."

"Yet we do when no one is looking."

"We do." He shook his head. "Your daed left before you were ready for him to go. Gott took him home. The days of his life were complete. For me, it's different."

"Why is it different? Gott made a mistake and took your mudder home too soon? Gott doesn't make mistakes."

"Nee. It was my fault."

His tone said he truly believed this to be true. Deborah grabbed his hand and squeezed. It took her a second to realize what she'd done. The billowing heat of the July sun seemed cool compared to the fiery embarrassment that raced through her. She jerked her hand back, but Phineas curled his fingers around hers and held on. The naked anguish in his face held her captive as much as any physical touch.

"It was an accident," she whispered. "You were a little boy. It wasn't your fault."

"I was wiggling around in the front seat. I blew this big bubble. It was huge and pink and I wanted to laugh, but I didn't want it to pop, so I turned and pointed at it to show Mudder. She was laughing at something Abram had done. My elbow knocked into Mr. Jenkins. The van swerved and I fell against him. He yelled at me to sit still. The next thing I know, I opened my eyes in the hospital and Daed was telling me she was gone."

Deborah tugged his hand into her lap. She smoothed her fingers across the wicked, grooved scars. "And you've been punishing yourself ever since."

"Gott punished me. I had a concussion, a broken nose, and a dislocated jaw. The asphalt ripped the skin off one side of my face. My left ear hung by a thread." He traced the outer edge of the ear with one finger as he listed his injuries in a tone that said he might have been reading a grocery list. "Daed brought my bruder Samuel in to see me because he didn't believe I was still alive. He didn't recognize me. He still didn't believe it was me."

"Our Gott doesn't punish little boys for having fun on a trip to the ocean."

Phineas closed his eyes and rocked. After a second, he took a deep breath and tried to tug his hand from hers. Deborah held on. He opened his eyes and stared down at her hand gripping his. "It's not the ocean. It's the Gulf."

"What?"

"It's the Gulf of Mexico."

"Don't change the subject."

"You don't have to feel sorry for me."

"I don't."

"I don't want your pity."

"Gut, 'cause you're not getting it." She stared at him, mesmerized by the welter of emotions on his face. A mixture of defiance and determination not to show her any more of himself than he already had. Too late. Phineas had let her in and she wasn't going to let him back down now. "Did you ever tell your daed about what happened?"

"Nee."

"Why not?"

"I already lost Mudder. I guess I thought . . ."

"You thought he'd stop loving you if he knew you thought you were responsible?"

He smoothed his finger over the skin on the back of her hand, his gaze never leaving her face. A shiver ran up her arm, across her neck, and lost itself in her hair. His Adam's apple bobbed. "I guess . . ."

She tried to follow his train of thought and not get lost in the feel of his fingers caressing her skin. "Mordecai would never do that."

"I don't know."

"I do."

"We shouldn't be . . . doing this . . ." He glanced around as if registering where they were for the first time. "People will talk."

"Do you care what strangers think?"

"I care that we set a good example that reflects what we know is right and proper in Gott's eyes."

"Gott doesn't want me holding your hand?"

He closed his eyes again. His grip tightened. His eyes opened and his hand dropped. "There's a time and a place for everything. I'd like to believe that includes holding your hand."

"It could." She cradled her hands against her chest, not wanting to lose the feeling of his skin against hers. "If you stop worrying about things that don't matter."

"Don't say that if you don't intend it. That would be . . . cruel."

"What makes you think I don't mean it?"

"Look at me."

"I am."

"I know I'm repulsive. As repulsive as this place you find so ugly. This place you want to leave so you can go back to the beauty of Tennessee. I'm sure the man waiting for you there is much more pleasing to the eye."

"You think I'm that shallow, then? It's all about how a man looks? I will get used to this place and there's no one waiting for me. Not anymore."

"You're not leaving, then?"

"I don't know."

Phineas scooted away from her. "Let me know when you make up your mind."

"I'm trying to—"

Her words were drowned by the growl of a bus engine as it strained and rocked past them, its brakes squealing as the white bus halted at the red light. DOCJ was lettered on the side. A man with a shaved head and a teardrop tattooed under one eye stared out at her. He waved. Surprised, she raised her hand and managed a small wave in return. He smiled, stuck out his tongue, and licked his lips in a complete circle.

"What are you doing? Don't look at him." Phineas's hand gripped her shoulder. He popped to his feet, taking her with him. "Turn around. Now."

"Ouch! What's the matter with you?" She had no choice but to follow his lead and face the building. "What? What is it?"

"You don't want the attention of anyone in those buses." Anger made his voice deep and the words sharp. "Never wave or talk or even look at them."

"Why? What bus is it? What is D-O-C-J?"

"Department of Criminal Justice. The men on that bus are going to the prison."

Her stomach rocked. She hadn't meant any harm. Even if these men had committed crimes, they still belonged to God. They still deserved forgiveness. A smile and a friendly wave might make them feel life still held promise. "You're judging them and you don't even know what they did?"

"I know they're in prison and they're dangerous and I don't want them doing anything to . . ." His Adam's apple bobbed. "Just don't do it again."

"They're locked up. They can't hurt—"

The growl of Mr. Carson's station wagon interrupted her bewildered reply. The engine backfired and black smoke rolled from it. Phineas moved back from the curb. He didn't make eye contact. "I'll settle the bill with Belinda and get Hazel."

"Phineas."

He stomped into the clinic, leaving her standing on the curb wondering if they'd taken two steps forward or three back. Why had her interaction with the prisoner made him so angry? Had she done something wrong?

Phineas surely thought so. Anger mixed with hurt. She hadn't meant to do anything wrong. Three steps back. Definitely.

TWENTY-FOUR

Her stomach rumbling and her mouth watering at the aroma, Abigail popped a juicy chunk of sausage in her mouth and almost sighed in bliss. Susan's venison sausage hit the spot. Still chewing, she speared another thick slice. A sharp, jagged pain shot along her jaw.

"Ouch." She slapped a hand to her mouth and tried to breathe through the fierce pain without spitting food on the plate in front of everyone at the table. In her haste to eat, she'd forgotten to avoid the sore tooth that had been plaguing her for weeks now. "Oh my, oh my."

"What is it? Did you bite your tongue?" Mordecai's fork, also laden with a plump chunk of sausage, hovered near his chin. "I hate it when that happens. Try a drink of water."

"Nee. It's not my tongue." She rubbed her jaw with her free hand, as if that would help. "It's fine. I'll survive."

"It's that tooth, isn't it?" Deborah picked at the fried potatoes on her plate. The girl never really ate. She simply pushed food from one side to the other. "How long before you'll admit you need to go to the dentist and get it looked at?"

"Yeah, Mudder. You always tell us not to be babies about it," Leila chimed in.

"Yeah, Mudder." Hazel mimicked her big sister's tone to a T.

"Hush, all of you." She sipped water, hoping it would ease the ache that throbbed from her jaw into her cheek and back toward her throat. "Dentists cost money."

"Not as much as you would think. Not around here." Mordecai tossed his napkin on his plate and leaned back in his chair. It creaked under his weight. "We have a dentist in Mexico we've been seeing for years. Real reasonable, he is."

"Mexico! You go to Mexico?" Deborah looked as animated as she had since they arrived in Bee County. "How do you do it? How do you talk to folks in Spanish?"

"Progreso is a town across from a place called Weslaco not far from here. A lot of those folks speak English." Mordecai pointed a finger in what Abigail surmised must be a southerly direction. "Enough to communicate, anyway. And I've picked up a few words of Spanish here and there."

"And the dentist is affordable?" Abigail brought the conversation back to the big issue, at least in her mind. Visiting a foreign country for dental work seemed a strange proposition fraught with hidden dangers. "And safe? Does he do gut work?"

Mordecai tugged down his lip on one side, displaying a tooth toward the back of his mouth. "He charged four hundred dollars for a crown. Less than half what a dentist charges in the States. And I can't complain. Seems to work just fine."

"I heard there's a lot of bad stuff happens south of the border." Abigail racked her brains for the tidbits she remembered hearing the men talk about back home—back in Tennessee. There wasn't much reason for them to worry about a faraway place like Mexico where she'd grown up. "Shootings and such."

"In the bigger towns, but Progreso is a little town and 'bout the only thing going on is the snowbirds popping across the border for pills and liquor and haircuts. The ladies get their fingernails and toenails painted."

Leila and Rebekah tittered. Abigail shot them a look. "Snowbirds?"

"Retired Englischers who come down here for the winter."

The throbbing in Abigail's mouth made her decision for her. If elderly Englischers could go there to get their fingernails painted, it must be all right. "When can we go? How far is it?"

"You're forgetting one thing." Susan stood and began to clear plates, a signal for Abigail and the girls to do the same. "Abigail doesn't have a passport card."

Mordecai tapped his knife on the edge of his plate in a *plink, plink, plink* sound, his expression thoughtful. "Jah, I did forget that. We'll have to get you into town to fill out the application and get your picture taken."

Abigail froze, the bread basket clutched in both hands. "Picture?"

"Since all that mess with 9/11, folks have to have a passport or a passport card to come back into the country. That means a photograph." Mordecai smiled up at her. "It's all right. The *gmay* voted. For this one purpose, it's allowed. It's the only way we can go to Mexico and get back into the country. I reckon you know plenty of Plain people who've taken family members to Mexico for doctoring. It's not a question of vanity."

He crumpled a piece of bread into tiny pieces. "It's a question of survival for our district. It's one more way to make sure we don't have to fold up shop and move up north."

"The kinner? They get their photographs taken too?"

"That's left up to the parents." He met her gaze again. "No one is forced to do it. But if one of your kinner got a sickness like cancer that needed a lot of doctoring, you'd probably want to get it done. If not, you can wait to decide."

"Can I think on it?"

"You can, but remember the emergency medical fund is for everyone's use, and we have to do what is right to keep the costs down. One way you can help do that is to go to the dentist in Mexico."

Another fierce pain stabbed her gum. She put a hand to her mouth to keep from moaning aloud.

"I'll get you some aspirin for the pain." Susan trotted into the kitchen. "I wish we had ice."

Her voice carried even as she disappeared through the door. The others began to disperse. Phineas, who'd offered not a word toward the discussion, fairly flew from the table, while the girls picked up dishes, their chatter centered on what life must be like south of the border. Men in sombreros with handlebar mustaches and serapes. What book that had come from, Abigail could only imagine. She thought of warm, soft flour tortillas, rice, and beans when she thought of Mexico. That and pineapple.

"It takes four to six weeks to get the passport card." Mordecai rose and stretched, his joints popping and cracking. "Don't wait too long or that tooth will rot in your mouth."

Four to six weeks. Could she stand it that long? Abigail rubbed her cheek, wishing she could will away the pain. Or pray it away.

"Get the picture taken." Mordecai's voice had gone gentle. "It's not a sin."

"The Holy Bible says no graven images." She glanced at Hazel and Hannah. They were engrossed in picking up the dirty silverware from the tables. "Who are we to say exceptions should be made?"

"There's nothing vain or proud about you, and Gott knows what's in our hearts when we do this. It's a matter of being good stewards of the bodies He gave us."

Something in his voice made the skin prickle on the back of her arms. She ducked her head, not wanting to meet his probing gaze. "It feels strange."

Mordecai slid his chair under the table, the scraping sound drowning the little girls' chatter as they scampered into the kitchen with their loads of silverware. "If you really don't want to do it, I can help with the expense of seeing a dentist here."

"Nee, there's no need. I can wait." She didn't want to be more indebted to him. "I should talk to Stephen about the passport card."

Stephen who had raised a bumper crop of grapefruit, oranges, tomatoes, okra, and cantaloupe this year. He had orders to fill from the state's biggest grocery chain. He was ready for the next step. His firm grasp on her waist said he was more than ready.

The concern on Mordecai's face drained away, leaving a neutral stare. He slapped his hat on his head. "I best get back to my chores."

At the door, he glanced back. "Stephen has never crossed the border."

"You make that sound like it's a bad thing." Stephen's conservative nature came as no surprise to her. "He's surely trying to do what's right."

"Not a bad thing, necessarily. I only wonder what that says about his willingness to put the community ahead of his own needs."

"He's cautious and steady."

"That's what I like about you." Mordecai's smile seemed genuine. "You always see the good in people."

"Stephen has done a good job with making the land here produce fruits and vegetables even though it's not meant to do so."

"You're right about that. He is a hard worker."

Still, Mordecai's tone said he found something lacking in Stephen. His assessment stung. Abigail wasn't sure why. His opinion shouldn't be more important to her than Stephen's.

The throb in her jaw seemed to take over her face. She swallowed against it. She needed that aspirin. She sucked in air and tried to breathe through it, but that only seemed to make it worse. "Ouch."

"I hate seeing you in pain . . . I mean, I hate to see anyone in pain." Mordecai paused, his big hand gripping the screen door frame. His knuckles were white. His pulse pounded in his jaw as he gritted his teeth. "I'll go to the store for ice."

"Nee—"

"I'm going."

He let the screen door slam as if for punctuation.

Mordecai was one opinionated man with a streak of independence.

Why did those qualities seem so appealing?

Stephen's steady, traditional ways should be important to a woman with five children to think about.

Still, here she stood with goose bumps on her arms and her hands shaking. Had to be the toothache.

Not the man.

TWENTY-FIVE

"I can't believe you're leaving." Deborah plopped down on the front step next to Frannie, who sat with a chipped cup of kaffi in her hands, staring at the streaks of pink and yellow beginning to stain the heavens as dawn stole the darkness from the horizon. Even before sunrise the August heat made her dress stick to her sweaty body. "Who will I talk to?"

"Esther, I reckon. And your sisters." Frannie sipped and lowered the cup. "You're blessed. You have sisters close to your age. Me, I got brothers and they aren't even close to my age. Hannah and Rachel are too young for much of anything."

Picking at a smear of dried jam on her apron, Deborah watched as the men tossed the last of the boxes and garbage bags of clothes into the back of the second van. In a few minutes they'd say good-bye to everyone who'd come to see them off, load into the vans, and head for Missouri.

And leave Deborah behind. She would miss Frannie. She already had a fierce ache where her heart should be.

"The new house is better than the one that burned down." Sighing, Deborah picked up a rock and tossed it at the rusted trash can sitting next to the broken-down buggy. It made a *plink-ing* sound and disappeared into the scraggly, brown weeds. "I don't see why Aenti Eve and Onkel John won't stay here."

"You were the one chomping at the bit to leave. You said yourself it's the ugliest place you ever been, and farming here is hopeless." Frannie set her cup on the step and slapped away a mosquito that buzzed her head. "At least you were until you started following Phin around. I'm guessing the feeling is mutual, him going into town for you and all."

"He didn't go into town for me. He went for Hazel. And I'm not following him around." Deborah had more sense than that. Phineas ignored her and avoided her even more than he had before Hazel's fall. Deborah had enough sense to know that meant he didn't want her around. No matter what he'd said outside the medical clinic. No matter how tightly he'd gripped her hand and how his eyes had sparked with a consuming heat. He ran hot and cold, mostly cold, and she refused to chase after a man who couldn't make up his mind.

"We live in the same house. I don't have much choice but to run into him now and again. But that's it. Nothing more."

Not as much as a person would think. Being a beekeeper gave him plenty of excuses to stay out in the fields. Lately, the production of finished jars of honey seemed to fill the kitchen every afternoon. Phineas stopped in only long enough to drop off the bounty, leaving the women to do the rest of the work.

"As soon as Stephen and Mudder get married, I'll go home. Or maybe I'll come to Missouri to visit."

"You still think Abigail and Stephen will marry?" Frannie wrinkled her nose. "I heard he was mighty peeved about the passport card."

"I don't think it's the passport picture so much as the fact she went against his advice."

"And took Mordecai's."

Deborah nodded. After two months in Mordecai's house, she'd found herself settled into a comfortable routine with Phineas's father. Much more than with the son. Mordecai told a good joke. He was kind. Hazel had taken to crawling into his lap for stories at night. He had a rare storytelling ability that held them all rapt. Stories about the pioneers who settled Texas and cowboys and cattle drives.

At first, it hurt to see Hazel there, like he was her daed, but then it had seemed natural. And Mordecai had an unfailingly kind and gentle way of speaking to Mudder that made Deborah want to shake her until she could see that the man had feelings for her.

True feelings. Not the possessive be-mine-and-let-me-tell-you-what-to-do feelings that seemed to billow from Stephen.

"You're gonna love going to Progreso. You'll stop at the beach on the way. Mordecai can't pass up a trip to the beach, you'll see." Frannie's words interrupted Deborah's morose thoughts. She sounded equally morose despite the optimism in her words. "No beaches in Missouri."

"Nee, but you saw that map. It had bunches of lakes. The Ozarks. You'll be fishing in no time." *They had to make the best of it.* Daed's words rang in her ears. Whatever *it* was. "Gott has a plan for you and me."

"Yep." Frannie stood and tossed the dregs of her coffee into the weeds. "I best get going. Mudder's been real tired lately and she shouldn't be lifting things."

To Deborah's surprise, Frannie enveloped her in a quick,

sharp hug that ended before she could reciprocate. She sniffed and wiped at her face with the back of her sleeve. "See you, cousin."

"Don't go yet." Deborah traipsed after her. "Stop."

Frannie scooped Hannah from her perch on a lawn chair and settled her on her hip.

"It's not forever. We'll see each other again."

Frannie deposited Hannah on a seat in the van and ordered her to climb into her booster seat. Then she turned. "I don't reckon I'll ever be back here. I'll find a man up yonder and settle down. You'll be here with Phin. Unless you can convince him to move too."

Her plain, freckled face creased in a grin. "That's it. Y'all can move up to Missouri and live next door to me and my mann."

"Your who? What husband?" Onkel John angled past them, bags in both hands. "You're getting way ahead of yourself, girl."

He tossed the bags in the back of the van and stuck his hands on his narrow hips, his expression self-satisfied. "Besides, Phin isn't going anywhere. He bought the Schrock farm. They've been trying to sell it ever since they left to go up north. He finally made them an offer they liked."

"Phineas bought a farm?" Disbelief made Deborah's voice high and squeaky. "By himself?"

"That's what he said." John rubbed at his beard with bony fingers. "I wish he would've bought this one, but it's a lot more land than the Schrocks had and he can't afford it. No young man just starting out could, and I can't afford to take less for it. Besides, he doesn't want to live so close to the store and all the Englisch traffic it brings out this way. You know how he is."

She did indeed know how he was.

Phineas had bought himself a farm as far from her as he could get and still live in their district. John's house was a stone's throw from the store. Phineas couldn't have that.

Did he intend to live there alone? Now? No more seeing him at breakfast? Or supper? Deborah didn't dare ask her uncle these questions.

"At least that'll give y'all a little more room at Mordecai's." John surveyed the van. "Looks like we're about packed. Let's get moving. Get your mudder, Frannie, and tell the boys to get a move on."

Frannie turned and scurried to the house. Deborah started to follow. John stepped in front of her. "You best take care of your mudder after we go." His expression had turned stony. "Do as she says and don't be giving her grief over marrying Stephen. You got that?"

"Jah."

His lips pursed. "Your mudder is doing what's best for all of you. Keep that in mind. Don't be selfish."

"I won't." She whispered the words, her throat dry and aching.

"And you might think of doing the same thing."

What did that mean? Her confusion must've shown on her face.

"Time you get serious about going to the singings. Those boys are interested, if you'd show a bit of interest yourself. Know what I mean?"

Phineas didn't go to the singings. "Jah."

"We'll be back in November for the wedding." He jerked his head toward the house. "I told your mudder to write and let me know how things are going. I expect a good report."

Like he was her father. Nee. He was not. She swallowed the angry retort. "Jah, Onkel."

"Gut. Go make sure Frannie didn't forget anything. I ain't

turning around for some little something she thinks she can't live without."

Deborah tore into the house without looking back. She didn't want to see the satisfied look on John's face. He'd given her a talking to. He'd done his onkel duties.

Didn't matter. She'd do her best to mind her mother. She always had. She didn't need John to tell her what her duties were. What was right or wrong.

Daed had taught her those things.

Head down, eyes blinded with unshed tears, she barreled around the corner anxious to find a place—any place—where she could be alone long enough to rein in her emotions. She smacked into something hard and solid. And warm.

"Hey! You have to stop doing that."

Phineas.

Deborah stifled a groan and closed her eyes.

"Are you going to look at me or what?"

She studied the wood under her bare feet. "Nee."

"Why?"

Because he would see the tears in her eyes and he would think of the day outside the barn and the night of the singing. He would think she was a big crybaby. She ran a sleeve across her face and lifted her chin. She was no crybaby. "You always do this."

"Do what?"

"Catch me at my worst."

The corners of his full lips turned up in a hint of a crooked smile. "You look okay to me."

It was his turn to duck his head and study his work boots.

What did he mean by okay? "Just okay?"

"Now you want compliments?"

"Nee, I don't fish for compliments."

"What is wrong with you?" His eyebrows rose and his forehead wrinkled. Phineas shuffled his feet, hands dangling as if he didn't know what to do with them. "Did I do something? Something more than usual?"

"Did you buy a farm out in the middle of nowhere?"

This time his lips widened into a real smile. A rare appearance, like a flash of heat lightning on a dark night. Like the rare birds he sought with his binoculars. "I did."

"You didn't bother to tell anyone?"

"I told Daed. He helped me." The smile died, much to Deborah's chagrin. He crossed his arms. "What do you care, anyway? You have . . . It's not like you and I have . . ."

"Have what?"

"You felt sorry for me and you got carried away and let me hold your hand and now you're afraid I'll think it's more than it was."

"Nee, it's the other way around. You held my hand and you got carried away and now you're afraid I'll think it's more than it was."

"What?" He looked as if his brain hurt. "I don't think—"

"Who's been holding hands?" Mudder stormed around the corner, hands on her hips, eyebrows so high they might touch her prayer kapp. "What's going on here?"

"N-Nothing," Deborah stuttered. "We were just—"

"I heard. You both best get yourselves out there to say goodbye. They're pulling out."

Phineas, a look of sheer relief on his face, hurtled past Mudder without looking Deborah's way.

Deborah followed. Mudder's hand shot out and grabbed her arm. "Just remember, dochder, there's a right way and a wrong way to do things. You've been baptized. You know the Ordnung. Your father might not be here, but Gott is."

"I know."

"Gut."

Her hand dropped. Deborah bit the inside of her lip to keep from saying more. Too bad Mudder didn't take her own advice. Open her eyes and admit she cared for a man who truly cared for her. And his name didn't begin with an *S*.

TWENTY-SIX

Deborah turned the lantern up just enough to throw light on Josie's letter. She shouldn't be reading it at what passed for the middle of the night, but the privacy she wanted was a luxury hard to come by. She couldn't sleep anyway, in the still, breathless heat of the tiny bedroom. The air didn't seem to have cooled at all after the sun disappeared into a starless, cloudy night. Maybe another storm was headed their way. Nothing to be done about it, either way. Sitting cross-legged on the floor under an open window, she smoothed the paper and peered at Josie's careful, penciled print.

Dear Deborah,

It's been awhile since you wrote me so I'm taking my turn again. Maybe that will jog your memory about your poor, forgotten best friend in Tennessee. I imagine you've made friends there so you don't feel the need to write so much. That's okay. We're busy here too, with harvest and canning and you name it. Still, it seems strange to be doing it all without you. I think of you every time I put a stitch in the quilt we started together back in May.

Surprise mixed with a touch of shame. Deborah had missed her turn without even realizing it. How had that happened? She'd written so much in the beginning, but then the days had filled up with the fire and moving and canning and honey. And Phineas. Not Phineas. Thinking about Phineas. Puzzling about him. Trying to ignore him. Trying to ignore her feelings. "Sorry," she whispered.

"What? Who's talking?" Leila muttered in her sleep, turned over, and tucked a flat, shapeless pillow under her head.

"Sorry. Go back to sleep."

Leila muttered again and rolled the other way.

It's strange to have both you and Aaron gone. The singings aren't nearly as much fun. I think he was really sorry about how things ended up with you, but your paths have gone in opposite directions so I'm thinking it's for the best. Easy for me to say, I know. On the happy news side, Milo Borntrager asked me to ride home with him Sunday night. I thought he'd never ask and now he has. We sat outside the house for an hour talking. I'm sorry you don't get to do that with Aaron anymore. I'm praying that your heart mends quickly. I have to run now. Mudder is calling me to help with supper. Write me soon. I'm dying to know if you're still thinking of coming back. If you come back before summer's end, you might be able to help Lotty teach at the school in the fall, but you'll have to write and tell me soon before they get someone else. Summer's almost over!

Deborah fanned herself with the paper for a few minutes, considering, probing her feelings. A faint ache, like a bruise that has almost healed, emanated from around her heart, but only a faint one. She hadn't thought about Aaron in weeks. She hadn't given much thought to going home either. Two months ago she would've jumped at the chance to be a teacher's aide. Now the heartstrings tugged in another direction. Gott's plan all along? A strange, meandering path that brought her exactly where she needed to be?

Mudder would say yes. That everything happened for a reason. Even Daed's death. The thought of it didn't pierce her heart the way it once had. She needed to think on that in the light of day when she wasn't so bone tired and fuzzy-headed.

Tomorrow she would write to Josie and cheer her on. Milo was a pleasant man, a hard worker, and he had a nice smile. Good for Josie. She folded the letter back into its envelope and laid it on the crate. At this rate, she would be walking through her chores in the morning. She slipped into the bed, trying not to disturb Leila.

"Stop tossing and turning, will you? I'd like to get some sleep 'fore morning."

The irritation in Leila's voice was deserved. Deborah rolled back toward the edge, keeping a narrow space between her sister and herself. "Keep your voice down. You'll wake Rebekah and Hazel."

If Frannie were here, she'd know what to think about all this. About Aaron and Phineas and Gott's plan. Deborah missed Frannie more than she thought possible, even more than Josie. Her cousin had made life here bearable with her tart observations on life, all delivered with her freckled nose wrinkled and her hands on her skinny hips.

Leila wiggled around on her side so she faced Deborah and put her hands under her cheek. "Do you think Frannie likes it in Missouri?"

Funny how Leila's thoughts always seemed to run parallel to Deborah's. "I think Frannie will be happy wherever she lands. She's like that."

"Not like you." Leila's mouth opened in a wide yawn. "Always moping around. Homesick."

"Hey, I'm not homesick anymore and I'm not moping. I'm just trying to . . . fit in."

"I'm not homesick anymore either."

Deborah couldn't see her sister's expression in the dark, but she heard the smile in her voice. "What changed?" As if she didn't know, but it was obvious Leila wanted to talk about it.

"Courting is private."

"Jah, jah. Spill the beans."

"Jesse slipped me a note after the service today." Leila rolled on her back as if she couldn't contain herself. "He's planning to shine his flashlight in the window soon."

"Good for you."

"It feels like my insides will explode."

Deborah knew that feeling. Her chest tightened. Her lungs didn't seem to want to do their job anymore. The feelings she had for Aaron were nothing compared to the morass of emotion that held her prisoner every time she talked to Phineas. If she'd never met him, she might never have known the difference. She would've thought her simple, sturdy feelings for Aaron were the best she could do. Could there be different kinds of love? A calm, steady love with no highs or lows. A love a person could count on. A love that lasted. Except it hadn't. Aaron had moved on.

Maybe that was because their feelings weren't deep enough or strong enough. As compared to the bedlam of feelings that made her want to pull her hair out, run screaming through the fields, and shake the man until he explained this whole mess to her. Was that love? "Your insides won't explode."

"How do you know?"

"You saw how Mudder and Daed were. Even after all those years together, they were in lieb." Deborah smiled to herself, remembering the looks Mudder stole at Daed during breakfast in the morning and supper at night. As if they couldn't wait to share a secret. "Their insides never exploded. They never died down either."

"You think she feels that way about Stephen?"

"Nee."

"Me neither." Leila slapped her hand over her mouth and swallowed another yawn. "Do you feel that way about Phin?"

"Go to sleep, Leila."

"Oh, come on, your turn to share. Everyone has seen how you two keep accidentally-on-purpose running into each other."

"You're dreaming." Deborah shoved back a sheet that felt as if it weighed forty pounds and sat up. "Go to sleep."

"Where are you going? The sun won't be up for at least another hour."

"I need a drink of water."

She slipped on her dress and slapped her kapp on her head. It wouldn't be right to go gallivanting about the King house in her nightgown. Grabbing the flashlight from the crate, she navigated down the hallway through the front room to the kitchen. The air seemed a little cooler. All the windows were open and a tepid breeze caught a curtain and lifted it. She could breathe again.

No chance she would run into Phineas. He'd moved out, lock, stock, and barrel. Most likely he slept fine in his new house where he didn't have to worry about running into her or sitting across the table from her at mealtimes. Or accidentally holding her hand. He had the place all to himself. Did he get lonely? Not likely. Sighing, she shuffled into the kitchen, one hand rubbing her burning eyes.

"*Guder mariye.*"

Deborah jumped and shrieked. "Mordecai!"

"Sorry. Didn't mean to startle you." His lean figure silhouetted by a kerosene lantern on the counter behind him, he cupped a mug of kaffi in both hands. "I figured you barely had your eyes open. Didn't see me."

"Nee, I didn't." Hand on her heaving chest, she took a step back. "I was just . . . I mean, I was going to—"

"I couldn't sleep either. Kaffi's ready."

"It's too hot for kaffi."

"It's downright cool this time of day—compared to what it's like out in the field, putting up silage in the middle of the afternoon."

"I guess that's a better way of looking at it."

"I guess it is."

She had so many questions she'd like to ask Phineas's father. She wanted to ask him why Phineas moved out and why he was so hard to talk to and why he couldn't see that she wanted to be his friend.

More than his friend.

"Phineas is coming over today. We have a hive that's lost its queen. We're shutting down the colony and shaking the bees into the one next door to it. We'll store the honey. It's quite the undertaking." Mordecai shifted and straightened. He set his cup on the counter. "I imagine he'll stay for supper. Susan's making that Mexican rice he likes with jalapeños and ground beef. It's spicy. One of his favorites. He really likes lemon pie too."

Phineas liked spicy food and lemon pie. Trying to figure

out what Mordecai was telling her in his man-roundabout way, Deborah grabbed a glass and filled it with water from a pitcher sitting on the counter. Mudder always said the best way to sweeten up a grumpy man was with a good dessert. "I have a hankering for lemon meringue pie myself. I might have to make one."

"If you cook like your mudder, I'll be first in line." Mordecai lifted his straw hat and settled it back on his head. "My son's not much of a cook, and living by himself, he's likely to starve."

"That bad, huh? He can't make himself a sandwich?"

"I reckon he can, but what he really needs is a good fraa to cook for him."

"Or Esther could do for him what Susan does for you." Deborah wanted to sink into the floor. The words sounded judgmental. She had no right to judge. Mordecai had lost his fraa in a terrible accident, and he was blessed to have a sister who helped him raise his children and keep his house in order. "I'm sorry. That came out wrong."

"Susan never met the right man." Mordecai strode past her, his boots clomping on the vinyl floor. "It looks as if Gott has blessed Esther with a special friend. The whole district is blessed by having your family move here."

It didn't feel that way to Deborah. "Because now there're a few more girls to marry the boys?"

"New blood is gut for the district."

"And that's more important than being happy?"

"The greater gut." Something in Mordecai's tone said he was trying to convince himself as much as Deborah. "We must submit to Gott's will for this district."

"How can it be for the greater gut if we're unhappy?"

"You have to choose your attitude." The grooves in Mordecai's face deepened into a frown. "We should all have an attitude of gratitude."

"I try."

"So do I."

"But it's not easy."

"Nee, but nothing worthwhile is."

"Why is it so important to you?"

"I try to practice what I preach. I know we need new families here." He strode past her and stopped at the screen door, his back to her. "It's also important to me that my son find happiness. I pray for that every day. That all his wounds be healed, not just the ones on his face."

He turned, his gaze drilling her. "No matter what's best for this district, I'm asking you to stay away from him if you're not really interested."

"I-Interested?" In her surprise at the raw emotion in Mordecai's voice, Deborah stuttered the word. "I'm—"

"He's had enough hurt for a lifetime. That he is still standing is a testament to Gott's lieb for him."

Before Deborah could point out the same could be said of Mordecai, he pushed through the door and disappeared from sight.

She had no intention of hurting Phineas. In fact, she was sure her heart was the one in danger of being broken.

TWENTY-SEVEN

Deborah shoved open the van door and hopped out. Her feet sank into hot, gritty sand that drifted over the edge of the asphalt parking lot. She inhaled the damp, heated air that wafted in a salty breeze from the endless expanse of gulf water. It had an odor the likes of which she'd never smelled before. Fishy, salty, and earthy all at once. She could almost taste the salt on her tongue.

Her mouth hung open at the sheer enormity of it. Waves crashed against the beach, dragging seaweed in great bundles back and forth, back and forth. The sun reflected on the water with such brilliance it hurt her eyes. Seagulls swooped and chattered over the roar of the waves. She stood without moving, one hand still on the van's sliding door, trying to absorb the idea of so much water all in one place. It stretched as far as she could see to the horizon and beyond, going to places she would never visit or know.

"What do you think?" Mordecai stopped next to her, hands on his hips. Butch, who had insisted on making the trip—according to Mordecai—kept going as if as anxious as the kinner to get to the water. There was no sign of the serious man who had taken her to task before dawn in his own kitchen only a week earlier. "Easy to see Gott's hand in all that yonder, don't you think?"

She nodded and managed to close her mouth. Words escaped her. All up and down the beach folks in skimpy bathing suits, funny straw hats, and dark sunglasses played in the water. They sat on plastic chairs that sank into the sand under windblown umbrellas anchored in that same sand. None of them seemed as awestruck by the sight in front of them as she felt.

"It's overwhelming, isn't it?" He slapped a hand on his hat to settle it before the wind snatched it away. "Go on, get closer. The waves won't grab you and suck you in. We have about an hour and then we need to get back on the road if we're going to get to Mexico and back today."

An hour. She would need at least that long to catch her breath. She wished they could stay here permanently. South Padre Island. Even the name was pretty. "What about all those people?"

"They may stare a bit, but mostly they're too busy having fun to care about a bunch of Plain folks getting their feet wet." Mordecai balanced on one foot and tugged off a boot. He stuck the boot in the sand, then tugged off the other. "I better get out there before Butch drowns. Come on. Wade in. It'll cool you off."

A grin stretching from ear to ear, he took off toward the water with a pace suited to a much younger man. He hippity-hopped a bit, zigged, then zagged, looking much like Butch had a few seconds earlier. "Last one in the water has to walk home!"

Deborah eased one foot onto the sand. Hot. She picked up the skirt of her dress to keep it from getting dirty and began the trek across the sand. Her feet sank. It felt as if they were encased in an oven. Mordecai was right. She could see God's hand in this. As she padded closer and the sand turned wet, the heat dissipated. It felt like sticky clay on her soles. Her feet made squelching noises as she walked. A little boy in a drooping, sand-smeared diaper chased a striped blow-up ball across her path, forcing her to sidestep. His delighted laughter mingled with the chatter of the seagulls.

Water lapped at her feet, leaving suds around her and tiny holes that filled again as the water drained away. Her footprints washed away as quickly as she made them. The water felt cool as it rushed against her ankles and calves, then swept away in a steady, rhythmic tide that rushed in her ears.

"Water, water!" Hazel shrieked and ran past her, arms flailing, dress flapping. She threw herself into the shallow water and rolled around. She staggered to her feet, mouth gaping. "Cold!"

"It's not that cold." Esther splashed ahead. "It feels like heaven."

Deborah wouldn't go that far, but it did feel good. "What are those?" She pointed at enormous birds flying in a line in the distance. They looked like flying dinosaurs. One swooped down and skimmed the water, its baggy mouth open. "What are they doing?"

"Those are pelicans, silly." Esther squatted and splashed Hazel, who shrieked and toddled away as fast as her short, fat legs would take her. "Haven't you ever seen one before? They're getting their lunch. They like fish for lunch and supper and breakfast."

"We didn't have pelicans in Tennessee. They're strange looking."

"Strangely pretty."

Deborah jumped in spite of herself. She hadn't noticed Phineas's approach. That he would come near surprised her. He still worked the apiaries with Mordecai and showed up regularly for supper, but he had nary a word to say to her. Nor had he spoken to her in the van or even looked her way, his nose stuck in a bird book. As if he, too, was haunted by the feel of his hand on hers that day in front of the medical clinic. His fingers rubbing the skin on the back of her hand. They hadn't done anything wrong. So why did she have this strange, queasy feeling in the pit of her stomach every time she saw him?

She kept her gaze on the birds, trying to ignore the catch in her breath at the sight of him. Every muscle in her body tensed at his nearness. He was only a man. A prickly, gruff, rude, unbearable know-it-all who had her all mixed up for no apparent reason.

Determined to ignore all this foolishness, she studied the pelicans as they soared, swooped, and bobbed. Unfortunately, the pelicans reminded her of that first real conversation she and Phineas ever had. The night he walked with her on the dark road back to John's house after the singing. He'd said then he'd like to know what it felt like to fly, a sentiment she shared.

"What about those, what are those?" Pleased that her voice didn't shake, she pointed at brilliantly colored sails that soared on the horizon. They seemed to hover and dip in the wind. "Are there people on those?"

Phineas lifted the ever-present binoculars to his eyes, then let them drop on their strap. "Parasails. And jah, those are people."

He moved away, splashing water that darkened the bottom of his black pants as he trudged in the same direction as the parasails. People were flying. Using sails like wings. Deborah glanced at Hazel, already soaked to the bone, her bonnet hanging down her back. Esther splashed water at her. "Go on, you know you want to."

"I should watch Hazel."

"I'll watch Hazel. Leila and Rebekah are right there." Esther jerked her head down the beach where the other girls knelt, gathering shells with Susan, Naomi, and Mudder. Caleb squatted in the water, examining something in his hand. Leroy had plopped down in the sand and was untying his boots. Esther grinned, looking particularly pleased with life and herself. "Go. Everyone's busy having fun. They won't care."

Wondering if she had a penchant for hopping out of the frying pan and into the fire, Deborah wheeled and trotted after Phineas, her feet making slapping sounds on the water. "Have you ever tried parasailing?" She lifted her voice to make herself heard over the noisy waves. It sounded high and childish in her ears. "It would be a little like flying, don't you think?"

"It costs a lot of money and it's not something we would do." Phineas kept walking, his bare feet making a *slap-slap* sound on the sand. "All those fancy, bright colors. Everybody watching."

"Everyone's watching us now."

"No more than they do anywhere else."

Three girls building an ornate castle in the sand stopped what they were doing to stare as Deborah and Phineas walked by. One sat up on her knees, hand to her forehead to shield it from the sun. "Look, Amber, they're wearing costumes on the beach." Her high voice carried on the wind. "They're like pilgrims or pioneers or something."

"No, moron, they're Amish." Amber waved with both hands. "Hey, you guys, come over here. Come join us. You're welcome to build our castle with us."

Phineas, apparently unfazed by this attention, kept moving. "Thanks, but we're taking a walk."

"Did you see his face?" The girl named Amber didn't wait quite long enough to ask the question. Even the crash of the waves couldn't drown it out. "He had a Frankenstein thing going on."

Phineas's speed increased. He probably wasn't even aware of it. Deborah scurried to catch up. "I'm sorry about that."

"Why? That also is no different from anywhere else." He glanced back at her. "Why are you following me . . . again?"

"Why have you been avoiding me . . . again? Is that why you bought the house? To get away from me? You couldn't stand to live in the same house as me?"

He didn't answer. Instead, he lifted the binoculars and let her hurt, angry words flow out with the tide. She had no right to be angry. He wanted to hide behind those binoculars and see the world without letting it see him.

He didn't want her to see him. Not the real him.

He'd talked to her at Choke Canyon and in town. Maybe Phineas needed neutral ground to be able to speak his mind to her.

"I wish we could live here all the time." The heat that burned her face had nothing to do with the sun. "I mean, I wish I could be here all the time."

The binoculars dropped. Droplets of water and sweat glistened his forehead and cheeks, giving his scarred face an odd glow.

"That's the thing about beauty. If you have it all the time, you can't truly appreciate it. If you lived here, you might start to take it for granted." His voice was so low and hoarse, she had trouble hearing him over the waves. "It's like if you had cake every day, it wouldn't be a treat on your birthday."

"I suppose that's true." She scrambled to walk closer, to hear him better, to be near. "But it would be nice to have it a little more often. Maybe birthdays and the Fourth of July."

"And weddings."

Why had he brought up weddings? From the startled look

on his face, he wondered the same thing. His pace faltered. He slowed, then halted, and turned so he faced the water.

"What is it?" Deborah planted herself next to him, determined to have this conversation. "Don't stop now."

"Daed used to bring me here . . . after the accident. The sound of the waves helped me sleep. This was the only place I could sleep for more than a few hours. I wanted to stay here forever."

"But you couldn't."

"Nee. Daed had work to do and the other kinner to think about. Samuel healed up fast, but Jacob had two broken legs and a broken arm. Esther needed Daed home. She'd just lost her mudder. We all had. He said I had to learn to be where I belonged. At home."

"But he still comes back here."

"Because it gives him some peace as much as me." Phineas's hands squeezed the binoculars, but he didn't raise them to his face. "He said it's like hard times. If we never had them, we wouldn't appreciate the good times when we have them."

"Like now." Deborah slid closer. Her shoulder brushed his arm. She held her breath. Waiting.

"Like now." He squatted and picked up a shell. A piece of sand dollar, one side partially gone and jagged. He held it up as if offering it to her. "Nothing's perfect."

Deborah knelt next to him and held out her hand, palm up. He laid his offering there. "It looks perfect to me." She rubbed her thumb across it in a gentle, careful motion, aware of the fragile nature of this broken shell that had once held life in it. She let the gritty grains of sand fall into her palm and looked at him, letting her gaze trace the scars before returning to his eyes. "It feels perfect."

He brushed the sand from her palm with one finger in a delicate touch that she felt from the tips of her fingers to her toes. His hand dropped. "Don't leave."

Two words. A simple plea. Deborah squinted against the sun that made a halo around his head. She tried to see through the man, past the ridged scars, to someone who had let down his defenses for the first time in twelve years. For her.

The sun beat on her face. The wind, laden with salt and humidity, cooled her at the same time. Exactly how Phineas made her feel. Hot and cold at the same time. She shivered and wrapped her fingers around his offering, careful not to squeeze too hard and fracture what was left of the shell or the strange, delicate thread that held them together in this moment. What was he telling her? What was he asking of her?

"Why do you want me to stay?"

He leaned back on his haunches. The waves washed over their knees and soaked their clothes. "I'm . . . I'm trying to—"

Shrieks filled the air. Someone in pain. One of the boys. Caleb or Phineas's brother. Deborah put her hand on Phineas's shoulder and used him to push herself to her feet. His fingers caught at hers. She squeezed and let go. He stood in one easy, fluid motion. "Someone's hurt."

"Wait, Phineas."

He was already gone.

TWENTY-EIGHT

The cry had ceased, but Phineas could see Caleb hunkered down on the sand, rocking and clutching his foot. Esther knelt on one side, Abigail on the other. Phineas picked up his pace. His long-legged stride outdistanced Deborah with no effort. He had experience running on the beach. She hadn't. And emotions she didn't understand were pursuing her.

His feet sank in the sand, his thighs ached, and he couldn't catch his breath. The last part might not be related to the sand and the wind and concern for Deborah's brother. It might be that he'd been about to admit something he shouldn't. Every time he got close to her, it happened. He couldn't help himself. She made him want more. She made him want to hold her hand and spend time with her. Forever.

Until he stepped away and reality set in. It would never happen. Never. She would not yoke herself to a man like him. She shouldn't. She should go back to Tennessee to a place where she could have the life she was meant to have. That was why he'd bought the Schrock farm. It would've been nice to help John out, but his farm was smack-dab in the middle of the district, on the main road, across from the store. It would never do. Not for Phineas. He needed the distance.

At least that was what he kept telling himself.

Seeing her on his beach, as he always thought of it, had been too much. She looked so pretty and sweet in her excitement at seeing something so magnificent for the first time. He remembered that feeling of being a tiny speck on God's creation. Nowhere did he feel closer to God than in this place, even as he railed at Him for all he'd lost. The comfort and certainty of God's existence had made him giddy enough to say what he'd longed to say from the first moment he saw her, flat on her back, scared silly over an armadillo.

He wanted her to stay with him.

It was one thing to admit such a thing to himself, quite another to say it. She'd been shocked. She had no idea. She had no inkling of his feelings. Or returned them. The look on her face made that obvious. No way she'd make a commitment like that—not to him.

He glanced back. She'd hitched up her skirt, and her bare legs showed above feet covered with sand. He faced forward. She was a strong runner. With strong legs. Shapely legs.

Gott, help me. A puny prayer, at best.

His job was to help and to stand back and let Deborah live her life as God intended. Nothing more. He could not expect her to feel for him—with his monstrous face and hands—what he felt for her. Telling her how he felt would only back her into a corner where she would have to dodge his feelings and feel guilty for it. He would let her off easy. Somehow. He'd stay in his house and keep his distance until she went back to Tennessee or on to Missouri.

Phineas focused on the cluster of folks ahead. Butch had taken to barking in a steady barrage as if calling for help. Rebekah hopped up and yelled over the din of girls talking and the dog barking. "It stung him or something. What is that thing?"

"Butch, enough!"

Butch ceased his caterwauling, circled the group, and plopped down next to Caleb, his intent to guard the boy apparent in the low growl still emanating from his throat. Phineas tugged Caleb back from a big, shimmering blob burrowed in the sand. At first glance, Caleb probably mistook it for a plastic bag filled with water and thrown on the beach like trash. On closer inspection, it looked like an iridescent balloon ready to pop.

Phineas knelt next to Abigail, keeping his distance from the sea creature, which for all intents and purposes had only been doing what came naturally to it. "It's a jellyfish."

Daed squatted on the other side of the boy. "Yep, those fellers are a nasty lot."

"It hurts." Caleb moaned and put a hand out as if to rub his foot. "It feels like my foot is on fire. Stephen said I shouldn't come. He was right."

"Stephen doesn't know much about these things." Phineas glanced at Abigail. Her fair skin, already pink from the sun, reddened. He grabbed a handful of wet sand and dumped it on the red, swelling welts on Caleb's leg. He wanted to tell the boy that Stephen's words came from jealousy and nothing more, but he didn't. Caleb was too young to understand man-woman things. "A little sand and mud will help."

"Hey, hey!" Caleb squirmed and pulled away. "Don't do that."

"He's removing the stingers. They're like little tiny harpoons and they have poison in them. We have to get them out."

Mordecai put both hands on Caleb's shoulders and held him still. "Esther, run to the van and get the vinegar and the first aid kit. They're in the back."

They always came prepared. The little ones always seemed to have to learn this lesson the hard way. Don't mess with jellyfish.

"You Lantz kinner have never seen a jellyfish before." Mordecai shoved his hat back as he surveyed the concerned faces of Caleb's sisters. Phineas recognized that tone. Daed was about to give a lecture. The man should've been a teacher. "This here is a garden-variety jellyfish. They sting their food to catch it."

"That's an animal?" Abigail wrinkled a nose already turning pink with sunburn. "Where's its mouth?"

"Don't encourage him." Phineas took the bottle from a puffing Esther's outstretched hand. He removed the bottle cap and poured vinegar over the welts, then dried them. "You'll just get more of a lecture."

"A jellyfish is an invertebrate animal." Daed tapped his temple with one long finger. "It has no brain, no head, no bones, heart, ears, or eyes. It's basically a big belly with a nervous system."

"How did it know to sting me?" Daed's tactic had worked. Caleb was so interested in his lecture, he forgot to be in pain. "He didn't see me coming."

"It has a nervous system. Its tentacles come in contact with something, it shoots out stingers. That's how it gets food." Daed began applying an ointment that would reduce the itching and pain. "You're lucky it's just a jellyfish. The Portuguese man-of-war is the one you want to avoid. It's purple and kind of pretty, but the venom can kill you."

Abigail sighed. Phineas glanced at the woman next to him. Her gaze was fastened on his daed, her expression a strange mix of concern and bewilderment. She looked mesmerized. He glanced from her to Mordecai. His daed's gaze skipped from the kinner to Abigail, who immediately ducked her head.

His daed was showing off for Abigail Lantz. Phineas couldn't help it. He grinned.

Gott was good. Why hadn't Phineas seen the thing going on between his father and Abigail before? Because he'd been too wrapped up in his own messy feelings. Too selfish.

Let Daed tell his stories. What impressed a woman never ceased to amaze Phineas. He wasn't a storyteller and never would be. Mordecai told the best stories Phineas had ever heard. The stories were true, but he and his brothers and sister had heard them hundreds of times. Along with the admonition: Stay away from creatures that might inflict pain and hurt.

"We're all done." Phineas patted Caleb's shoulder. "Time to go."

Daed handed Esther the first aid kit and turned to Caleb. "I'll give you a piggyback ride to the van. There're spigots in the parking lot. Everyone can wash off the sand before getting back in the van. It's time to eat lunch anyway."

Still grinning to himself, Phineas turned to lead the way until Butch took over, glancing back every few seconds as if to question why it took humans so long to cover such a short distance. The second Phineas squeezed into the van, clothes wet and sticky, Deborah plopped into the seat next to him. She shouldn't. The others would notice. They always sat boys in one row, girls in the next.

"Go away." He whispered the words while fumbling at the seat belt he never failed to buckle on every trip. The smell of sweat, ocean, and wet dog made his stomach roil. "Sit with the girls."

"You had been to this beach the day of the crash." Her voice was soft, meant for his ears only. "Why did Mordecai bring you here? It must've caused you pain. What made him think it would help you sleep better?"

"The pain was no worse than what I already carried with me." Phineas faced the window, ignoring the peanut butter sandwich wrapped in wax paper she extended toward him. "He knew this was the last happy place I would ever be."

"You've never been happy again?"

Phineas glanced at her. Emotion lit her blue eyes like fire in a woodstove, leaping and dancing in the air. She looked as if a wave of sadness took her breath away. He didn't want her to be sad for him. He had enough sadness for them both. "I've learned to be at peace. Most of the time. Until now."

"Until now?"

"I'd learned to not want what I can't have."

Her frown said she didn't understand what he tried so hard to tell her. "What can't you have?"

"I don't want to talk about this."

Her expression still puzzled, she laid the sandwich on his knee without touching him. "Fine. Eat."

She didn't intend to ask him the question again. He breathed a sigh of relief. "You're bossy."

She smiled. "I've been told that."

"Not a quality a good Plain fraa should have."

"Plain women run households full of children. Bossy is all they can be." She unwrapped her sandwich, took a bite, and chewed, her expression thoughtful. After a while she swallowed. "You're good with the kinner."

"As a man should be."

"Not all are." Her expression said she undoubtedly was thinking of Stephen. "Some leave it to the women and don't learn to be daeds."

"Or maybe they just need time to learn."

Her eyebrows rose and her nose wrinkled. She had a nice nose. "I suppose."

"They need their . . . the women to be patient with them. To let them figure some things out, learn how to do some things."

Would she hear what he was saying?

"I think I might find peace here too."

"Here?"

"In Texas."

Phineas's fingers tightened on his sandwich. Grape jam squeezed from the ragged sides of the white bread and dripped on the wax paper. His heart did a strange two-step that made it hard to breathe. "Why?"

"I can see it through your eyes now. I see how a cactus and a straggly bush passing for a tree and flat fields of milo can be pretty."

"How?"

"It has to do with the person who's doing the looking."

"Jah."

"That goes for people too."

What was she telling him in that weird, roundabout way women had? "It does?"

"Gott made them beautiful." She nodded, her gaze solemn, eyes sad beyond measure. "One of these days I hope you'll see things through my eyes too."

TWENTY-NINE

The palm tree–lined street that led to the international bridge between Weslaco and Progreso teemed with people and cars streaming south through checkpoints manned by men in green uniforms that were dark with sweat around their necks, backs, and under their arms. They wore guns on their hips. The air held the stench of sweat and human waste mingled with the sweet scent of pineapple sold by vendors and meat grilling on spits at street-side restaurants with doors flung open. Abigail sidestepped a cluster of barefoot children, all with dirty faces, all with their hands out, and all speaking a language she didn't understand.

She couldn't help but look back at them as Leroy and Mordecai hustled their little group through the doors and into a building filled with cool, damp air. The children's expressions spoke words any mother would understand. *I'm hungry. I'm tired. Feed me. Help me.* The mother in her wanted to go back and share what was left of her lunch with them. Filled with uncertainty and a strange sense of unreality, she hugged her canvas bag to her chest. Inside, tucked in her coin bag, lay the passport card that had arrived in the mail a few days earlier. The card featured the first and only photo she'd ever willingly taken.

"It's okay. We've been doing this for a long time. It's necessary for us." Susan held one of the double glass doors open for her. "It's a little discombobulating the first time, but I really enjoy coming here. Mexico is so different. It's colorful and noisy. Different from being out in the middle of nowhere, that's for sure."

If Leroy thought it was all right for them to do this, it must be all right. He'd drawn the holy lot. Abigail understood the reasoning. Buying medicine and going to the dentist across the border helped them stretch their funds. "Are you sure the kinner will be all right?" She asked the question for the third time, afraid the others would become impatient with her uncertainty. Parents decided if they would lift the ban on photos for their children. Hers didn't need medical attention, so she'd chosen not to get passport cards for them, but she hadn't realized she would be leaving them in such a vulnerable place while she traipsed by foot over a bridge into a foreign country. "No one will tell them to move or leave?"

Or worse, take them to jail for loitering too close to the border.

"They'll be fine. We've done this many times. They know to stay together. They know this is no place to mess around." Mordecai waved his passport card. "Be ready to show your card."

"Didn't you feel strange getting your photo taken?" She blurted the question, her neck and ears suddenly hot. Stephen had chosen not to be a part of this expedition, even though his teeth could use some work. He hadn't been happy with her choice, but she had an aching tooth and dwindling savings. "After so many years of being told to turn away?"

"I know many of our kind who take their families to Mexico

for medical treatment. This is a concession that makes sense, like having a phone in the store." Mordecai showed no signs of impatience as he shuffled forward in a line thirty people deep. "It helps the business thrive, which helps keep our families together. We do this in order to make sure our district survives."

Abigail understood all that. Leroy had offered the rule long before she and her family had arrived in Bee County. Still, whenever she glanced at the photo on the card she felt a shiver of apprehension.

The man behind the counter glanced from her card to her face and back in a split second. He handed it back and waved her on with barely an acknowledgment of her existence. She pushed through another set of double doors and stepped back into the blazing sun behind Mordecai, Susan, Naomi, and Leroy. A few more steps along the bridge, which featured a medallion settled into the cement at that spot that divided the United States from Mexico, and she, Abigail Lantz, stood on foreign soil. Slowing to peek over the edge at the scant waters of the Rio Grande, she giggled aloud. Who would've thought it possible?

"Are you coming?" Mordecai called. "We need to be quick about it and get back to the van. It's a long drive home."

"Jah, jah." She rushed to catch up. "Sorry."

"I understand." He grinned. "Even after all these years, I still like coming here to see what I can see."

"I'll take Susan and Naomi to the doctor." Leroy's expression said he didn't think much of what he was seeing. "Mordecai, you show Abigail where the dentist is. Stay there until we come find you. We'll return across together."

"Maybe we should all stay together." Naomi's frown seemed to settle squarely on Abigail. "It would be more . . . seemly."

"We don't have time for that." Leroy took off across the bridge, impatience evident in his long stride and hunched shoulders. "Be quick about it."

Abigail scampered after them, trying not to be distracted by the teeming masses around her. So much to see. The stores all opened directly onto the street, their wares spilling out in sidewalk displays. Many of the signs were in English and even the Spanish words like *farmacía* looked familiar. Everywhere, children begged for money and adults called out, "Miss, miss, one dollar, one dollar."

Blankets, huge straw hats with cones for tops, jewelry, masks, furniture, leather goods, candy, dresses covered with all colors of embroidered designs, liquor, papier-mâché animals. Abigail touched a turquoise-colored dress, marveling at the intricate embroidery of row after row of multicolored flowers done by some skillful seamstress. She turned to a large papier-mâché donkey hanging from a hook on the ceiling. Whatever did a person need a paper donkey for?

"Those are called piñatas." Mordecai's voice close to her ear startled her. How did he know she had this question? "Folks fill them with candy at birthday parties and the kids whack them with sticks until they break and everyone gets a treat."

"And this is fun?"

"The kinner think so."

"I wouldn't like hitting things, but I like candy." She touched a ceramic lizard painted in greens and reds. "So much stuff."

Mordecai nodded. "Most of it is of little use."

The crowd jostled them. Abigail stumbled and found herself toppling from the curb. Mordecai grabbed her arm and tugged her back. Her momentum sent her against his chest. His blue-green eyes widened as his big hands wrapped around her waist and held her. "Sorry about that."

"Not your fault." If she could melt into the sidewalk, she would. "How far to the dentist office?"

"Only two more blocks. Look, roasted corn. Would you like one?" He tugged a bill from the brim of his hat. "Add some lime juice and a little chili. You'll like it, you'll see. Just remember not to chew on the side that hurts."

Before she could protest, he paid the grinning, snaggle-toothed man behind the cart and presented her with an ear of corn sprinkled with red chili. He was right. Her mouth watered at the tartness of the lime juice and the spicy seasoning. "Good," she muttered after the first bite. "Very gut."

He paused from his technique of demolishing the corn with a steady *chomp-chomp* row by row and laughed.

"What?"

"Now you'll have corn in your teeth when the dentist works on them."

"Oh well."

"So what do you think?" He waved the ear of corn, oblivious to the juicy kernels that landed on his shirt. "I imagine it's different from anything you've seen before."

"It is. It reminds me a little of the market back home, though. Except for the border crossing and the language I can't understand."

"I imagine Bee County is different from back home too."

"It is."

"But you like it, right? It's an adventure?"

"It is an adventure." At least it had seemed that way at first. "I'm ready for things to be . . . everyday. I'm not in need of adventure."

"I can understand that. You want to settle down and feel at home."

"I do."

Mordecai dropped the bare corn cob in a rusted, overflowing trash can on the street corner. "You don't feel at home, living in my house?"

"It's your house."

"And that pains you? Having to be around me?"

"Nee, nee, that's not it. I like being around you." In her haste to correct his impression, she hadn't thought of how those words would sound. "I mean—"

"That's gut. Because I like being around you too."

Mordecai grasped her hand and squeezed past folks gathered around three young men who strummed guitars and played a violin while singing at the top of their lungs. She should pull away, but she found she couldn't. Instead, she let him lead the way. The singers seemed to be moving with them. They sounded as if they were in pain. *"Aye, Aye-Aye, Aye,"* they shouted in unison, the seams of the shirts straining across broad chests. They wore brown suits with rhinestones and black piping, a costume too warm for August in south Texas. She recognized none of the words, but their faces said they sang of deep emotions.

And they seemed to be following Mordecai and her.

"Another song for your *señorita*?" one shouted, his face creased by a big smile. *"Canción de amor*? Love song?"

Love sounded like *lob*.

She ducked closer to Mordecai. His grip on her hand tightened.

"No, *gracias*." He nodded to the man, who nodded back and moved away. "Another time."

"Mordecai, I didn't mean to say that." Abigail felt as if she'd been running. This no longer felt like an adventure. It felt as if she had entered a strange, alien world with no familiar landmarks—physical or emotional. "Forget I said it. Please."

"I don't want to forget it. I've been wanting to say it for a while now. At the right time."

In a foreign country on a crowded street. With love songs in the air. This was the right time? Maybe it was. They were far from the familiar dirt roads of Bee County. Far from all the usual everyday things. From other obligations. From their kinner. From Stephen. "I don't think we—"

"That corn made me thirsty. I'll get us some bottled water."

Changing the subject seemed like a good idea. "Isn't there some place we can get a drink of water that doesn't cost money?"

"Nee, not a gut idea. Stick to bottled sodas or water." He doled out more coins and took two plastic bottles dripping with condensation from a girl who looked to be six or seven. "I know this is a strange place to talk about this, but I don't want to wait any longer. I don't want it to be too late."

"Too late for what?"

He took a long swallow from his bottle, his Adam's apple bobbing. Water trickled down his chin and into his beard. When he lowered the bottle, his gaze locked with hers. "Are you committed to Stephen?"

"Courting is private."

"Then you are courting?"

"Not very well." She slapped her hand to her mouth. She shouldn't have said that. It wasn't fair to Stephen and it sounded mean spoken aloud. She kept saying things she shouldn't. Mordecai had her so befuddled. She lowered her hand, her cheeks tingling as if she'd been slapped. "Please forget I said that too."

"Sometimes when a thing is that hard, it's not meant to be."

"You have experience with that? You've courted another since your fraa's passing?"

"Nee. But I'm fixing to do it now, if I can get a by-your-leave."

"It wouldn't be fair to Stephen. I broke his heart once before, back in Tennessee when I chose my mann over him. It's not right that I do it again."

"Is that your heart talking or your head?" The pulse throbbed in Mordecai's temple. The words sounded like a growl. "You came out to see if there was something there now. Did you not consider the possibility that there might not be? That you didn't choose Stephen the first time because he was not and will never be the right man for you? That maybe Gott sent you here for a different reason, for a different person?"

It had occurred to her. She simply couldn't see how she could hurt Stephen once again. How could she justify such a thing? The stricken look on his face at the lake kept her awake at night. So did the fact that she'd wanted to back away both times he kissed her. "It's confusing. I've been praying Gott would show me His will for me."

"Me too. It would be far worse to be yoked with someone you didn't truly love."

"It takes work to build a relationship."

"Love shouldn't be that hard."

"Was it hard with . . . your fraa?"

All emotion drained from his face, leaving behind a stony facade. He tossed the plastic water bottle into the trash. "Doctor Martinez's office is right there ahead."

Talking about his wife still brought pain after twelve years. She'd had two to adjust and everyone seemed to think she should be ready to move on. "You brought this up."

"I know. I'm looking forward, not back. Are you?"

She stopped in the middle of the sidewalk, letting the tidal wave of people flow around her. "I'm in Mexico. What do you think?"

His frown eased and the smile she'd grown accustomed to seeing at the breakfast table each morning appeared and spread. "And I'm grateful to Gott for that."

"Why?"

"For the first time in twelve years, I feel . . . something."

He didn't know what he felt? "Something?"

"I've been like a block of cold, hard stone for twelve years. I couldn't feel anything. I feel now—happy, sad, mad, irritated, aggravated, uncertain. All at once every time I look at you. When I see you with Stephen . . . it's . . . hard, but it's gut too."

Good? The man must be daft. No, she understood what he meant. She had been numb with grief for so long, she'd forgotten what the highs and lows of new love felt like. "Because of me?"

"Because of you."

"How did that happen?"

"I don't know, but I'm glad. I'm glad and I'm not going to fight it or ignore it. If I thought you and Stephen were meant to be together, I would honor that bond. I would step back and hold my tongue." He grabbed her hand and squeezed. "But that's not what I see. Tell me I'm right."

She wanted to close her eyes and concentrate on the feel of his hand tight around hers, warm, capable, strong, even fierce. She swallowed against a wave of emotion that threatened to send her into his arms in broad daylight on a crowded street. Stephen's face hovered close to her, his eyes full of hope filling her mind. This wasn't fair to him. He'd done nothing wrong. Not twenty years ago. Not now. "I can't," she whispered. "I'm committed to another."

His hand dropped.

"Then I'll step aside." The stony facade had returned. He held open the door. "We best get in there and get back. The kinner are waiting."

She ducked past him and slipped into the dentist's office.

"So am I. As long as it takes." His last words were nearly lost in the squeal of the door hinges, but Abigail was certain she'd heard them. She glanced back. Mordecai's eyes held only distant politeness.

Still, those words caused relief to resonate in her head. Despite her denial, he would wait. For as long as it took.

THIRTY

Deborah flapped her hands, trying to create a breeze as she peered from the van window. From where they sat, she could see people trickling into the Customs buildings. Cars filled the parking lot, baking in an afternoon sun that beat down with no mercy. The asphalt seemed to shimmer. An ice cream truck made its way up and down the rows, tinny music blaring.

"It must be 110 degrees in the shade. Are we just going to sit here for two hours?" The whine didn't become her, but to come so close to a foreign land and not be able to go there seemed wrong. Why did Mudder have to be so stubborn about the photos? One little photo and she could be walking in Mexico. "Could we at least walk around on this side?"

"Daed said we could get a *paleta* if we wanted." Esther craned her head over the seat from the front row. "Or *raspas*. The ice cream truck is right there."

"What is a paleta?" For that matter, what was a raspa?

"Popsicle." Esther rubbed her hands together. She licked her lips. "I'd rather have the raspa. It's a snow cone, you know, shaved ice with syrup. You can get all kinds of flavors. I like coconut. It's blue. It makes your lips blue."

The closest they would ever come to wearing lipstick. "Let's go, then."

"We'll not all go running after an ice cream truck." Phineas lifted his gaze from the book he'd been studying ever since they left the beach. *Birds of North America.* He hadn't looked at Deborah once. "Daed also said for us to stay together."

"Come on, Phin, don't you want an ice cream?" Esther's wheedling tone said she knew how to get her brother to cave. "I'm sure they have Push Ups and rocket ship Popsicles."

He shut the book with a sharp bang as if he'd made a sudden decision. "Give me the money and I'll go."

"Nee, we all stay together." Deborah wanted out of the van. She wanted to get a closer look at the massive palm trees and the bright orange and red flowered bushes that mingled with trees covered with purple flowers. She thirsted for color after months in the brown south Texas oven-baked desert. "Mr. Carson will be able to see us from the van anyway."

"Fine, Esther, you, and me." Phineas's mulish gaze met Deborah's. "That's enough people to carry the ice cream back."

"The three of you, then. Take Butch." Mr. Carson shook one long, hairy finger at them. "He seems determined to be a watch-dog. And stay together."

Caleb's lip stuck out. "No fair—"

"Life isn't fair." Phin grunted as he shoved open the door and slid out. "Get used to it."

Surprised he'd picked her after giving her the silent treatment for the past two hours, Deborah hopped from the van before he changed his mind. The pavement singed the bottom of her feet. She hopped on one foot, then the other, hoping to get used to it. Esther did a similar dance a few steps behind her.

"Stay with me." Phineas glanced back, his tone aggrieved. Butch barked once as if voicing his agreement. "Anything happens to you, Daed will blame me."

A small grin on her sun-bronzed face, Esther slowed her pace even more, leaving Deborah with Phineas on one side and Butch on the other. The dog seemed friendlier than the man. He drew closer every time a person passed them, his growl a hum in his throat. Phineas didn't seem to notice. He kept his gaze on the ice cream truck, which had stopped for a cluster of white-haired old folks getting out of a travel bus three rows down.

"Push Ups are really your favorite?" Deborah couldn't think of another thing to say. "I like Heath ice cream bars."

"Those are gut too."

Not much to work with there. Sweating, her throat parched, Deborah concentrated on matching his pace. An ice cream would be a nice treat, and maybe it would improve Phineas's mood. Her statement about his seeing the world through her eyes hadn't improved it. In fact, it seemed to make it worse.

"How come you call me Phineas?"

Of all the questions he could've asked, he picked that one? She dodged a Styrofoam soda cup sitting on the asphalt and picked up her pace. Was he going to a huge fire? "What do you mean? It's your name."

"Everyone else calls me Phin. Not you."

"I like the way Phineas sounds." It rolled off her tongue. It was a strong name. "It's your given name. It's not like it's so long that it needs to be shortened. Why turn a perfectly good biblical name into a nickname?"

"Just wondered."

"Don't wander too far."

"Do you always have to be such a smarty?"

"Only when a person aggravates me."

"I aggravate you?"

"Only all the time."

"Then my work is done."

"Phineas—"

He held up his hand and turned his back to her, focusing instead on the man behind the counter who seemed to be sweating more than any man Deborah had ever seen. He smiled, his teeth white in a dark, shiny face, as he dabbed a wad of sodden, dirty towel at his slick bald head. "*Helado*? Ice cream?"

Phineas seemed right at home with this task. He recited the order and counted out the money to see how far they could make it stretch. In the end, they settled for an assortment of Fudgsicles, ice cream bars, and Popsicles. He pointed to each one and recited a name, then counted them again. "One more."

"That's everyone. Why one more?" Deborah glanced at Esther, who shrugged. "It'll melt in the van."

"For Butch."

An orange Popsicle for a dog? Deborah giggled and then put a hand over her mouth at Phineas's narrowed eyes.

He proceeded to count the money twice, to the man's chagrin.

"The ice cream will melt before we have a chance to *eat* it." Esther scooped up a bar and started tearing off the paper.

Phineas snagged the Heath bar from her hand. "Wait until we get back to the van."

Esther snagged it back. "Too late, bruder."

Deborah picked up her share of the load and turned. Immediately two children appeared in their path. They looked to be about Caleb's age, a boy and a girl, both so thin she could see their bones protruding in their arms and legs. Both were barefoot and their dark hair hadn't seen a brush in a long time. The boy wore a dirty gray T-shirt and ragged shorts while the girl's faded dress looked more like a flour sack than clothing. The dirt on her face didn't hide the bruises that darkened her brown skin. Her bottom lip was swollen and blood had dried on the end of her nose. The boy held out his hand. "Mister, mister! Helado. Ice cream. Hungry."

"They want our ice cream?" Deborah glanced from Esther, who'd already devoured a good portion of her ice cream bar, to Phineas. His gaze was locked on the girl. "Phineas?"

"Who did that to you?" He spoke to the girl. "Did someone hurt you?"

"Our *papá,*" the boy answered for her. "We no bring money. *Pow-pow.*"

He mimed punches being thrown. "Our job bring money."

"I'm sorry. We don't have any money." Phineas's tone was gentle and regretful. "I wish we did."

The little girl blinked back tears. Butch inched forward, his nose nudging her dirty hand. The girl disappeared behind her brother, her hands in the pockets of her dress. The boy shrugged. "She no like *perros.* Dogs." He grinned. "Ice cream, she like."

"Butch won't hurt you. He's a nice dog. We have ice cream." Phineas tugged Butch back with one hand while he held out the sack with the other. The boy's grin widened. Phineas pulled it back. "If it's all right with you, Deborah."

She nodded. Who could say no to these two waiflike little ones? Their job was to walk the streets begging and, if they didn't bring home money, be beaten. "We still have sandwiches in the van. And oranges. Cookies."

The supplies were for the trip back, but they'd all eaten plenty on the drive to Weslaco. Phineas's smile appeared. Deborah's breath caught in her throat. The scars disappeared and she caught a glimpse of a boy who liked to blow pink bubbles, fish, and swim in the ocean.

"Come on." Phineas jerked his head toward the van. The boy skipped to keep up, but the girl seemed entrenched in the cement. "Let's go. We won't hurt you. We have *comida*."

"What's her name?" Deborah didn't know how much the boy understood, but his English had been good so far.

"*Nombre*? Isabela. I'm Javier."

"Isabela. Come. Please. We won't hurt you."

The girl swiped at her dirty face with an equally dirty arm. Javier grabbed her hand and tugged her forward. "*Vámonos*."

In minutes, they were situated inside the van. Mr. Carson cranked up the air and the two children devoured their ice cream before it could melt, and then sandwiches, oranges, and cookies. No one complained about sharing their food, not even Caleb, who loved ice cream more than venison steak.

Phineas kept adding food to their paper plates, first more chips, then an apple, followed by Deborah's oatmeal cookies. The boy wolfed them all down, his gaze darting from the plate to Caleb as if he feared the other boy would steal his food. Deborah caught Phineas's gaze. He leaned toward her. "Thank you for being willing to share."

"It was your idea to share the ice cream." She patted her belly. "I could skip a meal or two and not notice it."

"Not really." He cocked his head, his gaze traveling head to foot. "Like I said before, you're a little scrawny."

"Am not."

The grin reappeared. She shook her head. Phineas could be

a tease and he took enjoyment from teasing her. She'd seen that grin on this trip more than in the entire time she'd been in Bee County. Was it the change in scenery or the company?

"We go now." Javier wiped grape jam on his shirt and tugged on the van door. "We work now."

"Wait." Mr. Carson had been watching over the impromptu feast with a thoughtful look on his face. He tugged a long leather billfold from the back pocket of his jeans. "Here's a little to tide you over."

He handed Javier a ten-dollar bill. The boy's face split open in a wide grin that revealed two missing teeth. "Gracías, *señor,* gracías."

Isabela, who'd mostly hidden behind her brother in the van, popped out long enough to join the chorus. "Gracías."

"God bless you." Mr. Carson waved them away. "Take care."

They scuttled away, still exclaiming in Spanish.

"Thank you, Mr. Carson." Phineas repeated the boy's story. "I was afraid they would get slapped around again by their father if they came home without money."

Shaking his head, Mr. Carson chuckled. "More than likely they fed you a line of bull."

"What do you mean?"

"They learn to tell tourists what they want to hear. The bigger the sob story, the better they do." Mr. Carson snorted when he laughed. "More than likely the girl got beat up fighting with another beggar over something they found in a Dumpster behind one of these restaurants."

Phineas's frown said he didn't believe Mr. Carson. Or didn't want to believe him. "So why did you give them money?"

Mr. Carson sipped from a soda can and then burped gently. "You did a good thing, bringing them here, feeding them what little you had. That's a generous spirit. They'll remember that and maybe somewhere down the line, they'll pay it forward."

"Even if they took advantage of us?"

"They were hungry and you fed them. They were thirsty for more than just water, and you gave them what they needed. They'll remember your kindness. They might think twice about pulling the wool over someone else's eyes."

"They'll remember the ten bucks you gave them." Caleb groaned. "And my ice cream bar."

Esther laughed. "Just like you to think of your ice cream."

"Easy for you to say. You ate yours before they could get it."

This time everyone laughed. Phineas slid from his seat and stood outside the van. Deborah took the opportunity to do the same, closing the door behind her. Phineas began to stalk up and down in the narrow space between the van and an RV. Deborah wanted to grab his arm and make him stand still. "He's right. Helping someone can't be wrong, even if they don't appreciate it or they try to take advantage of you."

"I feel . . . swindled."

"You can rest easy knowing your heart is in the right place."

He stopped pacing, his back to her. "What do you know about my heart?"

"Why are you like this with me?"

He traced a crack in the asphalt with his boot. "I don't know."

Deborah turned to open the van door.

"Did you know your mudder likes my daed and he likes her?"

She stopped, her hand on the door. "Jah."

"What do you think of that?"

She turned to face him. "I think it's a private thing between them only."

"And what about Stephen?"

"I don't think we pick the people we lieb." Of that she was sure or she wouldn't be standing here in the blazing sun talking to the most stubborn, prickly, know-it-all man in the world. In her world. He filled up her world, whether she liked it or not. Mostly she didn't. Like it. "I pray every day that Gott's will be done. Then I pray that Gott will favor Mordecai."

"For his sake or for yours?"

Phineas was also a very smart man. "Both. And for my mudder's sake. Your daed has waited twelve years. He's kind. He's good. He's . . . funny."

"You like him?"

"Jah." She sighed and turned back to the van. She didn't want him to see the feeling she couldn't hide. "I do."

"Give me time."

Deborah had given him time. She would give him more. She had no choice. That didn't mean she had to like it. She tugged open the door and climbed in, ignoring Esther's curious look from where she sat in the middle row. She shut the door and left Phineas standing in the blistering heat of the midafternoon sun a few yards from Mexico.

Deborah felt as if she were the one wandering alone in a foreign country.

———

Phineas raised his face to the sun. The heat felt good. Sweat slid from his temples into his hair, but he didn't bother to wipe it away. Deborah's question reverberated in his head. Why was he like that with her? Why couldn't he let down his guard and keep it down? Because he couldn't bear the thought of what would happen when she saw the real him. It had nothing to do with his face or his scars. How could a woman like Deborah Lantz have any interest in someone so messed up inside? Inside and out.

He kicked at a rock and stubbed the toe of his boot. "Whatever," he muttered.

The van door slid open and he turned, thinking he would have another chance to explain himself to Deborah. Or defend himself, he wasn't sure which it was. Instead, Esther popped through the door and hopped onto the steamy asphalt. She slung the door shut, turned, and planted her feet, hands on her hips. "What are you doing out here, besides getting heatstroke and sunburn?"

"I like the heat." He turned his back on his sister. "Feels good on my face."

He could say that to Esther. She had a way about her that was different from his brothers, who always seemed to be looking for a way to avoid the obvious. They worked side by side for days on end but, by silent agreement, kept their mouths shut. She shrugged and leaned against the van, arms crossed. "What were you and Deborah jawing about?"

"None of your business."

"When did that ever stop me?"

Phineas snorted. Esther was so like their father. She had more opinions than their momma cat had kittens. Which was saying plenty. "We were talking about Daed and her mudder."

"I reckon everyone can see what's going on there. What else?"

"What do you mean, what else?"

"You're an idiot, bruder."

"Name calling is never necessary."

"It's not name calling when it's true."

"Whatever you're wanting to say, schweschder, spit it out."

Esther straightened and sauntered over to stand next to him, her back to the van. "What I'm saying is Deborah got into the van just now looking like she lost her best friend. It's obvious she likes you. It's also obvious you like her. The problem is so do others."

A band like leather tightened around Phineas's chest. He struggled to draw a breath. He bent and scooped up another rock. It felt hot in his hand. He tightened his fingers around it until the sharp edges bit into his skin, a bittersweet pain. Others. Who? He flung the rock at a cement-and-dirt median bereft of plant life. "You don't know what you're talking about."

"I saw Will Glick talking to her at a singing." Esther's voice softened. "I see the way he looks at her during church. He's biding his time, working up his courage. He doesn't have a lot of choices when it comes to courting and Deborah will make a good fraa. What I'm saying is she has shown herself to be a kind person who longs to have something more with you. The question is what do you want?"

The sun had nothing to do with the heat that scorched Phineas's face. He longed to walk away, but he had nowhere to go in this town bordering on a foreign country. He wanted his open fields and his beehives. He wanted to stop talking and hear the wind blow and the bees buzzing with contentment. Will Glick wanted to court Deborah. Phineas shouldn't be surprised, yet he found it hard to draw a breath. "Not something I plan to talk to you about. It's private."

"I may be younger than you, but I know more about this man-woman stuff." Esther sounded pleased with that fact. "I know how Deborah feels. I feel that way about someone too. Her heart is vulnerable to you. It's a gift. Take it before someone else does."

She spun around and opened the van door, to Phineas's great relief. Esther couldn't understand. She was his sister, but even he could see she was pleasing to the eye and she might think he didn't know, but he had eyes in his head. Her special friend, Adam Glick, was unmarred as well. A hard worker and faithful. He would make a good husband for Esther.

Phineas worked hard at being solitary. He had his beehives and his bird-watching. He liked living alone on his little farm on the back road. He didn't like singings or social frolics. When he smashed into that highway face-first, he'd lost more than his looks, he'd lost a piece of his heart. In all these years, he hadn't found a way to replace it.

Esther looked back. "She's what you've been looking for, bruder. She's the peace you need."

She closed the van door behind her with a bang.

Peace. Phineas closed his eyes. A tiny sprout of hope burst from the barren soil in his heart and stretched, green and fresh, toward the sun. *Gott, please.*

It wasn't much of a prayer, but it was more than he'd mustered in a long time. He had no right to ask for anything, but in this moment, in this place in time, his heart's desire was stronger than any guilt or remorse, any shame.

Please.

THIRTY-ONE

Flopping one hand in the air to ward off a swarm of mosquitoes, Deborah ripped open the envelope the second she plopped down on the back step. Her favorite place for reading letters. No one looked over her shoulder or clamored for her to read aloud. She was selfish. She wanted to absorb Frannie's letter first, before she had to share her news with everyone. Frannie was a cousin and family, so the letter was considered fair game for everyone even though it was addressed to Deborah. But knowing Frannie, this would be a letter to be read in private first.

Trying to ignore the sunburn that had turned hot and made her skin feel as if it were about to peel off since their return to Bee County late the previous evening, she squinted against the early-morning sun and began to read Frannie's fat block handwriting.

Dear Deborah,

We're settled in with Onkel Keith and Aenti Lois. They only have four kinner, so there's plenty of room for us. Daed went right to work cutting hay, and Mudder is busy sewing baby clothes and making blankets for this winter. To think we might get to learn to ice skate on the pond and build snowmen and have snowball fights. I've only dreamt of such things 'til now. Onkel got me a job cleaning house for an Englisch family in town. I'll get paid next week. Can't wait. You need to come up here. There's more work. Lots of Englisch families wanting to hire Plain girls to clean. We're cheap and we do a good job. Even your mudder could get a job cleaning at the motel on the highway. The Ordnung here allows us women to work as long as it doesn't interfere with family. If Aenti Abigail isn't set on marrying Stephen, she can start over here as easy as there. She's moved once. What's one more time?

Deborah snorted, then looked around. No one lurked in the shadows to hear her. Leave it to Frannie to oversimplify. Of course, Frannie didn't know about Mordecai. No one did. Except Phineas. Who knew everything and saw everything—except how much she cared for him. Why did Mudder keep seeing Stephen if she had feelings for Mordecai? Why didn't Mordecai step up? People would have to be blind not to see how Mordecai looked at her mother when she wasn't looking. With this strange, mournful expression. How he looked away every time Mudder cast a glance toward him, her expression just as odd and bewildered. Did older folks somehow forget what all those feelings meant?

Deborah wanted to shake them both. Mordecai was a good father, a hard worker, he had a kind heart, and he told funny stories. His farm was neat and as clean as possible in the dust bowl of south Texas. It wasn't much different from the others, but he did his best. He and Mudder were right for each other.

Gott's will.

She wiped at the sweat on her forehead, sighed, and went back to reading.

We went down to the Ozarks for three days right after we arrived. Onkel Keith wanted to go before school started back up and before Mudder got too big. We caught some whopper trout and made fried pies and roasted marshmallows after dark.

Write me. I'm dying to know what's going on between you and Phin. You can tell me. Who would I tell? I don't know a soul here. My cousins are all too young to be any good to talk to. Come see us when you can. Drag Phin with you. I can't believe I'm saying this, but I miss his sourpuss face. I reckon he can tend bees anywhere. People do love their honey. Write me. Soon.

Hugs
Your cousin Frannie

Like she had a bunch of relatives named Frannie. Like Phineas would ever leave this place. Especially with her. She doubted her mother was interested in going anywhere either. Moving once had been enough. It cost money and uprooted the family. And she still seemed stuck with Stephen. Even if he had been stomping around with a peeved look on his face ever since Mudder decided to get that passport card and take a trip to Mexico. With Mordecai. Who came back looking as peeved as Stephen. These old folks had done this before. Why was it so hard for them to do it again? They had practice. They had years of experience. She had an excuse. She had almost none.

A squeaking noise made her jump.

"Deborah."

She looked back. Mudder stood with the screen door propped open. "Come on, I need you to help me pack."

"Pack?" Maybe she was wrong after all. The letter fluttered

to her feet. Her heart squeezed in a sudden painful hiccup. Did Mudder want to move back to Tennessee or to Missouri? What about Phineas? She couldn't leave Phineas. She hopped up. Much as she wanted out of this place, she couldn't leave Phineas. "We just got here. We can't leave. What did Stephen say?"

"I thought you wanted to go home." Mudder's smile lacked merriment. "One minute you want one thing, one minute, something else. Don't worry. We're just moving up the road to Leroy's house."

"What about Mordecai?"

Mudder winced as if her tooth still hurt her. "What about Mordecai?"

"I thought—"

Mudder let the screen door slam. "Hurry up. We've taken advantage of his hospitality long enough."

"Did something happen?"

"I asked Samuel to hitch the horses and bring up the wagon."

"Now? We're moving now?"

"Jah, now."

Deborah trotted into the house behind Mudder, whose pace suggested a pack of coyotes chased her. What was the hurry? In the bedroom, Deborah found Leila and Rebekah stuffing clothes into trash bags while Hazel sat on the bed, arms wrapped around her favorite doll. They looked as surprised as she felt.

"Don't just stand there. Help." Mudder swept a pile of Hazel's clothes into a worn suitcase that already held her own clothes. "I'd like to get this done before lunch. I want to help Naomi with the canning this afternoon."

"When did all this get decided?" Deborah asked, but it was too late. Mudder headed out the door, suitcase in one hand, bag in the other.

Deborah glanced at Leila. Her sister shrugged and dumped clothes into another smaller bag. "She didn't tell us either."

"I'll try to talk to her."

"A lot of good it'll do you."

"Try." Rebekah smoothed a hand over the faded patch quilt on the bed. "I like it here. Susan is nice, and Mordecai is funny and he tells good stories. Like Daed did."

"I know. Me too." Deborah hoisted a trash bag to her shoulder and made her way to the door. "I don't think Leroy will tell stories and be a fountain of useless facts."

And he wouldn't tell her what Phineas's favorite foods were either.

"And he won't play in the rain or give us bread and honey in the middle of the afternoon." Leila's dispirited tone matched her grim expression. "Mostly, I'm just tired of moving from one house to another where we don't belong."

"Me too." Rebekah plopped down on the end of the bed, her eyes bright with tears. "I'm so homesick."

Deborah dropped the bag on the floor and went back to her sisters. "I know." She hugged each one in succession. They returned the favor. Despite the fact that nothing had changed, she felt better. "We'll be fine as long as we stick together."

"Together," Hazel sang as she held up her tattered doll and made it sing with her. "Fine, fine, fine."

The other girls giggled. "Fine, fine, fine," Rebekah sang.

"Fine, fine, fine." Deborah joined in on the impromptu song. Nothing would ever be fine again, but her sisters needed her to believe. "Fine, fine, fine."

They all laughed.

"What are you girls doing?" Mudder stood in the doorway, hands on her hips. "We'll never get moved at this rate."

"We're fine." Deborah picked up her bag and brushed past her mother. "Can't you see how fine we are?"

Mudder followed after her. "I'm sorry this is hard for you girls. It's not easy for me either, but it's for the best."

Ignoring the sweat that trickled down her temples, Deborah dumped the trash bag into the back of the wagon that now sat in front of the house. Samuel was nowhere in sight. She turned to face Mudder. "Why are we moving out of Mordecai's house? All we've done in the last few months is move again and again. I thought we were staying here until you . . ."

She couldn't bring herself to say the words aloud. Until Mudder married Stephen.

"Leroy offered to take us in until . . . November."

Deborah waited for Mudder to elaborate. She didn't. She'd been prickly as the cacti that lined the roads on the trip back yesterday and barely had a word to say after evening prayers before bedtime. Deborah thought it had something to do with work the dentist had done on her teeth. But her mood seemed even blacker now, if that was possible. "Why?"

"Once we get to Leroy's, you're to keep an eye on your sister."

"Which one?"

"Don't be dense." Mudder dumped another bag of clothes into the wagon. Where was Samuel and why wasn't he helping with the heavy lifting? "Leila. Because of Jesse."

"How do you know about Jesse?"

"Mothers know everything."

"Everything?"

Mudder's grim smile spoke volumes. "Much more than you realize."

"What does that mean?"

"It means it's a good thing Phineas moved out on his own. It wasn't proper for you two to live in the same house. We'll be living in the bishop's house now. I expect you to be on your best behavior."

"I always am."

Mudder stopped shoving bags and looked back. Her frown eased. "I know. This has been hard for everyone, but we'll be settled by the end of the year."

"Maybe we should move to Missouri. Frannie likes it there. She says it's greener and it's already starting to cool off. They might even get snow this winter."

"You really want to move to Missouri?" Mudder blotted her forehead with her sleeve. Sweat darkened the bodice of her dress. Weary lines around her mouth and eyes made her look old. "Even though you have a reason to stay now?"

"It doesn't matter what I think. The decision is yours." Deborah avoided addressing her mother's oblique reference to Phineas. It was a private matter and much too big a mess to begin to explain. "We would all have to move, wouldn't we?"

"You're a grown woman. It's time I started treating you like one."

Since when? Mudder had sidestepped the underlying question. Deborah rubbed her forehead where the beginnings of a headache pulsed. "Do *you* not have a reason to stay anymore?"

"Truth be told, I'm not sure."

"After everything I've said and done, you're not sure?" Stephen's voice, filled with disbelief, boomed. "Where are you going? Are you leaving?"

He strode around the end of the wagon, his face red—redder than usual. His big hands were fisted. "I knew it. It's Mordecai, isn't it? He's declared himself to you, hasn't he?"

"Mordecai?" Deborah looked from Stephen to her mother. "Did he finally—?"

"Go inside." Mudder slapped her hands on her hips. "Now."

Deborah went, but not without casting another quick look at the two faces. She saw no love in either. She saw trepidation. A fear of loss in one and a fear of the unknown in the other.

———

"I planned to come talk to you after we got moved." Abigail edged toward the door. Stephen moved with her, the set of his broad shoulders rigid with anger. "We're moving in with Leroy's family."

It would make Stephen happy if he'd take a minute or two to calm down. His expression eased from anger to bewilderment. "Why?"

"We've relied on Mordecai's hospitality long enough." Her words were true, but they didn't encompass the entire truth. She wouldn't tell Stephen of Mordecai's declaration in Progreso. It was between him and her. "I don't want to become a burden. Leroy agreed. It's best to pass that burden around. He says to send Caleb over as well. He has room and he'll put him to work."

"What happened in Progreso?" Stephen followed her into the house, so close on her heels she could smell his man scent of sweat and hard work. "You haven't told me about your trip."

"Nothing happened. We went to the beach. I got the cavity in my tooth filled. We came home."

And she realized something that couldn't be denied. Mordecai wasn't the only one with feelings. She couldn't stay in his house. It wasn't proper. If he wanted to court her, he would have to do it the traditional way.

Abigail didn't want to move again. She liked it here, but they couldn't stay. It would only get harder. She didn't want to burden the bishop and his family either.

She needed her own place. *Gott, help me find my place here.*

Stephen grabbed her arm, forcing her to stop and turn. "I want to talk to Leroy about announcing the banns."

She tugged her arm away. "I'm sorry, so sorry." She would never be ready. How did she tell Stephen this? "I never meant to hurt you. I thought things would be different now, but they're not."

He crossed his arms, his face mottled red with anger. "I can't believe this is happening again. It wasn't enough that you threw away my affection for you the first time. You're doing it again?"

"What's going on?"

Abigail turned. Mordecai stood in the doorway. He let the screen door slam behind him.

Abigail hadn't heard him come in, such had been her focus on Stephen. As usual, Butch accompanied his adopted owner. His tail wagged as he trotted into the room and made a beeline for her, his nose cold and wet on her hand. She focused on giving him a quick pet and trying to collect her thoughts at the same time. "I'm packing."

"I saw your things in the wagon."

"I asked Susan if we could borrow it." Abigail backed away from the two men. Her hip bumped the desk. The kerosene lamp teetered. She snatched it back just as it would've tumbled to the floor. Her heart banged against her ribs. "I'll have Leila bring it back if you'll have Samuel give her a ride to Leroy's after."

"You're moving into Leroy's house?"

"She is." Stephen stepped into the gap between them. "Just until—"

"For now." Abigail cut him off. His face darkened another shade. He didn't like to be interrupted. Stephen should not speak for her. His thoughts and opinions would not govern her actions. She'd tried to fit herself into his mold and found it impossible. "Thank you for letting us stay with you. For sharing your home and your food."

"No need for thanks. Neighbors help neighbors. You more than made up for it with all the work you did around the house and the garden." Mordecai spoke as if Stephen didn't stand between them. "We enjoyed the company."

Deborah poked her head from the hallway. "Is everything—?"

"Go back to the room."

"But—"

"Now. I'll come get you girls when I'm ready to load the rest of our things. Go."

Her face set in disapproving lines that reminded Abigail of her own mother, Deborah whirled and disappeared down the hall.

"I need a word with Abigail." Stephen took a step toward her, but his gaze stayed on Mordecai. "You can get back to work. I'll take care of any help she needs."

"Jah. I'm sure you will." Mordecai's gaze stayed on Abigail. She could feel it boring into her, as if he wanted to discern what was in her head and in her heart. "Why not stay for supper? You too, Stephen. Susan has promised buttered noodles and baked squash. I smelled oatmeal cinnamon cookies baking earlier."

Abigail marched around Stephen. She didn't need him to speak for her, but the last thing she wanted was to eat while sitting at the table with these two men. "It's a long time until supper and we have unpacking to do. Naomi is expecting me. I told her I'd help her pickle the last of the okra and cucumbers this afternoon."

"Everyone has expectations that don't get met." His blue-green eyes full of a sadness that engulfed Abigail, Mordecai touched the brim of his hat. "See you when we see you, then. Come on, Butch. That honey isn't going to harvest itself."

"Mordecai, I—" The screen door slammed on her whispered response.

Stephen's gaze whipped from the door to Abigail. "What was that all about?"

"Nothing."

Not a thing. Not unless she stepped up and made it something. The sadness in Mordecai's face ate at her. She saw there a reflection of her own aching heart. Tomorrow morning she would get up and help Naomi make breakfast. Mordecai would not sit across the table and entertain her with little-known facts about the life cycle of mosquitoes or weather patterns in the tropics.

He wouldn't slather a piece of bread with honey and hand it to her as if it were a slice of the best cake in the world.

His voice wouldn't call to her from the swing in the backyard, reminding her to come out and enjoy the beauty of the setting sun before bidding her good night.

"See you when we see you."

"It doesn't look like nothing to me." Stephen crossed his arms over his chest. "Why are you standing there looking mournful?"

Stephen was better at reading faces than she had imagined. Abigail remembered to shut her mouth. She cleared her throat. "Stephen, I can't do this."

"You can't move to Leroy's? You're the one who said you wanted to do it, without even talking to me first. Now you've made a commitment. He's the bishop."

"Nee, we'll move into Leroy's house now. But then I'm going to look for a place of my own. For my family."

Time to stand on her own two feet. Time to figure out what she wanted from life on her terms. She would care for her family. She would do this right, one step at a time.

"You'll buy a house? By yourself? Why would you do that? You'll marry and have to sell it again. That makes no sense."

"I need to have my own place to raise my family. I have what's left of the money from the sale of my farm."

"What's left of our nest egg."

He refused to admit defeat. He refused to see what was right in front of him. Abigail couldn't marry him because she didn't love him. "My nest egg. When you have an income from the expanded orchards, you can pay me back. There's no hurry."

"Pay you back? I thought we were sharing in an expense for our future."

"So did I. But I no longer can see a future that we share."

"I don't understand. Is it you or all women?" Stephen put his hands up as if surrendering to unseen forces. Anger gave way to pain. The same heartbreaking pain Abigail had seen in his face all those years ago. "I've been patient. I've been more than patient. I've put up with more than any man would. No Plain woman buys her own farm. It's not done. It's not proper."

"I'm so sorry, so very sorry. I know I'm hurting you, but it's better to do it now before it's too late. I know you can't understand, but it's for the best. I'll talk to Leroy. I'll explain."

Her heart pounded at the thought. Surely the bishop would not have her marry for security. Marriage between a man and woman was more than that. It was a commitment between two people that bound them for life. Not for a farm.

"It's not me, is it?" Stephen lifted his hat and ran a hand through his hair. "It's you, surely. It has to be. I did everything I could, didn't I?"

"Yes, you did. You're right, it's me." No doubt about that. But it didn't make her a bad person. She knew that now. It made her . . . vigilant over her family and her heart. "I thought I knew what I wanted, but now I know I have to do what's best for my kinner, and being yoked to a man I don't love isn't best for them or me."

"There's someone else, isn't there? Just like last time." Stephen loomed over her. His pulse jumped in his temple. "It's happening again. You're in love with someone else. You led me on."

"That wasn't my intent."

He slapped his hat back on his head, his expression hard. "So there's no hope?"

"I'm sorry."

"I'll drop Caleb at Leroy's later." His Adam's apple bobbed. "He's helping me pick cantaloupe this afternoon."

"That's fine."

"It'll have to be. It's not the boy's fault." Stephen stomped through the screen door and let it slam. If this kept up, the poor screen door would be in shambles on the floor. He glanced back, his face blurred in the gray mesh netting of the screen. "It's your loss, not mine. I'll not waste another moment thinking of you."

His bellow likely was heard all the way to the barn. Mordecai might even hear it and know she no longer had obligations to another.

Abigail hoped not. She wasn't ready for what Mordecai offered her. She needed time and she intended to take it.

THIRTY-TWO

Deborah padded around the wagon, the withered, yellow grass cracking under her sneakers. The early September heat burned the back of her neck. Despite the bank of dark, rolling clouds glowering on the southern horizon, not a breath of wind stirred. The leaves hung listless in the live oak trees that dotted a yard more dirt than grass. The heat burned her nostrils when she inhaled. Her parched throat hurt with the effort to swallow.

She tugged a box loaded with the last of the grape jam from the wagon and marched toward the Combination Store. They needed rain. Soon. They still had some produce, thanks to the irrigation, but the chickens had stopped producing, and Naomi had resorted to butchering the older hens for frying. Some crops could be planted late into winter in this climate, much to Deborah's amazement, but putting meat on the table was another story. Talk at the supper table the previous night informed her that deer-hunting season didn't begin until early November. Same with turkey.

Maybe they'd have turkey in time for Thanksgiving. In the meantime, canned venison would do.

She needed to find a way to earn money to help with buying what they couldn't grow, raise, or hunt. If she managed to find a job in Beeville, how would she get there? Horseback? Her family didn't own its own horses or buggy. Mother had sold those too. Her mind running in four directions, she stuck her knee up to steady the box and tugged open the door with her free hand. Sultry air no cooler than what bathed her outside wafted in her face.

"Can I help you with that?" Mordecai appeared in the door, arms outstretched. "Looks heavy."

"Nee. I've got it." She wrapped her arms tighter around the box. She hadn't seen Mordecai since they moved from his house two weeks earlier. She hadn't expected to see him here. "It's the last of the grape jam."

Holding the door open for her, Mordecai backed away so she could enter. Butch, who lolled in the middle of the aisle in front of a display of straw hats, rose and barked as if announcing her arrival. His wide snout made it look as if he were smiling his welcome.

"Jah, Butch, we know." Mordecai wagged a finger at the dog. "You're glad to see her. We all are."

The dog flopped back on the floor, tongue hanging from his panting mouth.

"Hey, Butch." She settled the box on the floor next to the dog and gave him a pet, trying to hide her surprise at Mordecai's statement. "I figured you were pleased to get your house back."

"It's been mighty quiet without the gaggle of Lantz girls." He shrugged, but something in his expression told her the words were an understatement. He swept a hand toward the display of jellies and jams. "The shelf is a mite crowded still."

"The last batch hasn't sold?" She peered around him. Yep.

The dozen jars she'd delivered the previous week sat untouched next to Mordecai's honey. "I guess Leroy didn't tell Naomi her jars were still on the shelf."

"Probably not, right next to the honey." He leaned down and picked up a jar of strawberry jam, holding it as if it were precious and fragile in his big hand. "I'm not worried about the honey. It's good to have a supply. The bees will stop producing when it turns cold and then demand will exceed supply."

"It gets cold here?" Leave it to Mordecai to slip a bee fact into idle conversation. Deborah tried to imagine a crisp, cold fall day in this place. She simply couldn't. "When?"

He chuckled and settled the jar on the shelf. "Cooler, let's put it that way. Sometime around Thanksgiving. Maybe. Definitely by Christmas. In the forties sometimes. Doesn't last long, though."

"I can't wait. It's hot enough to fry an egg on the porch." And make toast too.

"Yep, doesn't help sales either. The hotter it gets and the less produce we have, the fewer folks make the trip out here from town. Broccoli isn't a big seller for some reason." Smiling, Mordecai picked up two more jars from her box and squeezed them onto the shelf. "Folks are spoiled by air-conditioning. They don't want to come out in the heat. Especially when the good stuff like the tomatoes and cantaloupe is all gone."

"Where're Leroy and Jesse?" The Glicks generally ran the store, started by Leroy's daed when he moved to Bee County from Tennessee twenty years earlier. They shared the proceeds, but everyone knew the store belonged to the Glick family. "They left the house this morning headed this way. Leastways, I thought they did."

"I came in to drop off some candles and lip balm. Leroy asked me to stay a spell while they went to look at a horse. Gilbert Berkley wants Leroy to break him to a saddle." Mordecai scooted the box under the shelf, straightened, and dusted his hands off. "And he got another order for a custom-made buggy today. Some lady down south who thinks she needs an *authentic* Amish buggy in her yard. Only she wants it to have orange trim."

Deborah giggled. Mordecai's gift of gab hadn't changed. He made her feel grown-up and an equal. Not like Stephen, who wanted her to be a daughter he could discipline and advise and boss around. "What did Leroy say to that?"

"He said she had to pay in full up front because no one else would buy it. Not in these parts."

They both laughed. Deborah ducked her head and busied herself arranging the rest of the jars. "How's—?"

"How's—?"

They both stopped. Deborah sneaked a glance at Mordecai. A red flush darkened his tanned face. She took pity on him. "Mudder is doing all right, if that is what you were planning to ask me."

"It was just an idle question."

"It's polite to ask about folks."

Mordecai's smile lit up the store. Phineas looked so like him. "And I'm always so polite. Almost as polite as the Englisch folks who come in here."

"I know when I get home, Mudder will ask me if anything interesting happened at the store."

"What will you tell her?"

"That you have a new job tending store and you do a fairly good job at it."

He chuckled again, a deep, rich sound. Phineas should do

more of that. Mordecai turned his back and sauntered behind the counter. "So, ask me your question."

Mordecai had eyes in his head. He knew what was going on between his son and her. Or not going on. He'd made that clear the night she'd stumbled upon him in the kitchen before dawn. "How is Phineas?"

"Pining away."

"Pining away?"

"Living alone and pretending he likes it, but all the while, pining away."

"I never would've expected such a flight of fancy from a grown man such as yourself."

Mordecai shrugged. "Looks can be deceiving. As we all know."

All Deborah knew was that she hadn't seen Phineas since their last conversation outside the van in Weslaco. No bumping into each other in the middle of the road. It had been an off week for services so no sneaking a peek at him during the sermon. Nothing. He'd said he needed time, and it was evident he meant it. She worked to keep her face neutral. She didn't need Mordecai telling Phineas she was doing her own pining.

"I hear your mudder is thinking about buying your onkel's property."

Mordecai had his own reason to pine, apparently. Deborah felt for him. She knew exactly how that felt. Despite the age difference and the fact that he was a widow with children, they were fellow sojourners on a road that seemed full of potholes and unexpected detours.

"She went to the bank yesterday, but last night she said she didn't want to talk about it." A woman owning a farm here and working it without a husband, that was a path not to be walked lightly. Deborah rearranged the jars, grape on one side, strawberry on the other. "Onkel John would feel mighty strange selling it to his own sister. He'd want to give it to her, but he can't afford it, I'm sure. I was thinking . . ."

"You were thinking. That's almost always a good thing."

Phineas came by his penchant for sarcasm from Mordecai apparently. "We don't have a horse and buggy. We'll need one to work and sell our own produce and such. How much does a buggy cost?"

"Better to get a wagon." He grabbed a pencil and began to add up the purchases of an elderly Englisch lady who had picked up a candle and some of the lip balm he'd made. "Cheaper. But your mudder knows enough to talk to Leroy about it. She's already talked to Andrew about two horses."

"She has?"

"Abigail knows what's needed to run a farm in these parts. She doesn't necessarily tell you everything."

But she told Mordecai? When? On those nights when she'd sat in a folding lawn chair a dozen yards from Mordecai's chair and they watched the same sunset, together but apart? Or had they talked since she moved her family from his house? Had there been a flashlight in the window and Deborah had missed it? "Why not?"

He folded the lady's bills and tucked them into a metal box on the counter next to a handwritten sign that listed the prices for a variety of produce—none of which they had in the store now. "She wants you to do your chores, watch out for your bruders and schweschders, and not worry. She's being both mudder and daed."

So she was. "I thought I could get a job in town."

"The district has permitted that a few times. Mostly with the boys, though. Have you asked your mudder about it?"

"Nee, not yet."

"Talk to her first." Mordecai waved at a young Englisch couple holding hands like newlyweds who slipped out the door without buying one thing. "She'll have to decide if that's something she wants her girls doing, and then if she does, she should talk to Leroy."

"I know. I don't think—"

The door opened and a man shaped like an enormous pear waddled through it, bringing with him a gust of hot, dank air. Butch hopped to his feet once again and barked, this time his tone surly.

"Butch! Stop it. Out. Out!" Mordecai waved the dog out the open door. Growling deep in his throat, Butch stalked through it. "Sorry about that, Jerry. Come on in."

"No problem. Good guard dogs are hard to come by. Good to see you, good to see you." The man started talking the second he crossed the threshold, his bushy, silver mustache bobbing in time. "Just stopping by because I know you folks ain't got Internet out here and it's not like you're sitting around the boob tube watching the weather channel."

"What is it?"

"The storm in the Gulf got upgraded to a category-three hurricane this morning." The man paused to run a red bandana across his forehead above round wire-rimmed spectacles and then across his sunburned bald head. "And it's gathering steam, could be a category four by late this afternoon."

"Where will it hit land?"

"They're thinking it'll be somewhere between Corpus and

Beaumont." The man stuffed the bandana into the back pocket of red-and-black checkered pants belted below his potbelly. His gaze went to Deborah as if registering her presence for the first time. "Sorry, ma'am. I guess you're new here. Jerry Cummings."

Mordecai made quick work of the introduction. "Deborah and her family have lived here about four months now."

"Welcome. I guess this will be your first hurricane."

Deborah reckoned it would. She'd experienced a tornado and some downright bad storms, but no hurricanes in Tennessee. "I reckon it's probably a lot like the tornadoes we had back home."

"Just as cantankerous. Hurricanes are straight—high winds and heavy rain like you've never seen before. Eighty-five miles an hour or more. Sometimes tornadoes spin off them to make the situation worse."

"But hurricanes come from the ocean. We're a long way from the ocean."

"The big ones, like this one, just keep on coming through the Gulf until they run out of steam, and this looks to be a big one. We don't get the full force of it, but plenty of wind and rain. Sometimes flooding."

"Nothing we can't handle." His features the picture of calm, Mordecai handed Jerry a bag of oatmeal chocolate chip cookies. The man took them with a nod and a smile. Mordecai grinned back at him. "We mostly get the rain and some wind. We board up the houses and hunker down in the basements if it gets too bad. Last time we told some good stories. The kinner get a kick out of it."

"True, true. I also thought you should know they've already set in motion the evac plan for the prisoners."

"Prisoners?" Deborah's mind's eye conjured up the bus with

its DOCJ lettering on the side that she'd seen outside the medical clinic in Beeville. "What does this have to do with prisoners?"

"If it looks like they're gonna take a hit in Cuero, they evac their state prisoners to McConnell. Just up the road."

"I see." She did. They'd lost a house to fire and now hurricane-force winds and torrential rains were next, bringing with them a herd of criminals. A different series of plagues? "But they never escape, do they?"

"You never heard of the Texas Seven?"

"Like I said, she's new." Mordecai helped himself to a cookie from Jerry's bag. Jerry chomped on one the size of a saucer and chewed. Both men made her wait for a response while they enjoyed Naomi Glick's best cookie recipe. "A few years ago seven prisoners escaped from the Connally Unit down in Kenedy, Texas. They was eventually all caught, but not before they shot and killed a police officer up in Irving."

Despite the heat, goose bumps rippled up Deborah's arm. "That's sad."

"It is, but it's the only time it's happened in all the years I've been here." Mordecai brushed crumbs from his beard and reached for another cookie. "No point in looking for trouble. We need to set our minds to getting ready for a nice storm. We can use the rain."

"Best batten down the hatches. We'll have the evacuation centers open in town." Crumbs settled onto Jerry's mustache. Grinning, he brushed them away. "A good mustache serves as a better cookie duster than a beard, you know. Y'all are welcome to come into town."

Mordecai shook his head. "We have basements."

"That's what I figured. Do you have enough plywood to board up your windows?"

"We'll be fine. Take some honey home to your wife." Mordecai held out a jar. "I know how she likes it on her toast."

Jerry pulled a worn leather billfold the size of a large waffle from his pocket, but Mordecai waved away his money. "On the house for taking the time to be so neighborly."

"Take care." Jerry waved stubby, fat fingers at Deborah. "Tie down everything that can't be brought in. Take care of your animals."

"We will."

Deborah watched him go, then turned to Mordecai. "What do we do first?"

"I'll close the store and start boarding the windows here." He tapped his fingers on the glass countertop, his forehead wrinkled. "Run back to the house and let Naomi and your mother know. Have them send the boys out to tell folks."

He paused, a pulse jumping in his jaw. "Send Caleb to let Phineas know."

Before she could take the time to reflect on it, her mouth opened and she made the offer. "I can do it."

After a fleeting second of indecision, Mordecai shook his head. "Nee, tell the women first."

"You could tell him yourself."

"I have to board up here and then get to Susan. My oldest son and his fraa are at the house today." His gaze dropped for a brief second, then met Deborah's. "There's a baby coming."

She ducked her head. "Everyone will be fine."

"I know. Go tell your mudder—I mean, go tell Naomi."

Mordecai was worried about Mudder. Surely he saw her worry for Phineas. "I will."

And then she would find Phineas.

She tromped from the store. The patches of blue sky that had lingered overhead when she entered it had fled, chased by the massive, roiling black clouds that had once hung on the horizon. The wind kicked up dirt in her face. Deborah shivered in the dank, heavy air. If Phineas hadn't been so intent on getting away from her, he wouldn't be alone right now.

She would find him and tell him that.

THIRTY-THREE

Rain clouds hung so low Abigail could feel their bounty of sweet water brush her face. The fierce heat and humidity pummeled her body, dampening her dress. Rain would be a relief. She tugged the basket of old towels from the buggy and laid the canvas bag filled with her birthing-baby supplies on top of it. Abram King's fraa had picked quite a day to have her baby. Rather, the baby had chosen a whopper of a day to come into this world.

She smiled to herself. She surely knew about that. Deborah had been born in the middle of a late-spring snowstorm, while Rebekah had caught her off guard at a school fund-raiser auction. Babies had minds of their own when it came to these things.

That train of thought naturally drove her right where she didn't want to go. Mordecai. Another one with a mind of his own. She didn't see him boarding up the windows on his house. Only Abram and Samuel. Maybe he had taken on the back side or was out making sure the livestock were tucked inside the barn.

Sooner or later he would come inside and see her.

Nothing she could do about that. Naomi and the kinner were busy boarding up their house and loading in supplies to the basement for the long night ahead. Leila and Rebekah would ride herd on Hazel and Caleb. That left Abigail to assist with this birth. She'd never been through a hurricane-spawned storm, but she had a passing acquaintance with all manner of bad weather. They would all do what they had to do, even if that meant being uncomfortable around Mordecai.

Uncomfortable. There was an understatement. Just the thought of his gaze made her stomach flop and her breath catch. *Stop it. Stop it now.* She wasn't a teenage girl suffering from puppy love.

The *clip-clop* of horse hooves made her look back as she approached the Kings' porch. There he was, coming up the road. Plain as day. Mordecai. She hadn't even made it in the door.

He eased from the saddle and tied the reins to the hitching post. "You're here."

"You're nothing if not observant."

"And I thought I was the one with the smart mouth."

"You are. It's catching."

He stomped up the steps, his boots leaving dusty tracks on the wooden porch. His expression was indecipherable. "Why are you here?"

"Susan sent Samuel to fetch me. It's time." Struggling for something to say in the awkward pause that followed that statement, she looked beyond him to the horse and then the road. No Butch. The dog hadn't left Mordecai's side since that first day they went to the lake. It seemed like a hundred years ago. "Where's your shadow?"

"I've been abandoned." He shrugged. "Butch apparently has taken a liking to your daughter."

A deliberate choice of words? She'd never abandoned Mordecai because he'd never been hers to abandon. But he wasn't talking about her. He was talking about a dog. She forced her tart comments back. "Daughter? I have four."

"Deborah. She came into the store to drop off the jam and he left with her. He wasn't with her when she got back to Leroy's?"

"I don't know. She stopped at the corral and told Joseph about the storm, then left again." Naomi had told her not to worry. Deborah had plenty of time to get back before the storm hit. "She said she had to go warn some other folks. How long until the weather takes a turn for the worse, do you think?"

"Not long, but there's no point in worrying about it." Mordecai tugged his hat down against wind that whipped up leaves and dirt in dervishes around them. He opened the screen door for her. "I reckon she's gone out to Phineas's place."

"What makes you think that?"

"I had to stay to mind the store for Leroy, so I told her to go back to Leroy's and tell you—tell Naomi about the storm. I figure Deborah, being her mudder's daughter and all, ignored me and went to Phineas's."

"I don't ignore you and neither did she. She came by Leroy's first. She's a good girl."

Mordecai stalked through the living room, leaving her standing there with her basket. "Theresa will be in Susan's room. I need to help the boys finish up outside and get the livestock battened down."

Gut. Better to put some distance between them. She whirled and gave him her back. A moan told her Mordecai had been right about the room. Ignoring the urge to say something snippy, she hurried back to Susan's room.

Esther met her at the door. "I'm fetching some clean sheets. Go on in. Susan could use someone to spell her."

"I'm here to help." Abigail squeezed up against the door to let the younger woman pass. Esther glowed with excitement. Probably thinking and wondering when her time would come. Every young woman did.

Susan sat perched on the edge of the double bed where Theresa huddled, her dress wrinkled and her sweaty face flushed a deep red. Susan looked up and smiled, the picture of calm. "Good, you're here. Could you bring her a glass of water to sip? Poor thing is parched." She dipped a washrag in a bowl filled with water and dabbed at Theresa's forehead and cheeks. "The wind was blowing in so much dirt, I had to close the window. We don't want the baby to get an eyeful first thing."

Abigail settled the basket on the floor and took a moment to squeeze Theresa's hand. The girl's eyes were bloodshot with tears and her fingers clammy. Abigail remembered what that first labor was like. It wasn't the pain so much as the anticipation and the uncertainty of being able do it. "The first one's the hardest. But it'll be worth it when you hold that baby in your arms, you'll see."

"I know. I'm fine." Theresa gasped and shrieked. "Another one already."

"That's gut. You're doing fine." Susan glanced at a pocket watch in her lap. She smiled up at Abigail. "About two minutes apart. It won't be long now."

"You sure you don't want me to spell you? I could sit with her while you get a drink of water and stretch your legs."

"Is Mordecai out there?"

What did that have to do with anything? "Jah, he just returned as I was arriving."

"Gut. You go. You two need to have it out, once and for all."

"Have it out? There's nothing—"

"I've been living with that man for the two weeks since you moved out, and I'm fed up with the moping around and the morose, vacant stares. I'm tired of talking to myself because he never hears me. And I'm especially tired of him not eating my cooking. The man refused a piece of pecan pie last night. This can't go on."

Mordecai wasn't eating. Most likely it had nothing to do with her. "Maybe he has a stomach bug."

"It's not his stomach that's hurting him."

"It sounds like the flu to me."

"There's only been one other time I've seen my bruder act like this." Susan patted Theresa's cheek with the wet washrag. "You're doing fine, honey. And that was twenty-five years ago. I'm telling you, it's his heart, not his stomach, giving him trouble. And there's only one cure."

"One cure?"

"Abigail Lantz, I know you're not that dense."

"Dense!"

"You broke it off with Stephen because you're a smart woman. Now do what needs to be done so the rest of us can have some peace."

Stephen had made it known to the entire community that she'd rejected his generous offer of marriage in November. Now he passed her at the Sunday service without speaking. Like a little boy denied a treat. "It's not my place—"

"I reckon Mordecai opened the door first and he didn't get the answer he wanted."

The heat of the sun on her face in Progreso and the feel of Mordecai's strong hand on her elbow assailed her. He had and she'd stumbled. She'd been weak and fearful when love presented itself in a strange, foreign country. The way love always did. Abigail turned and trudged toward the door.

"And don't forget the glass of water."

She must've answered, but she didn't remember. She marched down the hallway and out to the kitchen. Mordecai wasn't there. She proceeded out the back door. He was perched far up on a ladder, hammer in hand, a nail teetering on his lower lip.

"Could you come down here?"

He pulled the nails from his mouth. "I'm almost done. We need to move Theresa to the basement. The storm's coming faster than I expected."

"The baby's almost here."

"We have to move her." He slammed the hammer against the nail with more force than Abigail thought necessary. If he missed, he'd break a window. "There's no time. It's here."

Rain spattered against the sheet of wood and caught Abigail in the cheek. A sudden, fierce gust of wind brought leaves and pebbles with it. The sweet perfume of wet earth and rain wafted around her. "I'll tell Susan."

"What did you come out here for?"

"Nothing, I just wanted—"

"It wasn't nothing."

"Susan said you hadn't been eating."

"And you're worried about my health?" He clomped down the ladder and planted himself in front of her, the hammer swinging in one hand.

His scent of man mixed with wood enveloped her. She missed that smell. "My health is fine."

"You look a little peaked."

"So do you." He dropped the hammer in a toolbox and snapped the lid shut with more force than necessary. "Naomi's food doesn't agree with you?"

"Naomi's cooking is fine. My health is fine."

"Then we have that in common."

The rain came harder, bringing with it a wind that did nothing to cool Abigail's face. Heat burned her cheeks. Her stomach roiled. "What about other things?"

"I already told you what I thought about . . . other things."

And she turned him away. No wonder he was so bitter. "I was . . . mixed up. I had to do the right thing . . . with Stephen. Your timing was . . . off."

Another gust of wind knocked her against the house. The skies opened and the rains came. Mordecai grabbed her arm and pushed her toward the door. "As yours is now. Get Susan. I'll get Abram. He can carry his fraa down the stairs to the basement. Y'all bring what you need to finish up."

Abigail struggled with the screen door. Mordecai shoved it open. The wind ripped it from the frame and sent it sailing. "Go, hurry!"

She did as she was told. By the time she reached the bedroom door, Abram raced down the hallway. "Is the bopli here? We need to get to the basement."

"Nee, but soon—"

"Get her downstairs. Samuel, help him." Mordecai jerked his head toward the basement door. "Abigail, gather up whatever you'll need. We can put up sheets to make a place more . . . private down there."

She scurried after Abram. She grabbed her basket and dropped Susan's supplies on top of hers while Susan scrambled for a pile of blankets and sheets. Abram scooped up Theresa, who wrapped her arms around her husband's neck and buried her face in his chest, muffling ragged sobs.

They formed a single line, led by Mordecai, who held the kerosene lamp high. "Careful down the stairs, Abram. Watch your step."

The basement's still, dank air brushed Abigail's face as she inhaled its musty scent. Like every other basement in the district, the shelves were lined with canned goods, jellies, jams, green beans, okra, tomatoes, venison, and more. A bounty that would hold them over for the long winter. It also held a blessed quiet out of the whistling wind, thunder, and pelting hail.

Theresa groaned, then screamed. "Another one, another one. I'm sorry, it's another one."

Her screams echoed against the thick cement walls. Abram's face blanched. "I'm the one who's sorry."

"Nobody needs to be sorry." Susan set her lamp on a shelf and dusted off her hands. "It's the natural course of things."

"Esther, get the blankets down in the corner. We'll make a nice little bed." Abigail dropped her basket and grabbed a rolled-up rug from Esther's stack. "Mordecai, can you nail sheets from the shelves to the wall?"

"Got it."

A few minutes later they had a makeshift bed on the floor and a private, if not cozy, spot in the basement corner to deliver the baby. Not ideal, but women had been giving birth to babies for thousands of years in all sorts of places with little or no help.

Abram gently laid his fraa onto the blankets and backed away, his face, so like Mordecai's, filled with concern and a bit of relief, possibly, that he could retreat to the other side of the sheets. Theresa sank back on the makeshift bed, her breathing coming in sharp, hard gasps. "I need to push. I need to push."

"Gut girl. That's what we need now. That bopli will be here in a jiffy." Abigail grabbed her knee. Susan took the other while Esther held her sister-in-law's head against her chest, hands on her shoulders. "Push, Theresa, push. It's time for your bopli to see the world."

The basement, anyway. Abigail longed to know what was happening outside. As she encouraged and cajoled the frightened girl in front of her, she prayed her boy and girls were tucked safely away in Leroy's basement. And Deborah. Stubborn, headstrong Deborah. *Please, Gott, don't let her be swept away in this. Let her use the brain you gave her.*

The baby slipped into the world a scant few minutes later, his mouth open, his cry lusty and bewildered. Abigail grabbed a towel and laid him gently on Theresa's lap while Susan dealt with the business of the cord and the afterbirth.

"You and Abram have yourself a fine baby boy." With efficiency born of years of practice, Abigail wiped him down, cleaned his eyes, and examined him from head to toe. As perfect as only God could create. "He's a big boy, all ten fingers and all ten toes. Has his daed's nose."

Mordecai's nose.

Sobs mixed with hiccupping laughs, Theresa propped herself up, her face shiny with sweat and tears. "Abram," she called. "Abram, come see your son."

Abigail held up the sheet and slipped out as the new father slid past her, his face that sweet mixture of trepidation and elation she so often saw on men's faces at this special moment in their lives. Jacob and Samuel clapped as they followed.

She let the sheet drop on the family reunion and turned to see Mordecai sitting on the fourth step, a pocketknife in one hand, a chunk of wood in the other. His face held a different note, one of nostalgia, happiness, melancholy, longing, all combined in a bittersweet song she recognized.

"It's a boy."

"I heard."

"You don't want to see your grandchild, your first grandson?"

"Jah, but I want Abram to have his moment first." Mordecai gestured at the basement walls. "*Groossdaadis* take a backseat at these things. My turn will come."

"I can imagine how it will be when my first grandbaby comes along." She sank onto a rickety plastic lawn chair a few feet from where he sat. "I imagine I'll be thinking of Timothy."

"Jah."

Mordecai slid the knife along the wood, slicing away a sliver this way, a sliver that way. Nothing about his posture indicated a desire to talk about his own feelings. Or his fraa.

Fine. "What are you making?"

"Hmm." He held up the piece of wood and turned it back and forth in the flickering lantern light. "Looks to be a hund, I reckon."

"You're not sure?"

"The wood takes the shape it's intended to have. Kind of like our lives."

Maybe he could talk about his feelings in this roundabout way that most men had. She found herself holding her breath. Mordecai smoothed a scrap of wood away with his thumb. "You said you were confused. Do you still feel that way?"

"I was thinking . . . Everyone knows Phineas and Deborah

will marry as soon as they figure it out themselves." Keeping her voice soft to match his muted tones, she stumbled to find the proper words to express these thoughts that had been heaving themselves around in her head since the day she'd told Stephen she couldn't marry him. Thoughts that tried to find a path that would lead to a place where she could live and take care of her family until she knew her own feelings better. Until those feelings had a chance to take root and grow. "They may not know it yet, but it's as plain as the big nose on your face—"

"My nose isn't big."

"I like your nose, but that's beside the point."

Mordecai's bushy eyebrows shot up. "You like—?"

"Let me finish." If he didn't stop interrupting, she would lose her courage altogether. "I was thinking if they marry, Phineas might consider having his new family with him in that house until . . ."

Now he chose not to interrupt? She faltered. "Until . . ."

He cocked his head, his gaze fastened to the wood in his hand, the knife still moving in deft strokes. "Until what?"

She drew a breath. Now or never. "Until we have a chance to get to know each other properly."

His forehead wrinkled, but he kept whittling away at the wood. "You mean, like . . . court?"

She didn't like that word. She wasn't twenty and neither was he. "In a manner of speaking."

"I'm no young whippersnapper with a two-seater and a hankering to shine a flashlight in a window." Mordecai's tone didn't change, but he glanced her way, then ducked his head again. "I reckon you have your hands full too."

"Jah, I have little ones who need my attention." She forced herself to sit still despite the urge to squirm like a little girl. "Yet, for me, there has to be a time for two people to know each other. I need to go slowly. I had that with Timothy, and if I'm ever to have what I had with him again, I need time. Time to know if we're right for each other. Time for feelings to grow."

"Agreed."

"What?" After all the turmoil and the trepidation with Stephen, to have Mordecai capitulate so easily left her feeling like she'd been tossed from a capsized canoe into calm lake waters. "What did you say?"

"I said, I agree. The wait makes lieb all the more sweet." His gaze met hers. He held out the piece of wood, now a puppy with a whip tail and a pointed nose. She took it. Their fingers brushed. He smiled. He had a smile that caught her and held her like a bee drawn to nectar. "We'll take our time and we'll figure it out. There's no rush."

"There's not? We can't keep living with Leroy and Naomi."

"Have they complained?"

"Nee."

"Do you want to stay here, in Texas, or do you want to go home?"

She hadn't thought to go back to Tennessee, and since the brief time she'd lived in Mordecai's house, she never considered moving to Missouri with her brother. Now she knew why. "This *is* home."

A broad smile lighted his face. "Then stop worrying and trust Gott. He brought you here. You're home. The place you lay your head has nothing to do with it."

"How did you get so wise?"

"I don't know about wise. I only know what I feel."

Those feelings were written on his face, and they caused goose bumps to spring up on Abigail's arms and heat to brush across her cheeks. She swallowed, waiting for the batch of unruly puppies that had taken up residence in her stomach to settle. The road ahead no longer looked barren and deserted. She would not walk alone. Relief flooded her. Immediately followed by wonder. And uncertainty. Always the uncertainty. What came next?

She forced herself to look at Mordecai. Their gazes locked. No uncertainty lurked in that rugged face.

He stood and towered over her for a long second, his expression solemn now, his gaze piercing as if he'd peer into her heart, into her very soul. "No buying a farm."

She craned her head, caught by the emotion in his startling blue-green eyes. "No buying a farm."

"No Stephen."

"No Stephen."

Mordecai glanced toward the makeshift delivery room. Laughter and the sound of a baby fussing emanated from behind the sheets. He took her hand and tugged her to her feet. With his other hand, he slid his hat from his head and leaned down. "Gut."

His kiss was soft but sure, the kiss of a man who knew what he wanted but didn't take for granted that he could have it. It deepened with care taken and a kindness that made tears well and wet Abigail's cheeks.

The hat fell to their feet. His hands came up and cupped her face. Her own fingers covered his without her realizing she'd lifted her hands from her sides. He held her there until her heart fluttered, then smoothed into a new, steady beat. Everything that came before melted into a distant past. The clock started ticking on her new life. And his.

Finally, he released her. "That's gut, my sweet, sweet Abigail."

Indeed, it was.

THIRTY-FOUR

Fat drops of rain cooling his face, Phineas studied the undulating masses of gray clouds from the small porch that welcomed visitors to his home. They moved fast, whipped by fierce winds that had come off the Gulf and made their way willy-nilly across the plains. The rain pelted the house in a steady *ping-ping* that sang of ponds filling and plants growing green and tall.

He'd planned to inspect as many hives as possible today. He needed to make sure they were amassing food for the winter season when pollen would be scarce. If they weren't heavy enough, he would have to set up the feeders and buy some protein supplement to add to the syrup. From the looks of the sky, those visits would have to wait at least another day. High winds didn't bode well for the apiaries either.

Nothing to do about it now. Instead, he would board the windows on his home and make sure everything in the small shed that served as his barn had been secured, including the buggy and horse his father had loaned him until he could afford his own.

He shoved his hat back and picked up the hammer and a slab of plywood from the pile he'd stockpiled for this purpose. He slammed a nail into the wood. Swinging the hammer felt good. Better than it should. Maybe between the physical labor and the rain, he would be able to sleep when he descended into the basement to wait out the worst of the storm. He hadn't been able to sleep much since moving to the new house. Not with the steady stream of pictures that pestered him every time he closed his eyes.

Deborah, a look of wonder on her face as she saw pelicans for the first time. Deborah examining the bee sting on her finger, her expression asking him to make it all better. Deborah, angry and fierce, confronting him about buying this house. Deborah, sitting on the curb, holding his hand because she wanted to comfort him.

Deborah.

He went to sleep thinking about her and awoke from dreams that made his throat ache when he realized they'd only been dreams.

Ever since that day in Weslaco, he'd paced through the fields, debating what to do next. Hearing Esther's words echoing in his ears. *"She's made herself vulnerable to you. That's a gift. Don't miss out."*

Every time he saw Will, he wanted to tell him, "Nee, nee, you can't have her."

Yet he hadn't done the one thing he needed to do. Declare himself to Deborah.

He leaned his head against the solid wood for one second, trying to shake the feeling of disorientation. He had to return her gift. He had to make himself vulnerable to her. The thought made his stomach lurch. What if Esther was wrong? It seemed more than likely.

It didn't matter. He knew how *he* felt, and he had to take a chance or he would never know.

Gott, no more arguing. You win. Thy will be done. If it's meant to be, show me how. I want to be happy and I want to make Deborah happy. I can't do that without You. Give me the strength to tell her.

Phineas sucked in a ragged breath and turned to pick up another board. The long barrel of a rifle bobbing at chest level greeted him. He froze for an everlasting second. Then, with only the slightest of movement, he forced himself to look from the rifle to the man who held it.

He was tall, gangly, and his skin had the rough, red look of a man who worked outdoors. His Adam's apple stuck out in a long, skinny neck. A tattoo of a single upside-down thorny, long-stemmed rose covered one arm from the bottom of the sleeve of his grimy white jumpsuit to his wrist. His blond hair, highlighted by a smattering of silver, was wet and plastered to his head. The gaze of bloodshot eyes darted from Phineas to the house, out to the yard, and back.

Phineas worked to keep his expression neutral even as his heart took off like a buck startled by hunters. An escaped prisoner stood on his porch, a rifle in his hands.

Escaped prisoners were the worst kind. They had everything to lose. They'd already broken the law and they had no qualms about doing it again. They were desperate for the most precious commodity of all—freedom.

"Afternoon." He kept his voice soft and even, the one he'd heard Leroy use when he approached a horse that needed to be broken to a saddle. "Can I help you with something?"

"You can give the keys to your car." The man had the raspy voice of a smoker. "And whatever money you got in your pockets."

"I don't have a car." Phineas patted his chest. He had no pockets. Even if he had cash—which he didn't—he had no place to carry it. "I don't have any money, but I can feed you if you're hungry."

"Don't lie to a desperate man. You'll regret it."

The escapee shoved the rifle barrel into Phineas's gut like a man wielding a sword. Pain forced him to double over. Instinct or sheer desire to survive overcame him. Without thinking, he grabbed the weapon with both hands and fought to wrest it away from his attacker.

Gott, don't let it go off. Please, Gott, don't let him shoot me or me, him.

The escapee ripped the rifle from Phineas's hand and swung full force, catching Phineas on the side of his head. A second blow smashed into his shoulder. An explosion of sound blew up around him, ringing in his ears, the smell of gunpowder acrid in his nostrils. A white-hot pain sliced through his arm above his elbow, taking with it his ability to think about anything but the pain.

He slammed against the wall and found himself sliding, sliding down until he sat on the cold, hard, wet cement porch. He hunched over, left hand clutching at his right arm.

"You shot me." The wonder in his voice made Phineas want to laugh. How could he be surprised at such a thing? The man was a criminal holding a gun. "You didn't mean to do it, but you did."

"It's just a scratch, but there's more where that came from." The escapee panted, his face mottled red and white with anger. "Get up, get up, you moron, get up."

The rifle barrel hovered near Phineas's temple, the heat burning his skin. "Next time I'll blow your head off. Get up. We're going inside to finish this conversation. I know you've got money in there somewhere."

Maybe he *had* meant to do it. It didn't matter. Phineas knew one thing for certain. He did not want to die here on his front porch. He didn't want to die until he had the chance to tell Deborah he loved her.

Gott willing, he would survive this and he would tell her.

Gasping, he dragged himself to his knees and then to his feet. Legs and arms shaking, he forced himself to breathe, in and out, in and out, as he reached for the screen door.

"Easy, bubba, easy." The escapee gouged Phineas in the back with the rifle barrel. "You were stupid once, don't be stupid again."

"I don't have any money." His voice sounded odd in his own ears, like it belonged to someone else. "I don't have a car, but I have a horse and a buggy. You're welcome to both. I have food."

"Shut up and get inside. Someone might have heard the shot."

Phineas did as he was told despite the cold, hard fact lodged in his throat. No one had heard. No one would come. The other farmhouses in his settlement were miles away and everyone was hunkered down in basements waiting for the storm to pass.

He was on his own.

———

Deborah shoved her bonnet forward over her prayer kapp while she wrapped her other hand around the reins. Little good it did her. The wind whipped the bonnet back. Dirt pinged against the tender skin of her cheeks. A fat drop of rain smacked her in the nose, quickly followed by another that hit her right between the eyes. The horse shook his head and whinnied as if he'd suffered a similar fate. His head bobbed and the wet reins nearly slipped from her fingers.

"Come on, come on, it's okay." She shouted to be heard over

wind that pinned her to her seat. The wagon swayed and dipped in the rutted road. Only another quarter mile and she'd be at Phineas's new home. She had to get word to him that this was more than a run-of-the-mill thunderstorm. "Haw, haw, come on, you can do it."

Barking greeted her exhortation. She glanced back. Butch raced alongside the wagon, his short legs a blur. The dog didn't give up. She'd sent him back to the store twice, but he kept reappearing. "Butch, go find Mordecai!"

The dog picked up his pace, nose into the wind. He barked again. Butch had a stubborn streak about him that reminded her of someone else.

The King men maybe.

"Fine." She tugged on the reins until the horse halted, snorting his irritation and confusion. Butch didn't hesitate. He leaped and scrambled into the wagon. Not the most graceful entrance, but it did the job. His muzzle widened in the usual grin as he climbed into the seat, panting, his tongue hanging out.

"You belong to Mordecai, not me."

Butch's response was a breathless *woof.* He settled onto the seat, smelling of wet dog and whatever he'd rolled in earlier in the day, and surveyed his new view of the world.

"Fine, but after this, home you go to your owner." She snapped the reins and the wagon jolted forward. "I don't mind the company, but this isn't weather to be gallivanting about the countryside for you or me."

So what was she doing out here?

Same thing as the dog? Making sure a loved one was okay?

Life as a dog had to be confusing. People coming and going every which way. It confused her, and she had a little more book learning than Butch. The thought fled as she rounded the bend in the road and Phineas's house came into view. Two windows had been boarded, but the others remained uncovered, open, curtains flapping in the furious wind. If he didn't close those windows right now, he'd have wet floors or worse. She snapped the reins, spurring the horse on.

Phineas had started boarding up the house. Why had he stopped? Deborah halted the wagon next to the small porch with its two steps and let her gaze roam the property. A stack of boards lay on the cement-porch floor next to a rusted hammer and a coffee can filled with nails.

"Phineas?"

No response. Uncertainty assailed her for the first time. Phineas lived alone. The bishop would not look kindly on Deborah traipsing into a man's house. Just the two of them alone with a storm coming that most likely would prevent her from leaving right away. She'd flung herself into action without thinking ahead. Despite the steady patter of rain on her face, her cheeks heated. She'd come this far. Her only reason for being here was to make sure Phineas was safe. To make sure he'd received word of the hurricane's fury working its way north, flinging storms and tornadoes in every direction. She'd tell him and she'd go. Quickly, before the storm worsened.

No harm done. None whatsoever. In fact, it was the right thing to do. The neighborly thing.

Deborah hopped from the wagon and marched up the steps. She glanced back. "Are you coming with me?"

Butch cocked his shaggy head and took a flying leap onto the porch.

"I guess that would be a yes." A dog as a chaperone? Leroy

wouldn't buy that story even if she gave him a dollar to go with it. "Your feet are muddy, so don't be racing around inside."

His tail wagging, Butch lifted his nose in the air as if offended she would suggest such a thing.

"Phineas?" She knocked on the screen door. The inner door stood open, despite the wind and rain. If he was inside, he'd hear her. "Phineas, where are you? It's me, Deborah. I just wanted to make sure—"

"Go home."

His hoarse voice sounded distant and angry.

More so than usual.

"I drove all the way out here in the wind and rain—"

"Please. Go home."

Please? Something wasn't right. Phineas wouldn't stand on ceremony or use fancy manners. His voice held a distinct tone he'd never used with her before. Desperate to get rid of her. He didn't want her around. Fine. "It's raining into your house. If you don't want help from me, that's fine. But don't cut off your nose to spite your face. You better get out here—"

Butch growled, low and deep in his throat. A pulsating, feral sound that sent goose bumps racing up Deborah's arms. The dog's ears were back and his tail stood straight up. The fur on his crooked spine clustered in a long ridge.

"What is it, boy?" she whispered. The dog lifted his snout and howled. "Okay, okay. Stay. You stay right here."

She grabbed the screen door. Wind snatched it from her hand, tossed it open, then slammed it against the frame. She jumped back, saving her fingers by the skin of her teeth. Butch barked a furious bark that mingled with long, rolling thunder and the *snap, crackle, pop* of lightning.

The wind knocked her forward against the wall and sucked her breath from her chest. Gasping, she grabbed the screen door a second time and struggled to open it enough to slide in. Butch, still barking, darted past her and hurled himself into the front room.

No light shone in the interior, even though the storm had sucked the sun behind mammoth, furrowed clouds that looked like black, wrinkled cotton. It took a second for her eyes to adjust. And even longer for her mind to understand. Phineas stood in the middle of a room empty of furniture with the exception of a straight-back chair, a desk, and one of Mordecai's finely crafted rocking chairs. A pole lamp had not been lit despite the fact that day had turned to night in the middle of the afternoon.

Phineas had his hands in the air.

A man in a muddy jumpsuit stood a few feet from him, a long rifle pointed at Deborah's head.

At first, the weapon blotted everything out. Then the rest came into focus.

The man wore a white jumpsuit. His eyes were bloodshot in a red face with a five o'clock shadow in gray. Nothing else about him seemed important. A prison jumpsuit and a rifle. Those were the important details.

Forcing her gaze to Phineas, she took two steps in his direction. "I'm sorry. I didn't know you had . . . company."

"You never listen, do you?"

Deborah shook her head. She inhaled the scent of sweat and dirty feet and desperation. Phineas had a bloody welt below his right eye, and his lower lip was swollen and bruised. Blood stained his shirtsleeve. "You're hurt—"

"Shut the dog up or I'll shoot him." The man swung the rifle toward Butch, who bared his teeth and growled, the sound fiercer than any Deborah had ever heard. "If you think I'm kidding, you're crazy."

Her gaze glued to the gun, Deborah sank to her knees next to Butch. "Hush, hush." She wrapped an arm around the dog, suddenly grateful for his warmth, however wet. An icy cold invaded her arms and legs, making it hard to force them to obey her commands. "Shush, Butch, it's okay."

The barking subsided, but the guttural growl in the dog's throat made his entire body hum under her touch.

"Move over next to him." The man jerked his head, the gun bouncing from Deborah to Phineas, then back. "Now."

"Take whatever you want." Phineas inched toward Deborah. "Just let her go. She won't tell anyone you're here."

"Right." The man snorted, then winced. One hand went to his side and he stooped a little, his face creased in a grimace. "You Pilgrims have a sense of humor. The second I'm out of here, you'll call the sheriff."

"Pilgrims—"

Phineas shot her a look. She closed her mouth.

"We don't have a phone. We can't call anyone."

"No phone!" The man chortled. "You really are Pilgrims."

"We're not Pilgrims, we're Amish." Deborah ignored Phineas's scowl. "We believe in helping people in need."

"I'm definitely in need." A sudden, crooked smile covered the man's face, revealing gaps where teeth should've been and a dozen or more silver fillings. He eased closer to her, peering as if he needed glasses. "You're a pretty lady, despite the weird getup. You know how long it's been since I had a . . . date? Seven years, four months, and twenty-two days. But who's counting?"

Phineas shot forward, filling the space between Deborah and

the man. The rifle swung in an arch, smacked Phineas in the ribs, and sent him flying back.

With a half-stifled groan, he stumbled, his legs collapsed under him, and he slumped to the floor on his knees.

Butch wiggled from Deborah's grip and raced forward, his barking rising to a crescendo that filled the room.

"Phineas!" Deborah scooted toward him on her hands and knees.

A gun blast lit up the room and drowned out the sounds of barking and thunder and rain.

An unlit kerosene lantern shattered and clanged against the floor. Deborah's ears rang. She clasped her hands to them and hugged the wooden floor. No air filled her lungs.

Gott, Gott, Gott. Not Phineas. Lord, please not Phineas.

"That's a warning shot." The man's voice sounded cool. Dead. "The dog is next."

"Butch, stop. Now. Stop." She crawled toward the dog, reaching out with one hand. "Come on, boy, come on."

Panting, Butch circled and planted himself in front of her, teeth bared. Deborah wrapped her fingers around his collar and held on.

"Get up."

Gasping for breath, she gazed up at the man. She didn't move. Phineas's fingers touched her free hand. They were icy cold. She wrapped hers around his without looking at him. She'd held his hand once before. He'd said he wanted to believe it would happen again. Here they were, with a dog between them and an escaped prisoner. They were connected. They faced this danger together. She swallowed and took a breath. "What's your name?"

"What?"

"What's your name?"

"I'm not telling you my name."

Of course not. Silly question. Phineas coughed, his breathing labored. Deborah scrambled for words, any words. "I just wanted something to call you, that's all."

"Why, girlie? You like what you see?"

An acrid bile burned the back of her throat. She gritted her teeth against it, fearing she might vomit. *Breathe. Breathe.*

"I thought maybe you were hungry. I could fix you something to eat."

"Call me Joe."

His sneer told her this was not his name.

"Joe, I think my . . . friend has some fresh honey in the kitchen. He probably has bread his aunt made. Homemade bread. I could make you a sandwich. Peanut butter and fresh honey or home-made grape jelly. I'm sure you don't get much of that in prison."

"Why would you do that?"

"When was the last time you ate? Everyone feels better on a full stomach. I know I do."

Joe eased toward a window, took a quick look, then whirled as if sure she'd lunge at him. "I don't see no car out there. How'd you get here?"

"Wagon."

A wagon with Leroy's horse still hitched, standing out in a storm. *Gott, forgive me. I didn't know.*

"A wagon." Joe uttered a string of obscenities the likes of which Deborah had never heard before. "Just my luck, I stumble on to some backward cult in the middle of nowhere. I want to get out of here."

"We're not a cult." Phineas's voice was strong now. "We don't want any trouble. We'll share with you what we have. There's a bad storm bearing down on us. It might be best if we all went down to the basement together."

The basement, all of them together. Phineas, an escaped prisoner, and Deborah in an enclosed space with that enormous rifle.

"Don't you think I know that? Why do you think I was evaced here?" Joe laughed, a big, horsey laugh. He was someone's son, maybe someone's husband. He was a desperate man, but he hadn't always been. "Best thing that ever happened to me, that storm. I can't wait around. I gotta get while the getting is good."

This was good? He appeared to be hurt. He'd escaped in a hurricane-spawned storm likely to rip him from the road and land him on his head in a ditch somewhere. "I think Phineas probably has some doctoring things. I could fix you up."

"Why would you do that?"

"It's the neighborly thing to do."

"We ain't neighbors, lady."

Not in the traditional way, but he was still a human being. *Gott, help me help him. Don't let him hurt Phineas any more, please. Gott, You brought me here for a reason. Phineas. Please spare him. I promise to love and cherish him always.* "Maybe not, but you're a guest in this house."

"Honey, I'm no guest. I'm the kind of guy your mama told you to never talk to."

True, but Mudder would also pray for this man. Even if she didn't want to do it, she would.

Outside, hail pinged against windows and tree branches tore at the roof. A crack of thunder directly overhead made all three of them jump. Lightning lit up the front room for a split second, giving the man's face an eerie clown-like appearance, his features white against the dark around them. Rain filtered through the open window and wet the wooden floor.

"My mudder told me to be kind to strangers and to share." The words stuck in Deborah's throat. Mudder couldn't have imagined a scene such as this one. "We could fix you up and give you something to eat."

She tightened her grip on Phineas's hand and stole a look at him. His bruised face stared up at her, his eyes filled with concern and an emotion even she could identify. She saw no fear there, only determination. He struggled to sit up. She shook her head. He shook his right back at her. "I'll grab some provisions from the kitchen and we'll ride out the storm in the basement. As soon as the storm clears, we'll go."

"You think that horse and wagon will still be sitting out there?" Joe's derisive chuckle turned to a lung-rattling cough. "I'm a city boy and I know better than to leave an expensive horse sitting out in the middle of a hurricane."

"I can put the horse in the barn. I'll come right back. I promise—"

"He's right, Deborah. He needs to go now." Phineas growled, his hand on his side. He ignored her glare and focused on Joe. "We'll show you the way out. You can take us along for . . . hostages or insurance, whatever you want to call it."

Phineas must have thought they had a better chance out there than in here with a man who wanted nothing more than to escape his captors.

Ride out into the storm and then what? Out there in the wind and the rain, maybe they would have a chance to escape. If the storm didn't get them first. Or last.

"Phineas—"

He shook his head. She closed her mouth.

Joe pursed his lips, his forehead furrowed. After a few unnerving seconds of silence punctuated by continuous rolling thunder and lightning, he jerked the rifle toward the door. "Up." The gun bounced up and down. "Now."

Together, Deborah and Phineas rose to their feet. Phineas stooped, his lips pressed tightly together creating a thin, white line. Deborah slid an arm around his waist and braced herself to take his weight. "Can you make it?"

"I'm fine."

"Out the door. Now. Let's go."

"We need to get to the basement," Deborah pleaded. "He's hurt and there's a terrible storm out there. If we go out there, we'll all die."

"I'm fine." His teeth gritted, Phineas glared at her. "We can make it. You can let us go when we get to the highway."

"Your boyfriend's right. We gotta go now. They're looking for me right now. I need to put miles between me and that prison. If they find me, they're gonna find me with two hostages."

Deborah chose to ignore the word *boyfriend*. Whatever Phineas was to her, that word didn't come close to touching it. "They're not looking for you in this storm."

"You don't know how much it kills them that a guy slipped from their grasp. 'Sides, I hurt one of them bad and took his rifle. They don't like that. They're looking for me, you can bet on it. Go on, get out there. Stay in front of me."

Plain folks didn't bet. Deborah pushed through the screen door. Head bent against the onslaught of rain and wind, she tightened her grip around Phineas's waist. His quick intake of breath told her pain assailed him. His hand covered hers and squeezed. What did he have in mind?

The wind knocked her back a step on the porch. She stooped against its force, unable to move forward. "We can't go out in this." She had to scream to be heard. "We need to get inside."

"Nee." Phineas jerked her toward the edge of the porch. He whirled, his body blocking her from Joe's view. He stood between Deborah and the rifle. "Now, Butch! Now!"

Butch roared through the open door. The man swung his gun toward the animal. "Not you, you rangy mutt. You stay."

Butch ignored the command. Snarling, he leaped at the man as if he'd been released from a chain. His teeth sank into Joe's bare ankle. The man screeched and cursed. His arms flailed and his leg kicked out, shaking Butch like a rag doll. The dog hung on, his face contorted in a fierce grin.

The rifle clattered onto the porch.

Phineas shoved Deborah over the edge of the porch. "Run, run!"

She stumbled, caught herself, and took off into the wind and rain, sure that any second the man would scoop up the rifle, a blast would deafen her, and a bullet would strike her between the shoulders.

Phineas's grip bruised her arm. "Don't look back. Go!"

She slipped and slid in the mud, fell to her knees, then regained her balance. Phineas jerked her along. His hat flew through the air but he didn't stop for it. "Come on! Come on!"

She struggled to keep pace with his long legs. He raced, one hand on his side, the other gripping her arm. "Don't look back. Keep going."

They ran into a day darker than night. Blackness closed around them. Swirling rain and wind danced with tree branches that dipped and soared in a wild choreography. Lightning crackled and thunder boomed so close overhead she ducked without thinking. Hail pelted her head and pinged against her face in a painful pattern.

Please, Gott, please, Gott, please, Gott.

She inhaled rain, coughed, and struggled to breathe. Her sneakers sank in the mud and stuck, making it hard to lift her legs. Still, she kept moving.

They ran on and on, it seemed. The rain came harder, the wind more fierce, as if in collusion with the man who would hold them hostage.

"Here." Phineas veered right, taking her with him.

They raced into a stand of scraggly trees bent almost to the ground in the wind. Here they had a sliver of cover, both from the wind and from the man who called himself Joe. Deborah sank to her knees, her lungs ready to burst. "Here?" She gasped and sucked in air, not sure she could get another word out. "It's not much shelter."

"Just for a minute." Phineas squatted, his head down. His breath came in hard spurts. He inhaled, then rubbed his chest. "Just give me a minute."

"You're hurt." She pushed wet hair from her face, suddenly aware her kapp had slid down her back. She pushed his hand away from his arm. Blood soaked his shirtsleeve. "You're bleeding."

"It's just a scratch. The ribs hurt more."

"What possessed Butch?"

"Butch is a guard dog. I imagine his former owner taught him a thing or two." Phineas smeared his face with the back of his sleeve and laughed, a hoarse, breathless sound. "Besides, he likes you, and he's not keen on sharing you with a stranger."

"How did that stranger get in your house?"

"He took me by surprise. I turned and he was on top of me

on the porch. I grabbed at the rifle, thinking I'd take it away, I guess. It was . . . instinct. Stupid, I should've backed off right away. Instead I went for the gun."

"Not stupid. Like you said, instinct. Do you think he's chasing us?"

"If he's smart, he'll take the wagon and go. I'm praying he makes a run for it."

"If he was smart, he wouldn't be in prison."

"He's probably driven off into the rain, thinking he's making a big escape." Phineas laughed again, then gasped, his face contorted in pain. "If he was smart, he'd have taken you up on the offer of bread and honey. He won't get that where he's going when they find him in a ditch after this is over."

Lightning crackled in the sky directly overhead, illuminating black clouds that hung so low she might be able to touch them. She ducked again. Silly thing to do. "You think Butch is okay?"

"Butch has proven he can take care of himself."

"And Leroy's horse and wagon?"

"He'll understand."

He might, but the loss of an expensive horse and a wagon wouldn't sit well, regardless. Deborah prayed both would be recovered. "What do we do now? We're out in a hurricane."

"This is just the spin-off storm from a hurricane. It's nothing. We've seen plenty worse around here. We need to get to the store to call the sheriff."

"Don't you think we should get to a basement first, until the storm passes?"

"This wave is passing." Phineas coughed, his hand over his mouth for a few seconds, his breathing ragged. "There will be more, probably one after another all night."

They couldn't spend the night in the basement together, just

THE BEEKEEPER'S SON

the two of them. Better to go to the store. Deborah lifted her face to the sky. He was right. The rain had lessened, but thunder and lightning still warred in the heavens. Phineas's hand gripped hers. Rivulets of rain ran down his face, but he didn't seem to notice them. His face contorted in pain. "I'm sorry."

"Sorry about what?"

"That you're in the middle of this. Why did you come?"

"I came to warn you about the storm."

"You thought I wouldn't notice the wind and the rain?" He shook his head and snorted. "I've lived here my whole life. I know the weather. I saw it coming. Why did you come?"

"I came to make sure you were all right."

His blue-green eyes flamed with the same heat as the lightning overhead. "You risked getting caught in the storm to make sure I was all right? Why?"

"Because I love you."

The words came out of her mouth with no warning from her head. No taking them back.

She didn't want to take them back.

For better or for worse, she'd declared herself.

She waited.

No words echoing hers filled the air around her.

THIRTY-FIVE

Deborah stared up at Phineas. His face was inches from hers. His rain-soaked hair hung in his eyes, making him look like a little boy who needed a haircut. The emotion in his eyes did not belong to a little boy. The thought caused a hitch in her already-ragged breathing. Despite the rain on her skin, heat coursed through her. Phineas had the look of a man not sure he could contain himself.

They faced each other, on their knees, the deluge of water pelting them, soaking them to the skin, tree branches bending and dancing overhead. Deborah didn't care about the rain or the lightning or the thunder. She didn't care about escaped prisoners with rifles or what was right or wrong. This moment belonged to Phineas and to her. This was their moment, their showdown.

Take it or leave it.

"I said I love you."

"I heard you." The edge in his voice could've cut glass. "I'm not deaf."

"That's it? I heard you?"

"We need to get to the store before Joe finds us." He pushed back from the scant protection of the tree. Rain pelted his face.

He halted, the raindrops running in rivulets over his scarred face. "I can't . . . You don't . . . How could you?"

"I do."

He turned and stared at her, his lips twisted in a strange, sardonic smile.

Deborah refused to look away. She stared back at the man who stood before her, his need and his aloneness naked on his face. She fisted her hands and clutched them against her sodden dress. He had to take the next step. He had to take the chance. He had to trust that she would not reject his touch or his love. They would never have anything unless he believed she wanted him exactly as he was. She leaned back on her haunches, her dress twisted and muddy around her, and waited. He would have to come the distance to her.

His gaze faltered and fell to his scraped, bloody hands resting on the knees of his torn, wet pants.

Nee, come on, Phineas, come on. Don't run away. Don't hide. You can do this. Trust me. Please trust me. Gott, please let him trust me.

His gaze came up and met hers again. His hand crept out and touched her fist with one hesitant finger. Her throat tight with tears she would never let him see, Deborah opened her hand so his fingers could wrap around hers. She swallowed, afraid to breathe, afraid any sudden movement would frighten him away, like a wounded creature who didn't trust his would-be rescuer.

His gaze traveled from their clasped hands to her face again. With his free hand, he reached out. His fingers, their skin the rough texture of a working man's, touched her cheek. She leaned into his touch, never taking her gaze from his face.

Please.

Phineas leaned forward. Deborah couldn't restrain herself

then. She stretched to meet him. His gaze begged her to reassure him. She managed a quick jerk of a nod.

His Adam's apple bobbed and his ragged breath caught. Deborah tightened her grip on his fingers and willed him to understand.

Phineas closed his eyes and lowered his head until his lips met hers. They were soft, so soft and tentative, and warm, despite the cold rain. After one or two fleeting seconds, he groaned and tried to jerk away. Deborah threw her arms around his neck and held him close, forcing him to remain within this tight circle she'd created for the two of them. She felt his heart pounding in his chest under his soaking-wet shirt, pounding so hard she feared it would burst through his skin and collide with hers.

She drew away a fraction and turned so she could whisper in his misshapen ear, "Open your eyes."

"Nee."

"Open your eyes and look at me."

"If I do, I'll find out this is only a dream." A clap of thunder almost drowned the hoarse words. "I've dreamed this a hundred times and it's never been real."

"It's not a dream. This time it's real. I'm real. Open your eyes."

He did as she demanded. The firestorm of emotion in his eyes was almost too much for Deborah to bear. She raised both her hands, letting them stop just short of touching his face. She waited. A battle waged in his eyes. Still, she waited. The decision belonged to him. His gaze dropped, but he nodded.

"You are beautiful to me," she whispered as she let her hands travel the rest of that short distance to his face. She touched the scars and let her fingers brush his bruised cheeks in soft, gentle strokes. He held still, his gaze never leaving hers. She bestowed tiny kisses on his swollen lips, his cheeks, forehead, and his crooked nose. "So beautiful."

A sound like a half laugh, half sob brushed against her. His arms tightened around her waist and pulled her to his chest. "Because that's what a Plain man wants to hear."

She laughed, a wet hiccup of a sound. "You know what I mean. You're perfect in my eyes."

"Lying is a sin."

She tried to pull away. His arms were like a steel band, holding her in the exact place she longed to be. "I don't kiss a man and then lie to him."

"It's dark, we're in the middle of storm. You've been through a terrible ordeal—"

"And you think I'll change my mind on a sunny day when I can see you better? You forget that day at the beach? I loved you then. That day at the lake? I loved you then. That day sitting on the curb in town? I loved you then." She pushed back just enough so she could look him in the eye. "Most days the sun shines on us and I see you. I love what I see."

"How could you?" His whisper ached with wonder and near despair. "You're just out of your mind with fear."

"Is this the kiss of someone out of her mind from fear?"

This time *she* kissed him. She let him feel all the pent-up emotions of months of drought and uncertainty and loneliness. She let him see the future she wanted. The future that included no other man but him.

His response spoke of the longing of a man who had waited for a woman to love him as she did. To see him for who he was. To see through the damaged hulk of an exterior to a man who wanted only to be loved and to love.

The kiss lasted so long, Deborah thought she might collapse onto the muddy earth, but she didn't care. Should she fall, Phineas would catch her.

He pulled away first. "I love you."

Finally. Three words. The three most beautiful words one person could say to another. She cleared her throat. "I'm glad we've finally managed to sort all that out. I love you. You love me."

"I've waited so long . . ." He had the shell-shocked look of a man still trying to figure out how he'd arrived at this moment. Then he nodded, his smile still tentative. "You're sure?"

"Phineas."

"No going back."

"I don't want to go back. Ever."

He stood and pulled her to her feet. "We need to get to the store now. After this is over, I'll talk to Leroy."

She slid her arm around him and they left the shelter of the trees. The rain had eased a little, but it still soaked them. It didn't matter. "Tell him we don't want to wait."

"I'll tell him we have a life to live."

"Together."

"Together. Right here in Bee County."

Phineas made it a statement, not a question. Deborah knew then that he trusted her to love him exactly as he was physically, but also who he was as a man. A beekeeper who worked the land in this place, this beautiful place, made so by a God who created it, who loved it, and who inspired those who lived in it.

"It's a beautiful place to raise a—"

Barking interrupted her words. Butch bounded across the field and hurled himself at her.

"You made it, you brave, silly dog. You made it!" She sank to the ground and embraced a wet, muddy, stinky dog who came at her so hard he knocked her back. He proceeded to lick her face from forehead to chin. "Butch! Butch! Kiss Phineas, he's happy to see you too. Butch, go on."

Phineas knelt and tugged the dog back. Butch showered him with kisses for a few seconds but then returned to Deborah as if he hadn't finished the job with her. Laughing, Phineas tugged Deborah back into a sitting position. She leaned into him, breathless with laughter. "I don't know, Butch seems to be staking his claim as well."

"Nee, it's my job to kiss you and no one else's from this day forward. Starting right now."

He proceeded to make good on that promise.

EPILOGUE

Smoothing the cotton of his best church shirt with shaking fingers, Phineas heaved a breath and tried to concentrate. If Leroy's sermon over the first few verses of Genesis lasted much longer, he might keel over or throw up. The few bites of pancake he'd managed to eat for breakfast had swollen like balloons in his gut. His throat felt tight. Each breath he heaved made his chest ache. In a few minutes, he would stand and walk forward in front of every member of his district and all the visitors who'd gathered in his daed's house to help celebrate this special moment. He would make Deborah Lantz his fraa. A few short months ago he would never have thought such a thing possible.

Gott is good.

So much better than Phineas deserved. Grace poured out on him, wave upon wave, like the mighty waters of the Gulf. The thought conjured up the smell of sea salt on a wet breeze. It came and went, overpowered by the sweet scent of bread and cake baking. His body relaxed and the anxiety ebbed like the tide on his beloved beach.

Deborah loves me.

Gott is good.

Much as he appreciated the kindness and joy of all the folks who'd come together to celebrate this special day, Phineas would've been much happier to be alone in this room with his bride and the bishop. To speak the words to Deborah and Deborah alone. This binding of two hearts involved the two of them.

Nee. Deborah deserved a public declaration of his love. Before God and family. He leaned forward to catch a glimpse of her seated between Frannie and her good friend Josie, who'd traveled all the way from Tennessee to serve as Deborah's witness. The three had been inseparable for the last week, and he suspected a great deal of unsolicited advice had been dispensed by the two, who had become fast friends the second they stepped from their prospective vans. His bride-to-be looked beautiful in the blue wedding dress she'd finished stitching only the day before. But she always looked beautiful to him. Dressed in rags, she'd be the most beautiful woman he'd ever seen.

Her gaze caught his and she smiled. Her smile spoke the words he longed to hear. *Don't worry. I won't change my mind.* Even with all these folks surrounding them, they were alone in the room. She loved him. Just as he was. Scars and surliness and all. Deborah loved him. This plain-spoken woman who never backed away from an argument, who loved to probe his pain until she smoothed it away. No subject was taboo. No thought too scary to voice.

Gott had brought to Phineas the one woman in the world who could find beauty in his body and heal a pain that had nothing to do with injuries suffered long ago. Daed had been right all along. Gott knew what He was doing.

It had taken Phineas all of the past six weeks to get used to this new reality and still he awoke each day to find himself speechless with the joy of it. Much had happened since that storm. Two Texas Rangers had found Joe—also known as Raymond Southerland— hiding in an abandoned barn about five miles from Beeville. He'd taken shelter there with Leroy's horse and wagon. They found him curled up in some old hay, fast asleep, a nasty dog bite on one leg.

The sheriff had come out to the store to tell them and left, shaking his head at their decision not to press charges. Leroy had been clear. The man was forgiven, but that didn't mean he shouldn't go back to prison. The sheriff said Southerland's sentence would be increased for his assault on the guard and subsequent escape.

Phineas had no problem with that. It had taken time for his wounds to heal and yet another scar graced his arm as a result of the gunshot, but what was one more? He and Deborah had survived. Not only survived, but found each other once and for all amid the chaos. The broken ribs, bruises, and cuts were long gone and nearly forgotten in the preparations for marriage and the company that flooded their tiny community for the wedding.

In the meantime, Daed and Abigail had taken to courting and pretending not to do so. They weren't fooling anybody. One evening Esther and Adam had seen Stephen in his buggy with Ruth Anne Glick at his side. That news had made Daed and Abigail smile at each other, something they did quite often now. In a few days, Phineas and Deborah would help her mudder and the other kinner move into Phineas's—and Deborah's—house.

Until the next wedding, which Phineas suspected would be in the spring. Daed had waited long enough for his new start. So had Abigail.

"Phineas. Now."

Jesse's whisper, followed by an elbow to his ribs, made Phineas realize he'd missed his cue. Leroy's shaggy eyebrows were raised behind wire-rimmed spectacles. Deborah marched ahead of Phineas, her step sure, her witnesses scampering behind her, heads ducked, faces bright with smiles. Deborah turned. Her eyebrows raised, she cocked her head as if to say, "Hurry up, don't keep me waiting, we've a life to live."

He jerked to his feet. He couldn't wait another moment. He crossed the space in two long strides, holding her gaze as he walked. Together they turned and faced the bishop. Phineas's jitters dissipated, replaced by wonder and a curious light. Deborah would never change her mind. He was as certain of that now as he was of the presence of God above.

She answered the questions posed to her with an enthusiasm that made Phineas smile. His throat tightened at the sheer joy of knowing she committed to staying with him until death, to being loyal and caring in times of adversity, affliction, sickness, and weakness. Those times would come. They both knew that because they had weathered bad times before. Her character had been honed by circumstances. His also. They were evenly yoked, praise God.

When it came his turn, Phineas had to clear his throat. His voice was hoarse and low in his own ears. Heat flamed across his face. "Jah, I will."

Finally, Leroy took Deborah's hand and placed it in Phineas's. The bishop's big, bony fingers covered theirs. Deborah's skin felt warm and soft against Phineas's. Her blue eyes, filled with emotion and what surely must be tears, mesmerized him. She would yoke herself to him and he would try to be worthy of such an honor. The lump in his throat swelled. *Gott, make me worthy of her. And don't let me embarrass myself in front of all these people. Danki.*

"So then I may say with Raguel, the God of Abraham, the God of Isaac, and the God of Jacob be with you and help you together and fulfill His blessing abundantly upon you, through Jesus Christ. Go forth in the Lord's name. You are man and wife."

Leroy's hand dropped away, but Deborah slid her fingers between Phineas's, entwining them in a tight grip. He would never let go and he knew, without a doubt, neither would she.

They turned to face their church family. Everyone rose and stood before them, honoring their blessed union.

A shrill bark broke the silence. Butch bounded down the aisle toward them, his muzzle wide, tongue hanging over the side of his mouth.

"Stop that dog!" someone in the back yelled—probably the person responsible for leaving the door open a crack. "Butch, get back here!"

Caleb tried to catch him, but the wily mutt eluded them and made a beeline for Deborah. Laughter filled the air as their friends and family broke into a round of applause.

"I guess Butch is anxious for us to get on with living our lives." Phineas laughed as he dropped to one knee and hugged the dog, who showered his face with wet, sloppy kisses. He leaned back and looked up at Deborah. "I know I am."

Deborah knelt next to him, joining in the hug, but she kept her gaze on his face. All her hopes, her heart, her love, everything she offered him, shone in her face. "Let's go get started. Right away."

He rose and helped her to her feet. With Butch dashing back and forth in front of them, together they made their way through the crowd and out into a beautiful south Texas day.

— DISCUSSION QUESTIONS —

1. Today's society puts an enormous premium on physical beauty, from fashion models to actresses to elaborate homes and attractive automobiles. What does Scripture say about physical beauty? How would you answer Deborah's question regarding the barren "ugly" countryside she sees when she arrives in Bee County for the first time?

2. Hazel asks Phineas if the doctor can fix his "owie." Even at three she knows his face is different from hers. What does the world teach children about beauty, disfigurement, and disability? What can we do to counteract those messages about the beauty of others and of themselves?

3. Deborah is still grieving the death of her father two years earlier. Her faith demands that she believe that God had a plan for her father and his life was complete when he died young by our worldly standards. How is it possible to reconcile the loss of a loved one with your faith in God's plan for you?

4. Abigail believes she has come to Bee County to marry Stephen, but she finds herself drawn to Mordecai instead. Have you ever thought you knew what God's plan was for

you, only to find yourself facing a completely different set of circumstances? How did you react? What can you do to assure yourself that the path you take is the one God chooses for you and not the one *you* think is best?

5. Even after twelve years, it's hard for Phineas to understand why God would allow him to be so disfigured and his mother to be killed in a horrific accident. He suggests that only a cruel God would allow someone as beautiful as Deborah to experience similar disfigurement. Do you think God "allows" these things to happen or "causes" them to teach us lessons about life? If not, how do you reconcile these accidents and their repercussions in our lives with the knowledge that God loves us and wants what's best for us?

6. In order to accept Deborah's love for him—just as he is—Phineas has to learn to see himself through her eyes. He has to believe she finds him beautiful and worthy of her love. Ecclesiastes says God makes everything beautiful in His time. Do you believe God finds every one of His children beautiful?

7. When you look in the mirror, do you see a beautiful person, or do you find fault with your weight, your height, your hair, or the color of your eyes? How is your self-image shaped by the world's standards for beauty? What can we do to measure ourselves by God's standards instead?

8. Deborah's community chooses not to press charges against Raymond Southerland for assaulting Phineas and terrorizing Deborah. How do you feel about that? Would you be able to do the same? Does the fact that he's going back to prison regardless of their choice make a difference?

— A NOTE FROM THE AUTHOR —

My stories often start with the question, "What if . . . ?" What if this were to happen or what if that were to happen? Often that question and the subsequent answer have nothing to do with reality. That's why they call it fiction. All of this is my long-winded way of saying that the characters and situations in *The Beekeeper's Son* are products of my feverish, overactive imagination. The Amish folks who live in the tiny Bee County, Texas, district keep to themselves, and they appear very happy in their simple, industrious, conservative way of life. I respect their privacy and hope others do the same. I can only imagine what they would think if they were to read this story. If I have taken liberties with the rules that govern their particular district, it is for the good of the story. I hope my readers are blessed, entertained, and in some small way, edified. My thanks to the folks at Zondervan and HarperCollins who took a chance on something a bit different in Amish fiction. A special thanks to Mary Sue Seymour, my agent, who gave me a nudge—okay, a shove—in this direction. As always, my love and thanks to my husband, Tim, for his patience and support as my chief website guru, graphic artist, photographer, and business manager. And to my children, Erin and Nicholas, for understanding and sacrificing for my dream. Love you guys.

> But the LORD said to Samuel, "Do not consider his appearance or his height, for I have rejected him. The LORD does not look at the things people look at. People look at the outward appearance, but the LORD looks at the heart."
> 1 Samuel 16:7

> Those who look to him are radiant; their faces are never covered with shame.
> Psalm 34:5

> He has made everything beautiful in its time.
> Ecclesiastes 3:11

Read more from Kelly Irvin
in the Amish of Bee County series!

ABOUT THE AUTHOR

PHOTO BY TIM IRVIN

Kelly Irvin is a bestselling, award-winning author of nearly thirty novels and stories. A retired public relations professional, Kelly lives with her husband, Tim, in San Antonio. They have two children, three grandchildren, and two ornery cats.

———

Visit her online at KellyIrvin.com
Facebook: @Kelly.Irvin.Author
Twitter: @Kelly_S_Irvin
Instagram: @Kelly_irvin